White Knuckle

Daniel J. Gatti

Blackmore & Blackmore
Portland, Oregon

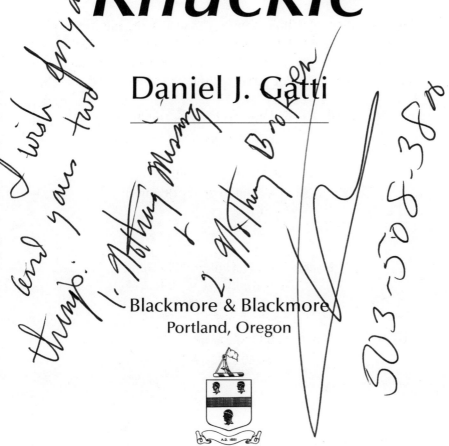

*and I wish for ya
things. 1. Nothing missing
& 2. Nothing Broken*

503-508-38__

WHITE KNUCKLE

Library of Congress Control Number:
2001 135627

All Rights Reserved
Printed in the United States of America

ISBN: 0-9666244-5-9

Blackmore & Blackmore Publishing
117 N.W. Trinity Place, Suite A
Portland, Oregon 97209
USA
Tel 503-228-6422
Fax 503-227-1261

Dedication

White Knuckle *is dedicated to those who have loved me
unconditionally, including my parents, my brother, Richard, and his
wife, Noelle, and to the greatest blessings God has given me:
my son, Danny, and my daughter, DiAndra.*

Acknowledgments

White Knuckle could not have been written without my editors:
Ann Kempner-Fisher, Bobbie Christmas, and Judi Thompson to whom I
am very grateful. I'd also like to thank my spiritual guide, counselor, and
friend, Lois Jean Kadera, and to the many others who encouraged
this work and gave me their support.

Most of all, I am grateful for the guidance, patience, input, closeness,
and insight of someone I will always love: Julietta Bauman.
My world has changed, and I am better. Thank you.

BOOK ONE

1

"Levi, I'm your dad, and I don't want you hurt. Getting divorced is never easy, especially on children, and I know how your aching feels. But Levi, the pain you feel is temporary. Believe that. Please? I'll do everything I can to take away your sorrow." Judd spoke the words, knowing he was out of control.

The father and son were sitting on the living room couch. Light from the Colorado moon streamed though the windows from the high skies overlooking the Rocky Mountains shadowing Denver. Judd's lips trembled as he held on to his young son's hand.

Levi stared at the most important person in his life and tried to understand. "I know you're only nine, but to me, you're ninety," Judd Saranno said to the uncompromising boy. "You're a giant, in my mind."

Levi wanted to believe his father. But Levi Saranno was just a kid, not a ninety-year-old. For reasons he didn't understand, Levi felt guilty, weak and helpless. Levi was just a kid. A kid whose heart was bleeding, all because of his father.

To Levi, Dad was his world. A world of happiness, love and kindness: fishing, playing ball, going to Denver Bronco games, and walking dogs while throwing sticks. Laughter. Protection. Peace. Dad was Levi's world, and Levi's world was exploding.

Judd Saranno was a trial lawyer. Some said a legendary one. Former president of the Colorado Bar Association, and voted National Advocate of the Year. An orator with the gift of words that had convinced juries to award millions. But Judd's gift of words meant nothing to Levi. They were just words, and no matter what his father said, Levi couldn't stop hurting.

Judd talked with his son in the home that would belong to his wife as soon as she became his ex. He didn't mind losing ten thousand square feet of brick and granite. The wife and opulent toys weren't much of a loss, or so it seemed to Judd. Leaving Levi's brother was tough, but not the same as leaving Levi. To Judd, Levi was the special child. Sometimes needful, always trusting, forever loving. Innocent. Levi, he was the son of sons.

"Levi, I know you don't want me to leave Colorado, but San Francisco's not so far away. We've got phones; I'll hook up to the internet, and I'll buy so many tickets on United Airlines that they'll think I'm a part of their profit margin. Levi, I'll always be available."

"It won't be the same. Never." Levi slowly shook his head back and forth.

Judd reached into a drawer in the marble end table next to the sofa and pulled out a pen and piece of paper. He thought carefully and started writing. Judd handed the inscription to his son. "Read this and tape it to your mirror. Read it every day, Levi. Read it now."

Levi held up the paper. It said:

> "A father who really loves his son will never hurt him. Not inten-tionally. Levi, you are my greatest treasure, my greatest blessing from God. I'll never hurt you. I promise. I'm here for you, and always will be. I love you. Dad."

The phone rang. Judd lifted the receiver. Levi could hear only one side of the conversation, but it was enough for him to know that something serious was getting his father's attention.

Judd's body stiffened, his voice grew stern and tense. "Bernie, don't do this. Bernie, please? Wait for me. Wait! I'll be there in ten minutes." He hung up the phone quickly, and with an ashen face, looked back at Levi.

"Son," he said, "we've got to go. I can't leave you alone. Hurry up, you're coming with me." Judd picked up his car keys and wallet as he bolted for the garage.

Levi followed; folding the paper with his father's words, he put it in his pocket. "Dad, where are we going?"

"To the hospital," Judd called back. "As fast as we can get there."

* * * * *

Bernie hung up the phone and waited twenty minutes. Finally he whispered, "I must have courage, Jordy. It's the right thing to do, isn't it?" Little Jordy couldn't answer his father's question.

Little Jordy was resting comfortably in the pediatric bed of the hospital where he had been in a coma for weeks. Bernie knelt beside his son. He looked at the electrical cord, and looked back at his only child. Weeping. There was nothing else to do. Bernie pulled the plug from the socket in the wall.

After the electricity was shut off to his respirator, it took exactly forty seconds for little Jordan Panzer to die. Forty seconds isn't generally considered a very long time, but, for Jordan's dad, the ticks of time felt like eternity. For Bernie Panzer, the seconds slow-danced forever, even though his son's dying waltz was uncomplicated by moans or grunts or contorted convulsions ricocheting up and down the small body. Instead, as death came, Jordan breathed a final tiny sigh that signified goodbye, and the little boy moved on to everlasting life at the right hand of God.

Bernie talked to the boy. "You were here four years, son. Just four years, but you gave your mom and me the greatest love we've ever known." Bernie held his child's small fingers in one hand, and with the other, he massaged an atrophied arm as if trying to keep it warm.

"I feel so helpless, Jordy, but you've got to understand *my* suffering. I just can't let you wither anymore. Remember when we wrestled? Remember how strong you were? God, you're tough, and now, God will make you even stronger."

Bernie smiled at his only son. Tousled brown hair strands crept from under the white bandages that covered the boy's scalp. Bernie's once stiff jaw hung like a willow.

"You make me so proud, Jordy. You could walk before you crawled. You always hugged your dad. Don't forget, big guy, you've still got your football. Someday, we'll throw it back and forth again. I promise. Even your teddy's right beside you." The puffy one. The one that had been resting in the boy's fetal grasp ever since the wreck. "And Jordy, I'm here too, son. I'll always be beside and you'll always be with me. I'm so lucky to have had you in my life. I'm the most grateful man in the world."

When Jordy got his electricity unplugged, red lights flashed, and the nursing station's buzzers blared. A white-coated trio blue-coded down the hallway, screaming as they tried to burst into the room of the powerless boy in the obvious grips of a mad-dog-dad gone nuts.

"Open this door. Open it!" The nurses pushed and pounded with their fists. "Get help! Call security!"

Bernie ignored the yelling and remained riveted on his son's final breath. "Jordy, wait there for me. Tell God to look out for you, and you look down and smile at me once in a while." Tears streamed down his cheeks. "I wish you could kiss me back, hold me just once more. Understand that I'm just keeping a promise I made to you. Remember? The one where I said I'd always take care of you. Where you'd never have to worry; you could always count on Dad to…"

The shouting outside the hospital room grew more agitated. "Open this door…goddamn it! We've only got seconds!"

White Knuckle

Bernie turned his head briefly, and saw that the barriers he'd placed between himself and the intruders were weakening. The furniture held for a few precious moments, but the pieces he'd placed in front of the door weren't deadbolts. Wrinkles crevassed around his narrowing eyes.

"Jordy, they're coming, baby. I've only got a minute. So hold me, son. Let me touch you and feel you and love you."

The boy's father lay on the bed, cradling his son like a goosedown pillow.

When the intruders broke through, little Jordy's father fell off the mattress and scowled at the predators like a cornered bobcat. Bernie Panzer wasn't about to attack, though. Not anymore. His fight was over. His sweet little boy was dead, and all Bernie could muster was to kneel by his son and pray – with the electrical cord clasped firmly between his palms.

* * * * *

The Mercedes screeched to a halt in front of the hospital and Judd leaped from the car. Levi quickly followed, trying to ask questions as his father sprinted toward the nurse's station. Levi stuck closely to his dad without his questions being answered.

Down the hall from the nurse's station, Levi heard nurses screaming. People pounded on a door. Pushed. Yelled. People in green and blue and white outfits ran in all directions. A buzzer kept buzzing. Levi couldn't believe his eyes. The scene was just like "E.R." on television, except he was there in person.

Judd stopped running and turned to Levi. His tense face frightened his son. He grabbed Levi by the shoulders. "Stay here, Levi. Don't come down the hall. I don't have time to explain. Just stay put. Understand?" His father's grasp was firm. He meant business. Judd quickly turned and left, running to the chaos as fast as he could, not looking back.

Levi quickly figured he was no one's priority. He was practically invisible as he carefully made his way down the hall, watching, afraid, yet morbidly fascinated. He crept along the wall to stay out of the way. The door to Jordy's room was finally broken open. Everyone rushed in, including Judd. Levi stayed back for several moments, but the boy had courage – his father had always boasted about that – and as he moved closer, Levi peered in the doorway and stopped.

"You fucking bastard," a man said, reaching for Bernie, who was curled in a corner, plug in his hand. Another man in a light blue hospital smock grabbed the cord and quickly plugged it into the wall.

"He's hypoxic," a nurse screamed as she grasped the Ambu Bag, attached it to Jordy's breathing tube and began pumping 100% oxygen by quickly squeezing the bag as hard as she could.

Another nurse started chest compressions of dead little Jordy, while a third injected an IV dose of adrenaline to jump-start the heart and injected sodium bicarbonate.

Little Jordy didn't move, and neither did Levi. The lines of the heart monitor were flat lined; cardiac standstill.

"Get the defibrillator!" the nurse commanded.

Levi watched as the nurse applied jelly to the paddles of the chest defibrillator, not knowing what it was. They placed the paddles on Jordan's body. Someone yelled, "Clear!" as the nurse pushed a red button on the paddle, 300 Joules of electricity shot through the dead child as his body jerked off the mattress and then down again, lifeless.

Levi never saw his father look so helpless as Bernie got lifted to his feet. A cloth belt from a smock was wrapped around Bernie's hands, and belted behind his back.

White Knuckle

The nurse jacked up the electricity on the defibrillator. "Work, oh, Jesus," she pleaded, as she slapped the machine. "Work, please. Jesus, oh, Jesus." Again she yelled, "Clear!" 350 Joules. No response.

The otherwise "flatlined" heart monitor jumped each time the nurse yelled clear and pressed the button. Each time, afterwards, the flatline returned. Levi wondered why she kept hitting the machine. It reminded him of a small TV set with a bad picture tube.

Everyone looked desperate except for the man the people kept shouting at.

The nurse's words seemed to be spitting from her mouth as she winced at the man being cinched with hands behind his back. "Why did you do this? Why did you kill him? He was your son, for christsakes."

Levi just listened, trying to comprehend.

Bernie looked casually at his accuser. "I did what I had to do. I had to let my son die. You just don't understand. All you do is prolong the agony."

"Be quiet, Bernie," Judd commanded. "Don't say anything else. Nothing."

"Who the fuck are you?" asked a man in blue.

"I'm Mr. Panzer's friend. I'm also his lawyer."

"He don't need no lawyer. He needs a noose. This dead boy had a pulse ten minutes ago. He had life. And your friend here killed him."

Bernie stared at the floor. "I killed Jordy because I didn't want him to suffer. Not anymore."

"Bernie, be quiet," Judd said between clenched teeth. "I mean it."

"I have to call the police." The nurse quickly turned, and almost fell over Levi in her haste to seek justice. Levi looked up to the towering figure, then

7

over to the boy's bed. Levi held his ground, but he was shaking as he watched the white sheet being placed over the dead boy's body and face.

The room fell silent. Judd looked helplessly at his son. "Nurse," Judd asked softly, "would you please take my son to a safe and quiet place? Please?"

A shiver went through Levi. Judd leaned down toward his son. Softly he said, "Levi, please go with this lady, and I'll be there soon. I promise."

The nurse nodded as she gently took Levi's hand. Someone else picked up the phone and called the police.

* * * * *

After the police cuffed Bernie Panzer and read him his rights, they knew they would get no more statements with Judd Saranno as the lawyer. The police could get the statements of those who had heard Bernie's confessions. Even without the confessions, there was enough factual and circumstantial evidence to put Bernie away for life. Bernie was done and gone. To one cop, Bernie seemed relieved, didn't even seem sad. The same officer tried to sneak an insight into the thoughts of the big-shot lawyer pacing the room.

"Get your work done, officer. I need to find my son."

"My work's done, Mr. Saranno. Yours is just beginning. Lucky lawyer, ain't you? You get to defend a confessed child killer. Good luck," he smiled, as they turned and headed Bernie Panzer to the county jail.

* * * * *

After searching for ten minutes, Judd finally found Levi sitting on a bench outside the hospital. The evening was warm and still. A lightpost guarded Levi's bench, and Judd saw his son sitting with his head bent down and shoulders slumped.

White Knuckle

Levi was reading the note his father had written. He looked up as Judd came toward him. The moon's fullness added light to the gentle breeze stirring the air. The people and the chaos had disappeared. No sirens screeched and no buzzers beeped. It was quiet.

Judd put his hand on Levi's shoulder. "I'm sorry, son. So sorry you had to witness that."

"It scared me, Dad." Levi's eyes widened. "Everything scares me."

"It will be okay, Levi. I'm here, and I'll protect you."

Levi handed his father the note Judd had written to him. "I've got it memorized, and I don't need to paste it on a mirror. You make promises, Dad."

"I keep my promises, Levi. I promise. Please take this back and put it on your mirror so you'll have the promises when I'm gone."

"Why did that man kill his son? Why did he hurt him? You said a father who loves his son won't hurt him."

Judd bent his head down and closed his eyes. "How do I explain it, Levi? I don't know what to say."

Levi stood up, took the piece of paper from his father's fingers, and walked to the car, leaving Judd behind. He didn't know if he should keep his Dad's note, or toss it. Judd heard his son mumble, "Maybe Mom can help. Something's wrong, and I don't understand."

Levi felt alone. Alone with the note crunched in his pocket.

2

"Why is Dad helping a killer?" Levi asked his mother. "I was there, and I didn't like it. They said the little boy had a chance, and his dad killed him. I saw it, Mom."

Sheryl Saranno didn't answer Levi's question. A grimace flickered lightly over her face as she opened the refrigerator door and took out the butter for breakfast toast.

"Mom," Levi persisted, "if Mr. Panzer killed Jordy on purpose, how come Dad's trying to get him off?"

"Probably because your dad's the only lawyer in Denver who can," she finally answered. "What's right or wrong doesn't matter to him. It's how he's been trained. It's really not his fault, I think it's in his blood. Nothing's his fault, or so he says."

Levi's redheaded older brother picked up a piece of bacon and took a bite. Joshua looked at Levi. "Dad thinks he can win anything," he said, "but I don't think he's gonna win this case."

Levi and Joshua sat in cushioned chairs at the granite table, waiting for the rest of breakfast. Orange juice had already been poured. Sheryl delivered full plates of scrambled eggs and hashbrowns to her sons. Levi stared at his mother impatiently.

Things weren't going well, and Levi didn't like it. Levi didn't like the changes. Joshua and Mom had teamed up together with nasty words and sarcastic comments about Dad, both of them working to get Levi to take their side. But Levi had a goal. Even at nine years old, Levi wanted to be like his father. To grow up like him. To be strong and powerful like Dad.

Levi was not only going to be like his dad, he was going to be *with* him, too. That's all there was to it. The decision was his, and one thing was certain. Levi's decision was final.

But Mom and Joshua were always cutting in. Getting in the way. Levi saw the changes in his mother's attitude. They were gradual, but now his mother's anger was an everyday occurrence. Levi didn't accept it, and he did not understand. All Levi understood was that Dad was leaving and that Mom and Joshua didn't seem to care. Levi did care, and his attitude was never going to change.

"Joshua," Levi said, looking back at his brother, "you might be seven years older than me, but you're not so smart. Well, maybe about computers you're smart. But why are you so mean at Dad?"

Joshua's freckled face leaned toward his younger brother. He raised his fingers and ruffled the red hair on top of his head. "Because Dad's leaving, Levi. Get it straight. He's hurting Mom and me and you too. Dad don't care about nothing except getting Panzer off, and getting off with his girlfriend."

"He cares about me!" Levi said defiantly.

Levi's mother looked at her boys. Sheryl never disputed that her sons were different. Same parents, but diverse sons. Levi had tenacity, his father's good looks and square shoulders. Joshua didn't have Levi's spunk, but at least Joshua had his loyalties straight. Straight to his mother. And Levi – she could change Levi's loyalties, once Judd left Denver with his whore.

White Knuckle

Sheryl sat down beside Levi. "Levi, you asked why your father would try to help Bernie. Can your dad win? Probably. No, I take that back. He *will* win. But he shouldn't."

Levi looked up from his eggs. His mother's thin lips got thinner. Tight. She looked bitter.

"What Bernie Panzer did was wrong. A sin against God...". She stopped speaking, and a sad look crept over her face. Her gaze wandered around the huge kitchen, with its custom-made cabinets of blond oak, the Corian topped counters and high-tech appliances. Modern, elegant and efficient. A room fit for the cover of *Architectural Digest*. A room that should have been filled with happiness.

As his mother's mind wandered, Levi played with his eggs. "I still don't understand, Mom," he said. "You always tell *me* to do the right thing."

"Of course." There was a touch of pride in Sheryl's voice. "But lawyers are different. They've got a different agenda."

"What's a...a genda?" Levi asked.

Joshua laughed. "Male? Female? Neuter?"

Sheryl smiled. "Don't tease him, Josh."

"Well, he's so dumb."

"I'm not dumb!" Levi shot back. He picked up a piece of toast and, as if he were tossing a Frisbee, hurled the bread at his brother's chin.

Joshua ducked, and grinned sarcastically at Levi as the toast landed on the tile behind his chair.

"Stop it!" Sheryl yelled.

Levi clenched his fists. Pushing himself away from the table, he started toward his older brother. Sheryl grabbed him by the arm.

"I said stop it! Both of you! No fighting. Sit down, Levi. The three of us need to talk, to make plans so we can get through the next few months." Her eyes looked heavenward, praying about something neither of her sons could hear.

Levi stared at his mother's pretty face. Her jaw was set, and it sent him apologetically back to his seat.

"It's so sad," Sheryl said, her shaky fingers reaching into the pocket of her slacks for a tissue. She blew her nose and spoke softly. "One day you have a marriage, a family, and the next day you've got nothing."

Levi and Joshua watched their mother as a palpable tension filled the room. Both boys knew what was coming. They had heard it before. Levi braced himself.

Sheryl's voice softened to a hush. "All I ever wanted was to be a good wife and mother. I look good, dress right; I keep a beautiful home; you boys are my heroes..." Sheryl's voice trailed off.

"Mom, I'm sorry," Joshua said.

Levi dove into the last of his scrambled eggs.

Sheryl suddenly slammed the palm of her hand on the table, startling the boys. Levi shut his eyes and waited for the angry words. Joshua stiffened. Sheryl's mood swings had become commonplace.

Their mother's voice jumped three octaves. "Your father has the most wonderful family in the world, a lifestyle other people would kill for. And what does your father want?" Sheryl no longer spoke to her sons, but *at* them. "A slut. He's giving it all up for a whore young enough to be your sister."

"I don't want Dad to move." Levi's words seemed to quiver with anxiety. "We're supposed to go fishing. Dad's going to show me how to shoot guns." Levi glanced at his older brother. "He's gonna teach me, Josh, not you."

"Big deal. I got better things to do."

Sheryl rapidly cleared the table, gathering strength as she moved about the kitchen again, her voice filled with bitter determination. "Levi, your dad's not going to teach you anything about guns. Guns are dangerous, and when the custody papers are signed, I'll set all the rules, and that means no guns. Your father's going to California with that girl, so he can run her dead dad's business. If he was so concerned about you, why would he go to California with a tramp?"

"Her name's Asia," Levi countered, "and she's nice."

Sheryl turned from the sink, her face flushed. "You've *met* her? I can't believe it," she screamed. "Did you know this, Josh? Did you meet her too?"

The slap came so quickly Levi had no time to get out of the way. His cheek felt like he'd been stung by a hornet.

Joshua shook his head. "No way, Mom. Honest."

Levi stared at his mother in shock. She'd never raised a hand to him. "Infidelity's bad enough," Sheryl cried. "Betrayal's bad enough. But how dare he humiliate me this way? Taking my little baby to meet that bitch! How dare he!"

"Mom, I never seen you so mad," Josh said.

Sheryl's fury arrowed toward Levi. "Nice?" she hissed. "You say she's nice?"

Levi's slender body grew rigid. His eyes narrowed. He was about to snap back, but instead, swallowed hard, and said nothing. He moved his hand toward his reddened cheek.

"Oh, my God, you're bleeding!" Sheryl cried, putting her arms around Levi as she pulled his taut body into her chest. "Look what he's done to us. To his family." She stroked Levi's dark curls. "I'm so sorry, Levi. I'll never hurt you again, baby."

Sheryl grabbed a paper napkin and dabbed at Levi's lower lip. She moved to kiss his cheek, but he turned away. Joshua sat and stared, a stunned look on his face.

Sheryl steadied her voice. "Levi, tell me when you met her. How you met her."

Levi gently broke loose. "It didn't seem like a big thing. When Dad took me to the Nuggets and Lakers basketball game, we stopped at her place on the way. He said he wanted me to meet Asia, so we'd feel okay together. Dad says I can visit them in the summers and maybe Christmas…"

"Holidays?" Sheryl's mouth quivered uncontrollably. Her eyes squinted with rage. "Levi, get this straight. Your dad will never get you for the holidays! He'll never get you, period!"

"Asia's nice," Levi said simply. "She didn't say nothing bad…"

Sheryl was pacing the large kitchen. "Bad?" she interrupted. "Why would she say anything bad? What's she going to tell a nine-year-old? How she wrecked his parent's marriage? Is she going to tell you Daddy's following his dick instead of his brains?"

White Knuckle

Levi looked at his mother and saw the Mad Queen in *Alice In Wonderland* shouting, "Off with his head!" Joshua sank deeper into his chair.

"Let's see," Sheryl ranted on, "she probably said, 'Levi, you're going to love San Francisco, and we're going to have so much fun there, riding the cable cars and going to Chinatown and Fisherman's Wharf.'"

Levi nodded. "I think she mentioned some, Mom."

Sheryl was striding around the room, looking for allies. "Joshua, explain it to your brother," she said, her hands gripping the back of Joshua's chair, but before he could say anything, she cried, "explain to Levi about the meaning of loyalty and betrayal. And abandonment." She didn't take her eyes off Levi. "Don't you see, baby, you're being abandoned by your father."

Levi's head bent so far down, his chin met his chest. "Dad promised it'd be okay."

"Bullshit. It's okay for him, honey. It's not for us."

Sheryl stopped pacing and studied her sons for a moment. Joshua was hers; Levi was Judd's. The fact was indisputable. Everyone agreed. Levi looked like Judd, acted like him, and they were a mutual admiration society of two. In retrospect, she couldn't even blame Judd for loving Levi best. She remembered what had happened in the past.

Joshua had been a colicky baby, sick all the time. Sheryl breast-fed him until he was two, while her husband worked sixty hours a week. For the first seven years of Joshua's life, Judd was obsessed with suing a "good-neighbor" insurance company for defrauding policy holders. For seven long years, Judd Saranno fought the giant. The giant never changed, but Judd did.

The case was Judd's first class-action suit, and his last. The good-neighbor company said Judd's suit on behalf of the company's own insureds was frivolous. The "frivolous" lawsuit finally ended with a verdict for fifty million dollars to his clients, and fifteen million to their lawyer. Judd Saranno got rich overnight, or so the newspapers said. The outcome brought huge financial success. It also brought disaster on the domestic front. Sheryl thought the money crippled the poor bastard.

While Judd was reaping a fortune, he lost his oldest son. Joshua didn't know him, didn't see him, and eventually didn't notice. Sheryl grew distant, accepting occasional sex at her husband's convenience. Then, Levi was born.

Judd got rich, and at the same time, God gave him a new son. He was blessed. Judd took the money, and he took to Levi as if he'd never had another boy in the family. Sheryl didn't understand it.

"I'm sorry," she said, sitting down again at the table. She took a deep breath and a temporary calm settled over her.

"What can we do?" Joshua asked.

"We can start by being nice to each other. Levi, I'm sorry I slapped you. It won't happen again. And you're not dumb. Joshua, quit telling him that. Panzer's trial will be over soon. When it's finished, your father's going to California. Then it'll be just the three of us, and we'll be fine as long as we're kind and trust one another.

"I trust you, Mom," Joshua said with sincerity. He looked apologetically at Levi. "I'm sorry I called you dumb."

Levi stared at his mother. "Dad and me are going fishing. He promised."

Sheryl remained stoic. "We can't keep every promise we ever make, Levi," she said. "Your dad tries, at least with you, but if you don't go fishing, well, don't be too disappointed."

"I want to shoot a rifle," Levi insisted.

"Levi, honey, when you go to summer camp, you can shoot arrows," his mother said. "Instead of fishing with Dad all summer, you can make new friends. If you'd like, I'll let you stay at camp longer this year."

"I don't want to go to camp. I want to go to California."

"California's not an option." Her tone was brusk. "Trust me, camp will be wonderful. They have great counselors. I'll even come visit you for a day. Besides, you'll only be there for two weeks."

"When can I go to California?" Levi persisted.

Sheryl's mouth tensed. She tried to keep her voice gentle but firm. "When I say so, Levi. Your life's changing. You're going to have to accept that."

"Why?" he wondered.

"Because I say so," his mother replied firmly as she walked over to the window and gazed out.

A dark cloud rolled across the sky, blotting out the sun, and Sheryl saw her reflection in the windowpane. For a moment, she also saw Judd, standing beside her on their wedding day, both of them radiant. Sheryl shook the image from her mind and turned back to Levi with her most maternal and protective smile.

"…and because I know what's best for you, Levi."

3

The facts were simple. Bernie Panzer got in trouble because a drunken driver's tire didn't squash Jordy's head by one more centimeter. If little Jordy had died like he was supposed to, the death would be the responsibility of the drunken bastard and his insurance company. Instead, the guilty ones managed to skate culpability by alleging that there was an "intervening act." That tire didn't kill Jordy. Bernie did.

But did he? Had Bernie waited a few days longer, Judd could have gotten a court order to pull the plug. But no, Panzer had to take matters into his own hands. Daddy-Death, and now Judd's responsibility.

Proving the innocence of Bernie was a responsibility Judd did not want to shoulder. Judd wanted a divorce; he wanted to take Levi fishing; he wanted to get in his car and head for San Francisco. But Bernie was his friend, and if anyone could get him off, Judd could.

The district attorney looked at his assistant, Jennifer Ottington. She would be handling Bernie Panzer's prosecution. "Judd Saranno might be considered one of the best trial lawyers in Colorado," he said. "Some have called him a fucking magician, but Judd puts his pants on the same way I do. Don't let him confuse the jury. Keep him to the facts. Concentrate on the law."

Ottington smiled confidently. "I'm going to nail him."

She was tall, slender, and looked like she'd be more comfortable in blue jeans and tennis shoes, but wore her tailored outfits with a simple gracefulness.

Her smile was warm, enticing. Rich brown hair flowed four inches below her neck and lay smooth and straight on her back. She was stunning.

"She's a ball-busting bitch, Bernie," Judd had cautioned his client and friend. "Don't let her lead you to saying things you'll regret. No matter what Ottington says to the jury or the witnesses, don't show anger. If the jury sees you angry, they won't like it. To win, we need to make the jury like you, and me as well."

"But, Judd," Bernie clasped his clammy hands as if trying to dry them with an imaginary towel, "you say she's got the law and facts on her side. Maybe we should take their offer for manslaughter. Maybe I can do five years without dying." Bernie's head dropped as his eyes closed. "Fact is, Judd, I'm dead already."

"Facts have nothing to do with justice, Bernie. Besides, your wife needs you, and you need her. Remember, getting you acquitted won't have anything to do with the law." Judd noticed beads of sweat on Bernie's forehead. "The verdict will live or die on emotions. Feelings. No parent would have wanted to be in your shoes. Most of the jurors, I think, are sympathetic."

Judd didn't know if he was trying to convince Bernie or himself. All he knew was that since the death of Jordy, only three months had passed, and the defendant was already on trial. On trial for murder. Judd had managed to get a quick court date. It only took a few days to get the evidence presented once the trial began, and the case was no epic of jurisprudence. There wasn't much in dispute. In the case of *The State of Colorado vs. Bernard H. Panzer*, the evidence showed beyond a doubt that Bernie Panzer severed the electrical charge to his son's lifeline. Everyone knew he was guilty. So what was there to talk about? What twist on the truth could untangle the noose that Ottington wanted to tie around Bernie's neck? As far as Judd Saranno was concerned, in this case, the facts standing alone were incompatible with a verdict of not guilty. Therefore, it came down to passion. Judd Saranno called it mercy. Ottington called it premeditated murder.

White Knuckle

Ottington couldn't stomach the demeaning Mr. Saranno, and that was just the way Judd wanted it. The bitchier she became, the better Judd liked it. A mean disposition wouldn't sit well with the jury. If Ottington got nasty, she didn't stand a chance of winning.

The trial itself became a goldmine for sensational and relentless press coverage. Some people marveled at the eloquence of Judd Saranno. Some thought he was a pompous jerk. Everyone knew he was a lawyer's lawyer.

As Bernie's trial approached the end, Judd Saranno made his way up the courthouse steps, passing cameras and professional protesters who carried signs that read: "BABY BUTCHER FROM HELL," "AUSCHWITZ IN DENVER," "LET BABIES LIVE – LAWYERS DIE!" Pro-lifers were angry Christians. Jews thought the trial was racial. Everyone seemed to hate lawyers.

Judd's briefcase bulged with legal theories and profound dissertations. He entered the courtroom for the final closing arguments. The courtroom seemed like a looming fortress for the carriage or miscarriage of justice. Larger than anything in the room was the judge's bench, with flags on each side, and the State of Colorado's official seal prominently plastered on the marble wall behind the judge's leather chair. When the judge finally entered, his bench looked like the throne of Solomon. Lives changed in the presence of a god.

In front of the judge's bench were tables and chairs for the prosecution and defense. To the left was the jury box, empty for now. The witnesses had all been excluded from watching the trial as it progressed. Each day, the gallery of citizens filled the benches behind Bernie and Judd's seats, listening and wondering. Waiting for each side to counter and rebut the other. The citizens came with their own thoughts, for their own reasons, with impressions and prejudices. As each day passed, the verdict was coming closer. Finally, the day of reckoning had arrived. Closing arguments were about to begin, and Bernie sat with his wife, Rhoda, while Judd took out his pens and yellow legal pads.

The gallery buzzed softly. Ottington finally made her way confidently to the prosecutor's table. Her eyes sparkled, an air of invincibility shone around her beautiful face as she moistened her lips in anticipation. The bailiff brought in the jurors. Everyone rose when the judge made his solemn entrance through his chamber doors. The gavel hit wood. "Court is now in session." A wave of goosebumps showered the room of spectators. Because she represented the state, Ottington got to go first, and last in delivering the closing arguments to the jury. "Are you ready to proceed?" the judge asked. Ottington stood up and paced the courtroom, her eyes focused on the twelve people who held the life of Bernie Panzer in their hands.

For two hours she spoke, grinding the evidence into mush, or so it seemed to Judd. Her arguments were not chicken soup for justice. Her statements were a potpourri of deceptive twists on logic. Ottington focused on a four-year-old boy with a pulse. Medical wonders and the possibility of miracles. Nurses and doctors. Hospitals. Caring and giving. Breathing and life. Dreams. Compassion. Death. The facts. The truth and the law. The finality of pulling the plug, taking any hope from a father who'd given up his child for dead. But the child was *not* dead, at least not until his father had barricaded the door and eliminated electricity, knowing no one could stop the ultimate act of humane criminality.

Finally, Ottington arrived at the end of her speech. Her remarks gripped the spectator's attention, and she had gotten into the hearts of some. Maybe. Nevertheless, she needed a final, probing comment.

"Why are we even here?" Ottington asked the jury with artificial indignation. Some jurors took notes. Some stared intently. Some crossed their arms and legs, pushing Ottington away with their body language.

Ottington shrugged and shook her head in mock disbelief. Her carefully plucked eyebrows furrowed. "Mr. Panzer admitted he did it." She backed away from the jury box and pointed her finger like a sword at Bernie's Jewish nose. "He *knew* the boy would die. Yet Mr. Saranno would have you believe it's justified. What nonsense."

She stared at Bernie's blank face. He looked straight into her eyes, not daring to turn away. He was a coward, she thought, and she knew in her gut that her finger felt like an ice pick in Bernard's heart.

"The defense says he was depressed." Still pointing, she went on. "Sure, Mr. Panzer was depressed. He was depressed because he doesn't believe in miracles. He was depressed because of how much this was costing him."

She moved closer to Bernie, her finger relentlessly pointing at him. "His depression continues," she said, "and I'll tell you why. It's not because of the murder he committed. It's not because he acknowledges his wrongdoing. He's guilty! He knows it, and so do you. He's depressed. So what? He's depressed because…because *he's* not God. He's even more depressed because of all the money. The money is what it was all about. It wasn't about little Jordy. All Bernie Panzer worried about was how much it was costing him. Money was the root of his evil act."

She sat down, smugly folding her arms across her breasts. She nodded the challenge to Judd, sitting at the table next to hers. "Your turn, Mr. Saranno."

The judge called a recess.

*   *   *   *   *

As the courtroom emptied, Bernie Panzer started shaking. "Judd, did you hear that? My God, the woman said I killed little Jordy to save money! Jesus, Judd, ask for a mistrial. She's lying. Can't they see she's lying?"

Rhoda Panzer tried to comfort her husband. "It'll be okay, honey. She's just doing her job. Trust Judd." She looked at their lawyer. "Judd?"

"She's worse than Hitler!" Panzer cried. He would not be comforted.

"No one believes her," Rhoda reassured him. Rhoda wore a dark blue dress that made her plump figure look less rotund. Lipstick was all the makeup she used. Rouge couldn't hide the worry and grief that etched her face. Her silky black hair hung to her slumping shoulders. Rhoda was a maternal beauty with a nourishing aura that shed light on her every movement. Today, her movements came slow, and the nurturing was difficult.

The torment in Bernie's eyes was clear.

"I'm being gassed." Sweat glistened on his forehead. He grabbed at Judd Saranno's coat sleeve like it was a life preserver thrown to a drowning man. Since Jordy's death, the tan on Bernie's face had faded. The wrinkles on his forehead looked deeper, the leathery skin more taut, his black eyes blacker, almost bleak. Bernie had the look of a boxer who'd just gone fifteen rounds. He was one big bruise.

"Judd, what are you going to do?" His hands moved from Judd's sleeve to the bald spot on his own head. His wife's arms went around the sagging shoulders.

Judd knew Bernie didn't kill for dollars. Bernie didn't care if it cost two cents or two thousand a day for a kid with tubes and shots and pumps and tests and air and monitors that beeped and left hyperventilated lines on machines that buzzed with sounds that blurted noise but never said anything except nothing was going to change, no matter what they wanted or how much they prayed. Nothing would ever change. Little Jordy was going to remain comatose and deteriorate and wilt and get bedsores until the machines quit buzzing and the little boy flatlined into eternity.

Judd touched the clammy hand of his client. "Ottington doesn't care about the truth, Bernie. She needs to prove malice. They need a bad motive. It's an old trick, a red-herring ploy. Nothing I haven't heard."

"This ain't a fucking game!"

26

"She's just throwing the jury a low curve ball, giving them something to think about except the real issue."

Judd knew the rules. He'd dealt with the nuances of trying to pitch a case to twelve people who had the collective legal intelligence of a nanny goat. For Judd, manipulation was easy.

He looked at Bernie and said, "In the real world after law school, one of the first things a good trial lawyer learns is this: If you can't dazzle them with brilliance, baffle them with bullshit."

"I'm losing, Judd."

"No you're not."

"I can see it in their eyes."

"Find a friendly face and keep your head up. Just find a friendly face, and I'll do the same."

He had been looking.

Find the leader of the pack, Judd had told himself. Judd's instincts picked her out from the very beginning. The foreperson is going to be the one with the tight, narrow twist on her mouth. The woman had salt-and-pepper hair tied tightly in a bun. She was a fading beauty, about Sheryl's age. No expression, just a knowing presence. Her imagination wanders, Judd thought, and she's watching everything I do.

For days she had sat in the jury box calm and polite, her hands resting discreetly in her lap. Now and then, she turned her chin and cocked her head. Sometimes she looked at the ceiling or at the judge. Most of the time she stared at Saranno. Judd knew this juror was his.

* * * * *

The recess was over and everyone was seated. Judd Saranno moved cautiously toward the jury and stood before them.

"I'm humbled," he said. "Humbled and proud to be defending this innocent man." His voice was soft, but firm. "Why shouldn't I be proud? Protecting the innocent is a privilege. And now, you as jurors have the right and privilege to stand up and declare, 'Yes, there are times when taking a life should be forgiven.' Not only were Bernie's actions right; the acts were moral and just. Merciful acts can never be wicked."

Judd moved closer. Not too close, but near enough to be a friend.

"There are times when mercy comes from an inner strength that might be perceived as weakness when, in fact, mercy is a virtue. Not an evil. Ladies and gentlemen, now is the time for you to speak up, and let your voices be heard throughout this community."

A sense of urgency echoed in Judd's voice.

"Stand up, now and forever, and shout it out. *Mercy* – say it people – mercy is not mayhem. And mercy..." For a second, Judd bowed his head; the silence was deafening. Suddenly, his jaw reared up sharply. The words seemed to scream from his lips. "Mercy is not murder," he said. "Mercy..." He was almost crying. "Say it please. Mercy is not murder."

Judd paused, letting his words sink in. The jurors were listening. How could they not understand? Judd looked like a general and his soldiers were at attention, waiting for his commands. The battling commander looked ruffled, but he was in control. Atlas, with broad shoulders proudly carrying the weight of Bernie's guilt or innocence on his back. His forehead wasn't wrinkled, his chin wasn't doubled, and his nose wasn't fat. His firm face and fit stature gave him an aura of character and strength, a confident bearing.

Judd was a protector, with Italian brown eyes and a smile that instantly put people at ease.

But the smile wasn't in the courtroom. "Once, not so long ago, someone called this man Dad," Judd said, as he pointed to Panzer. "We should all be thanking God Almighty that we have never had to stand in the shoes of this father. Ms. Ottington," he said with condescension as his voice lowered, "says this man committed premeditated murder."

Judd stiffened, like a guard standing before nobility. "I say, this father so loved his precious son that he gave his only boy…" sadness once again crept into his tone, "he gave his boy eternal life."

Judd's fingers reached to his eye as if to wipe away a tear.

"If you believe in The Creator Of All Things, you've got to believe that this father acted out of mercy. His actions were never motivated by greed. The final fact of death came from a final act of love."

Judd's eyes focused on the salt-and-pepper juror. She stared back at him, unblinking.

The courtroom was filled with spectators aching to hear every word. Reporters took notes as fast as they could. Bernie and Rhoda could hardly breathe.

"When Bernard Panzer cut off the current to his son's respirator," Judd pleaded, "he did not believe he was doing something wrong. Long before he disconnected the plug, the boy's brain had been irreversibly destroyed."

The lawyer walked over to his client and put a hand on his shoulder. Bernie's chin rested on his chest. He was a study in despair.

29

"In that hospital room, this father was suffering from overwhelming grief, which caused an uncontrollable psychological state of mind. It made him incapable of knowing his actions may be wrong in the eyes of the law. But in Mr. Panzer's mind, not only were his actions right, they were also moral and just. And 'justice,' ladies and gentlemen, is all we're asking for. If you seek justice, you will find this man not guilty. If you seek the truth, you'll forever set this father free."

His gaze lanced toward Ottington.

"This woman wants you to speculate," he said, foiling back at the opponent, "so let's speculate. But not on the cost of keeping a four-year-old brain-dead boy alive in a cold, sterile hospital room. That's a bogus motive trumped up by Ms. Ottington. Let's speculate on something real."

Judd's joust ricocheted as his gaze went back to the jury. He moved in close, to surround them with his presence.

"Speculate about the agony of a father disconnecting the lifeline from the body of his only son. That is anguish. That is real. Who among us doesn't feel the pain of a parent who stares helplessly at a loved one forever locked in eternal darkness? Without the possibility of embracing the light, Bernie couldn't let his son stumble alone in shadows. This dad had no alternative."

Judd backed slightly away from the jury box in anticipation of dropping the final, crushing blow. His eyes tried to pierce the heart of every juror. "Shutting off the electricity wasn't a choice between right and wrong," he said. "It was a choice between a life in heaven, or hell in a hospital with no hope."

Judd turned with solemn resignation, shaking his head sadly as he slowly walked back to the defense table and sat down. The hushed courtroom was spellbound, everyone watching Judd bury his face deep in the palms of his quivering hands.

Ottington stood up and crossed her arms in front of her chest. She wasn't smiling, but her face glowed. She stood tall and straight and walked with dignity. Ottington moved to within a foot of the jury box and paused. The prosecutor turned her head and looked sadly at Judd, and then Bernie. Finally, she turned back to look at the jurors as she bent forward and placed both hands on the jury box rail. She gave the shortest rebuttal argument Judd Saranno had ever heard.

There were twelve jurors, and Ottington said twelve words. One word for each juror, with one look at a time.

She said, "*Panzer's...depressed...because...of...the...money. He...knew... his... son... would...die.* His son's life was costing him money, so the dear boy had to die, to be murdered."

Slowly, she pulled away, turned, and with her head shaking back and forth, Ottington quietly sat down in her chair. The courtroom was dead silent.

*   *   *   *   *

The judge delivered his instructions to the jurors, reading from the standard text that the lawyers hardly understood, much less the average person. The judge read for thirty minutes before he came to what Judd believed was at the heart of Bernie Panzer's defense.

"Bias, prejudice, and sympathy have no place in deliberations," the judge read. "You must base your decision on the evidence at trial, not on guesswork or speculation."

Meaningless bullshit, Judd thought, as he did every time he heard a judge say it. Jury members always have prejudices and sympathies. Telling a juror not to speculate is like telling a toddler not to pee in his diapers. There was only one simple instruction Judd wanted: "Go do justice." But the judge wouldn't give that instruction. Justice and the law were often incompatible.

The judge finished reading the instructions, and the jury was sent out to begin their deliberations.

"Lunch will be brought in," the judge said. The jury went out just before noon. What mattered now was how long it would take for them to reach a verdict.

Judd and the Panzers left the courthouse, praying that within an hour the jury would come back with "Not guilty." A quick verdict usually meant that there was no doubt about the accused's innocence. If the verdict didn't come quickly, then Judd hoped it would take a couple of days. A couple of days would mean that there was disagreement and reasonable doubt among the jurors. The alternative scenario was clear: days of deliberations would hang the jury, not Bernie.

By five that afternoon, the jury still hadn't reached a decision. The judge politely told them to return so they could continue deliberating the next day, and longer if necessary. Bernie and Rhoda Panzer left Judd's office disappointed, despite their lawyer's assurances that the delayed verdict was a good sign, not a bad one. By six o'clock, Judd locked the door to his highrise law firm and left his briefcase there for the first time in weeks.

4

Waiting on the third day of deliberations, Judd Saranno and his client ate lunch in a restaurant near the courthouse. Rhoda Panzer was in the synagogue praying.

Judd put his cell phone on the table and said, "You did the right thing, Bernie. What else could you do? Those twelve will find you innocent, and you can begin your life over again. There's a lot to live for. You're young. You love your wife. You've got a future."

Bernie's eyes looked like a frightened buck which instinctively senses cross-hairs aimed at his head. The gun is somewhere in the distance, but the sense is real, and closer than it should be. Real close.

"Sometimes I wish they'd just shoot me, Judd. I don't have the courage to shoot myself." Two fingers went to his temple. He raised his thumb, pushed it down, and pulled the trigger. Bernie wasn't smiling.

"I've done my best to defend you, Bernie, but you've got to get a grip. Sometimes I think you've punished yourself more than the state wants to punish you. If you keep this up, your hell is going to last a lifetime."

"Maybe it should." Bernie's voice was resigned. He'd given up. Like a fighter on wobbly legs, one more punch, and a blackout would seem like a blessing. If he could only stay unconscious, then at least he'd find some freedom.

"How'd you like to know you killed your son?" Bernie asked. He looked withered and worn. Sad. Lost. "Jesus Christ, Judd, I can only take so much. There's nothing they can do to me I haven't done to myself."

"Oh, yes there is, pal," Judd said vehemently and patted Bernie's arm. "Trust me. Incarceration can turn you into a muttering loon. You're facing a life sentence, if they find you guilty in the first degree. Thirty years in prison for second degree, and with that you serve twelve to fifteen years for good time. You need freedom, Bernie, an acquittal. Even a third-degree manslaughter conviction puts you away for longer than you could stand. You need to get on with your life."

Judd looked out the window. "That's what I'm doing, Bernie. I'm getting on with my life. This divorce took longer than I expected. I have a few more things to wrap up, and then I'm gone.

"It's not quite the same, Counselor," Bernie cautioned. "You say get on with my life. You can. I can't. I can't replace my son, Judd, and God is a piece of shit." Bernie signaled the waiter and ordered another Scotch. "Have you ever played Truth or Dare?" he asked.

Judd shook his head. "No," he answered as he snapped his fingers toward the waiter. Judd motioned that the bartender should bring two drinks and Judd turned his attention back to Bernie. "Truth or Dare? Never heard of it."

"It's simple," Bernie explained. "You've got to tell the truth if I dare you to be honest. Then it's your turn. It's probably hard for a lawyer, but it's a diversion."

Judd nodded and took a sip of his gin and tonic. "I'm game. Who goes first?"

Panzer raised an eyebrow and moved closer to his attorney.

"I do. I dare you to be honest." He poked his head like a turkey as he leaned to within inches of Judd's chin. "You're not nice to anyone except your son,

Levi," Bernie challenged. "You drink too much, you've screwed up a good marriage, and even your kids are pissed. Besides that, you overcharge clients and friends. In short, you're an asshole, Judd. Why?"

"I should've charged you more money."

"You're not playing the game, Counselor. You're an asshole. Probably the only person who doesn't think so is Levi."

Judd smiled. "Every day when I go to work, Bernie, someone is trying to knock me down, prove I'm wrong, get me to cave in. When you've got to fight all the time, being an asshole comes easy."

Judd pulled out his wallet and flipped to Levi's picture. "But when the job becomes too tough, even for me, all I have to do is think about this kid." Judd looked at the photograph. "Levi's love is unconditional. Parents say they don't have favorites. Bullshit. Of course they have favorites, and every-body knows it." Judd looked proud. "It's not hard to love someone who thinks you soar with eagles."

"And what about Joshua?"

"Joshua doesn't think I soar with eagles. Levi does. Joshua's a good kid, and I love him, but Levi's great. I can't explain how I feel. Levi's strong and kind, gentle, warm and loving. I just know Levi is born for greatness. Levi's my legacy. And I'll never, never lose him."

"Then why leave him?" Bernie asked.

Judd didn't look at his client. He kept staring at the photo of his son. "Leaving Levi is the hardest part about going to California. But I need rest and a change. A new beginning. And I need Asia. Asia has to settle her father's estate, get the dealerships sold or under proper management. I'll help some, but I've got to simplify my life. Quit the race. I'm tired of juries and judges. I'm tired of fighting the fight. You're my swan song, Bernie."

"So what do you tell Levi?"

Judd paused. Thinking. Choosing his words carefully, he said, "I'll continue to tell Levi how much I love him, and that I'll always be there. Just a plane trip away. A phone call and I'm back. If he needs me to be there for him, for whatever reason, all he has to do is make a phone call. I keep my promises, Bernie, even though I am a lawyer."

Bernard chewed on an ice cube. "Watch out for your promises, Saranno. Some aren't realistic."

"Fuck you, Bernie. What about your reality? I dare you..." He paused.

"Dare what?"

Judd took a long swallow, draining his glass. "I dare you to tell me what you *really* think about what you did to Jordy in the hospital."

Agony. Bernie's face flushed. His eyes narrowed. He paused, and then put down his Scotch.

"Come close, Judd. Hear me." Bernie had a secret. "I've got to tell you about my dream. I haven't told a soul. It scares the piss out of me, and I have it every night." Bernie's hand trembled as it touched Judd's extended wrist.

"What is it?" Judd asked, his attention riveted on his friend.

Bernie whispered softly, "I see myself in a desert, nailed to a cactus. Like in Arizona. It's a hairy, prickly cactus. Sharp. Spines. I'm naked except for a rubber thing around my dick. But it's not a prophylactic. At first, I don't realize that. At first, I think it's just something or someone sucking down there. And then I kind of wake up. I wake up...wake up and go crazy.

"Keep going Bernie. I'm no shrink, but I am curious."

"You know what it is, Judd? You know what the hell's on my dick?" Sweat poured profusely from Bernie's forehead.

"No, what?"

"It's a fucking ventilator cord, Judd! Hanging my dick in a noose. It's not the mouth of a nymph giving head. It's a goddamn cord that's tied so tight, the tip of my dick is turning into a twinkling sparkler on the Fourth of July. It's like a Chinese finger-lock, the paper kind where the more you pull, the tighter it gets. I pull, and it gets tighter and tighter, and the head is turning purple. The blood at the tip of my dong is about to burst into the skies for the grand finale."

"That's awful, Bernie," Judd said. "That's painful."

"That's not all! It's after that when the real terror begins." Bernie's tongue went dry. His voice was so quiet, Judd could hardly hear him. Bernie clasped his hands on the table to stop them from shaking. "That's when I hear little Jordy. At first, I hear him in the distance. He's crying, 'Daddy. Daddy, I'm so thirsty. Please, Papa. Please don't hurt me anymore.' And then it happens. I try to wake up, but it happens, anyway. It's Jordy's way of getting back at me, no matter how hard I try to stop him from saying it…over and over. I try, but…"

"Jesus. What happens, Bernie?" Judd's head shook back and forth in dismay.

"It's Jordy at the other end of the ventilator cord. He's got a nose like an elephant thirsting in the dust of Death Valley. He's dry and parched. A little leathered mummy. He keeps trying to drink, and the cord gets tighter. Finally, the rubber snaps. It snaps as soon as he says, 'Thanks, Dad. Thanks for keeping your promises, you prick.'"

Bernie Panzer was really perspiring now. His shirt was tight and getting tighter as drenching sweat seemed to tighten the collar around his neck. His breath came in short gasps. For a moment, Judd thought his friend could pass out or have a stroke.

"And then I wake up from my dream," Panzer continued. His words were desperate. "I wake up. I wake up, wanting to die."

Fat tears flowed out of Bernie Panzer's eyes. He made no attempt to stop them, except to slightly bow his bald head.

Judd could hardly look at Bernie, could hardly stand witnessing so much pain. He was, for one of the few times in his life, at a loss for words.

*   *   *   *   *

The jury had begun its deliberations on a bright Tuesday morning, and by Friday afternoon it still hadn't reached a verdict. The wait became excruciating. Judd Saranno's office seemed to be getting smaller and smaller as he and the Panzers waited for the court clerk to telephone. The air in the office became heavy and stale. Occasionally, Judd swirled in his chair as Bernie and Rhoda held hands and tried to comfort one another. Rhoda nourished and rubbed her husband's back and arms. The tired look in her pale face gave way to the fear that surrounded her heart.

"How long does it take for them to decide?" Rhoda asked.

"The jury must be sharply divided," Judd replied. "The bailiff told me they were yelling at each other yesterday. Today, it's quieter." Judd slapped his hand on the onyx top of his desk. "All we've got to do is convince the leader of the pack that doubt exists, and the rest will follow like little ducklings." Judd stroked his chin. "I try to find the leader, Bernie. If I convince *that* person, it's a downhill slide on the way to the verdict."

Rhoda wasn't convinced. "I need answers, Judd. What if the jury's deadlocked? Can the judge declare a mistrial?"

Judd nodded. "If it goes on long enough, and the jury feels it's impossible for them to reach unanimous agreement."

White Knuckle

For three days, Judd had been assessing the possibilities. One, of course, would be acquittal, a stunning precedent for the defense. But how long does it take to determine that doubt exists? Three and a half days of deliberations spoke for itself. The fact of doubt on the part of some jurors was obvious. Maybe they were dealing with too many emotions. A dead child. Mercy. The right to live and the right to die. Money. Morals. Politics.

In Judd's mind, the final decision was probably being settled with a few jurors' sighs and moans or disgruntled abstentions that would eventually be worn down into frazzled acquiescence. Innocent. That, or a hopeless deadlock.

Finally, an excited voice over the intercom interrupted the anxious trio in Judd's office. "Mr. Saranno, you have a call from the courthouse. They have a verdict."

Bernie rose from his chair, grabbed his stomach, and sat back down. "I can't move, my guts are cramped."

Rhoda Panzer stood ramrod straight, but her eyes darted nervously in every direction.

Judd jumped up from his high-back leather chair. "Right on," he said as he pumped his arm back to his side like he'd just sunk a forty-foot putt. "I told you they'd come back before Friday night, Bernie. I've never seen a jury want to deliberate over a weekend. We're looking good, pal. Let's go."

Just before they entered the courthouse, Judd instructed his friend, "Stand straight when we're told to rise, and look proud if you can. Hang in there, Bernie. It's almost over."

The courtroom was still and quiet when the jurors returned to their seats. No one looked happy. No one looked relieved.

The judge turned to face the jury box. "Ladies and gentlemen, am I to understand you've reached your verdict?"

The thin-lipped woman, the one who Judd had predicted would be the leader, stood. She grasped a white piece of paper. "We have, Your Honor," she said without a quiver.

"Is your verdict unanimous?" the judge intoned.

"It is, Your Honor."

"Would the defendant please rise," the judge requested, glancing toward the defense table.

Judd gripped Bernie's elbow, more to steady himself than his client. He stared at the woman with the final verdict in her hand. She gave no sign. She showed no emotion.

"You may read your verdict."

Judd waited for a smile. A glint of light. There was nothing.

"We the jury, having been duly empaneled to justly hear and try this case, find the defendant..."

For Judd, and all trial lawyers, this part was the most excruciating, waiting for a jury to fill in the blank. Guilty or not guilty. This is why trial lawyers drink too much. Eventually they'll be able to deal with the end result one way or another. If they win, they're heroes. If they lose, they appeal. But at this very moment, the wait is dreadful. For one millisecond the time she took to spit the words out at a speed of 700 miles an hour to his ear – was torture. Judd felt like he always did at this point: naked before his peers. Not a stitch on his entire body. Really naked, and really small. Bare bones to the wind. Tiny.

White Knuckle

"…guilty, Your Honor."

The salt-and-pepper haired woman's head turned sharply. Her glare blasted into Judd's eyeballs, and then her stare turned to the prosecutor, Ms. Jennifer Ottington, as both their mouths wrinkled into slight, foxy smiles. Judd was numb with disbelief as he watched the subtle, prome-nading prance of the two fillies who had just won their first big derby.

"Guilty of murder in the second degree," she said.

And that was that. The gavel fell.

Sheriff's deputies moved toward the defense table.

Bernie looked for a sympathizer among the jurors who refused to look his way. Reporters leaped for the doors. Rhoda Panzer struggled to keep from fainting.

"What does this mean, Judd?" Bernie cried. "Judd, does this mean I can't…" His words were mushy. Both men gripped the other as they kept them-selves from falling into their seats.

"I can't believe it, Bernie," Judd said, his head shaking, his eyes blinking in amazement. "I just don't believe it."

Bernie's desperation oozed from every pore. "What now, Judd? What? What happens next?" Cameras flashed and the judge banged his gavel ordering the deputies to arrest anyone who dared to take a picture.

"What will happen to Rhoda, Judd? Can I…see my wife? Judd, can I?"

"Steady, Bernie. Steady. We'll have time to talk."

Rhoda Panzer couldn't get around the bailiff or the guards. A stranger's hand pulled her back as the jury was discharged and as Bernard H. Panzer was hand-cuffed in preparation for his becoming the newest ward of the state of Colorado.

"Thirty years, Judd? Thirty...fucking...years? I can't believe it," Judd mumbled helplessly. "I can't..."

The trial was over. Bernie Panzer got shackled and taken away from his wailing wife, the media, the prosecutor, the courtroom junkies, and his lawyer.

"I'll have lawyers begin the appeal tomorrow," was the last thing Bernie heard Judd call out to him as he was led from the courtroom.

Judd Saranno was left alone. A trial lawyer in defeat. No one to talk to and no one to care. Not even Rhoda waited for him. She was taken away by her friends with wet handkerchiefs and enough tears to keep them from ever drying.

Judd looked around. Exhaustion spilled over him. He felt a growing sense of relief, and yet despair. Acquiescence and acceptance. Adrenaline forced his breath to come in unsteady beats as he waved a silent goodbye to the judge's empty bench and walked out of the courthouse.

Judd Saranno headed absently toward his car in the parking lot. Now, he only had three things left to do before moving to California. First, he had to see Asia. Then he had to sign the last of the divorce papers. Finally, Judd would get to his son. They were going fishing. Levi and his dad. Fishing together.

The thoughts about the future gave him some consolation. His pace quickened as he moved to the Mercedes parked alone in an empty lot. Slowly and with effort, his thoughts distanced themselves from Bernie, handcuffs, chains, bars, and cells with cold, hard concrete. Those images were replaced as his mind began to focus on the friend he needed most. Asia.

5

Seventy miles south of Denver, Judd's Mercedes exceeded the speed limit on the freeway to Colorado Springs. His destination was the Broadmoor Hotel with its suites snuggled against the mountain majesty of Pike's Peak. In the Rocky Mountains, there were gems resting under purple skies. Peace could be found in the mother load, and the Broadmoor was a diamond sanctuary. It was a haven where lovers could cavort while spouses were forgotten as the minions rendezvoused to escape the stresses of "Life's a bitch, and then you die."

Judd traveled to be near the tall, green, and rugged Rockies. He needed to be with Asia, to escape the turmoil that was still boiling in the depths of The Mile-High City.

The farther away from Denver Judd got, the easier it was to stop feeling sorry for, or guilty over, Bernie Panzer. The faster he drove, the less he saw Panzer's pitiful face when Bernie realized he was facing thirty years behind bars. Bernie would have to serve about fifteen of those years, if he didn't do anything stupid, like commit suicide.

Judd hoped that Rhoda Panzer would hold her husband together. The lawyer could do nothing more about the verdict. There were a few futile motions, and a last-gasp appeal that could be handled by others. Judd had to get on with his own life, a life centered wholly on Asia Nichols.

Judd's heart raced when he entered the Broadmoor Hotel lobby and walked into a waiting elevator. Judd felt lightheaded, with a sense of invincibility. He knew that if the world caved in and covered him with dirt, he would either dig harder or buy a new shovel. For the first time in a long time, he was aware of possibilities, of choices, of renewal and hope. Judd's weight shifted from one foot to the other as he waited anxiously for Asia to open her door. The bouquet in his hand was a collage of bright, spring colors.

Asia smiled at the first sight of him standing before her. She was swift and gentle as she reached out and pulled Judd into the room. In seconds, her long nails caressed his cheek and the back of his neck. Her lips touched his as soon as the door behind them was bolted shut. In their own timeless world, they were finally safe from the one outside.

Judd put the flowers on the dresser, watching Asia's jade-green eyes filling with passion. She smelled seductive as she unbuttoned the tie around his neck.

"The only place I want to see a tie is around your ankle," she said.

Judd tossed his jacket onto a chair and pulled her close. Asia wore a man's silk dress shirt, Judd's, and nothing else.

His hands moved swiftly over the shallows of her back and down the sides of her hips as she stood poised on the tips of her toes, like a gymnast ready to vault the horizontal beam. Her long, runway-model legs stretched as she moved her fingers to unfasten his shirt and undo the zipper of his pants. She fell to her knees as his slacks slid to the floor. Her mouth was on him, and he was growing. Hard.

Then her lips and mouth and soft tongue...lick and caress and moist and moan and back and forth and forth and back as he balanced himself against the dresser.

Judd's eyes closed as waves crested through her mouth and he thought about shadows. Shadows that could vanish when a different light shined in his world. Darkness was a shadow's shelter. Judd relished the light. He floated in the luminous afterglow at the Broadmoor Hotel in Colorado Springs.

The beautiful, young lover finally freed Judd and looked up with a smile. "You're not always this easy," she said, slipping away. "I thought the verdict might dampen your spirit."

"It's been a long time since you did that, honey, and nothing will ever stop me from wanting you."

Asia spun in a circle like a ballerina. "I'm so excited, Judd. In just days, we'll finally be in San Francisco. No more hiding in hotel rooms or parking your car in my garage. Think of it. Just you and me and no more chaos."

"You make me feel alive, Asia."

"You deserve it, Judd. No matter what some people might think, you're filled with light and warmth. You're good and clean and deserve unconditional love. You're everything any woman would hope for. Now, and in the future, you'll be cherished. I love you more than anyone could ever love you."

"I thought my love for Levi was special, and it is. But, Asia, my feelings for you aren't like anything I felt before. Even with someone, I've been alone, like I was in a desert, hiding. You give me the right to live and be happy. Passionate serenity has been my goal, Asia, and with you, I've found it."

She kissed him hard on the mouth. "I want children, Judd. I want us to have a baby. Just one. A girl or boy. It doesn't matter. Tell me you'll be happy if I get pregnant. I'd be a wonderful mother."

"You're the baby I want," Judd said softly. "We'll talk about others when the smoke clears. There's a lot to do in California."

Asia sighed and frowned. "Stop talking business. I called the sales manager yesterday, and he's got two buyers bidding for the dealership. The estate is in great shape. My father said he'd protect me, and he did."

Judd reached for her hands, and quickly her arms were around his neck. Asia. Twenty-eight years old and beautiful and excited about the future. She was almost more than Judd could handle. Always dancing or skiing. Aerobics in the morning, running a travel agency by day, and forever planning to see the world.

He often wondered why she had picked him when she could have had anyone. At first, he thought it was his money that attracted her. He'd gone into Asia's travel agency a year earlier to pick up some first-class plane tickets. Usually, his secretary took care of it, but she was sick, and that day was the crossroad that changed Judd's life. Asia had handed him his airline tickets, thanked him for his business, and smiled. Her green eyes were luminous, and Judd Saranno was thunder-stuck. From that moment on, Judd's life kept getting better and better.

Asia made him feel young and powerful and loved and free. She was an uninhibited explosion of energy, with her own goals and her own recipe for happiness. A passionate beauty who somehow fell in love with the heart of a graying trial lawyer. She was the first woman to ever make him feel vulnerable.

She heightened his perception of life, offered him optimism and a bright new shiny day. Just when cynicism and bleakness were beginning to set in, Asia plucked him out of the maelstrom just in time. He was a lover again. The kind of intimacy he had with her was new to Judd. He'd never experienced it before, or if he had, he had forgotten.

Asia was like no one Judd had ever met. She was a giver, not a taker. A powerful passion radiated in how she looked, talked, laughed, and loved. Asia was a leader, commanding others to follow, to believe, to trust. She was real in spirit, and soul, and wisdom, and strength. Insightful. Spiritual. Happy.

White Knuckle

Peaceful, kind, and warm, with an inner goodness and loving nature that made Judd feel protected. She protected Judd, and no one had ever done that before. Judd was her champion. Asia was his warrior. Together, they were content.

Asia was smiling as she stood back and unbuttoned her silk shirt. Judd's shirt. "Now, it's my turn," she smiled.

He watched as white silk fell to the carpet and marveled at the tightness of her skin and the softness of her breasts. Her body was sleek and slender. Long and firm. The triangle between her legs was so small that when he made love to her in the past, he sometimes wondered why he couldn't feel the other side or why she didn't hurt. All he knew about that part of her anatomy was that it was tight. Damn tight. And he loved it. Moving inside of her.

Asia glided gracefully toward the king-size bed that had been turned down and was waiting. With her back to Judd, she bent down and poured two glasses of champagne from the bottle cradled in the ice bucket near the bed. Judd tossed what was left of his clothes onto the floor and moved closer to the softness of her body. He reached out to touch the sides of her waist and caressed the smoothness of her hips.

Asia sensed a growing need in herself. She wanted the warmth of his flesh next to hers. She turned and handed him the champagne-filled glass. "This is to us," she said, raising her glass to his, "and to our adventures in California." Stark naked and smiling.

Judd felt like a giant. He could conquer the world. "When I was younger," he said, "I had a dream. I walked on the sky and I held a cloud in my hand. I battled dragons and swam oceans in a day." They toasted the champagne glasses together. "There was nothing I couldn't do. But even though I could do it, I didn't want to do it alone."

Judd felt wonderfully alive. Exalted. "Thank you," he said, "for letting me truly fall in love. Loving you is easy; it's not work. The feeling you give me is something I've never found – until now."

Asia laughed. "You're such a pushover, Judd. One tough, trial lawyer who could be beaten every time, if anyone knew about your sex life. You're simply hard when you're soft, and soft when you're hard. When you really want something, you'll give away the farm. When you don't care, there's no point in discussing it. The problem with your contemporaries, Judd darling, is that they just don't know when to negotiate."

"Maybe you're right," he said. "But why the champagne? Are we celebrating something I don't know about?"

Asia took the glass of champagne from his hand, carefully placing the drink on the night stand next to the bed. She laid down on her back and propped her head up on feathered pillows. Uncovered and intoxicating, she tingled on the sheets, waiting for him to join her. She reached out and touched Judd's pelvis as he moved down to be closer to her.

"I'm negotiating," she said. "Good wine should go good places. Dom Perignon is not always for drinking, you know."

His lips moved toward her neck, but she turned his head and put her glass of champagne on his mouth. "Now it's my turn," she said. "Swirl some of this around your teeth, but don't swallow. I swallow. You don't. Dribble a bubble at a time, all over my body. Anywhere. Any place. Don't touch me with your hands. Use champagne and your tongue. Drop and flick it off at your leisure. Real slow, Judd. Real soft and slow."

"How are you feeling?" Judd asked and filled his mouth with wine.

"Wet," was all she could say as she drifted and waited to catch a wave. "I'm feeling wet."

"But I haven't started."

"I know." She paused. "I have."

Judd leaned over her breast, and let the moisture fall to the tip of her nipple. The wine flowed from the swollen peak of her bosom as his tongue flashed to capture the dampness before it streamed into her cleavage. He started over. Did it again. And again. One more time, and then to the next one. One sip. One drop. A flickering lick and then more places to dampen and water.

"Don't rush," she whispered. "Let it fall and catch it gently. Catch it all. But don't use your hands. Use your head and face and hair and chest. Not a finger, just your body. Your tits next to mine." Touching. Barely. "Pretend you're a cat, Judd. A sandy tongue…"

She fell silent. The stillness before the storm. And then the murmur began. Just a hush in the beginning as Judd caressed each curve. First a trickle of moisture, then a nudge with his cheek or chin or a temple with tender pressure up and down, in and out. There, then gone. Like a floating feather in a summer breeze. Nothing, and then overwhelmed. Hot, then cool turning into heat once more. Blistering damp. Her murmur became a moan.

"Everywhere," she whispered.

Her voice was muffled by her thighs.

"Judd. Everywhere."

Her eyes closed as images danced and fantasies waltzed freely in her head. And, then, out loud, an aching burst. She locked her lover's ears between her legs. "You're mine, Judd. I'm yours."

Daniel J. Gatti

The glass in her hand tipped softly onto the mattress, as her hands fingered his hair and pressured him gently into her groin. Harder now. Louder. The lull became a gust. The gust became a blow. Her passion consumed her as her back arched in a spasm that forced Judd to hold the sides of her hips as he held his breath and waited for the rumbling to soften.

She grabbed his head, his hair, his shoulders, as she cried, "Judd, I love you" Her entire body was shuddering.

When the quivering quieted, Judd softly kissed her stomach, her breasts, and then her lips. They held each other close, knowing that soon they would be sleeping next to each other on a constant basis. No more, "I've got to dress now." No more, "I'll call you in the morning." No more emptiness.

A new life loomed, a future. Hopes and dreams. Excitement. They knew it would last forever. Nothing and no one was ever going to get in their way. It was a promise they had made to each other. It was a promise they intended to keep. Consummating their love had changed their life. For a lifetime.

6

When Levi first found out his father was soon to be history, panic struck his inner soul, and there was nothing the boy could do to regain control. Levi was alone in a fragile canoe, riding the rapids. How could this possibly happen, he'd wondered. There was only one explanation: it was his fault.

Months before Bernie's trial began, Judd and Sheryl had first approached their sons like mourners about to drop flowers on a coffin going underground. Seeing the look on his parents' faces, Levi knew something serious was about to happen. His mother had called a "family meeting." Levi hated these events. Someone was always in trouble. Usually him. But this trouble was like nothing he could have imagined.

"Your dad and I are getting divorced, and Dad's moving to California," Sheryl had announced as she and Judd sat across from their sons on the two loveseats that flanked the stone fireplace.

Joshua stared stoically at his mother and father. Levi was terrified.

Sheryl continued. "There will be some changes in the next few months that you're going to find difficult to deal with, but understand that, in the end, everything will be fine."

More panic. Levi looked anxiously at his father.

Judd reached out and touched his son's knee. "Listen to your mother," he said. "It will be okay, Levi."

Levi stood up defiantly. "What do you mean, divorce? Dad's leaving?" His words were filled with incomprehension. Levi clenched his fists into hard, little balls. His face turned crimson as tears flooded down his cheeks. "Dad, you didn't tell me you were *leaving*. You said you'd never go anywhere."

"It won't be for a few more months," Sheryl reassured him.

But Levi didn't care what his mother was saying. Her words echoed in the large room. Levi's face was burning. He looked to his father for support and found none. Judd shook his head and bit his lower lip. He wasn't talking. Not yet.

Joshua sat silently, showing little emotion. For some reason, he didn't seem surprised or angry or alarmed. This was just another family meeting confirming that he and his father weren't going to be together. For Joshua, that wasn't much of a change.

"I don't understand." Levi was horrified. "Divorce? No! What are you talking about?"

Sure his parents fought, but didn't most parents? He'd grown up with it, it was a natural part of his environment. And there were lots of good times, like when he was little and had his nanny, Kit. And all the trips with his dad were the best.

Levi turned to his father. "You're not going anywhere, Dad. Not without me...are you?" His young, lean body started to cramp. His legs were aching. "It's not true. It can't be."

Sheryl quickly reached over to console her son. "Levi, I promise you, it's going to be okay."

"Get away from me," he lashed out. "You're lying!"

Judd tried to pull his son to him, but Levi was inconsolable. He stood his ground, guarding the gates to his guts, his fear, and with quivering hands, covered his ears. He didn't want to hear their words. He couldn't feel his father's touch.

His parents were right next to him, pleading and caressing but their actions and words meant nothing.

The second Levi understood the consequences of his parent's choice to divorce, he jumped into his Puckerbush Patch, and he didn't even know it. This was the place his nanny had talked about. The Patch. Levi remembered, once he got there. Once he understood.

Kit was Levi's nanny. Kit had told him there was a place where rabbits could scurry when they were afraid. People too. The Puckerbush Patch was a safe place to hide, but he'd never been there before. Somehow, he'd jumped in instinctively. Certainly, it was a better place to be than with people who were trying to justify the crime of abandonment.

They were outside, and he was in. Alone. Alone with his aching heart.

Every day since the family meeting, Levi Matthew Saranno had stood in front of the bathroom mirror, assessing himself. Even at age nine, he had the makings of an athletic body. He had a winning smile. And he had courage. He was a kid on a mission, not knowing that when a relationship dies it can't be brought back to life by the gallant gestures of a child.

There were lessons Levi had to learn. When he learned about the natural consequences of losing someone you love, then at least he could put up the first pucker and attach it firmly to the top of his patch. The Puckerbush Patch Kit promised he would find. Levi remembered the story. He just didn't fully understand it.

Weeks passed while Judd prepared for Panzer's trial, and more family meetings were called. At each meeting Levi tried to negotiate a peace treaty. Some sort of marital truce. When that didn't work, his panic grew worse.

"The divorce is my fault, isn't it?" he eventually confessed to his parents at another meeting. "You can't agree to be together, and it's because of me." His chin fell to his chest, and his eyes closed as if he were praying. Tears fell on the carpet.

Both parents were numb.

"Levi…" Again Sheryl started to reach for him, but Judd raised a hand as if to say, "Wait. Leave him alone and let him speak."

Levi looked up, through the redness in his eyes, and said,"What did I do wrong?" His body trembled like an icicle in the wind. "I'll be nicer to Josh. I promise I'll stop wetting the bed. It only started a month ago, and I can stop. I won't ever go to sleep until I do."

"It's not your fault, Levi." His mother's words were soft and gentle. "It's *not* your fault. You do fine with Joshua, and we know this bed-wetting thing is only temporary. You have a right to be upset, and sometimes feelings show in different ways. Come here, honey. Let me hold you." She reached out.

Levi stood still. He looked at his father. "Dad?" His head was turning in disbelief. The words wouldn't come out.

Judd's heart was ripping. "What is it?" his father asked. "Tell me, son. Go ahead."

Levi's lips were wet and quaking. "Dad…if I was little Jordy, would you have killed me like his dad did?"

Judd bowed his head. Levi backed away, looking frightened.

White Knuckle

"Would you, Dad? Would you have killed me?"

Judd's outstretched arms pleaded for Levi to come into them. "Never, Levi. Never."

Levi didn't move into Judd's helpless embrace. He looked at his mother. "And you?" he asked.

Sheryl could hardly speak. "Of course not," she said. "Not in a million years."

Levi was backing out the door, slowly, almost as if he was afraid to turn his back on them. "Then why are you doing it now?" he asked.

Levi's words were quiet as they left his mouth, but as the words entered his parent's ears, the noise was louder than a whip cracking in a silent corral.

Levi backed out of the room and ran up the stairs.

* * * * *

There's a lot of darkness in Puckerbush Patches, but it's a safe darkness, like sleeping with the covers over your head. They're your covers, and it's your space. It's a comfort zone only you can understand and sleep in. Alone. But in it, you're safe.

When you close your eyes, the dreams start and the light shines, and bad memories are forgotten, erased. Levi jumped into his patch and covered himself with a pucker he'd just discovered.

As far as he could recall, Levi was five when his mother first told him all people were sinners. But when Kit came all the way from Norway to be Levi's nanny, she told him that children weren't sinners. They were too innocent. This made more sense to Levi even if it did fly in the face of his mother's conviction that those who didn't dwell on the Savior at all times would surely end up in the fires of Hell. Mom was loving enough, but Levi never quite understood her ideas about what was right and wrong.

As Levi grew, he learned how to cope with life as a sinner, but from the very beginning, he learned he couldn't cope without his dad or his Kit. He quickly taught himself how to deal with his mother's righteousness. He ignored it. This was made easier because Daddy had bought Mom the nanny. With Kit, Levi was always honest.

Kit was Levi's real nurturer. Right from the start, she'd read him fairytales and stories about the hunters and the hunted, the takers and the givers. Kit would sit for hours in a rocking chair, and the back of Levi's head would snuggle into her bosom as she read to him.

Kit came to the Saranno family, and her job was to help with the boys while Sheryl helped the community and Judd did his job. Kit was soft and gentle. Her voice was always calm. She sang and laughed and sparkled. A Scandinavian blond with blue eyes and a small, lithe body, smiling constantly, always focusing on the boys. Kit loved her job and did it well.

Kit helped Joshua with computers and books and school. Joshua worked his brain. Levi worked his heart. Kit worked on the spirit. Kit was good and kind and tender. Loving and warm. A caregiver. Joyous and happy. Kit was only nineteen when she first came to America. At twenty-three she realized her time with the Sarannos was about to end.

Levi loved her scent and the gentleness of her touch. Even her voice reminded him of fresh air and springtime. But Kit didn't call him Levi. For her, Levi's *real* name was Matty. Only Kit and Levi's father called him Matty. Kit whispered it secretly; his dad used the name when Mom wasn't hanging around.

White Knuckle

Sheryl hated the name Matthew. "I don't want him thinking he's an apostle," she once told Judd. "You've got enough conceit, Judd, and that's a trait I'd just as soon Levi not inherit. You gave him the name Matthew, but someday he might drop it."

"Your middle name is Matthew, Levi," Kit said with reverence. "In the Bible, Levi was a tax collector, and not nice. He took advantage of people. He forced peasants to give money to the Roman emperor."

"Then, he met Jesus, and he became a disciple. Christ changed his name to Matthew, stopped his evil ways, and Matthew dedicated himself to goodness and spreading the gospel."

"Am I a sinner?"

"I don't think so. You're the best as far as I can tell. That's why I call you Matty. I think everyone should call you Matthew, and when you're older, you can change your name when the time's right."

One evening, just before Kit got her pink slip from Sheryl, she sat with Levi, both of them in rocking chairs on the huge screened porch. Levi had just heard about his parents' breakup, and he was frightened about his future.

Kit told him that God gives all his creatures, animals and humans, ways to protect themselves from danger and pain.

"How does he do that?" Levi asked.

"For instance, take rabbits," Kit said. "Can you tell me why God gave rabbits such big ears, and you've got little ones?"

Levi thought, and then thought some more. "I don't want big ears," he said. "If I had ears like a rabbits, I'd really look dumb."

"But the question is, Levi, why do rabbits have those ears? They have big ears so they can hear the predators. Their ears, speed, and patches protect them."

"Patches?" Levi stopped rocking to look at Kit.

"The ones they jump into for protection. If a rabbit is smart, he doesn't venture too far from his patch. When a fox tries to catch him, the rabbit runs to his patch and scampers in as fast as he can. The fox can only sniff and growl and scratch, but the rabbit is safe in his patch. The killer fox can be just a breath away, but he can't get to the bunny. As long as the rabbit's got its defenses, the attacker is helpless."

"Then how come rabbits die?"

Kit reached out and stroked Levi's hand. Her gentle fingers moved to smooth his pink cheeks and stern little chin. "They get eaten when they get careless or when they get stupid. People are the same. You and me too, Matty. We've all got to put up our puckers, or the fox might catch us by surprise."

"I don't get it," he said. "What are puckers?"

"Think of the thorns on a rose bush. They're only there to protect the rose. Or the porcupine with prickly spears all over its body for protection. We all have our puckers, and we all have our patches. If we hide in our Puckerbush Patch, no one can hurt us, even though they're breathing right down our necks or trying to blow the house down. If you can find your Puckerbush Patch, no one can touch you. You'll always be safe."

Levi stretched out his arms and jumped into her lap. "When I'm with you or Dad, Kit, I don't need a Puckerbush Patch."

Kit held him close. "I know, Matty. But we're not always going to be there. So always remember the rabbit, Matty. Its got its ears and speed. The rabbit also has his patch. Find yours, and keep it close. Keep it really close, so you've always got a place to hide. And beware of predators. They can look like a friend, but they can eat you like you were a rabbit. They are the hunters, and they'll consume you, if you let them. They'll take everything. Even your spirit."

Levi began to wonder who the hunters really were. First Kit was leaving, and soon it would be his dad. It didn't make sense. Levi looked for puckers, but didn't know where to find them. His situation was confusing, and he was helpless to do anything about it, but he tried. At night, he covered his face and hid under the blankets, looking for warmth and comfort and peace. Even at age nine, he tried as hard and as strong as his little mind allowed.

Levi wanted a Puckerbush Patch he could call his own.

7

For Judd, taking his son fishing was a big responsibility. Not like going to a football game and watching the Denver Broncos win or lose. If they lost, Levi could blame the coaches, the players, or the referee. In fishing, however, the accountability for success or failure falls directly on the shoulders of Dad. If Dad flops and the stringer stays empty all day, the kid's impression of the old man could be adversely affected for a lifetime. Judd knew this, and Levi figured it out quickly.

At four in the morning, Judd Saranno walked into his son's bedroom to wake him. It was dark outside, but moonlight through the window allowed Judd to see Levi's lean body stretched beneath the blankets. He prodded the boy. Levi instantly awoke, jumped up from the bed, and stood before his father, fully dressed.

Judd laughed when he saw his son all ready to go.

"You always tell me to think ahead, Dad, "Levi said proudly. "I never got undressed. Takes too much time."

After a quick bowl of cereal, father and son filled two Thermos bottles, one with coffee, and the other with hot chocolate. They stopped for doughnuts, and headed down the highway to Colorado Springs. As they drove past the Broadmoor Hotel, Judd acknowledged the hideaway with a tip of his hat and a smile.

They went through Manitou Springs, and the truck began climbing the winding, rocky mountainsides of the great Pike's Peak. Judd turned to his son. "Are you catching cutthroats or minnows today?"

"Browns, Dad. I read that brown trout are jumping on the Frying Pan River and the Roaring Fork. Actually, they could be anywhere. I'm going to get one.

"You've got big ambitions, boy. Maybe with *my* help, you'll be able to catch that guy and haul him home for dinner."

"I don't need no help, Dad. I got plans, and I know just where to go. We're at the same place as last year, aren't we?"

"Same place, Matty. If anyone else could get to it, it'd be famous. Levi's Choke Hole.

"*You* called it Levi's Choke Hole, I didn't. I just got too excited, and got a little wet."

"A little wet?" Judd slapped his son's leg. "You broke your line and damned near drowned trying to stab that fish to death with the tip of your rod!"

"I won't make the same mistake twice," Levi said with confidence as he tried to remember just where they had gone, and at what rock the fish had taken the fly.

"I think you were under water for thirty seconds before I grabbed your ass and pulled you free."

"I was holding my breath while I got my waders off."

"You choked, kid, and we're going to Levi's Choke Hole."

Levi liked his dad's driving, and his dad's guts when he got behind the wheel of his fishing rig. Levi knew that when his father found the spot to turn off the winding mountain road, Judd would jam the four wheel into first gear, and they'd head from the top of the canyon to the river below. The ride down the skid trail would be a thriller.

If a dead limb or a downed log got in the way, they'd go around it or through it. The truck would get scratched, the bumpers would get dinged, and the antenna would bend or become a part of the forest. This rig had character. They were going to Levi's Choke Hole, and they were fishing. Levi remembered the one time his mother came along. She lasted about two minutes down the rugged skid trail. First, she had to stop drinking coffee. Then she had to tighten her seat belt, and there was no shoulder harness for the person in the middle. She moved by the door, complaining that she felt like a basketball bouncing up and down. After one particularly large ditch, her head hit the cab roof and banged against the side window. She mentioned something about tits in her throat, and when a branch made a small crack in the windshield, she screamed that glass was going to scar them all for life.

They never did get to Levi's Choke Hole that day. His mother got sick, then scared, and eventually she got angry when his father couldn't find a place in the middle of the trail to turn around. She had to get out and walk. It was the one time they didn't go fishing as planned.

That was an adventure to be forgotten. Today, Levi waited intently for his father to stop the truck on the windy, mountain road. Judd finally put on the brakes, and exited his opened door.

Before his father took off the winch cover and started down to the river, Levi surveyed the area and etched in his mind the rocky ridge that jutted from a nearby cliff and pointed to the covered skid trail leading down to the water. The ridge was a natural marker that would always show the way to Levi as he got older and as the forest changed and grew. The ridge reminded Levi of a rainbow trout, with rock sides of pink and purple and speckled gray and brown. There were spots of black, and the rock rainbow's snout glistened red with Colorado clay pointing to the trail and the monster fish in Levi's Choke Hole.

"Fish aren't much different than people," his father once told him. "You can catch and control a person when his guard's down, when he's resting. You can't catch a fish when it's on the run and focused on where it's going. If you meet a person with a plan, he probably won't take your bait. If he takes your bait, then don't slack off until you've got'em in the net. If you let slack in the line, he might twist off and be gone forever."

"What do I use as bait?"

"Something he wants. Something you have, and he doesn't. Get him when he's hungry, not well-fed."

Remembering all the rules was difficult for a kid half the size of his fishing pole.

"Don't forget, Levi, you have to stay in control. You have to be flexible enough to bend, and to let him run, if he wants. At the same time, you need enough finesse to manipulate him into your net when the right time comes. All of us probably want power, but ninety percent of the people only catch ten percent of the fish. Ten percent of the people are destined to lead ninety percent of the men and women who willingly follow. If your hook is set, use your control wisely, and the followers come along with ease."

Levi thought about what admirable efforts were going to serve him well as they descended down the skid trail. Down the side of the mountain they thundered, in low gear. The brakes were on, and small limbs broke and dry brush crumbled beneath the bouncing tires.

"If you ever bring a girl down here Levi, be sure she's got pizzazz. Remember that word, 'pizzazz.' Find a woman with pizzazz, Levi, and you're halfway home. Hopefully, she'll have a zest for adventure, a yearning for excitement.

White Knuckle

There's nothing wrong with a woman who yearns for high tea and pedicures, but if the same lady likes her feet dirty and a cold-river bath, then good looks just add to her charm. Look beneath the skin, Levi, and discover the spirit. A woman with a reverent spirit is worth ten who've got nice legs."

"Mom says no fancy woman would come here. Look what happened to her. I mean, you and her."

"Levi, I can do *almost* anything, but I can't stay married to your mom. I can be your dad though. Parents can get divorced, but they can't divorce their children. I'll always be there for you; you can count on that."

"How can I count on you a thousand miles away? You leave tomorrow, and I go to summer camp. Mom says I'll be there two weeks. Maybe longer."

"You'll find friends, Levi. Kids go to summer camp so they can grow up. I know it might be scary, but you'll learn things about nature, yourself, and people."

"I don't care..." Levi said, his eyes starting to tear.

"There's no need to cry, Levi. This won't be the last time for you and me. I'll never get so far away you can't find me. I'm the *one* person you can count on. I promise that. As a kid, you count on your dad. As a man, you try to find a woman. If you find the right one, then you count your blessings and take care of her."

"How will I know who's the right one?"

Judd thought. "Look for someone just like yourself or like Kit." Judd laughed. "Someone just like me. If you ever find a woman who loves you as much as I do, then you'll be safe, and you'll be happy. It sounds sort of stupid, but I'm right. I promise."

About a hundred yards from the water, the once-narrow skid trail opened up into a broad meadow of lush green grass and brightly colored blossoms of wild yellow, blue, and purple. Miniature red bouquets were drinking in the morning dew that had formed on their petals during the night. Judd stopped the rig at the water's edge.

Air on a trout stream tastes and feels and smells and soothes and awakens unlike air any place else on earth. It's crisp and clean, and as it travels over the straits and shallows and holes, it brings with it a sense of awareness that anyone can feel and see if they take the time to listen and observe.

Levi was in the water in minutes. The cold water hugged his legs as he cautiously edged forward into the stream that swiftly flowed through the deep crevices of the purple mountain. His hip waders tightened as Levi moved deeper.

"I'm going to get you, big boy," he said to the water and the air.

The current swirled around rocks and over boulders and splashed against trees that had tumbled into the river after winter winds and eroding soil. In spots, the stream was too swift, making it unsafe. Levi knew there were few fish to be caught in the treacherous white water runs where the river surged dangerously, and he dashed downstream to reach calmer eddies around a bend or where the canyon widened.

The fish wouldn't be resting in the fast-flowing rapids of the river. Levi's prey could be caught either above the white water or below it, not in it. Levi concentrated his attention on the fifty yards of water above the spouting rapids. He was after the first and biggest fish, and he had to snatch it in a hurry, because his father was headed downstream to cast his luck below the white water's teeming current.

As Levi moved into the stream, he snapped the tip of his rod back and forth, to spin out the line. "Ten to two," he kept saying to himself. "Two to ten and ten to two."

Judd had taught his son to use wrist action, how to keep his elbow parallel with the ground. "Snap forward to ten, wrist back to two," his father had said. "Wait one second, and snap forward, letting the fly sail through the air until it gently falls above the suspected hiding place." The nimble bait was supposed to tiptoe on top of the water as it floated past the fish waiting for breakfast.

Levi selected several imitation bugs that he thought might work magic. Sub-surface nymphing with dead drifts was sometimes great, but gliding a dry replica of an insect on the top of the water was more exciting when a fish struck. Levi liked Mayflies, but on this day, he took out a #14 western March brown dry fly with speckled tan wings. If the presentation was authentic, and if the fish was hungry, the decoy would be swallowed and the adventure would begin.

Levi calmly edged his way to the middle of the stream. The fisherman marked his target as he moved slowly in an effort to lessen sounds that could distract or frighten the fish. The rhythm of his line was graceful as it arched back and forth over his head. The young boy sensed an early strike as he carefully laid the March brown down on the crest of the rolling current.

Judd Saranno had hesitated in his decision to start below the white water outlet. Instead of moving downstream and working his way back up the river, Levi's father stopped to watch as his son maneuvered the fishing line into the correct position.

Leaning against a towering tree, Judd knew Levi was aching for a thunderous strike at the end of his line. Each time the fly was thrown, it sailed with a purpose and an expectation of success. Judd watched his son proudly.

Levi threw the March brown wings near the bank, into calm shallows behind the giant boulders. The tan wings danced on top of the water beckoning the wary German brown or rainbow trout to take a chance, to try just a mouthful. Levi was working upstream toward a fallen tree, and although it looked like a holding spot, it would be very difficult for someone his size to manage, because of the protruding branches and snagging leaves.

Levi snapped his line out of the water and looked for a place to drop the fly upstream from the branches. The line had to be placed perfectly, to hover under the branches and next to the trunk of the toppled evergreen. The boy rhythmically whisked the line over his head three times, in an attempt to dry the fly, and on the third pass, he aimed toward the bank and shot the western March brown two feet from the threatening branch. The fly didn't seem to touch the water as it buoyed underneath the limbs.

Levi stared intently as the speckled wings neared the drowning trunk. Nothing happened. Levi had hoped for a strike as the insect bobbed under the branches. Nothing. If the fly hit the trunk of the tree, Levi would have to snap it in and try for another pass. Just as he began to twist up his wrist, a slight splash spurted, and a rippled circle moved outward from where his lure was drifting. Gone. It was gone, and in an instant, Levi reared his arm, and for an endless second, waited to feel the throbbing sensation at the tip of the pole and into his hands.

A second was all the giant needed. Levi had seduced a German brown trout. Small rainbows scampered away. Without hesitation, the sterling fish pulled to the right, ran toward midstream and with all of its savage strength, harpooned its way to the white water rapids where the river surged with power.

Instinctively, Levi had his arm up straight. He knew exactly where the fish was headed. Even though his arm was reaching for the sky, the tip of the rod was cocking with powerful thrusts toward the running water. The mighty German peeled off line like a runaway spindle. The fish's strength was incredible. Its speed was so great that when it ran, the line surf-boarded through the water, creating a wake as the trout scrambled downstream in an effort to escape.

White Knuckle

Turn it, Levi thought. He had to turn it before the line was gone, and before the trout hit white water and tried to hang itself up in the rocky rapids. Levi's stomach tightened as every bone in his body, each thought in his mind, concentrated on the trophy heading away from him. Levi was in an adrenaline state of red. He was glowing.

He thought of using his thumb, but a thumb abruptly smashed on the peeling reel would almost certainly break the fish off by jerking the fly from its mouth. The German had been hooked, but light gear could give way to heavy thrusts or a sudden burst and weaken Levi's hold in an instant. He had to do something. The rapids were too close, and too fast, too much extra pull between the hook and the boy at the other end.

Levi shifted the rod into his left hand and looked for the knob that would tighten the drag on his reel. He had to decide which way it should be turned. Moving the knob clockwise, Levi prayed he was making the right decision. How was he supposed to remember if it was left or right? Nothing happened. The fish kept increasing the distance between the hunter and the hunted. It was the biggest fish Levi had ever felt in his life, and he was losing it. Choking. Letting it run away. He tightened the drag even more, turning the knob clockwise, praying that he wasn't wrong. And yet, the gap was getting greater; the fish was more remote.

His mind raced. Lift the rod. Keep it up. Higher. Back up! Tighten the drag. Tighten it tighter. Let those fingers ache. Move. Stop. Hope. Pray. Jesus!

And then, it slowed. It stopped. There was a slight slack in the line. The fish was gone. No! The massive German brown trout rocketed into the air and flashed its silver sides in a blinding display of twisting anger. It dove under, and again torpedoed itself out from the crystalline water and into the cloudless sky. The brown fly flickered a quick, "Hello, Levi," and disappeared with its hook attached to the edge of the fish's outer jaw.

Fish on! Out from the water it surged. Flying into the air, it reached for the sky, arched its body and wiggled and curled and writhed in an effort to jolt the foreign substance from the side of its mouth. It landed on its sides, its head and its belly. Down. Slap! To the right, and then left, until out of the water it came again. Dancing on its tail, the enormous fish smashed the water in a valiant struggle for freedom.

The turbulent trout dove deep into the darkest part of the river. Just as quickly as it had attempted to run away from Levi, the colossal brute changed course and headed straight back toward the rod bouncing on the other end of the line. The fish shot like an arrow, taking the line back to the bow from which it had come.

But Levi didn't know. He couldn't see. The feeling was gone, because the line grew slack. It was a lethal error. The pole was straight. There wasn't any pressure, except on Levi, and Levi's line was limp. A limp rod never did any man any good, much less a fisherman. Levi's heart was filled with terror.

In an urgent act of recklessness, Levi shoved the rod between his shaking knees, and with both hands he desperately gathered the line back in and let it drift freely in the water. He didn't have time to reel in the line in the normal fashion, as his arms became the reel and his hands pulled the line and let it float in a desperate effort to shorten the distance between him and the fish before the trout spit the lure and swam away forever. Faster! Tighten that line. Keep control. Hurry.

Levi's gut said the fish was near, but without the line being tight, it was impossible to say just where. He pulled and pulled, hand over hand. His body weakened, as the nauseating thought of losing the fish swam through his blood and into his brain. It was the most monstrous fish he'd ever seen, ever come close to. Levi searched. He looked beside him, behind him. He looked in front. Nothing.

White Knuckle

Then it happened. Tension. Life. In the same time it took for the line to go dead, suddenly it was alive. The line tensed, and the tip of the pole strained downward, almost pulling the rod from between Levi's knees. God! Levi was certain the line would snap, the pole would break, or the hook would weaken and crack in the victim's mouth.

Levi held tight to the pole with his left hand and snatched the line between the fingers of his right hand. There was a lull. A moment's hesitation, as if the fish itself couldn't believe its jaw was still being twisted. When the fish paused, in that twinkling, Levi took back control. His fingers were able to dominate the pressure on the line. The sturdy fish waited. It waited to make another move as the two of them rested, saving their strength.

If Levi wasn't so bewildered by the change of command, he would have started celebrating. Like a boxer saved by the bell, Levi came to his senses, knowing that he and his opponent were in the final round. When he finally flicked his wrist; a jolt flew into the pole, and the German angered. The pole bent sharply as the fish powered back downstream. Levi was careful not to use too much pressure, and he was surprised when the fish shot up from the water, displaying its spotted sides of silver and pink and black and brown. Levi held his breath.

Get tired. Give up. Die.

The smart fish moved in the direction of the fallen tree where it had originally been protected. It tried to get back home.

Levi distanced himself from the tree. The mighty German brown followed. When the trout trailed without acrobatics, the fisherman knew that the prey had finally weakened. It wouldn't be water prancing anymore. The fish no longer tried to break water. Levi could feel its strength ebbing. The fish was his. He'd defeated the king fish in this Colorado river, and the defeat came at Levi's Choke Hole. There was no doubt about the trophy size of the swimming beauty.

Levi couldn't wait to show his father. When he looked up, his eyes fastened on Judd, watching from the river bank. The boy rejoiced, thanking God for the victory and his father's smile. Dad was even applauding, as he jumped an odd sort of Italian jig. The boy beamed with pride as the fish came into his net.

"Levi," his father yelled out to him, "be careful not to injure the fish. Turn the top of your net so it's closed, but keep the fish in the water."

Levi did as he was told and cautiously, but quickly, moved toward the side of the river where the currents were quiet and Judd was waiting.

"Dad, did you see it? Did you see it all? It was wonderful. That's the most wonderful thing that's ever happened to me. Wow! Look at that fish! It must be three feet long."

The fish bulged from the net, swishing helplessly side to side. Judd pulled a fisherman's tape from a pocket in his vest and bent down on one knee to measure the enormous trophy.

"It's beautiful, Levi. I'll bet it's over thirty inches and weighs more than twelve pounds. I know I've never seen one as big except in photos or in sport shops." Judd paused. "Now be careful you don't hurt it. We've got to get the fly from its mouth without damaging it or causing the gullet to bleed. If a gullet bleeds, the fish is dead, no matter what you do, but if the hook gets out without any bleeding, things will be fine."

"Gosh, Dad. Did you see it jump from that river? It flew in the air like it was on a trampoline! Man, it just kept running and running, and I thought sure I was going to lose him. I almost did lose him once, when he came back to me. He's wonderful, Dad. He's just wonderful."

"He's not a 'he', Levi. Look at the shape of its nose. He's a she, and she's remarkable," Judd said, drenching his hands in the chilling water. "Before you ever grab the sides of a fish, wet your hands, Levi. Otherwise, when you touch it, your dry skin takes the natural oil off the back and sides of the fish. It can be permanently scarred. It may even die after you let it go."

A bowling ball dropped into the young fisherman's stomach.

"Let it go?!" Levi was stunned. He couldn't have heard right. "Let it go? Dad, you're not letting my fish go, are you? You're not going to let it swim away after all that? I worked hard for that fish. It's mine!" Tears welled up as he envisioned his goliath prize cruising down the river, freed after the magnificent capture.

"Now, don't get yourself in a quiver, Levi. This is your fish. You earned it, and you can keep it if you want to. I thought that you'd let it go, that's all.

The fish was still in the net, but Levi had it so close to shore, there were only inches of water in which it could breath. Judd, with expert swiftness, snatched the fly out of the fish's mouth with a needle-nosed pliers. Judd guided Levi's hands, and together they moved the fish into deeper water, so the fish would not thrash and gasp for bits of air.

"It's a beautiful fish, Levi. I've only heard rumors that German browns were in this river. This is rainbow country. But you caught a German brown all right. And it's probably a record."

With a nervous voice, Levi asked, "Why do you want to let it go then? Why don't you want me to have it?"

"It's not that I don't want you to have it, Levi. I think you should set it free because it's a breeder, a champion. She's been spawning in this river for years. You caught her because you presented the fly like an expert. You caught her because when she struck, you lifted the pole and stuck to the fish like a gambler on hot dice. You outsmarted her. And you won. I was thrilled when you recovered from your error in letting the line go loose. It's this fish, and others like it, that make fly fishing memorable, special, something mystical."

"There are other fish in the river. Let them breed all they want. This is my fish."

"Yes, this is your fish. But do you have to eat it to feel victorious? What are you going to do with it? It's too big for a frying pan. It won't taste as good as one ten or twelve inches long. Now what? Do you want to smash its head with a rock and throw it on the bank while we catch others?"

His father surveyed the river. "Today, we'll net a dozen trout. We'll eat some for lunch, and clean some to take home to your mother. And we'll tell her a true story of remarkable adventure. And respect."

"What's respect got to do with it?" Levi pouted.

"If all of us recognized the value of producers like her," Judd said, looking at the fish, "maybe there would be more for all of us. For some reason, people want to kill the big ones. This fish has probably fed fifty people, and if you let it go, it'll feed fifty more. It's a matter of respect."

Levi was confused. One part of him wanted to listen to his father. The other part wanted to tell his dad to take a hike up the skid trail or a dive down river.

As he stood in the water by the riverbank, the only thing he really wanted to know was whether or not he had a right to keep his fish. "What if we don't eat it, Dad? Couldn't I just have it mounted?"

"It's your fish, Levi. You can do what you want with it," Judd said kindly.

Levi's confusion mounted. "If I'm supposed to let this fish go free, why shouldn't I release all of the fish I catch?"

"Because of pecking orders. There will always be more little fish than big ones. As a result, the little ones are more expendable. It's not the other way around. You might think it's unfair, but God promised equality in heaven, not on earth."

White Knuckle

Levi looked down at his captive waiting for judgment. Its tail moved back and forth within the confines of the net, its gills opened and closed. The trout had been a thundering opponent with colossal strength at the end of Levi's line, but in the surrounding mesh which hogtied its body, the fish had somehow grown smaller. When it was swimming for its life, jumping and dancing, and pulling against the line with Herculean effort, it was tougher, bigger, more brilliant, a radiant sparkling mass of energy.

Here, lying in the net, it was just a fish. It didn't look like it could fly, walk on water, or swim up a mountain. It was beautiful, but it was a fish, now it was bathing in the deep, waiting for a decision.

"Dad, in all your years of fishing, have you ever caught one this big?"

"No, I haven't."

"Then you don't know how it feels to let a giant go. What it really feels like."

"Oh yes, I do, Levi. Yes, I do."

Levi looked surprised, but remained defiant, challenging his father. "How do you know? How do you know, if you've never even been there?"

"Because, Matty," Judd said as he touched his son's face, "because – I'm letting you go. You're my giant, and I know how it hurts to let a giant go. If that giant is your son, then the pain of letting go is unbearable." Judd shuddered and the tears came. He didn't bother to wipe them away. "Just know this, son, that I love you more than anything in this world. And I'll always be with you."

Levi opened the net and freed the German brown. With the fish, the net slipped in the water as Levi put his arms around his father's waist. With all the strength he could manage, with all the feeling he could show, Levi squeezed and held tightly to his father's tall body. The two of them stood in the river and embraced, the water churning and caressing their silhouettes. They just stood there, holding on.

8

Camp Anakeegee was a YMCA summer adventure-land famous for contributing to the initiation rituals of boys on their journey toward manhood. Anakeegee was nestled cozily in the Colorado Rockies. There, deep in the forest, it nurtured young men and made them wise in the ways of folklore and crafts. Stallions and bows with arrows. Quivers. Headbands. Tanning leather and courage. Courage in many forms.

A massive mess hall had been built from old-growth timber before it became fashionable to protect spotted owls and minnows. Tents lined the lake at Anakeegee, and away from the mess hall were barns, corrals, stables and horses. Pastures and paths led to archery fields, picnic grounds, and at night, evening tales of horror and fantasy were told around flickering campfires.

Aspen leaves and towering ponderosa surrounded the encampment, protecting the children from the scrutiny of the outside world. A preserve from which there was no escape. An idle phone booth provided a link to the outside world, but if a young trailblazer was discovered by his peers calling home, he'd be labeled a sissy and shunned as a coward.

Boys came and went every week. Some stayed for as long as a month, others for seven days. The youngest kids were eight. The oldest, fifteen. Each boy was assigned to a cluster of other young campers, and each cluster had its "Chief," or head counselor. All chiefs reported to the head master, Barry Bates, an enormous glob of glyceride – fats and oils, burgers and gravy.

When Barry Bates' corpulent waste waddled into a crowd of campers, he didn't mind being called "The Beef" or even "Beefy Barry." They could call him "Barry" or "Big Bear." He did, however, go ballistic when he heard a reference to "Master Bates." It wasn't that Barry didn't whack off now and then. He did. He just didn't like kids thinking about it. For Barry, it was better if his private affairs remained as private as possible.

"I'm here for the summer," Levi heard him say at orientation. "To be your friend and answer questions." He was eating peanut brittle. "Your cluster chief assigns you a cot and takes care of everyday problems. I be around on special occasions. I make you safe. I'm the head warrior in this enclave, but mostly I stay by one or two of you. Occasionally, I go on special explorations. The trips I take are top secret. I'm usually on my own, because I can't trust children with classified information. The secrets that are here are mine. I ain't sharing everything with outsiders. Get that straight, *if* you want to be my friend. If the outside world knew about the gold, the Indian hideouts, they'd close this camp down and turn us into a fu… 'xcuse me, a natural museum. I got treasured stuff no one knows about. You either with me, or I don't give a damn. Ain't no middle. If they find out about stuff, you boys won't have a chance to become real men."

"How do we get the gold?" one boy asked.

"Only I know where it's at," Barry answered. "You can pan for flakes in the creek and get peanuts. I'm the only one knows of the nuggets."

"What Indians were here?" another boy called out.

"Geronimo, Sitting Bull, the Apaches, and Cherokees. All them came here. Some places are sacred, like Small Pox Canyon. I'm the only one who knows 'bout the hideouts and treasures."

"Will you share the treasure with us?"

"One boy. Maybe two. Depends on the fishin' pool. Boys who can keep secrets. That's all I want. Can any of you keep secrets?" Barry asked.

Everyone yelled and raised their hands. Barry's eyes embraced a stern-faced boy who stood up proudly with arms crossed like a stoic Indian. "What's your name, kid?" Barry inquired.

"I've decided to keep that secret, Sir. I'll tell only when I'm ready," Levi answered.

Bates admired the little warrior. "When you ready, let me know. You'll do, looks like. Do just fine." Bates smiled, and his upper lip moistened. Summer camp usually meant homesickness for some, especially at night, after the fires and darkness enveloped the world. Loneliness would crawl into the sleeping bag and stay until fatigue carried the youngster into the safety of his dreams.

After three days, Levi's dreams had nothing to do with despair or fear of being alone. Levi wanted action, and he didn't care about whittling wood or learning the names of fauna and flora on nature hikes. "I'm going to find nuggets," he told his tentmates, Red Spark and Mouse. "And I'll give them to my dad, so he can make a ring. I'll give some to Mom, so she can buy blankets. And the rest, I'll play with, instead of marbles."

"I'd do anything to find gold," Red Spark said.

"Me too," Mouse added. "But I wouldn't give none to my parents. I'd buy scooters and a new snowboard."

Red Spark was barely old enough to qualify for camp. He was small and frail looking. Meek. Red Spark and Levi became confidants and friends, teaming up with Mouse. Mostly teaming up so they could ward off the insulting onslaughts of Iron Horse.

Daniel J. Gatti

"People don't like me cause I don't do good at sports and keep twitching," Red Spark said. "Iron Horse says my twitching makes him nervous and shakes up the tent. Pee on that. Iron Horse still wants me sleeping outside the tent. The Beef found out, you know. Barry told him to back off, or he'd row him to the island and he could sleep there for the summer."

"Beefy tripped over me one night," Red Spark continued. "It hurt, so he held me. He'd been wandering around in the dark. Later, he says he liked listening to talking inside tents. He don't let on he's there. I shouldn't tell you though. It's confidential, he says, so forget I said it. Anyway, Barry says he's my friend. He's been meeting me for twelve days. I leave in two. We talk private. He's protecting me from Iron Horse. He trusts me, he says. And soon, I'll know the secrets."

"Honest? Barry's taking you to Small Pox?"

"Yup, and Iron Horse ain't gonna like that."

"Iron Horse is a bully. Must be he's mad because Bates likes you instead of him. Iron Horse's mean. You're different, Red Spark. You're nice; you sure are nervous though. You jitter a lot."

"That's 'cause I'm always leaving. No point in making friends if you keep leaving them. I need friends like Barry and you. Military's like that, you know."

Levi didn't know. He only knew a father, mother and brother, and Kit, all together. In the same house, the same town. They had never moved. He and Joshua went to one school. Levi felt sorry for Red Spark, whose father was always flying between Air Force bases or different countries. Sometimes he'd be stationed for nine months at the Academy in Colorado Springs, and the next nine in Europe or elsewhere. Sometimes, Red Spark joined his father, but most of the time he didn't.

80

White Knuckle

"I told Barry 'bout Dad leaving all the time. Never being around. Beefy understood, Levi. Barry told me he was orphaned as a kid. He says *he'll* be my dad. I'm excited." Red Spark's excitement shone on his expressions. "Levi, tomorrow I get to go with him into the land of the bravest warriors who rode the West. Barry says we're going to touch legends. They're in Small Pox Canyon."

"Wow," was all Levi could manage as a response.

Levi's like for Red Spark was genuine. Red Spark was nicknamed because his face flushed crimson, especially on nights when Iron Horse made him sleep outside the tent. Iron Horse, big and dumb, had boasted, "Red Spark's face blazes like the campfire! We could roast a hot dog on the steam coming outta his fuckin' nose."

Red Spark flushed, and curled further into his sleeping bag.

"You're jealous cause he's Barry's friend, not yours," Levi defended.

"Damn right, piss ant. Red Spark gets private meetings with Bates everyday. Don't tell us shit. Twitches cause of nerves, he says, but it takes nerve not to tell us what's up with Barry."

Every day after lunch for an hour, Red Spark disappeared with the fat man's hand on his shoulder. Levi and Mouse waited for Red Spark, and passed the time shooting arrows or swimming races to the island in the middle of the lake. When Red Spark returned, he had little to say except, "It's secret."

Red Spark was leaving in two days, and still kept the secrets when he rejoined Levi and Mouse as the boys shot arrows into bales of hay. When Levi saw Red Spark coming, he couldn't help but notice the look on his friend's reddened face, and he was shivering, not just twitching.

"You seen a dead indian, Red Spark?" Levi asked. "You look scared."

"It's secret. A top one." He was shaking, like he'd been in a snowstorm without a jacket, and it was eighty degrees in the field where they were standing.

"Tell us where you went. We're friends," Mouse implored.

"Look," Red Spark said with finality, "I can't tell anyone. Ever. I promised."

Mouse pulled a quivered arrow and missed the target bale from thirty yards. "I notice Big Beef spits a lot," he said as he watched Levi's arrow smack the bull's eye. "And he's always looking behind himself, and grabs his snatcher a lot."

"It's true," Red Spark muttered. "Today, he grabbed mine. Told me to take off my pants 'cause he wanted to see if I had hair on my balls."

Mouse's eyes bulged. His mouth hung open. "Whad'ya do?"

Red Spark looked guilty. "I told him I didn't have hair, and he said I was like Geronimo. He had no hair, and he got hanged from a tree when the army caught him. Seemed like he was threatening me."

"Did you show him your nuts?" Mouse asked.

"No. I got nervous. So did he, it seemed. But tomorrow, Barry promised big surprises. I get to go. I think I'll see the treasures." Red Spark was still quivering.

"Gosh you're lucky," Mouse said.

"Are you sure Big Beef said Geronimo was hanged?" Levi asked. "Last year my dad took me to the Grand Canyon. Dad said Geronimo became a carnival attraction and died of old age. He thought it was a sad way for him to go."

Mouse laughed. "Your dad's nuts! No Apache warrior ever joined a circus. Big Beef is the expert. If you ever expect to be his friend, Levi, you better listen to what he says and do exactly what he wants."

White Knuckle

Levi listened and decided his father must've been thinking about some other famous Indian. In any case, Levi agreed with Mouse that Barry Bates reigned at Anakeegee, and Levi wanted to please his new master.

Still, the child warrior was a bit uneasy when he found out he'd have to slice his wrists to become Barry's blood brother. It didn't help later, when the night was deep and dark and the boys sat around campfires and listened to terrifying yarns spun by the camp chiefs, counselors, and anyone with a quick tongue and a vivid imagination. Sometimes the moon peeked from behind a cloud and shed eerie light on the shadows between the trees. "How many dead people are buried in Small Pox?" one of the boys asked a counselor after the marshmallows were roasted and a few songs had been sung around the blazing fire.

Iron Horse piped up before the counselor could speak. "Hundreds. Women, babies, old people. The red man, wiped out by the plague of white man."

"How do you know? You never been there," Red Spark challenged.

"I know, 'cause I listen. I listen to the wind, and I can hear the screams of dying children and the wailing of mothers. You can hear 'em too, if you got guts enough to walk the shore when everyone's asleep."

There was silence for a moment, as if everyone was listening, trying to hear the terrible sounds. "I don't believe you," cringed a camper, hugging his knees.

But they all knew it was true. Maybe Iron Horse hadn't really been to Small Pox Canyon. But other kids had gone, and there wasn't a counselor who could remember one of those explorers returning the next year to Camp Anakeegee. One trip to Small Pox, and the child disappeared. He never came back.

"How did Small Pox get its name?"

Again, Iron Horse answered. "Smallpox came with the infantrymen hauling cannons. Soldiers had the disease. Some got buried, and some just dropped dead off their horses, and the pox oozed from the flesh. Bodies rotted in the sun. Sometimes a dumb Indian would come on a Yank, and steal his pants or a shirt or whatever else he could. What the dummy didn't know was he's stealing the pox. Pox makes holes on your face and eats you up from the inside out."

"Is that why they came here, to Anakeegee? To escape the pox?" Levi asked.

Iron Horse looked at Levi. "You're dumb, ain't you? They came here to bury their dead. The pox needed to go in a clean place where no white man ever been."

"Why can't we go there?" Levi pressed Iron Horse.

"Because of dead spirits and Bates. The dead defend their sacred grounds. Ghosts run wild with tomahawks. Indians don't like no white people around."

"How do you know all this?" Mouse wondered.

"Because I heard the story from outside a tent long ago. He didn't know I was listening, but now so many people know, I don't think it's a bloody secret. The place is the secret, not the story."

"Who told the story?"

Iron Horse smiled. "The Big Dick. You know, Master Bates."

"He ain't no Indian," Mouse said. "He's just a great big fat ass who keeps all the secrets to himself."

"Barry's okay with me," Red Spark said.

White Knuckle

Iron Horse was angry. "Red Spark, if you get into Small Pox, you better tell us where it's at. I'm tired of that jerk off's crap."

Someone spit, and a shadow merged deeper into the darkness.

* * * * *

The next morning, as a blazing sun crept over the mountains, the flap on Levi's tent, suddenly opened, and glowing like the sun behind him stood Barry Bates. He looked at Red Spark.

"Move out, Sparky. I got plans today."

Red Spark jumped off his cot and grabbed his backpack. Bates slipped outside, and just when his protege neared the exit, Iron Horse stepped into his path.

"Remember my present," Iron Horse warned. "I want a gift, and it better be a good one."

Red Spark nodded. "I'm going to Small Pox." The tone in his voice was smug. He looked cocky. "See what I can do," he said. Red Spark smiled and left.

The anticipation of Red Spark's return consumed Levi's thoughts. He went to breakfast with Mouse, where they pretended to eat Indian bread from rock ovens instead of flapjacks from the mess hall griddle. The trail ride on the painted horse was really a scouting trip for signs of mounted artillerymen coming back from finding sacred hideaways. Archery targets were antelope steaks for the hungry villagers dependent on the hunting skills of Chief Levi. His knife was a spear. His shoes, moccasins. His swimsuit was deer hide, and he climbed trees so he could talk to birds and watch for smoke signals from Red Spark.

Red Spark sent no signals.

Levi's day turned to dusk and dusk to night. The marshmallows burned, the stories were shallow, and the songs had no rhyme. Still, there was no Red Spark. Finally, taps played; the campfires smoldered into ashes. Levi waited quietly while his friend's cot stayed empty. All of the boys were in the dark, waiting for Red Spark's return. Waiting until they fell asleep.

An angry voice blew up the silence. It was Iron Horse.

"The little prick won't come back here. He got his backpack crammed with shit, and he's afraid I'll take the goodies." Iron Horse's fist punched the pillow.

No one answered.

Levi's eyes finally closed, and slumber hushed the tent. Once, Levi half woke, and in a sleepy haze, he thought he heard someone crying softly. When Levi asked, "Is that you, Red Spark?" the muffled whimpers outside the tent stopped. In the morning, Levi was the first to look for Red Spark. His dufflebag was still gone, but his clothes were underneath the empty cot. Quickly, Levi dressed and walked outside where he found Red Spark's sleeping bag folded next to the tent. He'd obviously been there.

Levi searched around the cluster of tents, and then went to the lake, the stables, the mess hall, and the activity center. Red Spark wasn't anywhere to be found. The YMCA bus back to town would leave right after breakfast, and Levi's friend was supposed to be on the bus. After an hour of searching, Levi hurried back to his tent. There he found Red Spark packing his suitcase, seemingly unaware of Levi's presence.

"Sparky, what happened?" Levi asked in a breathless voice. "Where've you been? I waited for hours last night."

Red Spark didn't even look in Levi's direction. He finished packing and was zipping up his dufflebag when Levi's eyes seized upon the ring of scabs and sores around both of Red Spark's wrists.

White Knuckle

"Jesus, Red Spark! Blood brothers doesn't mean you have to cut circles around your arm, does it? What happened in Small Pox, Sparky?"

His friend was silent as he zombied out of the tent and headed for the bus in a daze. There, but not really.

Levi stayed close. "Tell me what happened. Did you find any treasures? I know it's all secret, but you got to tell me. I'm your best friend."

Sparky abruptly dropped his luggage and put his hands on Levi's shoulders. "I don't want to talk about it," he said in an almost catatonic voice. "Just don't go. That's all. Don't go. Tell Master Bates to take Iron Horse; he wants to play rope tricks."

Red Spark picked up his belongings and waited inconspicuously among the trees for the bus to leave. Levi felt helpless. His friend wouldn't talk except to say, "Call your dad if you can find him, Levi, and don't play with ropes. Tell your dad to come and get you, quick."

"Why, Red Spark? Why? My dad's on his way to California. I don't know if I can reach him yet."

"Try, Levi. Keep trying."

When the bus started its engine, Levi watched his friend climb on board and take a seat in the back, away from the other campers. Levi wanted to wave good bye, but Red Spark never looked out the window. He kept his chin down and his shoulders slumped like a prisoner just released from an Indian sweat pit.

9

The clank of prison locks was the second loudest sound in Bernard Panzer's day, but no matter how loud the locks clanked and thundered among the dank walls of his prison cell, the noise was nothing compared to the shrieking cries he heard each night in his dreams. Little Jordy was always there. Always screaming, "Thanks, Dad. Thanks for keeping your promises, you prick."

"Judd, I can't stop the nightmares," Bernie Panzer said, sweat dripping from his forehead as he sat, wringing his hands, his fingers nervously intertwined with one another. "Every day I keep thinking that maybe there was a chance. Maybe my son had a miracle coming, and I took it away from him."

Judd looked at Bernie from across the table. The cement walls around them were painted grey, and a single bulb on the ceiling illuminated the room enough to show the ashen color on Panzer's face. Judd noticed his client seemed to age five years in a matter of days.

"You're not guilty of murder," Judd said. "I don't think the Court of Appeals will uphold your sentence when they learn that all the doctors testified that Jordy would have passed away within days, no matter what you did to intervene." Judd reached out a consoling hand.

"Guys in here tell me appeals take years, and almost none get any relief. My son didn't get a miracle, so why should I?"

"Bernie, we've got post-conviction motions already filed. If the judge denies our motions, we've assembled the best appellate team in Denver. We'll fast track it. You've got a chance. Hold on to that."

"I got nothing but my nightmares, Judd. And you're leaving. I can't even depend on you."

"Your intervention, Bernie, didn't stop the inevitable."

The prisoner pulled back. "Oh yeah?" Bernie answered sarcastically. "That's the same argument you used at trial, and look where I am!" Bernie's face no longer registered self-pity. He was now bitter and angry, looking for someone to blame. "Your arguments went over like a pregnant pole vaulter, and they'll do the same on appeal. Fact is, Judd, I'm fucked. You're headed for California, and I'm headed into a shithole for thirty years."

Bernie's sarcasm served to remind Judd of the old warning that a lawyer is better advised to take on a stranger's case before he takes on a friend's. Losing a case is one thing. Losing a friend is another. It's not worth any amount of money to do both at the same time.

Judd stood up to leave. "Bernie, I just wanted to visit and...say good bye." An awkward and long moment of silence stood between the two men. The guard started toward the table, but Judd shook his head and motioned for him to wait a minute.

Bernie looked at his lawyer. "I'm sorry," he said. "One minute I'm sane and hopeful, the next I'm crazy." He reached out to Judd.

"I'll keep in close touch with the lawyers appealing your case, Bernie. I'm not going to let you waste here for one day longer than necessary."

Bernie Panzer nodded and Judd smiled. Bernie stood up and Judd put his arms around him, patting his back. "I'll come and visit. I'm there if you need me; you know that."

"Right, pal." The sarcasm zipped back into Bernie's voice. He paused. "Sorry," he said. "I'll try once more, for old times' sake, to be a friend. It's not your fault Judd. I'm not blaming you."

"Thanks, Bernie."

"So, when you leaving for, what do they call it...'the Rock?' It used to be Alcatraz. Thank God it's closed."

Judd laughed. "Today. Now. Asia's outside in the car."

"In that case," Bernie said, "good luck, *mazeltov*, to both of you."

"Thanks, Bernie. One day soon, you and Rhoda are going to come and visit us in San Francisco, and we're all going to celebrate. Remember that."

"Don't make promises you can't keep," Bernie said. "Remember that."

Judd gave Bernie a final hug and walked out of the cold room filled only with a table, six wooden chairs, and a convicted felon. As Bernie Panzer watched Judd Saranno disappear, he began clenching his teeth, lips twitching uncontrollably, body shivering. The room felt like a snow cave, and Bernard Panzer had no blankets.

* * * * *

When the final prison door was unlocked to the outside, the bright sun hit Judd's face like a stage light. The tension in his body lifted as he walked quickly to his car filled with packed suitcases and the woman with whom he wanted to spend the rest of his life. Asia smiled lovingly as Judd got behind the wheel and started the engine. She bent over and kissed his ear, neck, and cheek as her hand went to his knee.

"Put on your seatbelt, baby," he said with a laugh.

As Judd drove, he glanced over at Asia and realized he never felt so full of energy. Joy and hope and plans for the future. Finally, *his* time had come. Finally, he had but one purpose in life, and that was to make himself happy. It was time to be selfish, to start a new life. It was time to take on San Francisco. Time to take on Asia and their life together. He'd been given the greatest gift, a second chance for happiness. This time he'd get it right.

Asia sat back in her seat as the engine purred, and the car sped over the Rocky Mountains, heading west. She knew her time had come too. Judd was older and wiser, and yet young and vibrant. She'd never seen him so happy. And Asia was the reason. That thought filled her with indescribable joy.

"Did you tell Bernie his…?" she started to ask.

"No," Judd interrupted. "I couldn't. How do you tell someone his chance of getting off scot-free is about as good as winning eight straight trifectas. Right now, all Bernie's got are a few shreds of hope. By the time hope dies, he'll have adjusted."

"How?" Asia wondered.

"I don't know. How does anyone go from having everything to having nothing? One day you've got a great life, and the next day you're just another statistic. Bernie's glory days are history."

Asia's fingers stroked the back of her lover's neck and pulled gently on the waves of his hair. "Promise me, Judd," she said, "that you'll wait at least fifty years before you become a statistic. By then I'll be in my seventies." She poked him kiddingly in the ribs. "You'll be close to a hundred, and even you won't be able to get it up by then."

"Liar," he said, laughing. "Fifty bucks says I'll die with my pants off."

"You're on. This is one bet I want to lose," Asia said, smiling as she looked

92

out the window admiring the majesty of the mountains and the beauty of the day. Sunlight dazzled and danced between trees, rocks, and rivers as the car cornered and curved up the slopes and over the Rockies toward their new life.

My dreams are just beginning, she thought. She kept glancing at Judd. I don't need to change him. I just need to love him, and that's the easiest thing I've ever done. The car kept churning on; hundreds of miles melting away. The farther they got from Denver and Sheryl and the Panzers and courtrooms filled with injustice, the younger and more joyful Judd became. He knew it was a selfish feeling and he didn't care. Like a snake shedding old skin, Judd felt an overwhelming sense of renewal. He felt reborn, and he didn't have to find religion to do it. He found Asia.

* * * * *

Asia's father had lived in San Francisco all his life. He also died there. On Lombard Street, "crookedest street in the world" the tourist brochures proclaimed, the one that weaved up and down Russian Hill. His three-story home overlooked the gardens in the middle of the lane that forced cars to take the one-way street downhill with brakes on all the way.

The veranda around the house was covered with purple bougainvillea and was a perfect place to sit, drink coffee, and read the paper in the morning. In the evening, a glass of wine or a snifter of brandy made the owner feel like the luckiest person on earth.

Seven days had passed since Judd and Asia had left Denver. The Lombard Street house was now Asia's, and she and Judd had settled into it. Judd sat on the veranda with his gin and tonic, breathing in the unpolluted air that had been strained clean by the ocean breezes blowing across the bay. Asia sat quietly beside him, chardonnay in one hand, her father's final papers in the other. Tourist cars and a trolley made their presence known with brakes that creaked or bells that chimed at the conductor's flick of a wrist.

"Judd," Asia said, putting down the legal papers, "you know my inheritance will mean we can live anywhere. Just think of it, darling. We can have a place here in San Francisco, maybe a house in Carmel, or one of those lovely Victorian houses in Pacific Grove or Monterey Bay. Or we could go to Maui or the Big Island, buy a condo."

Judd's eyes were closed. He was content.

"Such a life," he said. "As soon as your father's estate is settled, we'll make all those decisions."

"You've gotta marry me first. Right?" Her voice had a seductive, girlish tone.

Judd nodded and smiled, his eyes still closed.

"And then we're going to have a baby," she added. Asia put her drink down and moved to where Judd was sitting. She stood behind him, and touched her breasts to the back of his head as her hands caressed his chest. "I want to start trying now."

"I wonder how Levi's doing," Judd said, almost absentmindedly.

"Levi's fine. And I'll bet he'd love to have a little sister."

"You sure about wanting a child?" Judd's eyes were wide open now with a look of genuine concern. "Asia, I'd be sixty when she graduates from high school."

"So what? You'll be sixty anyway," Asia reasoned.

Judd laughed. "Good point. You know, maybe you should be a lawyer. You can talk me into anything."

Asia bent down and nibbled on his ear. "Good. Then how about I convince you to come to bed early tonight?"

White Knuckle

"Done," he said.

Asia took his hand and guided him off the veranda as she began unbuttoning her blouse, turning off lights on her way to the bedroom. She couldn't get the smile off her face, even if she wanted to.

*   *   *   *   *

In the morning, the lovers packed two suitcases and drove south along the spectacular Seventeen Mile Drive, past Pebble Beach and the opulent mansions overlooking the Pacific from atop the Big Sur cliffs. When they arrived at Quail Lodge in Carmel, they checked into the executive villa with its private gardens, Japanese hot tub, bar and fireplace in their private suite.

The next day the hotel made up a special picnic basket with champagne and cold lobster salad, French sourdough bread, fresh raspberries, and several exotic desserts. Judd and Asia picnicked in China Cove, a small beach surrounded by caves and cliffs, one of those places where Mother Nature outdid herself.

They waded into the icy waters, drank champagne, and giggled like teenagers as they fed each other morsels of desserts that looked too pretty to eat. Later in the afternoon, they shopped in downtown Carmel with its quaint shops and galleries and flower-lined streets. They stayed in one gallery for an hour, looking at sculptures of bronze and steel and glass. They were all elegant. They were all expensive. But none of them stood out and captured Asia's heart as did the Lorenzo Ghiglieri bronze sculpture of a man and woman sitting together on a stone, their eyes closed, her head on his leg. Their love looked real. Protected. Honored and trusted.

Asia could only exclaim, "My God, it's beautiful."

"It's called *Lovers*," the gallery owner said as he turned on a light so they could see the delicate detail of the man and woman.

"Honey, let's take the manager's card and get something to drink at that little bar we passed," Judd said as he started to usher Asia out of the gallery. Asia smiled at the owner and reluctantly followed. Once seated at the bar, Asia said that the sculpture was extraordinary and didn't Judd think so too? He nodded without comment, then excused himself to go to the men's room.

When he finally returned, Asia's first words were, "Sweetheart, can we go back to the gallery?"

"It's five and the gallery's closed. Have a pretzel," Judd interrupted as he popped one into her mouth. Asia picked up a pretzel from the wooden bowl and threw it at Judd as she squinted her eyes in mock annoyance.

The drive back to Quail Lodge was a quiet one. It wasn't until they were walking to their room that Judd finally broke the silence. "I've got a surprise for you. I was going to drop it on you later, but your disappointment just isn't worth the wait."

"You didn't!" Asia's voice rose with excitement. "Judd, you didn't buy the sculpture, did you?"

"Of course I did," he answered, amused by the flush in her cheeks. "Making you happy makes me happy. With you, Asia, all I want is to give, and to keep on giving. It's easy giving to someone who doesn't expect anything."

"Oh, Judd, thank you." Asia threw her arms around his neck and hugged him tightly. "You know what I thought the moment I saw it?" she asked, not waiting for an answer. "I thought it's us, sweetheart. It's the way we'll hold onto one another forever."

"I tried to have it boxed for the ride back to the city," Judd said, kissing her nose, "but the owner said it didn't have to be wrapped. He said it would ride nicely in the back seat of the car. So, on the way home, we'll pick it up and drive it to San Francisco."

White Knuckle

Two days later they stopped at the gallery to pick up *Lovers*. The owner carefully placed the sculpture in the back seat behind Judd, securely fastening it with the seatbelt. "This should hold, Mr. Saranno," he said. "Don't worry, it won't break. It must weigh forty pounds."

"I'll drive like the queen's chauffeur," Judd said. He smiled and pulled his car onto the streets of Carmel, slowly heading for the freeway to San Francisco.

Even on Sunday afternoons, California freeways were not considered country rides. At first, the scenery was beautiful as they coasted along the Pacific, through Monterey and up the peninsula, but then it changed to city traffic, a cement desert of signs and speeding cars. Cars slamming on brakes, accelerating, weaving and coughing black smoke.

The traffic irritated Judd, forcing him to slow down to forty miles an hour as they passed the San Francisco airport. From nowhere, a car swerved in front of Judd's Mercedes, missing it by less than a foot. Asia screamed, "Jesus, Judd! That kid almost hit us!"

Judd pulled sharply to his left, and back into his own lane when a pickup truck blew its horn warning that the fast lane was taken. Beside them, veering back and forth, was a carload of teenage boys obviously wanting trouble.

Judd slowed to thirty-five miles an hour, his face flushed with anger. "You crazy bastard!" he yelled, at the kids who couldn't hear him. "You trying to kill someone?"

They were laughing. Laughing at him.

Asia could see their faces. Grinning as they raised their fists and blew her kisses. The driver looked like a grungy skateboarder, probably no more than sixteen, waving a lit cigar as he drove. Smoke billowed from his mouth, momentarily obscuring his view through the windshield. Again, his car came into Judd's lane. Judd hit the horn and stepped on the gas, hoping to pull ahead of the rusty Dodge with its raised rear tires, dents, and collage of psychedelic colors painted on the hood.

"Judd, get us out of here," Asia pleaded, trying to control her fear.

The Mercedes darted into the right lane as Judd slammed on the brakes, displaying his anger. He was boiling. The bronze sculpture held its place in the back seat. The Dodge fishtailed behind them, missing their car by inches.

Looking into his rearview mirror, Judd's foot pounded the pedal to the floor. The juvenile delinquents were no longer laughing pranksters. Now they were enraged, making obscene gestures.

"Jesus, Judd! Stop this! I don't like it. Please, get us out of here."

"Fuck 'em," Judd shouted. The Mercedes careened in and out of traffic. Fast. Slow. Sharp and jolting. The Dodge wasn't getting lost.

Asia turned to look out the rear window. The boys were waving their arms and fists and snarling as their car came closer. Traffic was all around them. There wasn't a chance for a clean escape.

Judd miscalculated as his Mercedes got caught behind the cars trying to make their way to another freeway. In an instant, the hell-bent teenagers were beside them. Then in front.

A window rolled down, and an empty quart bottle of whisky was hurled like a javelin toward the windshield of the Mercedes. Judd couldn't stop or turn in time. The glass was crushed, air whistled through a hole, and the rest of the windshield looked like a broken mirror, with silver lines splintering up and down and out to the sides. A broken mesh of glass blinded Judd's ability to see clearly.

White Knuckle

Judd's adrenaline exploded as the Dodge leapt forward, weaving in and out of traffic toward the Third Street exit near Hunter's Point. "I'll kill those little bastards!" he bellowed as his eyes bulged, trying to see the Dodge. He felt like a hunter stalking a crazed Rottweiler as his hands gripped the steering wheel, choking it as if it were the other driver's throat.

"Stop this, Judd! Stop, please! I've never seen you act like this. Please."

Judd couldn't hear her. He couldn't hear anything except the voice in his head screaming, "Get 'em, Judd! Those punks don't know who they're fucking with. Turn their car into scrap metal and bust their stinking heads into the gutter where they came from!"

An exit was clear of traffic. The Dodge swept to the right, heading off the freeway. The Mercedes went into passing gear, shooting from forty-five to sixty in seconds. The Mercedes kept accelerating.

Judd slammed the steering wheel with his fist. "Faster!" he yelled as the light in front of him turned red at the intersection coming off the exit. The Dodge was three hundred yards ahead, but Judd could see he was gaining, even though his vision was distorted by broken glass and lines and white and blurred and splintered and...

Asia wasn't looking at the Dodge. The last thing she saw was the red traffic light and the huge tires, the truck, and the word "Mayflower" coming at them like an bomb in a 3-D movie. The Dodge swerved. Judd tried.

Asia's hands went to her face, and apart from her own scream, the last thing she heard was two explosions from the airbags that were meant to save their lives. Unconsciousness stopped her from hearing the breaking of bones in her leg and the sickening crack of Judd's head as the bronze sculpture crunched into the back of his skull.

* * * * *

"Watch for fire!" But there was none.

"I think they're dead!" But they weren't.

"We can't get the doors open!" And they couldn't.

Asia didn't see the ambulance coming. She didn't hear the call for Air-Life crews. She didn't feel the pulling and twisting at the car doors with the jaws of life used by the paramedics.

The Mercedes was twisted and crumbled and curled into a mangled heap of pulverized steel. Spectators gathered as the emergency crews urgently tried to figure out if the passengers were still alive, and if they were, how the bleeding could be stopped, and how the man's airway could be kept open.

Through the haze, Asia heard voices in the distance and felt a cool mist come over her face. Her body was numb, her mind confused, her brain scrambled. A finger reached to her throat, taking her pulse, as a cool, wet washcloth wiped away blood and sweat and glass.

Slowly, the numbness in her head cleared. Slowly, she woke up, opened her eyes, and realized she was alive. Asia heard a voice echoing sounds in the distance. "Take it easy, lady. Take it easy."

She tried to listen carefully as the voice grew louder and closer. Her senses worked desperately to clear the dust and fill her brain once again with consciousness.

"You'll be okay," The voice said. "We'll get you out just as soon as we can. Try not to move. Stay calm."

She listened, but barely understood, at first. Her body ached. All she could do was turn her head. She turned it to her left. Her vision was restored enough to see him. Her eyes blinked. They blinked again. She saw him. She saw Judd's body next to hers. His clothes were awash in red. Blood was flowing as a paramedic squeezed through the window of the back door into what was left of the back seat, reaching forward and encircling Judd's head with white bandages and tape and drainage pads and dressings.

"Get the goddamn door open!" he kept hollering. "He's waking up, but he's got blood coming from his ears! I think we've got a cerebral hemorrhage here. Hurry!"

The scene sounded like a war zone with chainsaw-like sounds from the jaws of life, sirens, horns, and helicopter blades flapping.

"Judd! Oh, Judd." Asia tried to speak over the sounds from the outside. "Please, baby. Please don't die." She was desperate to touch him, to hold and comfort and warm his chest and arms and legs, but she could hardly move her head.

The paramedic looked at Asia. "Just try to relax. I'll stop the bleeding, and you just stay calm." The medic searched for a flashlight. "Get that door off!" he screamed again.

Suddenly, Judd's eyes opened. When they did, he was looking straight at Asia. He tried to speak. "As...ia. A...Asia."

"I can't hear you," she cried. "I can't hear you, baby."

When Asia tried to move closer, the medic squeezed between them and peered into Judd's eyes and ears.

"He's dilating!" the medic screamed. "He's dilating, for christsakes, and blood's draining from his ears."

The medic moved back and the driver's door burst open. Asia's ear made it to Judd's mouth. Judd's mouth was moving, trying to speak. The medics reached in, but stopped, as if they knew they needed to wait ten more seconds. Out of respect or sorrow, they paused while Judd whispered into Asia's ear.

Judd spoke, and Asia cried. Asia listened carefully, listened hard, knowing Judd was fading and knowing that he had something important to say before he passed into unconsciousness again. Judd whispered, and Asia strained to hear – and remember. Then, her lover's eyes closed, his mouth stopped, and medics grabbed him as the lead paramedic barked orders to others.

"Get him to neuro. We've got to get him to neuro, now!"

Asia heard their words but didn't understand any of it. Her brain and body, it seemed even her soul, had become mummified. Her eyes closed and opened and her thoughts crawled in and out of the dark recesses inside her head as the remaining members of the rescue crew pried the passenger door away from the frame of what was left of the unrecognizable car. Judd was lifted out and instantly put on the Air-Life gurney. He was securely strapped in. The helicopter rose over the street amid the chaos, blood, tears, and amid the prayers of bystanders.

Asia's own pain was making itself known through the numbness and tingling, seeping its sharp daggers in and around the broken bones in her leg, the blood on her face, and the contusions and abrasions covering her body. Asia pleaded to the medics for assurance. "Please," she said. "Please tell me he'll live."

"Ma'am, we're gonna do the best we can; I promise you that. The sculpture thing hit his head hard. If the neurosurgeons can stop the bleeding and release the pressure in time, he'll make it. He was breathing and almost conscious when we got him out. It's a question of time. That's all I can say."

Asia grabbed the front of his white coat with what little strength she had. "Tell me there's time," she cried. "Tell me!"

The paramedic was sympathetic, but firm. "Right now, we've got to take care of you, Ma'am. There's time. But now we've got to get you to the hospital."

White Knuckle

Asia tried to say something else, but the words wouldn't come out. Her fingers released the white jacket. Her body was lifted onto the gurney and placed into the ambulance where she was hooked up to tubes and bags of liquid hanging above her head. An oxygen mask went over her nose, and an injection went into her arm.

As the ambulance sped away, several paramedics all spoke at once around her, but she didn't hear them. All she could hear was the piercing sound of the sirens and Judd's voice whispering words to her. She had to remember them, she thought, as she floated into unconsciousness.

10

"I'm going to Small Pox today," Levi boasted to Mouse and Iron Horse. "Barry said we'll be searching for gold.

Mouse scowled at Levi and shook his head. "I still don't like what you told us about Red Spark. Maybe you should've called your dad."

Levi shrugged, unconcerned. "I tried to call, but his cell was off, or maybe he was just out of range."

The three boys in the tent were getting dressed for breakfast. Iron Horse was irritated, as usual.

"Red Spark's a weasel. If I could've caught him, he'd of left with a broken nose."

Levi put on his red swimsuit and tied his tennis shoes. "Sparky seemed pretty weird," Levi acknowledged. "But I talked to Barry, and he said Red Spark was just scared of ghosts and the dead warriors that protected the burial grounds. He said he also panicked when an elk herd busted through Small Pox. Took it as a sign Indians were about to attack or something."

"Do you believe him?" Mouse asked innocently.

"Who knows what you can believe about Master Bates?" Iron Horse interjected. "He's never even offered me an arrowhead. I've been coming to this toilet for six years, and I'm not coming back."

"Well, I am," Levi said confidently. "Barry told me that if I was afraid of graves, he'd take me bingo fishing instead, but I told him I wasn't afraid, and he said we could do both. Pan for nuggets and bingo fish."

"What's bingo fishing?" Mouse asked.

"I don't know," Levi replied. "Must be some kind of fish I never heard of. Barry said it was special, and not many people got bingo fish. It'd make my dad real proud if I caught a bingo *and* got gold nuggets, too."

Iron Horse was still thinking about Red Spark. "That cowardly little prick was always twitching," he said with contempt. "Didn't even bring me a memento."

"I'll bring back bingos, and we can have a fish fry," Levi said, trying to cheer his campmate.

"I want a tomahawk," Iron Horse challenged.

"I'll do the best I can," Levi said as he left the tent, certain that he was about to embark on the adventure of a lifetime.

Barry Bates was waiting at the phone booth that seemed so incongruous there in the wilds of the Colorado Rocky Mountains. Bates smiled as Levi came up to him. "Where're the fishing poles?" Levi asked.

"Don't need poles for bingo fishing. You need rope and a good place to hide." He bit down on a piece of peanut brittle as Levi eyed him curiously. "That's why we go to Small Pox."

"Where's the canyon?" Levi wondered.

"About a mile is all. We just go out the gate, turn down the road, and my cabin's in the woods. That's where we play with bingos and artifacts from warriors. But it's a secret, Levi. You can't tell nobody where it is or that you've been there. Got it?"

Levi nodded. "Of course," he said as he climbed into the head counselor's truck.

"Eat some peanut brittle," Bates said, offering the candy to the kid. And Levi ate.

The ride lasted only a few minutes. "You mean Small Pox is only a mile from camp?" Levi asked in astonishment. "I've been looking everywhere, and it's been right in front of me all the time. This is great!"

Levi jumped from the truck as soon as it stopped in front of an old log cabin tucked inconspicuously in a dense grove of trees. The roof was covered with moss and pine needles that had been falling for decades. The facade was weather-beaten, surrounded by tall trees that shaded the sun and kept it dark inside the cabin during the day.

Levi stood anxiously on the little, creaky porch while Barry Bates locked the truck and looked around surreptitiously. Barry ate his peanut brittle and smoked a cigarette at the same time.

"Where are the burial grounds?" Levi asked. "Do we need shovels?"

"Small Pox has already been dug out," Barry replied. "The treasures are stored in my cabin. Small Pox is behind us, but we're after bingos right now, and there'll be plenty of time to shovel dirt later. Let's see what's in the cabin."

Levi felt a brief tinge of disappointment, but didn't argue.

Bates opened the old cabin door but stayed on the porch and said, "Bingo fishing died about the same time Queen Victoria came to the throne of England and brought in what's known as the Victorian Age. Before that bitch took over, the crusaders, the aristocrats, and the artisans *all* went bingo fishing. It was real popular." He sighed. "I wish I could've lived back then."

Levi looked puzzled. "Barry, how do you catch a fish with a rope? You need hooks. Hooks or nets. You just can't tie a fish's fin under water."

Bates smiled at the boy.

"If the fish are walking and not running, you can get a loop around them," he explained to Levi. "If they don't start fighting and screaming, you can tie one up pretty quick. The crusaders used to bring their bingo fish with them, and the aristocrats could always just buy them. The artisans of Florence, Italy, even Leonardo da Vinci, had bingos supplied by his benefactors. Leonardo and Michelangelo were notorious bingo boys, but the historians usually leave that out of the history books. Bingo fishing was everywhere."

The look of longing and nostalgia on Barry's face was like dog's glare at a turkey leg. "It must've been a grand time to be alive," he drooled.

"I can't wait to try it, if you say it's so great. How big do bingos usually get?"

"Oh, about your size," Bates answered with a barely controlled chuckle.

Levi's eyes widened. "Wow, and I thought the trout I caught was big!"

Bates' smile was becoming a leer. "Most of the time, bingos are somewhat smaller, unless you're going for a filly. I caught one in Denver I still can't forget. It was my first black experience," he said with profound pride. "Bingo hens are okay, but once you've nailed a tight tom or a baby rooster, you don't much care for a young biddy with no tits."

Bates planted two huge paws on Levi's shoulders and leered down at him. "You do what Barry Bates says, and you'll do it all, because I know the secrets, and you said I could trust you. But I don't pick just any kid. Not every little buck can be my buddy. Understand me, boy?"

"Yes."

"Do you keep promises?"

"Yes."

"You don't lie, do you?"

"Not very often, and never when I promise."

"Then listen to this. If I can't trust you, and if you can't keep secrets, then you might as well be dead. Do you get that?"

Master Bates's scowling face was an inch from Levi's nose. The boy could smell smoke coming from the ugly brown and yellow teeth. He couldn't help staring into the fat man's mouth.

Bates looked distraught. "Dead! Did you hear me? Dead!"

"Yes. Yes, I hear you."

"Then get it straight, Levi. You're the lucky one. You're the one I've chosen. You and me, buddy. And, if you ever tell a soul, I'll skin your fucking neck like a banana."

Zip. Tension shot in, and then out like a comet. It left no trail and no sound. Zip! The tension was gone. It lingered briefly on Levi Matthew Saranno, who shrugged it off as a misunderstanding.

Bates turned the boy with a friendly, gentle twist and guided him into the cabin.

"Yup," Barry said as they stepped into the darkness, "You and me are pals. Joined at the hip, so to speak. And the two of us are...guess what?" he asked with a jubilant little grin.

"What?"

"You and me are going bingo fishing right this minute. Bingo fishing. Just the two of us."

Levi smiled back and nodded eagerly.

"Great," he said. "I love fishing."

Bates turned both locks on the door and looked around to see Levi holding a blue-light-special tomahawk with feathers and beads. It wasn't quite what Levi imagined *this* tomahawk would look like. He thought it should seem more, well, ancient, or made of stone. But maybe Geronimo had done some trading with the white men and had gotten steel in exchange for hides and furs. He ran his fingers across the blade and was impressed to see it was as sharp as a steak knife. A real scalper, Levi thought.

Levi smelled the mustiness of the room as his eyes adjusted to the tiny bit of sunlight that was seeping through the curtained windows. The cabin had no electricity, but it did have running water for the bathroom and sink, and a small kitchen took up most of one wall. A tattered throw rug decorated the wooden floor. The bed jutted prominently from the wall into the center of the room. Levi looked at all of it, not caring. He cared about the trinkets and treasures and tomahawks. Levi didn't see the concave in the mattress worn down by the weight of Barry Bates each night. He didn't realize the significance of the two rusting hooks welded to the metal bed frame about eighteen inches apart.

"This tomahawk is awesome," Levi said, genuinely impressed. He hoped he would be able to take it back to Iron Horse as a present.

"It was used to kill white people," Bates explained, then smirked, "Especially children. Make yourself at home. Get comfortable. There are bows and arrows, and that spear in the corner was owned by Sitting Bull. In the jar, you'll find old arrowheads of stone and on the dresser, there's a rock knife that slit the throat of a wolverine. It's all here. Everything you wanted."

"Where's the gold?"

Master Bates threw Levi a roll of quarters. "Take these," he said. "You can use quarters easier than you can cash nuggets."

"But I want to see the gold," Levi insisted, as he caught the roll of quarters. Levi put the money in his swimsuit pocket.

"Then come here," Barry said as he sat himself down on the edge of the mattress. The bed squeaked. "Let's talk."

He stretched out his arms and beckoned the boy to come closer. Levi was still holding the tomahawk when he spotted the rifle.

"Is that a musket? Does it work?" he asked, fascinated by the artifacts he was discovering in this mountain hideaway. Levi lifted the gun, which when stood up straight, was taller than the nine-year-old holding it.

"Be careful, it might still be loaded," Bates warned. "Davy Crockett owned that rifle and gave it to my grandfather. Crockett was a friend of the family. You know, I have powerful friends all over the place. Friends who'll die for me. Do anything I ask."

Levi couldn't take his eyes off the gun. "This is so cool. Let me go outside and shoot it."

"The door's locked. Come here." Barry's courage was concentrated on the potential exploitation bouncing before him in the little red swimsuit and shirt with the Nike logo: "Just Do It." The irony did not escape the burly fat man.

Levi continued to wander around the cabin, carefully examining the dusty fossils, not noticing when Bates reached for a jar of Vaseline and the beach towel draped on the night table next to the bed. Bate's hands went to his zipper, and with a subtle push, his trousers fell to the floor, while the towel was neatly placed over his distended belly. Two fingers were all he could get into the Vaseline jar, and with expert swiftness, he scooped some jelly and quickly shoved it under the towel and into his crotch. Slowly his pants fell from around his feet as his hands moved back and forth under the threads that covered his flabby thighs.

The fat man couldn't take his eyes off Levi, or his hands off the growing hardness in his groin.

"Jesus you're a beauty, kid," he stuttered. "Young precious plucking."

"Thanks," Levi answered without looking away from his memento exploration at the other end of the dim room. "Do you think it's possible for me to have a souvenir? Something little, like a piece of pottery or some beads?"

Levi had his head in a box. "I like feathers, too."

"I'll give you a feather, Levi. I'll tickle you with one, and you can do the same to me. We'll feather each other until we think we've died and gone to heaven." His hand kept its ugly rhythm, up and down, up and down.

"Thank you, Barry. Thanks a lot."

"No problem, son," he said in a huskier voice. "You can keep the feather and the quarters and the beads. They're yours, if you want. You can even have the tomahawk."

"You mean it?"

"Yes. Yes I do. Come here. Sit on my knee, and we'll talk about it."

"Gee, thanks. This tomahawk's great." Levi grinned to himself. He'd have a gift for Iron Horse. Maybe it would even make the older boy smile.

"My pleasure, Levi. Here. Sit on my knee." Levi moved closer. Within reach. The fat man was starting to pant with anticipation.

Levi smiled at the blubber face as Barry's outstretched hand caressed the curve of the young boy's spine. One hand down to the swimsuit, and one hand on a greased-down javelin. Both moving imperceptibly, but moving all the time, sparking a twitch, holding back the bomb. From Levi's back to his waist, along the trunks, and on the side of his skinny, tanned legs, the big hand caressed. Levi was thrilled that he had such fine treasures. Barry's breathing was heavier now, the clawing more private. One hand was under the towel, on the serpent. One hand was on Levi.

"Sit on my knee, and we can discuss the finer things in life, including the gifts that Barry has to give." With a gentle sweep, Levi was on the man's left leg looking at the tomahawk imagining whose scalp it had taken when the West was won.

"Barry, this is so neat."

Twinkling eyes and flushing cheeks. Bates saw that his mark had a perfect body. A small tight ass. A perfect face.

"Levi, have you ever had an erection?"

"A what?" Levi looked up, startled.

"An erection." The big man smiled. His stubby tongue whipped out and moistened his bulky lips. Perspiration beaded on his forehead. "You know, when you rub your peter, and it gets hard."

Levi shook his head. "Gosh, I don't think so."

"You're such a sweet innocent."

"Whaddya mean?"

"A hard dick feels good, Levi. It feels good to touch it. To kiss. To suck. You can get one, if you try. It grows and grows. Even little dicks like yours get tall and tough. If you work it. How big is your dick, Levi?" One arm held Levi's waist. One hand wandered under the towel.

The tension rose. Bates's hand went around to the front of Levi's stomach and then reached down. The circular rubbing was gentle. Into Levi's groin.

Levi tried to pull away. "Stop that, Barry! I don't want you to do that!"

"Be nice, Levi..."

"Barry, stop it! I don't want to be here." Levi was squirming. "Let me go!"

"No, baby boy, no. Not now." The words sprouted quickly in breathy gasps. "Stay here. It's okay. There's nothing wrong."

His hands were moving faster. Both of them. Under the T-shirt and to the child's chest, beneath the towel. Grasping. Holding on tight. The jowls of his fat cheeks puffed. His eyes were a watery glaze.

Levi rammed his elbow into Barry's neck and raised the tomahawk. Barry's huge hand grabbed the top of Levi's leg above the knee and squeezed ferociously. The pain was intense.

"Barry! Stop!" The child's hands tried to pull away the squeeze. "That hurts!"

The grip loosened, and Levi was crying. In an instant, the brute snatched the tomahawk and threw it to the floor at the head of the bedpost.

"Let me see your dick, pal." Bates tore at Levi's trunks, reaching in, fingering skin. "We'll touch it and kiss it, and it'll grow and feel good."

"No! Leave me alone!"

Panic was ballooning into Levi's brain. But Levi couldn't move. With all his strength, he couldn't pull away from the grip that Barry had on him. His legs twisted, his buttocks arched, and his arms thrashed wildly.

"Settle down, Levi," The big sweating beast tried to placate the boy. "Nothing's wrong. This is good. I'll show you. Trust me. Let me touch you. You touch me. It's so good." Bates was in a tither. The excitement was over-whelming. His hands caressed each part of his new lover's body. Grabbing his stomach and chest and legs and knees and balls. "Beautiful. I want, I need you. Oh, Jesus."

Levi pulled and wriggled and twisted.

"Please don't struggle," Bates pleaded. "I won't hurt you. I'm your friend, your counselor. I'm here to take care of you. To love you. We're here to love each other."

Levi squeezed out from between the fat man's legs. The boy almost got away when the other fat hand flashed from under the towel and grabbed him by the elbow. Levi was terrified. Barry viced him with his legs as he bur-rowed his fingers into each thin arm. He had a straddle-hold on the boy who stood, facing the repugnant blob, locked against his will.

Levi could barely hear Barry's pleas. He was looking for an escape route that was impossible to find.

Levi didn't hear, "I'm your friend."

He scarcely heard, "I'm going to show you an erection, Levi. We can play with it together. If you touch it and kiss it, it'll make us feel good."

Levi didn't believe, "Don't be afraid. There's nothing to fear."

He did believe, "I'm going to show you something you've never seen before."

Bates said the words with unmistakable glee. Lascivious, wanton lust.

Levi almost crumbled in absolute terror as the fat man flipped the towel to the floor. Springing skyward was the slick, pulsating erection with the petroleum jelly sides, jumping from a pubic pillow of black, nappy hair. The one-eyed snake stared directly into the petrified face of the fragile cowboy about to be saddled.

"See the penis, Levi? See? You'll have a big one too someday. When I touch it, it feels good. Touch it. It won't hurt you."

Paralyzed with fear, the face of the incredulous young boy was inches away from the greasy pink and purple monster with the acorn hat. Levi paled. Barry's erect dick was right in front of his nose.

"No! Never!" he screamed as he shook his head in crazed disbelief. The thing stared back. Goggling. Right at him.

"Then watch. I can touch it." The fat man stroked it with a ferocious whacking that left Levi frozen.

White Knuckle

Fear and panic were shutting down Levi's nervous system, blanking out the madness from which there was no escape. Levi could no longer feel the fondling over the back of his swim trunks and on his ribs, legs, thighs, armpits, and chest.

"You must touch it," a disembodied voice demanded. "You must kiss it and suck it hard. Put your mouth on this popsicle."

"No!"

Barry's self-control had stroked itself into oblivion, as he pulled Levi's face toward him, almost for a kiss, and then down. He opened his greasy legs and shoved Levi's horror-filled face into his corpulent groin.

Levi strained, flailed, pushed, hopped and jumped. Kicking and shoving and pounding. But fat was everywhere. Like quicksand. Sinking. One big claw held onto the back of Levi's neck, while the other gripped his trunks, shaking them loose, pulling them off.

Levi twisted and punched and pulled, but he didn't scream. He wouldn't dare open his mouth. Not there. Not while he was still running. Running in place, like a football center practicing with a tackle machine. Hit it! Head down! Hit! Hit! Hit! His little red suit rested on the dirty floor. Bare-assed to the wind, and Master Bates now looking for a place to probe with a fat finger. A tight hole to enter. Barry's eyes closed in ecstasy.

Both hands went to Levi's buttocks. The child's head instantly lifted out of the darkness. Vaseline was on his forehead and nose and mouth and chin. He screamed. But Barry pulled him close, suckling his neck, tonguing his temples.

"Let me lick your dick, Levi. You'll lick mine," he panted.

Levi bit him, his teeth dug in like a piranha on fresh liver. He bit the rotund lobe of an ear so hard, Barry thought he'd lost it. The man howled as he flung Levi across the room, tossing him like a blanket in the park. Then Barry stood, livid with rage, his dick staring skyward.

"I'm not taking any more of your nonsense," he yelled, cupping his hand on the side of his head. "You almost bit off my goddamn ear! For that, you're going to pay. I was going to be nice, but no, what do you do? You get violent, you get mean. All I really wanted was a blow job, a little head, and maybe I'd do a suck or two. Now, you little bastard, we're going bingo fishing! Bingo fishing, and you're the fucking mackerel."

Barry Bates moved toward Levi like a sumo wrestler flopping after his opponent. The child stood, shrinking in a corner. The floor boards creaked under Barry's weight. Levi blindly grabbed the rifle and cocked the hammer.

"Get away from me, or I'll shoot. I swear to God, I'll kill you."

Barry kept coming. Levi took feeble aim, squeezed, and the hammer came down with a thunderous…click. Nothing. In the split second of Levi's surprise, Bates pulled the rifle from his grasp, propelling him closer. Close enough for one hand to seize a shoulder, and the boy was his again.

A squealing Levi was lifted up like a dumbbell by the blubbering behemoth, up toward the ceiling, and down into Barry's face so he could get a taste of the morsel between those weakened legs. One brawny hand held Levi under an armpit, the other hand was on his thigh. He lifted the boy up, opened his mouth wide and tried to get to the wiggling little penis he dangled in front of his wet lips.

Barry moved to the bed and flipped Levi onto his stomach so hard, the belly-flop took the rest of his breath away. When Levi's face hit the mattress, Master Bates had his wrists handcuffed between five fat fingers. The predator straddled his wailing victim with a dexterity born of experience as

118

the blue ropes were cinched onto Levi's wrists, then firmly attached to the cracked, welded hooks.

The bed buckled under the strain. The ropes were taut and the hooks groaned. Barry bounced up and down, with Levi buried beneath him. One big butt on a little one. Two fat knees on each side of a tight-assed virgin. Unable to escape, move or breathe.

"You're a quick little buck, ain't you boy? But not quick enough." Barry pulled back to look at his prize, to appraise his target and find his mark. The throbbing soldier between his legs was craning and crowing at attention as Master Bates slowly rubbed the little boy's back, and the cheeks of that fabulous ass. He pulled the boy's legs apart and began singing, "B-I-N-G-O, B-I-N-G-O, B-I-N-G-O, and BINGO was his name-oh."

Levi hung like a skinned rabbit. His arms over his head, and his hands firmly attached to the ropes. The hooks were strong, but they were old, and the weight kept getting bigger, heavier, and more burdensome. And then the bouncing. Each pull gave another strain, broke another fiber of rusted metal. The big man paid no attention. His focus was elsewhere.

"You're going to love this, Levi. Here comes Daddy." Barry held the cheeks apart, poking and prodding with the swollen organ, trying to get the opening to give a little. Barry was determined to carry his rod to the depths of Bingo bliss. But the unruly little rabbit kept turning and twisting. The bed kept bouncing. The walls creaked and the wrists bled from the rope burns and the pounding.

"I'll get this in, buddy! I'll get it in. Here I come!" Barry reached for the Vaseline again and pulled apart the victim's cheeks once more. With frantic, careful placement, he aimed the poker and with a final, mighty jump, he pushed. Hard and down and in and...

The bed broke. The crashing weight on Levi's back knocked the air out of the boy's screaming voice. Barry's dick was slightly in Levi's ass for a second. In another second, it would have been Bingo. Instead, the bed collapsed to the floor as torn hooks came down with the bodies. Barry popped away and out, and in the confusion, Levi squirmed to the side of the mattress. His arm reached to the floor to pull himself away. He didn't get away, but his hand found the handle of the feathery, beaded tomahawk and he blindly held onto it. Instantly, Barry was back, trying to mount him.

"Levi, now! Give it to me now! I'm ready to go." Barry had the boy by the waist. Frantically, both hands dragged the little torso in position, while his knees spread the legs again. "I'm ready, baby. I'm ready for a fucking." Bates reached down to guide his slickened penis into the bingo fishing pond. "Fuck me, son! Fu..."

With whatever strength he could muster, Levi's free hand raised up and came smashing down on Barry's head. The tomahawk hit, right above the eye.

Bates rolled off the mattress like a tire bumped from its axle. He tried to recover. Blood poured from his wound, gushing into his eyes, blinding him.

"You're a goddamn cocksucker!" Barry shrieked. "You'll pay for this! And when I'm done with you, your asshole will feel like the Columbia Gorge!" he thundered as he stumbled up.

Barry grabbed the knife that slit the wolverine's throat and staggered toward Levi. The boy still held the tomahawk. Levi stood, menacingly alert, but shivering like a sickly doe surrounded by a pack of wolves. Levi's arm reared back, and with a white-knuckle fling, the weapon went flying.

Barry caught only a glimpse before the blade smashed into his skull. He was nearly scalped with the single whoosh from Levi's memento.

White Knuckle

The crevasse in Barry's head was so wide, a team of Clydesdales would be needed to drag together the stitching between the bleeding ridges. For a second, the tomahawk remained poised in a deep red wrinkle on Barry's forehead, before it fell to the floor. He swayed and stumbled into a corner of the room, confused, unable to see through the gush of hot plasma that poured like lava from a volcano.

In the semi-darkness, Levi found his shorts and pulled them on in an instant. He unlocked the door as fast as he could, and when it opened, the sun burst in.

Levi looked back at Bates, who was babbling and cursing, struggling to stand up. Blood drooled from his jowls to the floor. He looked like a gored bull.

"I'll kill you, you little bastard," Bates croaked in a paroxysm of agony.

"No, you won't," Levi yelled back, his eyes blazing. "I'm going home!"

Bates gurgled, "If you ever tell a soul, I'll find you!" Rivulets of blood gushed from his head. His ugly teeth were red with blood.

Levi thought that Master Bates's fat hands looked like they had been drenched in ketchup.

"You're a dead man," Bates gasped. "Tell anyone, and I'll hunt you down and fill your asshole with a whisky bottle!"

The fat man Bates fell into a pool of blood. If his head had been in a bucket, he would have drowned.

Levi heard the threat, but he was running, running as fast and as hard and as strong as he could. He couldn't stop. Not until he reached the telephone booth in the middle of nowhere and dialed the cell number and talked to Judd. He had to get to his father.

11

A four-minute mile wasn't easy for a nine-year-old, and when Levi passed the lodge after running seven long minutes from Small Pox Canyon, he was too tired and intent on his mission to notice his mother standing near the lake. She was holding herself, anguishing like she'd been kicked in the stomach, trying to catch her breath. A concerned counselor had his arm around her shoulders, attempting to comfort her. Sheryl was sobbing. Her eyes were glazed and streaked when she first saw Levi running.

"There he is!" she cried to the counselor. "What do I say to him? How do I say it?" She absently twisted a tear-stained handkerchief in her distraught hands.

"I don't know, Mrs. Saranno, I don't know. There's no easy way." The counselor shook his head sympathetically. "I hear Levi's pretty strong. God will help you find the words."

Sheryl looked up at the young counselor. "If ever I needed God, this is the day," she cried. "I surely need him now. Joshua's so sick, I had to come alone. You understand, don't you?"

"Yes, Ma'am. Yes, I understand. Levi's coming. Now go to him. You'll find the words. I'll get the rest of his things and meet you at the car."

"Thank you," Sheryl Saranno whispered, and hurriedly tried to compose herself.

This is the time to be strong, she thought. You're in charge now, and now you've got to be Mom and Dad and give comfort and strength. He's just a little kid, but so gentle and wise and needful. Loving.

Sheryl reached out her arms to Levi as he ran toward her, but to her shock, he whipped past his mother and headed straight for the phone booth. He seemed obsessed. Nothing could stop him, nothing could get in his way. He saw only one thing. The phone. Levi clung to a solitary hope. His dad. Levi dialed his father's number and waited for the answer. Sheryl walked over to him as quickly as she could. Levi didn't hear her coming. He dialed, and waited for an answer. Out of nowhere, his mother pushed down the clicker, and the ring went silent.

"Levi, what's wrong with you? Didn't you see me?" She extended her arms to hug him. "Darling, I have to talk to you. Something terr…"

"Don't!" Levi lurched back like he'd been cornered. He held the phone like a hatchet. "Don't touch me. Don't ever touch me!"

Sheryl reached out to stroke her son's hair. Those fine curls, the strong, young temple. "Dear, dear Levi. It's been the hardest day of my life. Coming up here. Trying to figure out a way to tell you that everything will be okay, that we're going to be fine, that our life must go on."

Don't touch me!" He flicked her hand off his head like it was a gnat. "Leave me alone! I have to talk to Dad. I need the other number. Give me another number, Mom, so I can call Dad. His cell phone's not answering!"

"Levi, you can't call your dad. That's what I came here to tell you. That's why I'm early," Sheryl said weakly.

"I have to call him!" Levi screamed. He swung at his mother as hard as he could. It was the first time he'd ever pushed her. It wasn't intentional, no premeditation, just a spontaneous act of aggression.

White Knuckle

"Get away from me! I'm calling Dad, and I'm calling him now! Leave me alone!"

"Levi, you can't call your Dad." Sheryl cried out, trying to grab hold of her son.

"You're crazy!" Levi dialed. "I got quarters. I can make the call direct. I thought I remembered the number, but there's no answer. What's his new number? Give it to me, Mom!"

Levi turned away from her. With all his strength, he concentrated on the phone. He banged his fist on the steel coin box. "Work, you son-of-a-bitch, work!"

In the background, Sheryl was shouting and crying.

"It wasn't really your father's fault; it was an accident. A yellow light or something. Maybe he was drunk. Not your dad, Levi, the other guy, the other driver. It was such a terrible accident. Daddy hit his head very hard."

Levi paid no attention. Her words made no sense. He was waiting for the connection. Silence. He slammed the receiver against the wall.

"Please listen to me, Levi..." Sheryl pleaded through her tears.

The boy listened instead for the connection. The recording on the other end said, "We're sorry, the party you have dialed is not on service or is out of the service area. Please try again."

Levi slammed the phone, pressed the clicker, and got another dial tone.

"Honey, you've just got to listen to me," Sheryl was begging. "Joshua's so sad, he can't get out of bed."

Levi's mother pulled another handkerchief from her purse. "I can't...oh Levi, I can't explain how it happened. Asia could hardly talk, but she said it was a horrible accident. She said..."

Levi dropped in more quarters and listened to the ringing on the other end of the line. A ring. But no Dad. No hello. No voice, except in the background, behind him, where his mother spoke in anguished tones. Heartache. Real. From a foggy distance, Levi heard her words for the first time.

"When I saw how upset you were, I thought maybe you already knew, but I didn't know how you could've found out. Asia called me. From the hospital. Can you imagine? It's the first time we've ever talked. She's badly hurt, but she's going to recover. She seemed rather nice..." Sheryl's word's started to trail off, then seeing that Levi was finally listening, she snapped back to the moment, and her son.

"Levi, you can't reach your dad anymore. You just can't reach him."

Now, she was crying hard again. Levi slowly and cautiously hung up the phone.

Sheryl reached for him once more. "Baby. Please, let me hold you. Please know that things'll be okay."

"No." His head shook back and forth. In disbelief. It wasn't possible. "No!" he said, over and over again.

"Levi, it was the other driver's fault, sort of, but God has a plan for us. Each and every one. Even your dad couldn't change that plan. It was his fate. To be in that car. On that highway. He's with God, now, Levi. God wanted him. It was time for him to go."

Back and forth. Levi's head kept turning, slowly one way, and then the other.

"Your dad lived long enough to tell you something. Asia will be there, at the funeral. She's got a message from your dad. She wanted to tell you herself, so…"

"No," he said, so silently only an angel could hear.

"Your father is dead, Levi. He's gone. He's not coming back."

"No…" Levi's voice sounded barren and hollow. Like a faraway faint wail in the moonlight from a forsaken coyote on a lonely mountaintop.

"No," was the echo that broke the silence. A murmur from an abandoned oasis gone dry.

"No," was the only sound that could be heard.

Levi had finally found his Puckerbush Patch, and he jumped in. Levi was gone for good. Good and gone.

Into a swirling tornado he flew. A tornado with no sound or rain or air or wind. It took him into the clouds and over the seas and beyond the world he knew and loved and wanted. Needed. Like the earth needs the sun. Like a stream needs water. Like a baby needs care. He needed, and they went away – the warmth, the water, the caring. Gone.

Levi floated into another world, where nothing was familiar. A place where he had to make it on his own. There, he would have to find his own warmth, his own way to quench a thirst. Caring might or might not come. That came with trust, and trust was left in the world behind him. Trust would never be found in the new world, at least not as far as Levi was concerned.

* * * * *

Levi sat silently in the front seat of the car as his mother slowly drove down the winding Rocky Mountain road that led away from Camp Anakeegee.

Sheryl had one hand on the wheel and the other clenched tightly to her wet handkerchief.

Levi swirled in the tornado, quietly staring into the trees and dirt and the road that he couldn't see. He couldn't see because he was whiting it out. Whiting out the old world so he could paint a new one. But at nine years of age, Levi didn't know what memories *really* needed painting over.

Sheryl glanced over at her son with red, tear-swollen eyes. "Asia's hurt, Levi. But she was able to tell me that your dad's final words were about you. Asia's got a message, and she's asked permission to come to see you, to tell you what your father wanted you to know."

Sheryl's voice was so sad and confused that Levi wouldn't have recognized it, even if he wanted to. Which he didn't.

Levi didn't speak, either. Sheryl couldn't tell if her son was listening, things had to be said, and plans had to be made for the future.

"I know you're young, honey." She reached her shaking hand out to touch his naked knee. Levi recoiled as far to the corner of the car as he could get. Away. Quarters fell onto the seat, clicking like the bells that guard the doorway of a pawn shop. "You'll always have your happy memories of Dad."

His mother didn't hear the quarters, but to Levi, they were rattling tattle-talers, begging for a question about where they came from. He couldn't hear his mother, but he could clearly hear the clanging quarters. Levi understood their meaning. Clearly they were evidence, like a trail of crumbs from an empty cookie jar and a dash of milk on a child's upper lip.

Carefully, Levi grabbed the coins and rolled down the car window, watching his mother out of the corner of his eye to make sure she wasn't aware of his clandestine move to throw them away, out the window, to be forever lost in the old world. The evidence was tossed into the blowing wind, and the quarters silently rolled into the past as Levi's body curled into a fetal hunch as close to the door handle as he could get.

"Levi, you've got to be strong, now. Try to remember all the good things your dad wanted for you. The good things were so many, the good times were so close. Especially for you and your father."

The candy! More evidence! Carefully, Levi reached into the small pocket of his swimsuit, and his fingers delicately rummaged for brittle or beads or arrowheads or feathers. Feathers! There were none.

A silent, heavy sigh of relief oozed out of his small, trembling body as he resumed his fetal clutching, his left hand on his right shoulder, the right hand on his left. Knees crunched to his chin. His face, looking dazed and bewildered and empty. Twirling further into his new world, flying with the tornado over the seas and into a different dimension. Levi was like an astronaut, floating in space, without gravity, without a lifeline.

"There's so much for us to do, Levi. So much to think about and so little time. Your dad..." she started crying again, tears impairing her vision. Quickly, she pulled the car off to the side of the road before she lost control of the vehicle completely. "Your dad wanted bagpipes. Bagpipes!" She blew her nose and wiped away more tears. "Where do you find bagpipes? He wanted them to play *Danny Boy*."

Sheryl stopped, remembering Judd in happier days. She had her own memories, just as Levi did. Husband and wife, with dreams and hopes and recollections of how they'd been in the past, before the break, before the failure. Sheryl reached out to bring Levi closer.

The boy refused to move.

Her trembling fingers gently touched his shoulder.

129

"Don't!" Levi screamed. "Don't touch me! Don't you, or no one touch…"

His mother's hand ricocheted back.

"Levi," she soothed, "Levi, it'll be okay, honey. Please, son. Try to understand. I know you're upset, baby, but you've got me and Joshua and…" She could hardly believe she was about to say it, "…and you've got Asia. Asia's got something to tell you."

"Never! Never, never!" Levi wailed as his hands covered his face and lips and mouth and cheeks and chin. His legs shot straight to the floor boards, as his body bent forward to the dash. His little fists pounded the leather above the glove compartment, rhythmically slow at first, and then faster and faster as he cried, "Liar! No! Liar! No! Liar!"

Sheryl knew she had to let him get it out. The anger and denial and pain and disbelief. She also knew that he would be strong again. Sheryl desperately wanted to soothe and reassure and comfort her little Levi. "I understand, baby. I understand your pain. I feel it, too," she said softly as her son continued to punch the dashboard, screaming, "Liar! Liar! Liar!"

His hands swelled, bruised and bleeding. Hammered, like his heart.

* * * * *

At nine, Levi's mind stopped growing. Parts of it. He didn't tell. He didn't tell anyone, because it was all so bad. Levi was bad, and he didn't know why. Raped, and he didn't know why.

I didn't like camp, Mom. You! *You* made me go. Listen to me. Listen! Where's Dad? Gone? Why? But I need him, because it scared me. What? Nothing. I forget! Lies. I can't remember, and I don't want to be bad. I'm not bad, am I? I'm bad? Tell me! And I won't tell. I don't want to go to camp anymore. I don't want to go. Where's Dad? He said he'd always be there. Gone? I want to hide. Hide. Alone.

White Knuckle

Levi was a child to be loved, but he didn't love being a child. A boy who could tell no one. And he never did. He knew Kit was right after all. It was safer, necessary, to collect puckers. Giant, huge, colossal puckers. Everywhere. Collect them and put them firmly in place, because there was too much shame and too much guilt. Too much for a small, lonely sinner.

Too much for any kid to tell at the age of nine and growing. Growing within a Puckerbush Patch, and growing alone.

12

Sheryl had to wait eight days for the body. Eight days to find bagpipes, coffin, and priests. To make phone calls to friends and relatives and to find a suitable place for a burial. A headstone. What kind of inscription? "Judd Saranno. A loving husband, father, and warrior for the oppressed." That wouldn't work. "Judd Saranno. Faithful. Humble. Kind and gentle "wouldn't work either. You have to be honest, Sheryl thought. She finally decided it was better to just inscribe Judd's name in granite, put a picture someplace, note the day he was born and the day he died. You have to be dignified, she told herself, and kind.

Sheryl waited eight days, and so did Asia. The police investigated and Asia anguished. Her wounds had been stitched by plastic surgeons as orthopedists sliced into her hip and inserted a steel rod through the femoral head and into the center of the biggest bone in her body. Her right femur had been shattered. She saw the X-rays afterwards.

"Looks good," the doctor said, admiring his own work. "You'll be on crutches for about nine months, but the bone grafting looks secure, and by putting the rod through the center of the femur, you won't need casting."

"Thank you," she said politely, and continued her crying. Crying for Judd and their future and plans and hopes. Dreams. Dashed and gone and nothing to show for them except a bronze statue of two lovers, smeared with the blood of Judd Saranno.

The police never found the Dodge or the other driver. "I'm not sure it would do us any good, anyway," the investigating officer had told her. "I'm sorry, Ma'am. I've got to close the case and put the blame on Mr. Saranno. It's just too bad he got so angry. People get like that, you know. It's road rage," he said. But she didn't want to hear it. Asia didn't care about fault or drunken kids or police officer opinions. What she cared about was getting out of the hospital and getting Judd's body back to Denver. And telling Levi that Judd's last words were of hope and love and promises. And about the funeral. She cared about that.

Asia, she knew, was an outsider. The mistress. The "other woman." More importantly, *she* felt she was the reason for Judd's death. How would it look for her to be at the funeral? How would people react? Would she even be allowed to attend? The fear of calling Sheryl had been overwhelming. Asia didn't think anyone would go out of their way to extend an invitation to the funeral. She would have to ask for some kind of permission to attend, and she had no idea what Sheryl would say. Then again, Sheryl *had* sent flowers to Asia in the hospital. That gesture gave Asia some hope. She made the call.

Sheryl's response was unexpected. "Asia, I don't know you, but if Judd loved you and you loved him, of course you should be at the funeral. And of course you can talk to Levi."

For the first time, Asia questioned why Judd had divorced this woman.

Sheryl's tears kept falling as she made funeral arrangements. Joshua watched his mother and cried almost as much as she did, mostly because of her sadness, not his. But Levi never started crying. Tears never came into his eyes.

The world around Judd's favorite son was changing so rapidly that Levi had to be deaf, dumb, and blind not to know it. He was all of that. He didn't see the flowers streaming into the house every day. He didn't hear the conversations about eulogies and music and memorials. Numbness blocked out every word of consolation, every tender touch of sympathy. There was no light. Just darkness.

But there was a life for Levi. It was just that no one could see it. The outside of Levi's patch was bristling with thriving new puckers. Sharp and tingling as they tangled up barriers. They built moats and shields of armor all around his heart and soul and thoughts. Mostly, around his feelings.

* * * * *

Judd's broken remains were waiting at the Catholic altar, the closed coffin surrounded by flowers.

"Levi," his mother pleaded, "please hurry, honey. Put on your tie and sport coat now, so we won't be late for the rosary. Comb your hair nicely. Please? It's time to go."

Time for Levi to visit the dead body of his father. Even Levi had to climb out of his patch for this one.

For Sheryl, the eight-day delay was a blessing. Judd Saranno was about to get the most beautiful sendoff Denver had ever seen. "Prominent Trial Lawyer Dies," was the front-page headline of the *Denver Post* a week before, accompanied by an article about the car crash in San Francisco. Nothing was said about Asia, and for that, both women were grateful.

Sheryl had arranged for a rosary to be said on the night before the burial, followed by dinner. Dinner with close friends, and at noon the next day, the mass would begin, and then the internment.

Sheryl knew that Judd wouldn't have wanted a private funeral. He'd want a line of cars so long it would stop traffic for blocks. A wavy line of cars with lights on, following his hearse to the grave he'd inhabit forever.

No cremation for Judd Saranno, and at least six motorcycle cops would be needed to block all the traffic. It was going to be one big parade of mourners. Judges, lawyers, clients, employees, friends, and relatives. Even old lovers could attend. No one would know who they were or would even care, because the focus wasn't going to be on a forgotten liaison.

Although Asia was invited to the rosary, mass, and interment, she would find her own pew in church, and she had to make her own arrangements for a driver and a car. Of course, Asia wasn't expected to attend the wake afterwards, not at the Saranno house.

Sheryl was convinced that she had handled every detail perfectly. Judd Saranno was going out with dignity and class. She had even convinced herself he deserved no less.

Levi's bedroom door was locked, and Sheryl tapped on it gently as Joshua walked down the hall toward the waiting limousine outside. "Levi, it's time to go," she said softly.

His mother waited, but heard no sounds. "Levi," she said, "it's going to be okay, honey. Open the door."

Finally Sheryl heard the lock click, and the door opened slowly. Her son stood alone in his bedroom. Levi didn't speak.

"Is there anything I can do?" she asked anxiously.

Except for shaking his head, Levi's body was stiff and motionless. Sheryl pulled a handkerchief from her pocket and handed it to her son. Levi took the handkerchief, and as his mother led him into the hall, he dropped it in the garbage can by the door.

* * * * *

White Knuckle

Asia was one of the first people to arrive for the rosary. She passed the guest book without signing her name.

"I don't want to stand out any more than I have to," she told her friend, Julie, who accompanied her to the funeral. "We'll come early and leave as quickly as possible. I hope no one will really notice."

"Yeah, right. Black eyes, bandages, and crutches. You're practically invisible."

In the middle of a wooden pew, they sat as inconspicuously as possible. People sat in the benches around them, and the organ music played softly, filling the church with an aura of somber formality.

In front of the altar lay Judd's casket, an ornate, white box with lacquered paint and golden handles. On the top, there was a huge bouquet of roses, lilacs, gladioluses, lilies, and carnations. Wreaths were all around the casket, and next to it was a picture of Judd, more like a poster, framed in gold underneath clear, crystal glass. Judd was smiling, looking confident, strong, happy. Alive. Behind his dead body was Christ, His thorned head bowed as He hung from the cross.

The organ played as Levi, holding his mother's hand, walked to the front pew, knelt dutifully, and sat down between her and his brother.

Levi could see his father's picture smiling at him. He could see it clearly. Levi stared back. His eyes never strayed from his father's, except to look at the coffin. To wonder.

"Why?" he whispered. "You promised."

The priest walked in and the music stopped. Levi heard some of the words. The introduction. Acknowledging the rosary's purpose. Thanking the people for attending. Telling the throng to respond, "The Lord is kind and merciful."

"Look at the beauty of the flowers," the priest said. "Colors add to this celebration. A celebration because Judd Saranno is one step ahead of us, headed in the right direction."

Celebration, Levi thought. Headed in the right direction! Even priests were liars. "God does not judge us for our sins...." Could that really be true? "Jesus will rise him from the dead...." Okay, rise then. "Why do you sleep? Get up and pray...." It was a story from the Bible. If Jesus did it for that guy, will he do it for Dad? But nothing happened. They were just words. More lies.

No one kneeled during the rosary. They stood for readings from the gospel. Levi heard the mourners respond, "The Lord is kind and merciful." Levi stayed quiet.

Liars. All of them.

And then one of Judd's lawyer friends got up. Billy Barton spoke, but Levi didn't listen to everything he said. Levi heard, "And if you had Judd Saranno on your side, you knew you had a winner. He could always be trusted. His word was his bond. He fought fights no one else had the courage to consider, and won. But most of all, if Judd Saranno made you a promise, he kept it. He was a legend in his own time. A giver. A friend. A protector..."

Levi hissed under his breath. All bullshit. The priests were liars, and so was Billy. Billy and all the other friends that praised his father. Them and God and his mother and brother and Asia, too. Except for Kit. Kit was not a liar. She didn't leave him on purpose. It wasn't her fault; she was forced out. And now she was gone. He had no way to reach her. Away. Away so he'd be alone and defenseless and they could all keep on sinning against him.

For eight days his mother had watched Levi go into a shell. He wouldn't come out of his room. He barely ate; he barely slept. And he never spoke.

White Knuckle

Sheryl talked with friends, consulted her priest, and read a book on dealing with grieving children. Nothing helped.

Sheryl held her son's hand tightly as the mourners lined up to pass the casket and offer tear-filled condolences. Sheryl and Joshua acknowledged the consoling words, the hand held, the cheek kissed, the whispered grief. Levi watched the procession blankly. The last person to come down the aisle was Asia.

Asia was wearing a black suit. A white pearl necklace swung around her neck as she slowly maneuvered the crutches forward. Her hair was neatly trimmed, but there were bruises on her face, and it was filled with pain.

"I...I'm so sorry," she said to Sheryl. Asia took one hand off the handle of the crutch as she balanced it under her arm. "You, you've been so kind. I..."

Sheryl touched her arm. "Please," she said. "You don't have to say anything."

"But I need to talk to Levi," Asia reminded Sheryl.

The boy stiffened and sharply turned his head away from Asia. Sheryl leaned forward slightly and gently rubbed Levi's back. "Honey, you've got to listen."

Asia wanted to reach out and bring Levi to her breast. This was Judd's son. The child he loved and cherished the most. Maybe Judd loved Levi more than he loved her. His last words were about Levi, not about them.

"Levi, your dad...he wanted me to tell you..."

At that moment, and for no apparent reason, Judd's picture fell from the stand next to the casket, exploding as it hit the stone, sprinkling diamond-like pieces of glass across the altar.

"Judd!" Sheryl screamed.

Levi bolted over the pew and ran for the door yelling. "Kit!" he cried. "Kit!"

Sheryl and Asia stared at the altar, horrified.

* * * * *

The caterers arrived at the Saranno house the next morning to prepare for the wake, setting out folding chairs, extra tables, punch bowls and plates, glasses and utensils.

Sheryl stood in the doorway of her youngest son's bedroom. "You've got to be strong, Levi. Do this for me, and do it for your father."

"Dad's dead."

"But, Levi," she answered reassuringly, "he's up there, watching over you."

"Right," Levi said, as he reached for the remote control on his television set.

Sheryl's patience faded. She looked stern and angry and old. "This isn't time for TV. It's time you promise me you'll behave. No more scenes, like when you ran out of church. Act like your father would expect."

"I don't care," her son answered. "How long will this take?"

"The limousine will be here shortly. The mass will take an hour or so." His mother tried to stop the stammering in her voice. "And the other services will be about the same. Your dad always told me what he wanted if he were to pass away." She paused. "I'll bet he would've wanted you to make him proud."

She put her trembling hands on Levi's shoulders. "Promise me you'll do what's right."

White Knuckle

Levi looked directly into her eyes. "I won't promise *you*." Sheryl's face filled with disappointment. "I'll promise *him*." Levi looked toward the dresser at a framed photograph of his father and him taken at a rodeo the summer before.

A rush of relief swept through Sheryl's body as she pulled Levi next to her, rocking him like a baby. "My son. My perfect, perfect son," she whispered in his ear.

* * * * *

Sheryl left home with her sons, and as their black limousine parked in front of the church, they could hear the bagpipes playing *Danny Boy*. Again, the church was full. Sheryl proudly noted the crowd of people who had come again to mourn the untimely death of Judd Saranno. Levi just watched, walked, and followed, like he'd promised.

Everyone held hands when they said the *Our Father*, and they turned to each other and said, "Peace be with you," as a guitar player sang *Margueritaville*.

"Judd wanted that song," someone said. "Judd never wanted to die. He just wanted to go to Margueritaville, to bow out of the life that made him a prisoner to his job and responsibilities."

"Well," an old friend mused, "if he doesn't make it to heaven, I hope he makes it to Mexico with a shotglass and some tequila."

"He'll make it to God's house. He wasn't perfect, but his heart was generally in the right place," Levi overheard someone say.

After another eulogy by yet another friend, the priest finally sprinkled holy water over the flower-covered casket. *Ava Maria* was played on bagpipes during the blessing, and mass ended. Six pallbearers lined up beside the casket. The priest headed for the door, the crowd stood, and just as Judd wanted, *Danny Boy* was bag-piped again as the Saranno family walked behind the casket into the sunlight. The priest bent down, kissing the coffin. The pallbearers lifted it into the hearse, and the limousine doors opened. People headed for their cars, and the procession to the cemetery began.

"Now what?" Levi asked.

"Look at all the cars." Joshua exclaimed. "It looks like a ten-mile train!"

"We're going to the cemetery, Levi," his mother answered. "Then, we're going home. Then it's over."

"Good." Levi looked out the window, wondering what *Margueritaville* meant.

The procession was long and slow. Motorcycle cops kept zooming past the caravan of cars, stopping traffic ahead of the hearse, then zooming forward again.

Joshua laughed. "Wouldn't you know it," he said. "Dad's going out breaking the law all the way. We've gone through a dozen red lights already."

Sheryl smiled weakly, and finally, the cemetery came into view. Levi saw the canopy hung on four poles surrounding the open grave. The dirt was in a pile, neatly covered by a white tarp. Somehow, the flowers from the church had beaten them to the burial grounds.

Hundreds of single, white roses were in boxes. As people came up to the gravesite, each was given one of the flowers. Carefully, the pallbearers placed the casket next to the hole in the ground as the priest asked the mourners to gather closer. Sheryl and the boys were at the head of the coffin. The crowd parted, and Asia made her way to the front.

Several people stared at Asia, others murmured about her presence, while still others watched Sheryl's reaction. Sheryl nodded to Asia, communicating that it was acceptable for her to be there.

There were more prayers. More words. More tears. The casket was lowered into the ground. One by one, everyone holding a rose tossed it into the hole.

Asia cast her rose and said some inaudible words, but her pain was so obvious, it hurt just to look at her. She turned to Sheryl and asked, "May I have just a few moments with Levi?"

Sheryl nodded, took Levi's hand and led him off to the side, away from the crowd. Asia followed.

Sheryl backed away to give them privacy, then walked toward the priest who took her hands into his and held them.

Asia and Levi stood away from the mourners. Asia trembled. Levi was stoic. They were alone.

"How come you're not dead?" Levi asked

"Oh, Levi, please," Asia begged. "I loved your father. I loved him with all my heart and soul." She paused. "Your father and I had so many plans, Levi, and you were a part of them."

"Then how come I wasn't there?" His voice rose. "How come I got to go to Small Pox?"

Asia looked at him quizzically for a second. She didn't understand the reference, and chose to ignore it. "Your dad's last words were about you."

Levi wanted to run from her as fast as his legs could carry him. He glanced toward his mother. She was dabbing tears, acknowledging the visitors who nodded or spoke quiet condolences. The guitar player was strumming *Greensleeves* softly in the background.

"Please don't go away, Levi. Let us be friends." Asia was so sincere, it made him wonder, but only for an instant.

"No," he said.

"It's how your father wanted it."

"I don't care."

"But, Levi, it's what your dad wanted you to hear. That's part of what he asked me to tell you."

"So tell me. What did he say? What's the big-deal message?"

Asia's body leaned heavily on the crutches beneath her arms, as she held her hands out to Levi. She wanted his hands in hers, but he didn't reach back.

"He told me," she said. "to tell Levi I love him. No matter what happens, I'll be there for him. Tell him to reach back, back to the Choke Hole and fishing and the good times, and there, that's where he'll find me. That's where I'll be. And that's where I'll protect him. It's a promise."

Levi's hands started to move to Asia. Through her tears she could see that something was stirring in the little boy's heart. In Levi's face, she saw Judd.

Then the palms of his hands hit her chest so hard, she stumbled backwards. Before anyone could rescue her, Levi pushed her again. His right fist hit her in the shoulder. The music stopped, as Sheryl and several others ran toward Asia, on the grass, crying.

Levi was gone. He ran into the cemetery, into a desert of graves and head-stones. Running as fast as he could. The last thing anyone heard Levi say on the day his dad was buried was, "Liar! Liar!"

And into his patch he sprang.

BOOK TWO

*"'I was bred and born in a briar
patch, Brer Fox – bred and born in
a briar patch! There's no place I
love better!'
And with that, he skipped off
as lively as a cricket in the embers."*

– Joel Chandler Harris
The Wonderful Tar-Baby Story

13

At the moment of her birth, her parents knew she was going to shine, which is why they nicknamed her "Sunny." Sunny sparkled. She danced in the light. Her real name was Erica Lynne Jacobson.

Mary and William Jacobson doted on their lovely child, all through the years of her growing up. They adored her, supported her, approved of just about everything she did. But they weren't always pleased with her choices, particularly in boyfriends. The current one was the most worrisome.

"I don't think Levi can be trusted," her mother said, looking at the daughter she'd raised for nineteen years.

"But he's just like me, Mom. I know it – at least I *think* so. He just doesn't express himself very much. He's closed off. It's like Levi's afraid or confused."

The two women were arranging the last of the garden's fall flowers in vases around the living room. "Maybe so, Erica, but last night he didn't even have the courtesy to cancel your date until nine o'clock. He's unreliable. Levi's got *some* charm, and certainly good looks, but lots of boys have that. You deserve better." Mary smiled at her daughter.

There was some truth in what Erica's mother was saying. Levi and Erica were sophomores at Colorado State; she majored in psychology and had ambitions for graduate school, maybe law. Levi, on the other hand, had dropped out of the psychology class where she'd first seen him after only four weeks. He was pursuing "social science," which everyone knew meant studying nothing, just going through the motions of getting out of college. So why was she attracted to him?

"It's a feeling," she had tried to explain to her parents as they watched TV. "Intuition. I've got to trust my instincts."

"You're trusting something else," her irritated father had said. "Common sense tells you he's spoiled and rich, but he's not measuring up on his own." He reached for his pipe. "You deserve a young man with ambition, a sense of direction. Levi seems like a hustler, hustling what, I don't know. Maybe you."

"Now, Bill," Mary cautioned, "Erica's a big girl and instin..."

"Instincts, intuition, same thing," he said, staring at his daughter. "Use your brain, honey. It'll keep you out of trouble."

Erica thought her father might be right about some of his thoughts. But she didn't tell him why he was right. The *real* intuitive factor stemmed from the tingling sensation she felt whenever Levi walked into her space. Erica felt it the instant he first wandered into her classroom, in her pulse and stomach and legs. The juice just started to flow, alive and seductive. She'd never felt this way before. And it happened every time she saw him. The dampness came. There was no explaining it. Then, suddenly, Levi dropped out of psych class. Without having ever said anything to her, he had disappeared for weeks. Erica remembered that, and the feelings of emptiness that came with his being gone. She had never been ignored by someone she instinctively wanted. Rejected. Rejected before he'd given her a chance. In retrospect, maybe her parents were smarter than she was.

When Erica had first gotten to know Levi – even just a little – she quickly found out he was different from the other guys who would do anything they could to impress her. Not Levi. Even after he stopped coming to class, Erica's fantasies continued. Whenever she walked on campus, Erica wondered if she'd see the boy who obviously never saw her. He wasn't in the halls, didn't go to rallies, wasn't at games and didn't mingle with other students. Levi was gone, and Erica's hopes had eventually faded.

After weeks of staying dry, Erica instantly felt the wetness again. She hadn't seen him approach. Her nose had been buried in the large textbook she was studying for a psych exam on what adrenaline does to the body and mind during a crisis. Sitting in the Alferd Packer Cafeteria, with the book in one hand and a sliced turkey sandwich in the other, Erica was unprepared for Levi's appearance from out of nowhere. He was carrying a tray with a hot roast-beef sandwich slathered in brown gravy, mashed potatoes, a Coke and a thick slice of peach pie.

"Mind if I sit down?" he asked, and without waiting for a response, pulled out the chair opposite to Erica's and plopped into it. She looked up from her book, looked into his eyes, and the juices took over.

"Do you know the real story of Alferd 'Frank' Packer?" Levi asked mischievously.

"I think so," Erica replied, feeling the heat rush to her cheeks. "Didn't Packer eat some prospectors he was guiding to the gold mines in Colorado? Wasn't he a cannibal who would have starved to death, if it weren't for his food fetish?"

Levi grinned. "It's fitting they named this cafeteria after him, don't you think? Do you know why they didn't hang him?"

"Why?" Erica asked with genuine curiosity and a mouthful of turkey sandwich.

Levi slapped the table with the palm of his hand. "Because he was a Republican!" He laughed. "Can you believe that?"

Erica stared in disbelief.

"It's true," Levi insisted. "The judge was so pissed off during Alferd's sentencing, he said, quote: 'There were seven Democrats in Hinsdale County, but you, you voracious, man-eating son-of-a-bitch, you ate five of them! I sentence you to be hanged by the neck until you're dead, dead, dead; as a warning against reducing the Democratic population of the state.'"

Erica was laughing, almost choking on her sandwich.

"Alferd appealed the verdict on the grounds that the judge was a Democrat and, therefore, prejudiced against Republicans. Court bought it. He got forty years, but was pardoned after eighteen. Then he allegedly died of a gastro-intestinal disorder."

Erica was laughing so loud, several other students turned to look at them.

"Now what does that tell you?" Levi asked as he took a swig of his Coke.

"I don't know," she replied, still smiling. "Maybe prison food wasn't as good as what he could get in the mountains?"

"It tells you that if the judge had just hid his feelings, they could've put a rope around the cannibal's neck and saved the state eighteen years worth of holding costs."

Levi, too, was laughing with Erica as she looked into the eyes of the young man whom she desperately wanted to know better. He had never said a word in class and had never started a conversation, not with anyone. He'd been so quiet. And now, Levi Saranno, the handsome loner, sat in front of her, smiling, talking, and being more than just civil.

Erica didn't want the conversation to end. "But shouldn't the judge be entitled to express his feelings?" she asked.

"Doing that was stupid," Levi said, his face clouding. "It always is."

150

"Always?" Erica's voice sounded a challenge. Levi said nothing. "You have feelings," she reasoned. "Don't you express them?"

"No," he answered over a forkful of mashed potatoes. "Not if I don't have to."

Erica stared into the deep brown eyes. Almost black, but filled with warmth and kindness, except for occasional flickers of uncertainty. Sometimes, his eyes seemed to impart a sense of loneliness, a sense of disenchantment. Detached. Like he was there one moment and off in some nether world the next.

But Levi was real for Erica. And finally, they were talking.

"My name's Erica."

"I know. I'm Levi Saranno." He started to fidget and averted his eyes. "I'm in a hurry," he said. "Sorry if I've bothered you." He stood up as quickly as he'd sat down.

"No!" Erica reached for his sleeve and gently tugged on it. It was almost a plea. "Don't leave. I've been hoping we'd meet sometime."

"I think it's better if I go," Levi said, then paused. "What the hell, you can't eat me, even though we're in Packer's Cafeteria. Alferd's not contagious, is he?" Grinning, he sat his lean, tall frame back down.

Erica loved his outdoorsy look. Boots. Wrangler jeans. Blue denim shirt. She admired his chiseled chin and confident jaw. He had undoubtedly worked his magic on a lot of girls, but he didn't smile very often. In class, she'd never seen it happen. Often, she would see him sitting there, just day-dreaming. At least that's what it looked like.

"Are you from Colorado?" she asked.

"Yeah. Grew up here. Live with my mother. My parents divorced."

"Where's your father?"

"Dad's dead. Killed when I was a kid."

Erica's face clouded. "Oh, I'm so sorry."

Levi leaned back and glanced out the window. "I don't remember him really," he said. "People say he was an asshole, and so I figure I didn't lose much." He looked back into her inquisitive eyes.

She sensed a vague sadness. He didn't sound sad, but Erica felt it.

"He died when I was nine. He'd just divorced my mother, when he was killed with a whore in California."

"Murdered!" Erica asked, astonished.

"No. Car wreck." He looked out the window again. "Dad was never around, so I don't really miss him." Levi's eyes met her sensitive stare. He seemed nervous. He started to stand up once again.

"I was wondering, Levi, could you help me with my homework?"

"How?" Her question didn't make sense to him. He knew she was smart, at least she stayed in class and didn't drop out like he did.

"In psych class, we have to do personality profiles," she lied. "I've got to ask strangers about themselves and try to categorize them into types. You know, type "A" or "B" or something like that."

"I'm not interested," he said with casual indifference. "Besides, I don't like talking about myself. I'm passive, not aggressive."

Erica didn't want to overwhelm him with personal questions, but she didn't want him to walk out the door and be gone again, maybe this time for good.

"Well," she said, "you could at least tell me a *little* bit about yourself. I'll change names to protect the guilty," she joked. "And I promise I won't make you a main character in my essay."

"Don't make promises, Erica," he said, as if scolding her. Pushing his tray aside, he pulled out a pack of cigarettes. "If you don't mind my smoking, we can take a walk outside, and I'll answer some of your questions."

He stood up and started toward the exit, not waiting for Erica, expecting her to follow.

The day was cool and sunny. Blue skies touched the mountaintops that had been lightly glazed with fall's first snow. Pumpkins were on the way. Levi wandered down a paved path, flicking ashes and looking distant. Erica caught up to him.

"I grew up in Denver," he said matter-of-factly. "And then moved to Colorado Springs with my older brother and mother. Joshua's at M.I.T. in Texas. My mother's into charity work, the Assistance League, that sort of thing. Other than that, she reads books and lives alone in a house with a view from every window."

"How come she didn't remarry?"

"The black dago was all she could stand," Levi said wryly.

"Your father was black?" she asked, surprised.

"Of course not," Levi laughed. "I think she calls him 'The Black Dago' because she's still bitter. I don't know why, exactly. Maybe because he was always lying, but he left her so much money, she ought to speak better of him, hmm?"

"Money's not everything," Erica said. "Maybe your mother still loves him."

"Oh sure, right," Levi said sarcastically. He noticed her frown and the soft look in her eyes. He didn't want her compassion. "All I want is my inheritance when I'm twenty-five, and then I'm moving to Mexico or Thailand."

"Why are you so cynical?"

"Never mind," he said.

"But you said you'd answer my questions."

"I said I'd answer 'some.'"

"I believe in hard work and honesty," she said. "I was brought up to trust people. And you?"

Levi looked at her cautiously. "I got some values I suppose. Somethin' had to wear off on me. Trust ain't one of 'em though."

"You're being difficult, Levi. There's no need," she said, thinking Levi was hiding the truth behind bravado.

Levi had an aura of mystery and his acting the loner excited her. He was different than the other boys she'd met. She knew that from the very beginning. Erica was sometimes Sunny, and sometimes, Erica was stupid. Dancing in the light all the time could be blinding.

"Right now," he was saying, "the only thing that matters to me is whether or not I'll ever be able to run all the balls on a snooker table. That really means something."

Erica stopped and put her hand on Levi's arm, and turned him so she could look straight into his eyes. "Do you have a girlfriend?" she asked. She hadn't meant to ask the question – it just popped out. She really wanted to ask something profound and insightful, hoping he would give her an answer she could care about – something about Levi besides his good looks and the tingling she felt flickering up her thighs.

The question took Levi off guard. His expression changed. He looked startled and uncomfortable.

He's afraid, Erica thought. He doesn't like you being so direct. He's going to lie.

"Tons of them," he said, looking up at a distant cloud. "If I'm not playing snooker, I'm fucking 'til I drop."

"I take it that's a 'no,'" Erica said with a mischievous smile.

"Only the snooker part," Levi said, and without warning pulled her body next to his, her head on his chest, as the two of them laughed and hugged right there in the middle of the campus quad.

The sudden intimacy was so unexpected that neither of them realized what was happening until they felt the closeness. Erica felt his hands and arms and smelled his breath. He felt her softness and warmth, and it reached deep into his being. Too deep. Pulling on dormant feelings inside his patch.

Embarrassed, they pulled back from each other at the same time. "I – I'm sorry," Levi said nervously. "Something must of just got in..."

"No, no. It's my fault," Erica stammered. "I shouldn't have asked..."

"Forget it," he interrupted. Silently they both began walking. Levi lit another cigarette to calm his nerves. The unspoken fire they'd felt was cooling rapidly. Both had regained control.

"Why'd you drop out of psychology class?" Erica asked.

"Because it's bullshit made up by neurotics who need more 'shrinkage' than the rest of us."

"It's not bullshit, Levi. Maybe you left too soon."

"Oh yeah?" Levi said, disinterested. "What did I miss?"

Erica gave him an exasperated look. "The 'Whiteout Phenomenon.' That's what we're studying right now."

"What's the 'Whiteout Phenomenon?'" Levi snickered. "Oh wait, isn't that when it snows so heavily, like in a blizzard, and you can't see two feet in front of you, so call out to your inner child, screaming for Mommy?"

"It sometimes has to do with rape."

"Oh, that. Not interested. I don't think rapes happen as much as people say." Levi tossed his cigarette on the ground and put it out with the twist of his shoe. "Victims are so fucking dumb, half the time it's their own fault."

"Levi, I'm going to ignore the fact, for now, that you just said something so foolish, and I'm going back to your question."

"A 'whiteout,' is different from a blackout." Erica continued, trying to steady her voice. "A 'blackout' happens when the body shuts down and there's no recollection of what happened, because there's no memory to hide. The person was unconscious when something happened to the body. The *body* may have experienced an event, but the *mind* didn't, so there's nothing to remember.

"A 'whiteout' is a defense mechanism created by the psyche. During trauma, the body and mind are awake, except the *mind* doesn't want to be. When something happens to the body that's so terrible and frightening, the mind's defense is never to revisit the horror. The psyche finds a place – a recessed corner – puts the event into it, and whites it out. It no longer exists. It's gone. The body may have felt it, but the mind made it disappear.

"And the brain can't find it again, unless there's a triggering event, sometimes similar to the whited-out one. Otherwise the whiteout stays in the subconscious or unconscious. Maybe it's never brought to the conscious level."

Levi blinked, as if he were only half listening. His gaze wandered up to a large bird, flying high in the sky.

Erica ignored his lack of attention and continued. "Usually, just portions of the trauma are whited out, and some parts still remain at the conscious level. Either way, a whiteout is the mind's way of escaping horrors of the past."

Levi realized she had finished explaining. "Seems to me, you'll pass your test," he said casually. "So if you don't have to study too hard, why don't we grab a pizza and check out a movie tonight?"

Erica's mouth dropped. "You're asking me on a date? Why?"

"I don't know. Maybe it's because you remind me of someone."

"Who?"

"I don't remember," he teased. "Must've whited it out."

Erica punched him on the shoulder. "Quit joking," she said. "Whiteouts are serious. They explain why girls remember predatory uncles twenty years later."

"More psychological bullshit," he said.

"Like rapes are the victim's fault?" Erica challenged, putting one hand defiantly on her waist. "Levi, have you ever 'whited' out something?"

Levi let out an ironic laugh. "Now isn't that a dumb question? I mean, if the phenomenon really exists, then how would I know if I blanked something out?"

"Oh, forget it," Erica said with irritation and then turned apologetic. "I'm sorry about all this psychology stuff, it's just that I've been studying hard – maybe I'm just too immersed in it."

"More like obsessed."

"I admit to that," Erica smiled. "Personality tests tell me I'm addictive in some ways. It's not a good way to stay in control. But if you're serious about the movie, I promise I won't try to analyze you, if you promise to be on time."

"What's your address? I'll be there at six."

Erica nodded. "It's 3971 Mountain Drive."

As she spoke, Levi noticed how white her teeth were, how blue her eyes, how translucent her skin. She was the most beautiful, the most desirable girl he'd ever met. If only she would drop the psychology crap.

"See you at six," she said. Levi nodded and watched as she turned and hurried off.

Erica wasn't usually late for class, but today, she didn't care. For reasons she couldn't explain, Levi affected her like no one ever had.

Levi Saranno showed up at seven-thirty that night. Without apology or explanation, he said, "Hi," lit a cigarette and walked her to the car.

Erica's parents watched from their bay window. "Definitely not a ten," Bill Jacobson said. His wife shook her head in agreement.

White Knuckle

When Levi brought Erica home three hours later, she didn't quite know what to make of it. He didn't try to kiss her goodnight, didn't hold her hand, and didn't open any doors for her – except the one into the pool hall. The Cue Ball Bar and Grill was a sleazy, smoky pool hall for vagrants, migrants, and a few middle-class drifters, waiting for a place to drift. It was here where Levi felt most comfortable. And here, was where he took Erica on their first date.

Erica thought it was amazing. Amazing the way he shot the balls. Amazing the way he played on the pool and snooker tables. Amazing the way he avoided any attempt to play with her. With the pool stick in his hand, Levi had the confidence of Minnesota Fats. With Erica Lynne Jacobson, Levi had the confidence of an older boy being circumcised.

Erica hated the place, but Levi, she thought, was someone worth knowing. Intuitively, Erica knew. She watched him, wide-eyed as he shot the balls. She tried her hand at knocking in an eight ball a few times, and they finally left, smelling of smoke.

When Levi parked in front of Erica's house, the porch light was on, but the street was dark. Erica sat still in the passenger seat, waiting for Levi to turn off the ignition, waiting as the muscles in her stomach tightened. She felt a sensual chill.

"See ya around," Levi said, breaking the silence. His hand didn't move toward the keys, nor to her arm or shoulder or waist. Nothing. He just sat there, and waited for Erica to open her own door, to exit without a kiss or a small embrace. The pool hall hustler didn't utter a word of romance. He didn't mumble the idle words of courtship.

"You're fascinating," Erica said.

"At pool or at snooker?"

"Neither. Maybe 'fascinating' isn't the right word. 'Different' is probably more descriptive."

"Why?"

Erica hesitated, weighing her words. "I'm not complaining," she said, "but I've never met anyone like you. You're so down to earth it seems, but different. Most guys would try to impress me with big stories or big ideals or promises, and then make their move as we're parked here or on some viewpoint overlooking the city. Instead, you take me to a pool hall.

"Where'd you rather go?" he asked.

"I don't know." Erica paused, waiting for the quiver in her stomach to pass. "I've just got the feeling I'd like to go there. I can't explain it."

Levi opened his side of the car door. "I'll give you a call, Erica."

Erica watched and waited as Levi came around the car and opened her door. Instinctively, she reached out her hand, expecting him to take it as she started to get up from her seat. One of his hands was on the door handle. The other stayed in his pocket. Levi might not be emotional, she thought, but he certainly seemed nervous as he stood there, almost fidgeting.

The fidgeting continued as they walked to her porch. Erica turned toward Levi instead of opening the front door to her house. Her suitor didn't move in, didn't come close. Both hands were now in his jeans.

Levi looked awkward. Erica felt empowered, almost giddy as she realized that Levi's outside bravado or indifference really masked a shyness she'd never expected.

As he stood stiffly with his hands still in his pockets, Erica boldly moved closer. She reached for his waist as her ankles rose and her lips gently touched his. She could feel him tremble.

There was no embrace. Their mouths had touched for only a moment, but it was smooth and warm and gentle. Soft. Levi seemed startled. Erica felt like dancing.

"Goodnight," she said, backing away and opening the door. "I can't wait for the next time."

"I...I can't either," he stammered.

Erica smiled as the door closed behind her.

Levi watched until she vanished. He paused on the porch, slowly shaking his head. Wondering. Wondering what they'd do next.

14

For months after their first date, Levi still found himself standing over pool tables on most nights. "Rack 'em up, Saranno, and I'll play you for another three bucks."

"Losers rack, Sampson," Levi boasted. "So rack 'em tight, but let's play nine ball and see how big your balls are." Levi chalked his cue-stick. "Five dollars on the three, five, and seven balls. Twenty on the nine."

Sampson pulled on his beard. "That's thirty-five bucks!" he complained. Sampson was almost twenty-one years old and looked like a porky biker who'd just lost his Harley-Davidson to a clean-cut college kid, no less. Levi and Sampson had been friends since Levi was eleven, when Sampson's family first moved to Colorado Springs.

Sampson grew up looking like Burl Ives, with a raspy voice and a live-life-like-you're-going-to-die-tomorrow attitude. Mostly, his life was about music, specifically, the blues. Some people said that when Sampson sang the blues and played the guitar, he was almost as good as a white Otis Rush.

Levi smiled. "Glad you can add, big guy. When I get your last fifty, I can afford to take Erica to dinner."

"Fuck dinner, and fuck my fifty. In fact, why don't you just go fuck Erica, and leave my wallet alone, tonight."

"Erica isn't ready for it."

Sampson lit a big, black, foul-smelling cigar. "My ass." He laughed sarcastically. "She'll do anything you want. It's you who ain't got balls."

Levi threw his cue stick on the table. His eyes squinted, his lips became tight and narrow. "I said she isn't ready, Sampson, and if I hear any more, 'you're-a-dickless-wimp,' I'm gonna…"

Sampson held up his hand. "Okay, okay. Forget it, pal." He wiped the sweat from his forehead. Smoke curled up from Sampson's cigar as he puffed on it.

"You look uptight about Erica again."

"Drop it."

"You just hate the facts, Levi, and the fact is, I see it."

"Women and relationships I hate. Sometimes."

"Well, pal, they turn some boys into men, others into stalkers. You just don't understand your feelings, let alone Erica's. You got not a clue on how to deal with your anxiety. Pressure's on. You're feeling it."

"How come you think you know it all, Sampson?"

"'Cause the closer she gets to ya, the more pool you want to play."

"It relieves pressure." Levi was sweating.

Sampson understood his friend. "It's a hide'n place for you, Levi. Like a safety zone, at least for a little while."

"You and Erica's psych shit is boring. Know that?"

Sampson shrugged his shoulders. "I ain't playing no more. I've got a gig in a few days, and the band's got to work out some new material. If you don't want to do Erica, why don't you come with me tonight? We're rehearsing in Sheila's basement."

"Don't quit now, Sampson. I…" He hesitated. "I need to talk," he said, hating himself for sounding like the wimp Sampson accused him of being. "This Erica thing's getting – I think – out of control."

"Jesus, pal, just sleep with her. You ain't gonna find anyone better looking, and she's got the hots for *you*, God knows why. You don't have to marry her, or even pay the rent. Make the move, see what it feels like. Trust me, you'll love it."

"Thanks a lot, Sampson, you're no help at all. Hey, listen, about San Francisco during spring break? You interested? I'll pay your ticket, if you want to come with me."

"San Francisco?" Sampson's eyebrows rose. "Isn't that where your father's girlfriend lives? What's her name?"

"Asia." Levi looked down at his keys. "Yeah, she lives there. But I'm not planning to visit. Christ, I haven't talked to her for more than ten years, and this is the first year she skipped sending me a birthday card."

"Then why San Francisco?" Sampson asked.

"It's a thousand miles away from Erica, isn't it?" Levi answered.

Sampson turned his head sideways, like a cop hearing a suspect's lie to a critical question. "Problem ain't with Erica, Levi, and a thousand miles apart's not going to fix it."

Levi didn't respond. Denials and defenses and half-truths or outright fabrications weren't going to work with his best friend. Lying to Erica came easy, but not to someone who knew him as well as anyone could.

The friends left the Cue Ball Bar & Grill. Levi drove slowly. He looked at Sampson and said, "I'm sorry. I lied."

"So what else is new? What'd you lie about this time?"

Levi pulled an envelope from his jacket pocket. "It's a birthday card from Asia." Levi handed the card to his friend.

Sampson turned on the tiny dome light and squinted as he read aloud:

Dearest Levi:

Happy Birthday! My hope is that you're safe and content, but most of all, healthy. You're twenty, now, and I'll bet you look just like your dad when he was your age: handsome and tall. I wish you'd send me a picture. The last one I have is of you and a fish in Colorado. I miss Colorado, but San Francisco is a good place to live. More than anything, I hope that you'll come and visit someday. And that we can be friends, maybe in some ways, family. There's good reason for my saying this, but without seeing you, there's no need to explain how or why I feel this way. Just know that my feelings for you are very real, and that I'd like so very much to see you. You might be surprised at how good you'd feel about coming here. This was one of your father's favorite places.

I hope you'll at least consider stopping by if you're "in the neighborhood." Remember, Levi, you're always welcome in my life, and in the lives of the ones I love most. Again, I hope you have a happy birthday – the happiest ever.

Love,
Asia

Sampson put the card back into the envelope and handed it to Levi. "Sounds like a pretty nice lady to me."

White Knuckle

"'Whore' is more like it," Levi retorted. He rolled down his window, crumbled the letter, and threw it into the black, night wind. "My father's dead because of her, and she's still trying to screw with me. I don't get it. What else does she want?"

"Maybe a piece of your old man."

"Hah! My mother said she got two hundred grand for the accident and has plenty of her own money, besides."

"You dumb fuck, that's not what I meant." Sampson laughed. Then, as if explaining something to a five-year-old, he said, "I meant, first old, then young. Both Sarannos. Maybe she wants you now. Dad must've been pretty good. Maybe she thinks it runs in the family." Sampson laughed hysterically. "Your old man could get laid by someone in her twenties, and you can't get it up for a virgin who looks like a *Sports Illustrated* cover girl. Jesus, what a joke! Huh?"

Levi's right hand swung over and hit hard against his friend's chest. "You're such an asshole, Sampson." The car swerved and Levi tried to hit him again, not out of real anger, but out of irritation.

They'd had similar conversations in the past. For ten years, Asia had been sending birthday cards, letters, even Christmas cards, to Levi. Sometimes she would write a newsy letter about her life in San Francisco, and as Levi got older, she wrote about her feelings. Seldom did she mention Judd. Through the years, Levi never responded with so much as a thank-you note, even when the occasional holiday present arrived.

Levi was glad of one thing. His mother didn't go nuts when she saw the return address on the envelope or when Levi opened a gift from Asia. Joshua tossed his presents and letters, and Sheryl acted disinterested.

For eleven years after Judd's death, Sheryl had made her sons her first priority. "Husbands you lose. You never lose your children," was what she told her sympathetic friends and relatives. Men never stayed overnight, and the boys were a perfect excuse to escape the arms of an overwrought lover if she was at a man's house. Besides, Sheryl always wanted to be home to comfort Levi who, for five years after his father's death, had violent, recurring nightmares, the kind that woke him up, sweating and terrified, then caused him to shiver from the chill that came over him.

He had the terrible dreams, sometimes as often as two or three times a week. The doctor assured his mother that they would eventually stop, that the boy was temporarily traumatized. The dreams didn't stop, but Levi did learn how to deal with them himself. He sprayed graffiti on every YMCA wall he could find, and he lied, telling his mother that the nightmares disappeared as soon as the memories of his father were safely stored on a cellar shelf inside his head.

 He turned his stare to Sampson. "I don't think it's a good idea for me to visit Asia," he said almost absentmindedly, as if trying to convince himself. "My memories of Dad aren't going to change."

Sampson kiddingly poked his friend in the shoulder. "They change all the time, if you ask me," he said. "Why not visit her and get it over with? Besides, you might learn something. Even if she is a whore, at least she's loyal."

"To an asshole! Not even that. To an asshole's memory." Levi pounded the steering wheel again. "That's what I remember, and that's the way it's going to stay."

"Maybe," Sampson countered, knowing that Levi usually said one thing but meant another. He'd never known anyone quite like him. People lied on occasion, but Levi lied all the time. Some people hid their true feelings from strangers or casual acquaintances, but everyone had one or two confidants to rely on. Not Levi. Even Sampson didn't feel trusted often. Once in awhile, but seldom.

Levi lived in his own world. He wasn't a leader or a follower. He was just there. Alone. On the sidelines, but barely observing, and definitely not participating. It was a world without trust or feelings. Sampson was a friend, about the only one Levi ever had. Now Erica had captured Levi's attention; at least he was intrigued with her – and, whether he admitted it or not, with Asia as well.

"Erica wants me to take her away for a weekend. Her parents are going on vacation," Levi said matter-of-factly.

"You need all the friends you can get, Levi."

"I need a vacation, but I don't need it with Erica."

"Erica's the best thing that's ever happened to you," Sampson said. "She's the best, and I mean it."

"She's too demanding."

"You don't know what demanding is, pal."

Yes he did. Levi knew. Demands meant honesty and trust and commitment and loyalty. Understanding. Giving. Truth. No games and no escape routes. How the fuck could anyone be so stupid? To become vulnerable. That'd be like sitting on a carnival bench over a tub of water while strangers threw hard balls at a bull's eye, praying they would hit the target so he could be dunked and drenched and maybe even drowned.

And who'd pull him out of the water while he gurgled in love and kindness and warmth and feelings? Feelings. What were those? And who cared? She didn't *really* care. No one ever did. It was just a game. One filled with promises to be broken. And Erica was just another predator cloaked in a white veil of innocence. Smiling, as she reared her arm back and threw the ball as hard and as fast and as accurately as possible, hitting him square in the head, knocking him out, just before he went under, choking. Then he would drown and die for certain.

It was so fucking obvious, even a dead man could see it.

15

"You know what's wrong with your precious Levi?" Reni Bourland asked.

"No, what's wrong with him?" Erica replied, hoping she wasn't in for another lecture from her friend and confidante.

"I'll tell you," Reni said. "He's too much work. That's what Levi is: work. Either that or he's gay."

Erica did a double take. "Listen, Reni, Levi might be a challenge, but he's definitely not gay."

The two women were sitting by the window of the Lakeside Terrace restaurant. Spring was in the air as birds built nests and new flowers danced in the breeze. But Erica wasn't dancing. Erica's relationship with the snooker-playing Italian was going nowhere, fast. And yet her instincts kept telling her to hold on, that things would change.

Six months earlier, Levi had told her he was passive. Erica decided Levi wasn't just passive, he was downright apathetic, immobile, and frigid. She thought frigid applied only to women, but he gave the word a whole new meaning.

"Levi's not just hard work," Reni continued, "he's a goddamn undertaking. It's no wonder you're depressed, Erica. He's the kind of guy who thinks his parental responsibilities end as a sperm donor, and he ain't even willing to do that."

Erica watched the ducks swimming in the lake. She thought about her dates with Levi. All casual – a pizza or a show or a few cozy walks in the park. No candlelight dinners, no necking in cars, no moonlight romance, or dancing to the saxophone of Kenny G in some solitary boudoir. There was never a mention of a weekend in Vail. Still Erica hung on.

"Okay, so Levi's straight," Reni said. "But he's still work. As in 'effort.' It's a fucking chore to even like him. Are you sure he's worth it?"

"Of course. Why else would I be so depressed?" Erica answered.

Reni may have been a bossy, hyper redhead, but she was also a concerned friend. She looked at Erica and said, "You deserve better."

"My head says one thing, my heart says another. It's all so confusing. I want him, but I keep asking myself, 'Why?'"

"Jesus, you've got a right to be depressed."

Reni looked up at the waitress who had just poured more iced tea into her glass and said, "Please bring us your darkest, most sensual, chocolate mousse with raspberry truffles immediately, or my friend will be passing out."

The waitress nodded and hurried off. Erica grinned, "You're bad."

"Why?" Reni feigned hurt. "For ordering something you need? You need more than you need wimpy."

"Stop it. You shouldn't say Levi's not worth it. You're not exactly the one to talk. You've bedded some first-rate assholes."

"That's *exactly* why I'm an authority on the subject! Erica, I'm just trying to protect you."

"Levi needs time. He's…"

White Knuckle

"You're a glutton for punishment."

"No, I'm not."

"Look, girl, the guy's stood you up more times than he's taken you out. One day he says he's going to come around and the next day he's playing pool and doesn't even call."

"Snooker," Erica interrupted. "He's just…"

"Then you go out, and he barely speaks." Reni's voice grew louder. "Or he goes off into some vacuum in his head."

Erica looked around, hoping no one at the other tables could hear her friend. "And then he has the nerve to ignore the body to die for that you're just begging to have deflowered." Reni sat back and smiled facetiously. "I rest my case."

"I know as sure as I'm sitting here, Reni, Levi's hiding something, but it's not deliberate. I'm positive. If I can just get it out, talk about it, if he'll just let go."

"Give it up. Levi's a lizard and you're taking a course in Advanced Suffering. You're like Don Quixote, on an impossible mission riding a broken-down horse named Rocinante."

"I understand what you see," Erica said. "But when I see Levi, I'm not on Quixote's horse. I see and sense something no one else does, and I know I'm right. Levi's not a Rocinante, he's a Secretariate. I believe in him, and God's going to show the truth to me, and to Levi."

"How's God going to do that?"

Erica's face dropped into her folded hands as she slowly shook her head back and forth. "I don't know," she whispered. "But I believe in miracles, and I believe in myself."

The waitress arrived with two plates and a giant slice of dark chocolate mousse pie drenched in fresh raspberries, its butter-cream topping nestled with fine chocolate shavings.

"We call this Death by Chocolate," the waitress said as she portioned out two large pieces.

Reni smiled up at her. "As soon as we're finished, you can call 911."

Erica put a forkful into her mouth. "Reni, Levi's just afraid. I know it. He's afraid of letting anyone get close."

Reni sighed. "Well, admittedly guys have trouble with expressing intimacy, at least that's what therapists say, but I've never seen a guy who couldn't get it up if he wanted to. I've seen 'em nervous, but with a little ingenuity and imagination, you can take care of that."

"I'm not sure I'd know how."

"Yeah, right! All you've got to do is let him see you naked, and his pecker'll pop out like a nipple in November."

Erica didn't laugh. "Levi might be afraid, but so am I. I'm not exactly an expert."

"Okay, here's the – you should excuse the expression – bottom line." Reni leaned closer and lowered her voice. "You're almost twenty years old. Levi's been groping himself too long, and now it's your turn."

Erica raised her glass of tea and clicked it to Reni's. "I think you're right," she said, "but I can't just rip down his zipper and pull off his pants."

"Why not? It works for me."

Erica laughed. Reni took a huge bite of chocolate. "Much as I hate to see you giving your maidenhead to this undeserving lout, maybe, just maybe, your first experience will be romantic, sensual, and wildly..."

"Enough, you're embarrassing me." Erica's face flushed. "All I know is, I'd like Levi to be my first – and last – lover."

"Whew," Reni whistled. "You are in trouble. Good thing I'm Catholic. If ever I get around to saying a rosary, I'll dedicate it to you."

"Thanks. I probably need it."

Erica wouldn't admit it to others, but the truth was, just maybe, that Reni, her mother and father, and even Sampson, were right about Levi. On the outside, Levi was strange, selfish, and passion-less. Aside from her own intuition, what made her think he was any different inside?

Maybe Levi had toyed with her for the last six months and never had any intention of opening up and letting her in. That was bad enough, but it was the lying that bothered her the most. She always knew when he was lying too.

It had taken Erica two months to figure that one out. The insight gave her power, and Levi hadn't a clue about what he had given her. Knowing when he was lying was so simple, really. Rather transparent. Whenever he lied, Levi *always* looked away from her. That was the Levi most people knew, the liar. But whenever Levi was telling her the truth about himself, he looked straight at her and his eyes didn't wander into outer space.

When Levi looked at Erica, when *that* person spoke, Erica listened. When the other guy talked about feelings, Erica heard the words and immediately knew they were fabrications, made up to shut her out.

Reni stopped eating and stared at Erica for a moment. Her voice was gentle, protective. "Here's what I'm really concerned about, girlfriend. I don't want to see you get hurt. Not even a little bit. Besides, are you sure if Levi does open up and let you in, it's somewhere you want to go?"

Ducks were still swimming in the pond and the snow was still melting on the mountaintops, as Erica gazed outside the restaurant window.

"Yes," she said. "I don't know why, but yes."

*   *   *   *   *

As she drove home from the restaurant, Erica remembered the winter picnic she and Levi had, up in the mountains past Manitou Springs. That was when she first discovered when Levi was lying and when he was telling the truth.

The day was sunny and unusually warm for February. Blue skies and tall evergreens brightened their path as Levi drove along the curving pavement until he took a rocky dirt logging road that led into the wilderness. They were high into the canyons of Pike's Peak. Levi seemed to know where he was going.

"We'll find a spot along a river," he had said confidently.

"Did you bring a fishing pole?" Erica asked.

"I don't fish."

"Why not? Didn't your dad ever take you?"

Levi kept his eyes on the road. "No. He didn't have time for me. He was too busy making money and screwing. He was good at both, but he wasn't much as a father."

Her hand reached across the seat and onto his shoulder. "I'm sorry," she said. "When you talk about him, you always seem so angry. Why?"

"He'd make promises and forget to keep them." Levi reached for a cigarette as he accelerated the car. "Dad never kept a promise I can remember. But then I don't remember much – not about him, anyway."'

For Erica, it was a bold question, but she asked it anyway. "Are you like him, Levi?"

He was driving too fast and his eyes left the road for a second to look at the girl beside him. "Exactly," he said without hesitation. It almost sounded like a threat.

Erica wasn't scared. "I won't break any promises, Levi,"she said softly. He looked at the dusty road, and then back to her.

"Everyone does," he said. "It can't be helped. Promises are made to be broken."

They were bouncing over potholes and rocks. For miles Levi raced down the jagged dirt road. The tires of the Toyota Four-Runner were spitting rocks and twirling dust. Erica said it felt like a roller-coaster ride. Levi had been expecting her to tell him to slow down, to complain about ditches and turns and skidding around blind corners. Instead, she said, "This is fun."

"You like this?" He was astonished.

"Why do you act surprised? Of course I do. This is great."

Levi slammed on the brakes. The car came to rest on the edge of a deep canyon. Levi wasn't looking down the cliff. Instead, he was looking at a rocky ridge colored with spots of pink and purple and speckled grey and brown. There were spots of black, and red Colorado clay pointed to the bottom of the canyon and the trail leading to the river below.

"Get out of the car, Erica, and come around and tell me what you see."

They both got out and Erica went to his side of the car.

Levi pointed down into the woods. "What's there?"

"Trees. A canyon. It's beautiful," she answered.

"At the bottom, there's the river. If you've got courage, we could make it to the bottom by going straight down, by following the skid trail."

"What's that?"

"It's right in front of you."

"I don't see it, but I'm game."

"I don't understand you. You're crazy sometimes," he said. His voice held a hint of fear and the tone seemed distant, like he was remembering some long-ago words. But they were far away, deep inside his head.

The two of them stood beside each other, looking into the canyon. Erica turned and put her arms around his neck. She pressed her body against his. "I am crazy," she said. "About you." She kissed him gently.

Levi turned his face away, but held her close.

"Why do you always turn from me?" she asked. "Levi, tell me the truth. Am I wasting my time?"

Levi thought about it. Erica was a beauty. Gentle, wholesome, and honest. A centerfold with virtue. She wanted him, and he'd been fighting her for months. She tried hard to get close, and he always pushed her away. The worse he treated her, the harder she tried. He lied constantly, still she kept coming back. He couldn't understand her loyalty. It made no sense to him.

As they stood beside the car, Levi asked the question he'd been contemplating since the first time they'd met. "Can I give you a nickname that's just between us?" He looked nervous, uncertain.

"A nickname? Sure." Her soft, fresh face smiled up at him. "What would you like to call me?"

Levi looked at the rocky ridge pointing to the canyon below. He stared through the trees and smiled as if he'd just seen something or someone familiar. Someone he wanted to see. He turned back to Erica. "Sometimes, I'd like to call you Kit. It's a special name that's important to me. Can I call you Kit?"

"Yes," she whispered and then looked into his eyes. She saw tears. "What's the matter, Levi?"

"Nothing. Just feeling sentimental." Levi gently pushed Erica slightly back, both his hands on her shoulders. "You've got pizzazz."

"Thank you."

"I love that, Kit." He didn't avert his eyes as they started to tear up. "I love Kit. I really do." His lips moved toward her, and she kissed him again. This time, he kissed her back. It was the first time he'd ever returned her passion. She could feel his trembling. She could feel a sorrow and she wanted to soothe it, to make it go away.

"Let's walk down the trail a bit," Levi said.

"I don't see a trail."

"It's there. We'll only walk down part of it. I can't take you to the bottom today."

Levi took Erica's hand as they moved into the canyon. Ten years of growth had obscured the trail, but he could see it, even if she couldn't. With the right rig and the right driver, it could still be mastered.

After a hundred yards, he stopped. "If you're real quiet, you can hear the river down below," he said.

She listened. "I hear it! Have you been here before?"

Levi suddenly appeared as though he were traveling through time. Erica could almost see his thoughts weaving through the trees and over the rocks and down the covered trail. He had been there. She knew it. She was reaching something. She watched him. The river was talking to him, and he was listening. Levi shook his head as if to shake off the memory.

"What's wrong, Levi?" she asked. He sunk back into some hollow recess. She had lost him again.

"Nothing, Erica, nothing's wrong." He rubbed his eyes and said gently, "Let's get in the car and drive back down the road. We'll get close to the river some other place. There's a public campground about ten miles back."

They walked up the hill, and as Erica started to get into the car, she noticed Levi turn, and give a final look through the trees below. She could almost see him touching a memory.

When they arrived at the campground, Levi spread out a blanket, and Erica opened the picnic basket she had prepared. Cold chicken, potato salad, a loaf of French bread, some cheese, and a bottle of white wine. They sat beside the stream and ate and talked. The river was cool and comforting as it rippled over the rocks. They talked about their parents, Erica hoping Levi would reveal more.

"Even though my father's a minister," she said, "he wasn't around much either, not when I needed him. My dad's always on call for emergencies and funerals and hospital visits. My mother's always there, but there's no perfect recipe on how to parent. I'm sure your father loved you."

Levi stared at the flowing water. "My mother's the only one who tried to be a good parent, but she couldn't do everything after he ran off and got killed."

"Levi, you can't blame your father for dying."

"Bullshit. You don't understand. It's almost like he killed himself. What'd he expect? Going to California with some chick who got little more than a whiplash from the accident that killed him. She could've bedded him in some motel instead of letting him drink and drive."

"I thought you told me it was the other driver who was drinking."

"What difference does it make?" Levi snapped. "He's still dead, and she's had ten years of new lovers."

"Come on, Levi," Erica interrupted. "Give the woman a break. She lost too, you know. And didn't you once tell me that she tries to keep in touch with you, but you never respond?"

Levi hurled a rock into the river. "There's no point. I don't care about her." He turned and stared directly into Erica's eyes. "Look, Kit, it's like this. I'd like to trust you and my dad and my friends. But when you've been betrayed – and as far as I'm concerned, Dad betrayed me – and you're left alone, it makes you strong, but it also makes you wary.

"I feel as if I grew up isolated from the rest of the world. The only person I could trust was myself. My mother relies on God. My brother's into cyberspace twenty-four hours a day. My father is history. But sometimes I remember things. Sometimes his words come back to me, and I feel like there's someone else, somewhere inside of me there's a person I'm trying to protect."

He kept looking at her. "Kit, I want to feel love and joy and be kind and gentle, but it's not safe. You've tried to make me open up, and I've resisted, because I'm afraid. The fact is, I'm really a coward. And too much has happened. Too much has gone wrong."

"What are you hiding, Levi? Tell me. I can be trusted." She moved closer and put the palm of her hand against the side of his face.

He blinked and looked at the water again. "Nothing happened, Erica. I've got trust accounts and money and good looks and good health. What else could a guy ask for?" He looked back to her. "Kit, I need help."

And that's when she figured it out. That's when she knew she loved him. It was as close to him as she'd ever gotten. It happened when he called her "Kit," and it happened when he looked her in the eyes. He was honest with Kit, not with Erica.

Erica's discovery was profound. Her goal was clear. To find the other Levi. The one who called her Kit was filled with promise.

Her intuition had been right after all. And she had just made some progress. Now she needed to break down the barricade and reach the love that huddled inside a shell that she'd just begun to crack. Light was on the other side. He had opened the door for a precious moment, and in that moment, she saw illuminated brilliance.

16

Setting up a seduction takes careful planning, especially if the seductee might not be a willing participant. But Erica was convinced that her love for Levi would conquer every obstacle, even the ones he'd pounded into place.

"How long will your parents be gone?" Reni's voice bellowed through the phone.

"They're on a Caribbean cruise for ten days," Erica replied. "Levi doesn't know it yet, but he's spending the night."

"You're both virgins. If you're not careful, you could scare him to death. Remember, you're not the problem, Erica. He is."

"Look, Reni, I know that, in spite of himself, he loves me. I'll make it work if I have to tattoo 'Kit' across my chest and forehead."

"That's the problem. He loves Kit, not you. You think it's a fantasy. I think it's psycho."

"He's everything I've ever wanted."

"You're the only one who can see it, then. I still think he's impotent. There's a screw loose somewhere."

"Tonight, that's going to change forever. Believe me, if I can crack through his armor, there's a guy on the other side who is going to make me happy for the rest of my life."

There was a deep sigh on the other end of the phone. "Well, I guess the only thing I can say is good luck. You'll need it."

Erica had thought about it for a long time. Making the decision hadn't been easy. She remembered a dinner they'd had one evening after a movie, two months earlier. The movie told a story about fathers and sons and fly fishing. About streams and mountains, love and courage. She knew it was about Levi.

They sat in a quiet Italian restaurant drinking cappuccinos and looking at each other in the semi-darkness.

"The secret's not in the water, is it?" she said. "The secret's in how the water makes you feel."

"It brings back memories, Kit," he answered, staring into her inquisitive eyes. "For some reason, I've forgotten a lot of my childhood. I remember some things vividly, and other things are just a haze."

"How far back do your memories go?"

"I have a clear vision of going to summer camp. Except for some fairly distinct memories there, that's where it stops. Somehow, I remember leaving camp and driving home. Then it's blank for about five years. It's like I disappeared.

"I recall being with my father, but I don't remember it all. They seem like selective memories of him and me before he died. In spite of what my brother says, I know he wasn't an asshole."

Levi's mind wandered, searching. "I know I don't hate him, but I don't know how much I loved him, or if he really loved me. I blank it out."

"Why?"

"Because it hurts. I hated his dying, and I forget a lot of what he said. Sometimes. Then zoom, he jumps in and out of my head. I know I needed him and he wasn't there. I guess I got bitter and started to forget."

Erica held his hand across the table. Levi wasn't sad, but rather reflective. His openness encouraged Erica to ask, "Do you usually come up blank when you try to remember the past?"

"Not always," he said. "If I try, if I really, really work at it, then I can remember. Sometimes when I'm afraid or get scared, then I remember, too. But not everything."

Erica tenderly caressed his hand. She waited, wanting him to reach back, back into whatever past he was willing to conjure up.

"My father called me Matty when we were alone together," he said in a distant voice.

"Can I call you that?"

"No!" His response was quick and non-negotiable. Startled, she pulled back and sat straight in her chair.

"I'm sorry," he said, reaching for her hand. She gave it to him. "For some reason, it makes me feel bad. It's like, it's like that's who I should be, but I'm not. I don't know who *he* is or how to find him." His eyes never left hers. "I feel like this Matty kid died when my father did, and so did the memories. *Except* when I go into the mountains or sit by a river. Then the good memories try to come into focus. There's a peace there I can't find anywhere else."

"You could find it with me, if you tried," Erica said gently. "Someday, you'll let me call you Matty. I know it. I think it's Matty in you I love."

Levi didn't answer her.

* * * * *

Erica knew that seducing Levi Saranno wasn't going to be easy, but she'd give it her best shot. Her lack of experience would not become an obstacle, she promised herself.

Erica prepared everything perfectly. The salad was in the refrigerator, the vegetables were ready for steaming, and the steaks were marinating. She had bought French bread and two bottles of expensive cabernet sauvignon. Candles glowed on the ornately set dining room table.

As sinful and improper as it seemed, Erica decided to use her parents' bedroom suite. It boasted a king-size bed, a double shower, fireplace, and a Jacuzzi. Unfortunately, it was all for show. Erica's parents hadn't made the best use of it in many years. Now, it served as testimony to her mother's decorating skills and her father's indulgence of his wife's favorite pastime: spending the money she'd inherited. Erica's parents never invited the parishioners into the bedroom, and certainly, the elegant suite wasn't intended to be their daughter's playground. But on this night, Erica decided that taking this outrageous liberty would be worth it.

The food and the bedroom were ready. Erica was, too. There'd been a quick trip to Victoria's Secret, a new perfume, and a luxurious bubble bath that made her feel clean and crisp and cool. She stood in front of the mirror, naked. Long legs, manicured toes, a tight, tapering stomach leading down to a perfect triangle of golden hair between her white, slender thighs. Levi arrived at eight. He had promised he would be there at seven-thirty. Well, at least he was only a half hour late, this time. She thought, we're making progress.

"I won a hundred dollars playing snooker," he boasted. "I promised Sampson I'd be back in an hour and see if we can't set up another pinch."

Erica handed him a glass of wine. "Levi, tonight's our night, and I'm not going to let you break your promise to me."

White Knuckle

"Erica, I promised Sampson…"

She moved closer to him. "Tonight I'm not Erica, I'm Kit. The one you can trust."

For the first time, Levi looked around. He began to sense something was different. "Sure," he said, as his natural defenses began to stir.

He took in the fresh flowers, the soft music playing in the background, and the candlelight. And Erica. The blond beauty that stood before him. Almost dancing. Always smiling.

Her voice was seductive. "Levi, I want us to play a game tonight." Her touch was gentle. "There's nothing to be afraid of. It's me, Kit."

"Erica, I…"

"Kit. Remember? You drink your wine, and I'll start dinner."

Levi sat in a tall chair at the kitchen island as Erica cooked. Her actions were delicate but focused. Levi sensed she had a plan. Erica was on a mission, and he knew he was it. His defenses mounted.

Her low-cut yellow blouse revealed the top of her breasts. Her tan, suede skirt barely reached the middle of her thighs. No nylons. No shoes. Barefoot floating around the kitchen, humming, sipping wine, and casually rubbing up against Levi whenever she had to move past him.

Levi knew it was a setup, the one he'd been avoiding for months. He hated setups. He remembered the pig. The blubbery monster he should've killed. If nothing else, two inches lower, and the tomahawk would have blinded the fat, filthy bastard.

"What are you thinking about?" she asked.

"Next week," he lied. "I'm thinking about going to San Francisco for spring break."

"I'd like to go, Levi. Would you take me with you?" She brushed her breast against his shoulder and put her arms around his neck. Her lips touched his, but his lips stayed closed. "I'll just tell my parents I'm checking out a law school. Mom would invade her inheritance for that."

"I don't think so, Erica..." his voice trailed off.

He didn't see the disappointment cloud her face and he barely heard her say, "Kit, remember?"

Levi wasn't in the kitchen with her anymore. His body was, but Levi's mind had him going elsewhere. He was going back. Back to Small Pox. Back to betrayal and horror and loathing. And then the subsequent years of darkness. The lonely, loveless, adolescent nights of guilt and fear. Camp was his fault. What right did he have to be loved? And how could he love anyone, much less someone like Erica? She was just like Kit and his dad. And what did the two people he loved the most do? They left. He gave them his heart and his innocence and joy. He gave them his trust. And then they fucked him, just like fatty did. Lied to him, banishing him to a shameful world of aching emptiness.

Erica wouldn't be any different. She was just like everyone who said they loved him, who made him promises. She won't stay, he told himself, so what's the point? Dead or gone or changed or plain fucking sick and crazy. How could he trust that? How does anyone get a hard-on for betrayal and lies and gone and forgotten? Lies. They all just lied about caring and love and kindness. Being there. Protection. Lied about feelings and commitment. Relationships. It was so much safer to just stay hidden.

Except, of course, from his mother. Her love was real at times. She loved God and old memories, and as long as Levi did what he was supposed to, she'd pat him on the head like he was an obedient Collie and tell him he was a good boy. But if he screwed up, then he was like his dad. "A liar and a cheat," she'd said. Levi didn't know if she really meant it. She only said those things when she'd been drinking or crying or looking at old photograph albums with pictures of them as a family. "All your father ever did was screw loose women," she had cried to Levi.

Joshua was also adamant. "That's what killed Dad. It was his dick, Levi, and what it led to."

Their words made sense to Levi. Everything was obvious. Dicks did that. They had a mind of their own. They got men in trouble every day of their lives. Look what the counselor's dick did, and that almost killed him, too. It should have.

Levi was deep within his Puckerbush Patch. And just outside was Erica. Close. Too close. He could feel her touch, whenever she got the chance. She would manipulate and mold him, play with him, get tired of him. And then he'd be tossed aside like a rag. He'd have been squeezed and pinched and ultimately left. He'd be alone. Always alone, and in the darkness.

Fighting back was the only way to survive. Hiding was the safest way. If you never let them in, they can't hurt you.

The perfect dinner had been perfectly cooked and silently eaten. Silent on Levi's part, anyway. For an hour, Erica valiantly talked about dreams and plans, parents being away leaving just the two of them alone, free to explore new feelings. Levi responded with blank stares. A mind that was mindlessly foraging in the clouds or shooting snooker balls between his ears. Except for a few words like "good," "fine," "thank you," and "pass the salt," Levi had become a complete stranger to Erica.

Finally, she held out her hand. "Come with me," she said. "I'll fill the Jacuzzi, and you can sit by the fire." Levi blindly grabbed the wine bottle and a glass, and unconsciously followed her into the bedroom. He'd never been there. There, or anywhere close.

Levi sat in one of two chairs that had a small table between them. Erica was bending over the Jacuzzi, testing the water temperature. He could see her legs, trim and long, and the black lace of her panties.

Erica was lighting rose-scented candles and placing them around the Jacuzzi. She turned, facing Levi, and started to unbutton her blouse. Smiling. Eager with anticipation and warmth and excitement. She'd never let anyone see her naked.

"What are you doing, Erica?" Levi looked terrified. It was clear Erica was expecting him to do the same.

"Kit's my name tonight," she said softly, as softly as she tossed the blouse to the thick, beige carpet. A hand went behind her back, another to the bra strap, and before Levi could blink, Erica's bosom was bared. Levi didn't know where to run. Where to hide. As her hands reached for the zipper of her skirt, panic coursed through his veins.

Erica knew how she looked. Even though she pretended not to notice, she'd seen and felt the stares of strangers whose breath she could take away with just a slight twist or wiggle, a hint of cleavage.

Trapped! She was taking off her skirt and panties. The scene would have been comical, if he weren't so pathetic, Levi thought, miserable with guilt and fear and rage.

"Erica, don't. Please, you've got to stop." How could she be so impulsive and so certain he wanted sex, when he'd never gotten over his shame? Levi was completely confused, upset, and frozen. As much as he wanted to be in the present, his mind kept ushering him back into the past. Into dark recesses and corners, behind doors and locks without keys or light. He'd lost control. Erica had it all.

"Levi…" Erica reached out with her arms, imploring him to hold her, to clothe her nakedness with his body.

"You're acting like Asia. Kit would never do this. You and Asia are…"

Instantly, Erica's nudity became her shame. "How dare you!" she shrieked. "How can you be so humiliating?"

"It's not my fault I…"

"You're an asshole, Levi," she screamed, quivering with outrage and contempt.

Out of nowhere, Levi burst out, "I should've killed that fat, fucking freak."

This was a Levi she'd never heard. His words were slow. Deliberate and mean. If eyes are the window to the soul, then voice is the echo of the heart. Levi's heart was bent on destruction. His voice was deadly.

Erica backed away. The tone of Levi's words startled her, but she was ready to fight.

Reni had called him psychotic. Maybe she was right. Levi didn't care about her or how she felt or what she wanted. Erica's feelings of passion vanished. She should have listened to Reni. Loving Levi *was* too much work. I'm not a masochist, Erica silently told herself.

Sweat was pouring from Levi's forehead. He was frozen with fear. Fear of what? Erica no longer cared.

Levi stood up from the chair, swaying. He looked as if every drop of blood had drained from his face. Ashen and pale, his whole body shook. Erica thought he was going to faint, and she didn't give a damn.

"You can take a lot of things from me, Levi, but you can't take away my dignity. I loved a part of you. The other part, I hate."

"That's tough," he said. "Go find a different rabbit. I'm going to San Francisco."

"Good! Maybe you'll meet the man of your life there!"

Before Erica could say another word, Levi slapped her so hard, she almost fell down. Her cheek blotched red. He roughly pushed her aside, almost leaping for the hallway. Erica's body started to crumble as she watched him leave.

Abruptly, Levi stopped and turned back to her. "I'm sorry, Kit. It's not you. It's me. Someday, I'll tell you why."

"I know all I need to know." she yelled. "I hate you, you sick son-of-a-bitch!"

Levi was appalled. Not at Erica. At himself. He was tormented, weak and feeble. A pathetic neutered farce, hiding behind a facade of lies and spineless bravado. Levi Matthew Saranno deserved all the torment he got. He had earned it.

He stared at her watering blue eyes. "I love you, Kit," he said. "Kit, I really do love you."

"My name's Erica. Erica Lynne Jacobson, you pig!"

Levi's shoulders slumped. He turned, moved down the hall, and left the front door open as he walked into the Colorado Springs night air. A shooting star fizzled toward the western horizon.

It reminded him of himself.

17

You can live your entire life in San Francisco, but you'll never get buried there. Even the unfortunates who got smoked in the great fire of 1906 had what was left of their bodies carted off to Colma, or their remains ferried off to lesser lands in northern California. San Francisco is a place to party, not a place to die.

In 1901, the San Francisco city council passed an ordinance that prohibited burials within city limits. Later, those in charge went a step further and ordered disinterment of the dead and removal of all remains from any cemetery with less than five acres. Apparently, even at the turn of the century, the hills of San Francisco were too beautiful to be cluttered with tombstones and rusting photos of departed loved ones. Dead people have their place, and it wasn't within the San Francisco city limits.

"Don't plant bodies, plant trees." The citizens complied. With their toes in fertile, sandy soil, residents dug holes and filled them with saplings. Every tree within the 44.6 square miles of the city by the bay was planted by someone other than God.

Cypress, eucalyptus, pine, and acacias grew and flourished. The city also opened its arms and welcomed anyone and everyone who wanted to express themselves freely and release their inhibitions. No one to censure, point fingers, condemn, or run out of town. People could search for themselves or anyone else, without fear of judgment or ridicule. San Francisco let you be.

Perhaps that's why Levi was heading there. His trip certainly wasn't to look up Asia. Maybe he just had to get as far away from Erica and the humiliation he had caused her and himself. Maybe he had to be in a place where no matter who he was, no one would judge him, study him, or analyze his actions. Hell, no one would even know him in San Francisco.

Levi looked out the window of the plane and saw the Golden Gate Bridge come into view, its awesome span glittering in the early morning sunlight. He felt like he was embarking on an adventure. If only he could shake the gnawing guilt, he might even have a good time.

He checked into the Clarion Bedford Hotel, recommended by a travel agent who said it was located near Union Square. In reality, it was squarely in the middle of the Tenderloin. Whore heaven.

"How long will you be staying with us, Mr. Saranno?" The clerk was a well-dressed Hispanic, who offered him a friendly smile.

"Probably a week or two. I'm looking for an apartment here. I thought I'd check out the area. Any ideas as to where to live?"

The hotel clerk squinted his eyes and looked Levi up and down. "Depends on what you want and what you can afford," he said. "Lifestyles round this town vary. You into boys, go to the Castro. You into money, go to Nob Hill. Music? North Beach. Whores? Stay here. If you've got lots of cash, and want it all, try the Marina. You got no money, go to Lower Haight. Hippie shit? Try Upper Haight. Hell man, we got it all."

"I don't know what I want, exactly."

"Well, if we ain't got it here, I don't know where you'll find it. You got any friends in town?"

"No, not really. But a buddy of mine's coming in a few days. He lived here last summer, so he'll help me scout around."

The clerk came from behind the counter and picked up Levi's two suitcases.

"This is a big town, but a small town, if you know what I mean," he said, walking to the elevator. Levi followed him. "It's all divided up into little sections with little pockets of people who hang together because they think that they think alike. Some places are safe. Some ain't. Most of it's clean."

The clerk continued talking as they got off the elevator and walked down a short hallway to Levi's room. "But don't let it fool ya. Nothin' you see is necessarily what you get. I don't believe nobody. I finally got me a straight girl, and we just hang together. Can't trust no one." He unlocked the room door and ushered Levi inside.

"Well, sir," he said, putting Levi's suitcases next to a chair by the window, "just keep your dick in your pants, your hand on your wallet, and you'll be fine. If I was new to a town, you know what I'd do?"

"What?"

"I'd get me a cab driver who speaks English, if you can find one. And I'd have him turn off the meter and give me a tour for fifty bucks or so. Cab drivers know more about what's happenin' than anybody."

Levi reached into his wallet and pulled out a five-dollar bill. He handed it to the clerk. "Thanks for your advice," he said.

After the clerk left, Levi laid down on the bed and stared up at the ceiling, through tears. He closed his eyes, and he slept.

Sleep came easy. At least through high school and the beginning of college. Sleep escapes started with puberty. In sleep, Levi didn't have to think. Or feel. Or try. Usually. At least it would begin that way. Then some demon would wander in and dangle an old memory in front of his subconscious. Levi would try to kick him out, or if he sensed the demon coming, he'd charge into another room within his mind and close the door before the demon reached into his bag of tricks and pulled out another nightmare. Nightmares. Always there and always the same ones.

Levi got up, unlocked the door, and walked quickly to the elevator. He needed to be in a place with people. "Friendly, sane people," he said to himself as he got onto the elevator. The doors closed, Levi pushed the lobby button, and slowly the elevator descended.

The elevator continued going down. Slow. Real slow. Deeper and deeper. Then it jolted. As if the cable had broken. Falling. The elevator was in a free-fall! Levi panicked. The elevator shot downward like a skydiver without a parachute. Levi smelled blood, broken bones, crushed organs, death, and in a town where you couldn't even get a proper burial.

Just before the elevator hit bottom, the cable locked, and Levi came to a lurching halt. Maybe it had actually fallen only a floor or two, Levi thought, sweat pouring down his face. It didn't matter. Levi needed out. He started yelling. He pushed the emergency button. Bells rang. The phone didn't work. "Get me out of here!" he screamed.

Levi pounded on the door. Finally, he heard the pounding on the other side. Saved! But he couldn't hear their words. He couldn't understand what they were saying. Giving instructions. Telling him what to do. He kept trying to listen. To grasp their meaning. To communicate.

Nothing. Levi could think of nothing but escape. He had to get his bearings and get control of the rush of adrenaline. To find strength. Nothing was in the elevator except the button panel, a useless phone, and two doors tightly shut. There had to be a way to get out before the cable broke completely and hurled him to inevitable doom. Overhead, Levi saw the panel leading to the top of the elevator. If he could get through the hole, at least he'd be able to find a ledge, or a rope, or something to hang onto. A hatch to safety. Safety, in a dark elevator shaft, if he couldn't get out the door. But the door was the best avenue for escape. And people were on the other side. Friendly people, pounding on the door, trying to help him, trying to talk and comfort him. That's where he wanted to be. With them. On the other side.

Levi placed his fingers between the cracks in the door. He pulled so hard, the tips of his fingers felt like they were digging into a hot charcoal. "Help me!" he hollered. "Get me out of here!"

Suddenly, what looked like a sword slithered between the crack of the doors. The pointed tip almost hit him in the eye. Levi was so startled, he fell backwards onto the floor with his back to the wall. "Thank God," he said. The crack was opening. Finally he could hear their voices. "Oh, thank God you're there. Can you get it open?"

The voices replied, "We're coming, son." "We're here." "You'll be safe soon." "We'll get you out of there." Panic. Fear. Claustrophobia. "Help me," Levi kept pleading. He had to get out of the hellhole that would serve as his coffin, if they didn't hurry.

"Don't worry, Levi. If you're hungry, take this," a man's voice said. And through the little crack came chocolate. The crack was opening slowly. At least it was opening. Peanut brittle popped in and shattered on the floor. Little tan spots of hard candy and nuts bounced into the elevator.

Levi looked down at them, confused, then turned toward the voices of his rescuers. "I'll help," he cried as he reached for the crack that was continuing to creep open. His fingers could now easily get between the doors. His cheek was red and hot against the steel frame. His nose was in the crack. He could smell musky breath on the other side. His ears could now hear the words, "We're coming for you, Levi. We want you. We need you. We love you. Wait for us, son. We'll take care of you, and you'll be ours, and we'll be yours."

"Now!" he yelled.

"Yes, now!" Suddenly a fist from the other side was able to punch through the widening crack of the doors. A hand. A fat, hairy, clammy hand. The fist opened, and wet quarters and greasy peanut brittle fell to the floor. "Take my hand, Levi. Take my hand, and let me hold you and touch you and protect you," he heard the voice say from the other side of the door. "First me, and then the others. We all want you."

Levi was up against the wall. A body was desperately trying to squeeze in. First the fist, and then the forearm, and then the shoulder. Pudgy and pink. The crack got bigger, and Levi could see fat faces and glowing eyes laughing and looking in at him from the opening in the door. Wet lips and drooling smiles. Levi swung at the fist like a boxer hitting a tethered ball. He missed the arm that was moving up and down, flailing between the constricted portals. Again, he pushed the emergency button. Nothing. He hit the button to close the door. Nothing. The crack kept creeping. Opening wider.

A throng of fat hands on fat shoulders and fat feet jumped to get to the front of the line. The hall was full of endomorphic whoppers, all in a line leading to Levi.

"Nooooo! Leave me alone! Stay away!"

"But we want you, Levi," they said in unison. "We'll take care of you. You'll like it. It will make you feel good. Feel real good."

"I'm not like you!" Levi shrieked. "I'm not like you!"

"Nonsense, Levi. You are." The panting grew louder. Hurried. Foul and sticky. "You're just like us," they exulted in harmony. One gravelly voice said,

White Knuckle

"You've had it, boy. Remember? It happened because of you. You wanted it."

"No!" Levi yelled. "I didn't! I...I'm not...not like you!"

Another voice laughed, devilish and haunting. "You're just like us, Levi. Accept it. Let us in."

"Fuck you!" he bellowed. "Fuck you!"

"Yes. That's it, Levi. Yes," they tittered. "Fuck us. All of us. All the time! We're coming. It's so hard, Levi. So stiff."

A head was almost through the creeping crack. Brittle breath and quarters were flying through the opening. Levi remembered the hatch. Fat fingers grappled for a shirt to hang onto. Shorts. Pants. Anything.

With his hands clenched together and his arms straight over his head, Levi jumped, shooting at the ceiling hatch like a human cannonball. His fists hit the ceiling panel with a booming crunch. The hatch popped open. Levi fell back to the floor. He looked up. There was no light, but in the darkness there was safety.

"You fat fucks can't get through *that* hole!" he screamed. Hands lined the doors. Prying them open. Quarters flew. Peanut brittle broke.

With all his strength, Levi crouched down and then hurled himself as high as he could possibly jump. If he had a basketball in his hand, he could've dunked it. Instead, each palm grabbed a corner as he pulled himself up through the hole and into the darkness.

The doors below opened, and the people rolled in like a massive slab of bread dough that had come to life and was running amok. White flab, tumbling all over each other. Blubber. Looking for Levi. Snarling. Grabbing. Wet flabby flesh. Levi closed the ceiling hatch of the elevator and shut out the sights and sounds and hisses and fears. He was alone in the darkness, and he was safe and secure.

When he knew he'd survived, his eyes opened, and he could wake up once more. The nightmare was over, again. It had come back, but again, he'd escaped. He never wanted to wake without first getting through the hatch. That part of the dream was an absolute necessity. He couldn't understand, why the demon kept coming back, over and over again, carrying the same old suitcase full of fears.

Levi got off the bed, went into the bathroom, and put a wet towel on his face. He looked into the mirror. "Someday," he said, "I'm going to throw that suitcase away."

Levi turned and left his hotel room. He bypassed the elevator, walked down the stairs, and out onto the street. It was night-time, and Levi was in the Tenderloin.

18

Outside Bedford, Levi looked around, trying to get his bearings. Across the street was the Pence Gallery, the Burma House restaurant, a laundromat, and more businesses up and down the street. He wasn't hungry, he was thirsty. He turned left and wandered up the street, watching people as he tried to find a bar. Levi wanted a drink and something else, not knowing what that something else was.

Girls and cars were everywhere. Everyone scanned everyone. The girls kept walking back and forth, waiting to catch a glance, for a car to stop, for a question to be asked. A price to be fixed, and then for a ride. Blacks, Asians, whites, and all blends in between.

"Looking for some action, honey?" She was in Levi's face, smiling.

"No. I'm looking for a drink," Levi replied.

"I drink, baby. You buy me a drink, and we can talk."

Levi kept walking. At a small grocery, he found fresh apples, bought two, and stood on the corner surveying San Francisco's Tenderloin.

This isn't Colorado Springs, he thought.

The hookers were working hard. It was a Saturday night, and the town was alive.

A steady stream of cars cruised the Tenderloin. Bumper to bumper traffic, and no one honked a horn. Music blared from stereos, rap and rock and loud.

If a car slowed and a window went down, the girl hustled over and she and John talked. Some cars had a lone driver, some with three or four teens or young men in their twenties. Old guys, short guys, smokers. Everyone looking for a date or acting like it. Levi thought he was in an Italian fish market on a Saturday morning, except instead of selling fresh mackerel, they were bartering over blow jobs.

Sometimes a deal was struck, and the lucky lady laughed and jumped into the car with the stranger. Off they drove. Levi saw a black man taking down a license number. Her pimp. Her safety net. And then the pimp yelled an order to another girl in his stable of prancing sluts.

When a police car came into view, things changed quickly. The women walked down the street as if they had a purpose and a place to go. No more sashaying. Maybe a quick dive into the grocery store for a bottle of Snapple or another pack of cigarettes. The police passed, and out they'd come out again.

"You sure you don't want nothin', honey?"

"No thanks. Not now," Levi said politely.

"Why not? Don't like my looks, or you lookin' for boys?"

"Just looking," he said. "Just looking."

Levi found himself on the corner of Polk and Larkin. The Mother Lode bar was on the corner, and Levi walked in. The bar was filled with liquor, and customers searching for liaisons. It was loud and smoky. Marijuana smells floated in the air.

A man approached. "You got ID," he asked. Levi gave him the driver's license that showed his age as 23. Fake ID's were easy to get.

"Colorado, huh?" The man looked Levi over carefully. "You sure you're twenty-three?" Levi nodded. "You look younger to me."

"Yeah, well, I've had an easy life," Levi said.

The man seemed satisfied. "Okay, behave yourself. You can stay, but act right. Ain't a place for kids."

"I'm not..." but the man was gone before Levi could finish his sentence. A singer sat in the corner moaning some bluesy song people didn't seem to hear. Levi made his way to a barstool beneath an AIDS banner. He ordered a gin and tonic. His drink arrived quickly, and he downed the liquid empty with a few fast swallows. He ordered another and glanced around. A hand landed on the inside of his thigh. Smiling white teeth were within inches of his face.

"You want some company?" she asked. Her breasts were next to his chest. Her shoulders were bent down so he could get a clearer view. Soft, pearl-white skin. No bra. The dress was tight, and her legs were thin and smooth. Her hand moved on his stiff leg.

"Not right now," he answered. "Right now, I feel like getting drunk." Levi softly pushed her hand off his thigh. She put it back, closer to his crotch.

"Maybe later, then," she said. "Maybe after you get loosened up a bit. But don't go with any of these sushi girls without talking to me first. Understand? You don't need a sushi girl."

She leaned over and kissed his cheek. Her hand gently whisked over his groin. She stood up, adjusted her breasts so Levi could have another look, and got ready to move on to another score.

"My name's LaToya," she said. "Remember, now, I don't want to see you with any little thing. You don't need no sushi. They like raw meat."

203

"What's a sushi?"

"Thailand, man. You know, Indonesia, Taiwan, Oriental. Not me. Some dudes like those little girls with small tits. Japanese men like us dark ones. Whites too. You, you'll like the likes of me. Tight and horny."

She slid two fingers up and down the front of her pubic bone, smiled, winked, and left.

Levi was in the heart of whore country, and he was getting scrambled. He noticed purple tassels that were hanging on all the walls of the Mother Lode. Leftover party tassels that were never taken down. Thin purple strands of foil, eight feet long and hanging everywhere. On the ceiling, blinking red and white lights were strung around naked branches of bleached wood. Little lights strung around the hanging limbs as if they were preserved Christmas trees that no one had bothered to recycle.

The singer sang on a two-step, black stage, with green silk leaves that made an archway around a stone fountain, like a plastic garden in the den of sin. A long-haired biker dressed in leathers, a cowboy hat, and wearing sunglasses in the darkness of the bar, sat at a table, drinking beer.

A Marilyn Monroe poster hung on one wall, and a half-naked poster of a buffed, handsome, white stud hung on another. He was wearing shorts, and the poster said, "Determination."

Determination for what? Levi wondered. Determination to get laid? Me, too. I need determination. Jesus. Erica. Why? He ordered another drink.

Levi listened to the singer croon and eyed the people playing with each other. Girls kept coming at him with offers, but he hadn't enough booze to drown out his fears and insecurities. Determination hadn't quite set in yet, but his courage was building.

204

White Knuckle

In and out of the Mother Lode they came. Prostitutes left with guys, and then came back without them, looking for another trick, another score. Levi kept drinking. He noticed that the girls inside the bar were prettier than those walking the streets. The girls inside wore fancy dresses, their hair carefully styled, their long nails perfectly manicured. High heels, colorful scarves, jangly earrings and fanny-struts.

Levi glued to his barstool, getting drunk and dizzy. If he didn't have to talk, he wouldn't slur his words. One red-haired hooker was especially attractive. If he could stand without falling, he decided he'd finally exercise his determination and courage. But then, he felt LaToya's hand between his legs. Out of the darkness she'd found him again. Through the haze in his eyes, all he could see was her smile.

"You loosened up yet?" she teased.

He rubbed his eyes as if to make them see better. "I…I'm so loose, I don't think I can stand. What time is it, anyway?"

LaToya looked at her watch. "Quarter to one, Jacko. Closing time. Time to go to my place and have a good time. You ready?"

"How…how much?" he stammered.

LaToya laughed. "How much you got, honey? And what do you want?"

"Don't know. I never, oh shit, where's my drink?" Levi looked at the bar. His drink was gone. "Hey, asshole," he yelled. "Where's my goddamn drink?"

The bartender ignored him. LaToya grabbed his arm. "Don't be yelling at him, man. It's not cool. Come on, let's get to my place."

"I want my fu…cking drink."

205

"You're too drunk as it is." She pulled him off the bar stool. Levi stumbled and grabbed a chair to steady himself. LaToya was strong, a five-foot-six-inch beauty from the Bronx. Moderate breasts. Full ass. Big hands. She put one arm through his and escorted him out of the Mother Lode like they was walking up the aisle in church. Levi was staggering, but LaToya managed to keep him upright and walking.

Outside on the street, Levi started laughing and swatting drunkenly at invisible demons. "You see that?" he asked, stumbling backward.

LaToya grabbed him. "What, honey? I don't see nothin'."

Levi broke from LaToya's grasp, shadow-boxing the vision dancing and hiding in and around the night lights of the street.

"I'm gonna kill you, you fat ape!"

LaToya grabbed Levi before he fell off the curb and into the gutter. She steered him toward her apartment building on the corner and pulled him up the stairs to the second floor and opened the door to her world.

A world of trash and total disarray. Levi could barely see, let alone notice the chaos around him. Nothing was in place – except ten videos of pornographic couplings neatly centered between twin dildoes that acted as bookends. A blue and white tube of K-Y jelly came into view. The videos were stacked on top of the TV set with a built-in VCR. A hot plate and dirty dishes and glasses cluttered the tiny kitchenette area.

Clothes were crumpled and thrown into corners. Trousers. Dresses. Blouses and nylons. A brightly lit vanity took up one corner. Makeup, perfumes, hair sprays and silly little bottles with cheap rubber bubbles were on a vanity.

"Now tell me what you'd like, and I'll tell you how much it costs," LaToya cooed as she sat Levi down on the bed, in front of the television. She shimmied and moved in close and away and then twirled around in circles. She turned her back on Levi, and bent down with her hands beneath the dildoed videos. Her ass swayed in front of Levi's mouth.

"You want pussy, it's two hundred. A blow job costs a hundred and fifty. You just want me to dance and get naked while you get yourself off, that's just a crispy one."

"I need a drink."

"That's the last thing you need, pretty boy."

LaToya turned and began to unbuckle Levi's belt, kissing him on his ears and cheeks and neck. She licked an ear lobe and pushed her breasts around his nose.

Levi fell back on the rumpled bedspread and sheets. In the same move, he pulled her body on top of his, kissing her neck and chest and trying to kiss her lips. Soft, but thicker than Erica. Levi didn't notice, he was hungry.

LaToya pushed away. Levi was flat on the bed.

She stood over him, unbuttoning her blouse with one hand and turning on music with the other. She knelt on the floor between his legs. Her hands went back to the buckle.

"What you want from this girl?" she asked. "Let's get them pants off, and see what we've got inside. Don't know, but if it's big enough, I may just cut the price tonight. All I've seen tonight is one little dick. I want a big one."

Levi lay still, his head swimming, dizzy with tension and booze. His mind couldn't concentrate. He closed his eyes, while LaToya unbuttoned his pants and slowly took down the zipper. Levi was quiet. Submissive.

"Before I pull this baby out, honey, where's the cash?"

Levi mumbled.

With sturdy quickness, the hooker rolled Levi to his side. Her fingers found his wallet, opened it, and took out three new hundred dollar bills. She put them up to the light to check their authenticity. Levi was half asleep when LaToya hit the VCR and began taking off her clothes. Her panties stayed on. The music and voices from the video brought Levi back to half-life.

She looked at herself in the mirror. Long, wavy hair, multicolored plastic earrings, firm breasts, smooth, thin arms. Strong, muscular legs, collagen lips.

"Watch the video, honey. Now don't that get you horny?" She grasped Levi's hands and pulled him up so he could see three girls doing it to each other on the screen.

Levi's head seemed to lose blood as he sat up. He tried to shake the cobwebs and lights and stars careening back and forth inside his brain. The figures on the screen were blurs. LaToya was standing close, with firm hands rubbing his shoulders and chest as her mouth and tongue wet his neck and ears.

Levi pulled her onto his lap. His uncoordinated tug nearly landed LaToya on the floor, but she grabbed his neck and hung on as Levi began to massage her breasts and squeeze her nipples. His fingers moved to her legs and thighs and to the outside of her panties. Groping. Clumsy fondles. One arm around her taut back, with a hand to her breast, and his mouth and tongue on the other. Then back. His fingers plunged back to her panties.

LaToya quickly stood up between his legs, and kept wiggling her breasts back and forth across his face. Levi's hands grappled to pull down the panties. LaToya backed up and stood straight with her legs pushed tightly together.

White Knuckle

"You want to see a pussy?" she asked. "A tight, cute, aching pussy?" Slowly, she shimmered and pulled down her panties. Cautiously, they came down to just below the basket between her legs while Levi's head swayed and his eyes opened and closed. LaToya moved her nakedness next to Levi's face.

"Put your hands on my titties and your tongue on my pussy." Levi reached up, but his arms and hands felt like limp Chinese noodles. Floppy and stringy and floating in all directions. LaToya grabbed the back of his neck and guided his face into her crotch. She started to moan as she bumped his lips and nose back and forth into the pubic hair carefully shaved in the shape of a triangle. A triangle, with the point leading down.

"Oh, I like it," she said. "I like it…yes, I like it."

Levi's hands were at his sides. He could hardly hear her words.

"I want to lick you," she said. LaToya moved her hand from behind Levi's neck, and with a swift flick from her palm and fingers, she pushed Levi's body back onto the covers and she fell to her knees.

Levi was about to pass out. But through the boozy muddle, he could feel LaToya's fingers reaching into his underwear. She pulled his penis out, into the light of the room, and through the clouds clogging his mind. Levi felt it growing as her mouth sucked over him, and the wetness of her tongue encircled his feeble erection. Her nimble fingers magically and rhythmically stroked him up and down and around.

"My God," she said, "You're the most beautiful man I've seen in my life."

LaToya's mouth and hand moved up and down in unison on her trick for the night. Her other hand went behind her back, and she rubbed between her legs. Hard and fast. On her knees. She yelped out a fevered cry, confirming the release of unexpected passion as her body shivered and tingled.

209

"Holy shit, man. That almost never happens," she said. "But you're 'bout the most handsome thing I seen." Her mouth and hands went back onto Levi. "I've got to make you feel as good."

But Levi wasn't listening. He hadn't heard a word. When LaToya reached for him, she saw that his erection had shrunk right back into his shorts, hiding like an ejected little-leaguer in a dugout. Levi had passed out cold.

"Baby," she said, "Wait till morning. When we're through, you're going to have fucked me so hard, I'll give you a refund." She got out of bed and carefully undressed Levi. He was naked and unconscious as LaToya easily pulled him under the covers and carefully tucked him in. "I think I'm in love," LaToya said to herself. "I'm gonna give him that refund right now." She took Levi's wallet out of his pants pocket, and put three hundred dollars back into the billfold without a moment's hesitation or regret. She turned out the lights and laid down beside Levi. She stroked his brow and ran her fingers through his hair and over his chest and shoulders.

"I've got myself a lion," she said, as she put her head on Levi's chest and fell asleep, smiling.

19

After a drunken blackout, it was difficult for Levi to even open his eyes. For twenty minutes he tossed and turned before it slowly dawned on him that he wasn't alone. When his hand touched LaToya's leg, Levi woke up with a start and hurled himself out of bed like a lover caught with another man's wife. He stood by the bed, staring down at his smiling mistress, trying to remember how he'd gotten there and who the hell she was. He recalled the Mother Lode, but he didn't even know her name.

LaToya's smile was at its most erotic as she pulled the covers down so he could see the beauty of her body. Her long fingernails caressed the thin waist and tight stomach. She cupped her firm breasts with both hands. Levi stared in astonishment, and then realized that he was as naked as she. He blushed as he pulled part of a sheet from the bed to cover himself.

"What the hell happened?" he asked. "How'd I get here? Who are you?"

"My name's LaToya. What's yours?"

"A hooker?"

"No," she said. "Check your wallet. It's on the TV. Money's all there." She stretched, arching her breasts into the air. "Come here, baby. Lay beside me."

"I'm thirsty. Feels like someone stuffed cotton in my mouth."

LaToya pointed to a miniature refrigerator next to the vanity. "There's orange juice in the fridge. Grab some and lay down beside me."

A confused Levi dropped the sheet, went to the refrigerator, took out the juice, and carefully slipped into bed. He covered himself quickly and took a long, cold drink, trying to replay the previous evening's events.

"Did we have sex?" he asked.

"Sort of," she said. "Don't you remember me sucking you? You've got the most incredible body I've ever seen."

"I remember you touching me, and then, it's all blank."

LaToya took a swallow of juice and put the carton on the table next to the bed. She popped a mint into her mouth and said playfully, "Open your mouth, and let me put something in it."

Levi's mouth opened, she put a mint on his tongue, and then jumped on top of him with a naked embrace that was startling and consumed with passion. LaToya rolled and pulled his body on top of hers.

"Be a lion, baby. Be my lion, and take me hard and quick."

Levi had no time to think. She was under his naked body, and he could feel his chest next to hers. Blazing with erotic warmth, tingling every nerve in his nervous skin.

He softly bit her neck and shoulder and moved his mouth to her breasts. It seemed natural, natural for the first time in his life.

"Bite me," she said. "Please, baby. Between your teeth so the nipples hurt." Her hand reached toward his crotch. Excitement began to overwhelm him. Levi's hand reached for her panties and his fingers searched between her legs.

White Knuckle

"No baby, don't," she said. "Stay away from my panties. Just touch my tits. I'll direct your dick, honey. Let me show you the way."

But Levi was consumed with determination. A determination he'd never known. His senses never felt such need. He was hungry, bursting, wanting in. LaToya pushed him away from between her legs, but Levi was stronger, as his hand reached for her. LaToya crossed her legs in an effort to keep her thighs together, tight.

"Baby, wait!" she pleaded. Pushing away. "Wait, honey, I've got to explain."

Levi's knee squeezed between LaToya's legs. Her thighs spread under his urgent fury. His fingers were there, searching for the lips that would open and invite him in. He would at last know what it really felt like. The warmth and wetness. And then he felt it. Not lips. Not a soft, inviting spot. He felt skin. Hard. Small and erect and hard.

"Jesus!" Levi stopped and looked straight into LaToya's eyes. His body tensed, then recoiled. He bolted from the bed and threw off the covers so he could see all of LaToya's body. Tits and crotch and long, thin legs.

"Baby!" she cried. "Let me explain!" Her legs were together again, as tight as she could hold them.

Levi bent down, grabbed her knees, and violently pulled her legs apart. He stared in shock at a small, stiff dick in a cloth sheath, strapped with elastic between the cracks of LaToya's buttocks.

Levi went numb.

"Honey, listen," LaToya begged. "It's not, it's not like it seems. I'm a he/she. I'm really a girl." LaToya cried. Sadness echoed from her throat. "I'm not a guy. You got to believe that. Baby, listen. I'm a transsexual. Not a transvestite. I'm a girl, stuck in a boy's body. A real girl, with real tits and real feelings."

Levi's feelings froze. He didn't speak as he dressed. He wasn't in a hurry, but he didn't say a word. His mouth was closed as he automatically put on his shorts and pants.

LaToya cautiously got off the bed, covering herself with a robe. She moved to put her hand on his wrist, and then saw the hatred in his eyes.

She'd had Johns figure it out before, but this was a look she'd never seen. She moved into a corner, giving Levi as much space as possible, leaving him a direct path to the front door.

"I'm a girl, honest!" she said. "I didn't want this dick. I should've been born a girl. Look," she cried, as she grabbed a handful of prescription bottles and showed them to Levi as if she was making an offering. "See these pills?"

Levi didn't look or speak. Another sock on, and then another. Levi was slow. LaToya was fast.

"I get Estrogen and Estron," she said. "Shots, two times a week. And I take Spardalin and Perenon and B-12 pills two times a day. B-12 boosts the shots, and they give me softer breasts and a softer ass. Spardalin is a female hormone. It breaks down the male hormones, too. You listening? I'm telling you, I'm a girl." She sounded desperate. And pathetic.

Levi ignored LaToya. He looked inside his wallet.

"I told you, I didn't take no money. I just want you."

Levi put the wallet in his pants pocket and slipped on his shirt, slowly buttoning it.

"Honey, I take Provera," LaToya went on. "Gives my breasts milk, and stops hair from growing on my face, and makes my skin smooth. All of this stuff makes my voice high. Don't you see? I didn't want to fuck you as a man. I want to fuck you as a woman."

Levi opened his pants and tucked in his shirt. He secured the zipper and fastened the inside hook of his trousers. He didn't look at LaToya as she prattled on.

"I even get a shot that's smuggled in from Mexico," LaToya shouted. It's called Peretal. Some girls inject it direct into their tits. I inject into my ass. Someday, when I get the money, I'll have the operation, and I'll get real breasts and this dinky dick of mine will be gone. I'm a girl, baby. At least in my heart."

LaToya's mascara smeared, and it gave her a clownish look. Behind the tears, her face wrinkled with fear.

Levi finished dressing and stared at her. A cold, blank stare that terrified LaToya. Her legs could hardly keep her standing.

She tried another tack. "What's your name, baby? You live here or visiting?" The words crawled out of her throat. "Tell me," she pleaded.

Levi interrupted angrily. "How many men find out you're a man?" He walked toward her as he spoke. His movements were deliberate. Slow.

Anxiously, she looked to the door, but her feet were frozen to the floor as her lion closed in.

Levi's fury blazed toward her like a blowtorch. "Answer me!"

Words sputtered from her mouth. "Two, maybe five percent. But, but they don't care."

"How many men fuck you, thinking you're a girl?"

"Lots." Her whole body shook.

"How? I mean how do you do it?" His voice thundered.

"I..., now baby, honey, you're scaring me."

"How?" he screamed. LaToya stood, quaking in misery.

"I, I direct it in. They, they think they're fu – fucking pussy, but, my ass, you know..."

"Blow jobs," Levi spit at her, "how many get blow jobs?"

"Please, baby. Please, you're scaring me to death." LaToya was crying. "Okay," she stammered. "Okay, 'bout half want blow jobs. Most like my dancing and playing with themselves. They're so horny"

She tried covering herself. Levi grabbed LaToya's shoulders and pushed her hard, reeling her across the room. A chair fell, sending clothes to the floor as she hit the TV. She tried to steady herself, but she tumbled to the hard-wood floor.

"Goddamn you! Why'd you do this to me!" Levi screamed. "Why's every-body so fucking crazy?" Levi cried. He stood over her sobbing, not knowing which one of them was in more pain or anguish.

His tears were still falling as he slammed the door of the apartment and walked out onto the street.

"Why?" he kept asking himself. "It's so sick. Why?"

20

Walking San Francisco streets in the early morning light can make people feel alive and fresh. Wholesome and energetic. Blue skies above, cool ocean breezes from across the Bay, the sun starting to shine on El Dorado.

But Levi didn't feel fresh and clean. Levi didn't want to walk the streets. He wanted to crawl to his room so he could slither under the sheets and hide in the darkness. Safe from all the madness and guilt and shame. Safe from the demons. Demons lurking in the shadows of his thoughts, confusing his sense of reality as they gathered and readied themselves for another attack.

And attack they would. They always did, no matter where he tried to escape. Like mosquitoes on horse tails, they swirled and bit themselves into his hair and head and around his skin. Mosquitoes clinging on, drawing one drop of blood at a time.

Over time, Levi knew he'd bleed to death. A slow, but certain death, unless he found a cure. A fix. Something to push away his past, so Levi could live in the present and dream about the future. A cure that someday, maybe, would fling him into the light.

For a moment he wished he'd kicked LaToya into unconsciousness. But what good would that do, he thought."She's just another victim like me. I wonder how many others there are? Different lives, different twists. Same story."

After getting off the elevator, Levi opened his room and locked the door behind him. Double-bolted it, turned on the shower and undressed. The water warmed, and Levi waited, staring into the bathroom mirror. His naked shoulders were broad and strong, his eyes, bloodshot and glassy. Shaking fingers brushed against the stubble on his chin as he scrutinized his own reflection.

"You need help," he said aloud. "But who? Who could help a piece of shit like me?"

The reflection stared back and answered his question without speaking.

"No," Levi replied. "Erica's not much different than the rest. Is she?"

The question was stupid. Even Levi's reflection knew that. Of course Erica was different. When he was honest with himself, Levi knew, he just didn't want to admit it. Mostly, he didn't want to accept it. Admitting and accepting the truth would make him vulnerable. Lying was easier than becoming vulnerable.

Dad lied; Erica didn't. Kit left; Erica didn't. Erica wanted to be close, and he pushed her away. Why?

It was clear to Levi that the two people he had loved the most in his life were liars. They said they would be there forever, and then they disappeared. He couldn't forgive them. They were liars, and the rest like Barry Bates and LaToya lied to get what they wanted from him. But Erica didn't lie. She was honest. And that's what she wanted him to be. Honest. To himself. And to her.

Maybe she did love him, he thought. Did. That was the operative word. Past tense. His eyes darted to the window. "So who cares?" he said aloud with cockiness in his voice. But he still wanted her friendship. Somehow he knew it was important, but he wasn't certain why.

Levi turned from the window. The cocky tone disappeared. Erica's history. She'd never let him come back into her life. Or would she? She who was the best thing that had ever happened to him, and what did he do? Lied. Kept her from being close. And how could she take back a guy who slapped her? She was forgiving, but she wasn't stupid.

He closed his eyes, and his chin dropped. "But I'm not worth the effort," he said to his image in the mirror.

Levi was in the shower, scrubbing and shampooing and lathering. Removing the grime, grease and sweat. The smell. Trying to wash away the night before, a he/she's mouth around his limping erection, the passion he felt as he barely remembered touching LaToya's chest, thinking it was real, a girl's, not knowing hair was trying to grow on the soft, smooth skin he kissed and even wanted. Sick sex, just like in the past. A repeat performance. Would it ever be right? With anyone? Or was he an emotional cripple who would stay that way until the day he died?

Levi got out of the shower, dried, dressed, reached for the phone, and dialed Erica's number. His heart ached for a touch of her kindness. If nothing else, the least he wanted was to hear her voice.

The shaking in his body coincided with the ringing sound in his ear as he waited for the phone to be answered.

The "hello" in her voice was soft and gentle.

"Erica, it's Levi...I...I just wanted to say hi, and see how you've been. You've been on my mind...and I..."

There was no response.

"Erica, it's been over a week, and I can't not talk to you any longer. Please don't hang up." Levi couldn't believe it. It was so unexpected. Suddenly, he found himself needing her.

"Maybe," he said, "maybe we could try again."

She was silent.

"Erica, you've got to understand. At least try. I...I'm asking you to forgive me."

She still didn't speak.

"Can't we at least be friends?" he asked. "There's only you and Sampson. I know you deserve someone better than me. But I need you as my friend, Erica. I don't know what it is. Why. All I know is you're special, and I messed up bad."

Levi was holding the phone and shaking. Thinking about LaToya and Bates and Dad and Kit and camp and being alone with no one but himself and his dreams of the past and present. Where did it all come from, and what did it all mean? He hadn't done anything wrong, had he? Erica was the only light that had come into his life in ten fucking years, and now she was gone, too. He knew it was his fault. In the past, and again, now. The truth crushed him like an avalanche. His fears whispered to him, filling his ears, heart, and mind.

Levi couldn't hear Erica's breathing. He couldn't feel the tightness in her stomach, or sense the conflicting feelings – hang up or listen? Speak or be quiet?

Erica could hear the real pain in his voice. This wasn't one of his lies. She could feel his anguish.

Erica knew that if she didn't hang up soon, she was bound to say something kind, something he wanted to hear. Her natural instinct was to help, and his words resonated with despair, but she was still angry, still hurt. A part of her didn't want to give a damn. She had heard it before.

White Knuckle

"Erica, listen to me, please," the voice on the other end pleaded. "I'm gonna stay here in San Francisco awhile. Can I just call you from time to time? To talk? I need us to be friends. We can be that, can't we?"

She pulled the phone from her ear held it in front of her face like a hymnal. She'd never been so ambivalent about anything in her life. Why the hell should she care? Was he worth it? What did she really feel for him at this point?

Erica could barely hear Levi's voice, but she did hear it enough to know that this was the voice she had seldom heard in the past. The one that didn't have the bravado or the arrogance.

"Erica, say something. Say anything. But please, please don't say you won't be my friend. I need to tell you something. I need..."

That's all he thinks about. That's all he ever thought about. His needs. His life. His problems. What about hers? Did he ever consider the fact she loved him? And what did he have that made her feel that way? Good looks – there were lots of guys with those. Charm? Seldom. Wisdom? Never. Feelings? Hidden.

"I'm sorry, Erica. I couldn't help myself; I couldn't be who you wanted..." His voice trailed off.

You couldn't do a lot of things, she thought. You couldn't feel. You couldn't be honest. You couldn't trust. You couldn't even get it up.

Silence. The voice on the other end of Erica's phone grew quiet. Levi had stopped talking.

The silence told Erica that Levi could be lost for good. The weak one could leave, but the strong one, she wanted. A small part of her still wanted him.

Levi isn't talking, she thought. He's giving up. Giving us up. Erica reached out to him, but her voice was so soft, he didn't hear her say, "Levi, I…"

"Talk to me!" she heard him bawl. Slowly and gently he said, "If you won't talk to me, at least know this: I…I really think I do…I love you, Kit."

Except for his own voice, Levi heard one more sound, the click of the receiver, before the line went dead.

* * * * *

Her face was red with embarrassment and rage. Duped again. Stupid again.

"Erica Lynne, it's time to go to church," her mother said, entering the bedroom as she primped the last straggles of graying hair under a hat. "Daddy's left, of course, but I'd like to get there early and talk with some of the folks as they come in."

"I don't feel good. I think I'm going back to bed," Erica said, trying to avoid her mother's gaze.

"Honey, you look feverish. Maybe I should call the doctor." Erica's mother reached down to place a palm on her daughter's forehead.

Erica flicked her mother's hand away, like a petulant child. "Leave me alone, Mom. I don't need a doctor."

Ever since the Jacobsons had returned from the Caribbean cruise, Erica's mother had noticed her daughter's behavior had undergone a dramatic change. Instead of being kind, open, warm, and friendly, Erica was angry, aloof, cold, and abrupt. Overnight, her daughter had become an angry adolescent. Although William Jacobson chalked it up to the minor frustrations of growing pains, Mary knew it had everything to do with Levi.

"Just because your boyfriend's away is no reason to treat me this way, Erica."

"He's not my boyfriend. He's history."

"Oh? Why didn't you tell me you broke up? What happened?"

"He's a liar!" Erica shot the words out bitterly.

Mary saw the tears well up in her daughter's eyes. "Honey I can't bear to see you hurt by Levi. Sweetheart, he's not worth it. You're better than he is."

"I know." Erica laid her face into the pillow.

"You can try to tell your heart what to feel or forget, Erica, but it's not going to listen. Hearts are on their own, honey. Time's the only friend they've got."

Her mother turned and walked out of the bedroom, closing the door quietly behind her. Erica lay on the bed, crying. Crying and battling. But she wasn't alone. There were all those voices within, screaming for attention.

"Let him die!" said vengeance.

"That's stupid," answered a hopeless, love-struck tinge. "Matty's who she wants."

The mocking voice of reality said, "She wasn't fucking Matty. That's what's stupid. She went for the other guy, Levi."

Another quipped, "I think he's too much work."

"That's why you're called logical. I think he *is* worth the effort."

"You're irrational. Let him die."

"Who cares if someone thinks he's worth the effort? She can live without a man. Any woman can."

Wherever she turned, Erica's voices shouted. If she slept, they invaded her dreams; awake, they pounded and pounced on her brain. She listened to them all, but there wasn't one she felt she could trust completely.

But one voice, one quiet feeling, stayed hidden. One voice remained silent, waiting for the cacophony to die down. With the others constantly roaring in the hollows of her head, this voice didn't have a chance of being heard.

* * * * *

Reni offered her wisdom over coffee at the most popular Starbucks in town. "'Don't look back on a love that's dying,' Erica. That's what the song says. There isn't a man in the world who's loyal to anything more than his dick. Big or small, they still think it's the most important thing in their life, and wherever it leads them, they go."

"It didn't lead Levi anywhere."

Reni leaned over the table and placed her hand on Erica's. "He's in San Francisco, isn't he? What does that tell you?"

"It's time to let go of him, I know."

"You know what my grandmother would call you?" Erica looked up quizzically. "She'd say you were a regular Florence Nightingale, and she'd be right. You see Levi as some kind of fallen warrior that you have to bring back from the brink of death. Me, I see a bushwhacking guerrilla who could easily become a goddamn predator."

Erica looked into the eyes of her friend. "Part of me says you're right, Reni. The other part says I'm crazy to let go. Both parts hurt. I can't make any sense of it."

White Knuckle

"Of course it makes no sense. It's too complicated. Love's not enough for men. They can't express their feelings, and they're afraid of getting close. Look, why don't you start dating some other guys?"

Erica took a sip of iced tea. She noticed some of the other people at Starbucks. Couples talked softly and gazed into each other's eyes. Some couples sat together reading newspapers or eating, but not saying a word. A well-groomed, older woman sat alone. And she wasn't the only one. Maybe they were all alone, and just didn't know it. Maybe being alone was everyone's fate, and they should just accept it. People kept passing out promises like they were candy kisses. Promises they had no intention of keeping.

"Reni, you tell me to date, and in the same breath, you say no man's worth it. So why bother?"

Reni quickly pointed a finger at Erica and started to blurt out an answer, but she stopped, shook her head, and placed her chin in the palm of her hand.

"Why bother?" she asked thoughtfully and closed her eyes. Thinking. Looking for the truth. She opened her eyes. "Because we have to. Because with all the shit we've got to slog through, somewhere there must be a pony worth saddling."

Erica smiled, then her eyes turned sad again. She whispered, "Zorba The Greek said, 'Madness. We all need a little madness or else – or else we never dare cut the rope to be free.'"

"Waiting for Levi to change will drive you crazy for certain, Erica. That madman isn't capable of setting you free to do anything but hurt yourself, at least if you're with him."

A memory zipped through Erica's mind. One of the few good ones left. "Reni," she said wistfully, "you should've seen him the day we went picnicking and driving through the mountains. It seemed like an angel flew inside his head, and I could see and feel the transformation. He was sincere and honest. Gentle and kind. That was the moment I fell in love with him."

She remembered it all like it happened the day before. She remembered the rocky ridge with its spots of pink and purple, speckled grey and brown, pointing to the bottom of the canyon and the skid trail leading to the river below. The far away sound of his voice, and the feel of his body pressing against hers. In the mountains, Levi loved.

She remembered his telling her she had "pizzazz," and she recalled Levi's trembling passion when his lips touched hers. She would never forget seeing him gently blow a kiss to the river flowing quietly below, and to some distant memory. "I'll never forget it," she said, not knowing or even caring if Reni was really listening.

And that's when Erica heard the voice. The one that stayed silent while the others clamored for her attention. The voice with quiet feelings. When all the other voices fell asleep, finally it was safe to speak.

"Believe, Erica. Believe. If Matty can be found, he's everything you've ever wanted. The word is 'if.' The answer's out of your control."

"But it hurts so much."

"Then let go, until…"

"Until what?"

"Until *he* finds himself. Maybe then, *he'll* find you."

21

It wasn't how Levi wanted the phone call to end. If she cared half as much as she'd said, she could've at least spoken a few words. Instead, she hung up the phone, just when he was telling her how he felt. Really felt. A lot of good that call did.

So much for being honest, he thought, as his fingers started dialing another long distance number. So much for reaching out and baring your soul and...

"Yo, Sampson. Levi, here. Thank God I got one friend left in the world. When you coming to San Francisco, Sampson?"

"I think I can make it in a few weeks."

"Great. I'll find an apartment by then. Maybe. Maybe I can..."

"You sound weird, Levi. What's happening?"

"Nothing. Things are fine. Great. Went out last night and almost got laid. "

"I don't believe you, man. Sounds like there's more."

How could Sampson sense anything through a long distance phone line? "Honest," Levi countered. "Me and this chick were ready to go, but then some jock showed up, and I was ushered out the door. But, man, was I ready."

"How ugly was she?"

"What do you mean, ugly? No way. This girl was another Erica, but with a better attitude."

The conversation didn't last long, and it made Levi uncomfortable. He didn't like lying to Sampson, but Levi lied to everyone. Sampson was his best friend, and he needed a familiar face, someone who knew and cared about him. Levi was feeling alone in San Francisco. And lonely. Weariness overwhelmed his feelings as exhaustion forced him to lie on the bed. He was hungry, but too tired to go out and get something to eat. Within ten minutes of his head hitting the pillow, he fell into a sound, peaceful, nightmareless sleep. He slept until noon.

His belly woke him, aching with hunger. "If you want fish," the desk clerk told him, "go to the wharf. But North Beach's got Italian. You're Italian, right? Saranno?"

Levi nodded and smiled. "I think I'll try the wharf. How do I get there?"

"Jump a cable car up Russian Hill past Lombard Street, stay on till you get to the bottom and they throw you off. This town's easy to get around."

"Lombard?" Levi asked. A vein on the side of his head throbbed.

"Yeah. The crookedest street in the world. Car stops right at the top of it."

Levi turned right as he left the Clarion Bedford and walked several blocks toward the center of town. As soon as he saw the opportunity, Levi jumped on the outside steps of a cable car that was clanking its way up the steep slopes leading toward the wharf. Levi loved the way people rode the cable cars, either crammed inside or clinging onto the outside with one or two feet on a metal step, and one or two hands grasping a rail for balance.

White Knuckle

It's a game, Levi thought. Passengers defied the cable conductor to stop suddenly and jerk the lumbering vehicle knocking someone off. Like a ride in an amusement park, it was a risk, one that exhilarated Levi, challenging him to be brave, to take a chance. Maybe, he thought, he should chance letting go of the past. Hanging on the outside of a cable car was a small risk. Letting go of the past was a bigger one.

Levi jumped off the cable car at the top of Lombard Street and looked at the one-way road, twisting and turning down Russian Hill. Tourists were snapping pictures as a guide told them, "This was an artists' neighborhood. Painters and writers lived around here until it became too expensive. Now only rich folks live here, while gardeners tend the flowers."

"It's so beautiful," said someone standing behind him.

Levi picked a flower and began to tear off the petals. One by one he dropped them as he slowly walked down the steps.

And he could feel it. He could feel the closeness. She's here someplace, he thought. Close. Asia and her goddamn cards and letters and phony words of, "Gee, I'd like you to stop in and visit me sometime."

Why did she do it? Why did she take his father away? She didn't care that Judd left his family. Left Levi. All she cared about was his money and his time and taking him away. Away, so she could have him to herself. Well, look how long that lasted. He got buried before she could even marry him. Serves her right. God's punishment. She may have taken him away for a few weeks, but God got him forever. Now that was good for at least one fuck you.

The homes on Lombard Street were striking, but one was especially well-dressed with green vines of purple bougainvillea draping its windows and curling up to the veranda and onto the roof. Levi studied the house for a moment. A white-doored garage was at the bottom of its three stories. The outside facade was a light blue, with dark gray trim boards crossing at different angles leading to the designer-iron railing protecting the deck on top.

So this is what his father died for. Here's where he wanted to be instead of Colorado Springs. Levi grabbed more flowers from the gardens blooming in the middle of the street. He raised a fistful of blossoms into the air. A bouquet of pink and white and purple.

"Get your ass out here, Asia!" he yelled. "You've wanted to see me all these years, well, here's your chance! Here's your big opportunity, bitch."

* * * * *

Levi hurried away from Lombard Street and headed to the wharf. His thoughts felt like an inflamed pile of embers – burning an old life into smoldering ash.

Block out the past, he'd told himself. Everybody in this town wears a different costume or a mask, so why not join in? Join the fun, Levi. Jump right in. It's time for the new and improved Levi to reach out and grab life by the jugular.

You've got the courage, don't you?, he asked himself. If you can't crank it out of your gut on your own, at least you've got cash. Money buys booze, and if you need a pill or a line or a puff, who gives a damn? If they put you into any new lifestyle, it's a better place than where you've been. Fact is, boy, it's time you grew up.

Levi was in Chico's Seafood Grill & Bar, eating a plate of fish and chips, when the man sitting next to him reached out.

"My name's Detroit Willy, son, and I'm the only real bohemian hippie left in this town. Everybody else is fakin' it."

There was no doubt about it. Detroit Willy looked, acted, and smelled like a hippie. Long hair, dirty hat, an earring on one lobe, and crusty, tanned skin that made his fiftyish face look like a cowboy who'd gone too long without a hat in the Mohave. One look, and Levi knew Willy had been around. One look, and Levi also knew that wherever Willy went, Willy made friends. This guy was outright hospitable.

"I'm Levi Saranno." He smiled, shaking Willy's calloused hand. "I just got to town, and I'm looking for a place to live. Got any ideas?"

"I'd say try the Upper Haight. You want some excitement, Haight-Ashbury's borderline, but it'll get you a good start."

"Is it clean?"

"You don't have to deal with garbage on the street, Levi. You have to deal with the garbage around you."

"How do I get there?" Levi asked.

"Get in my cab, and I'll drive you," Willy answered.

* * * * *

By day, Detroit Willy was a cab driver and tour guide. By night, he was a guitar-picking, party-going drug dealer. His drug of choice, both as merchandise and for personal use, was cocaine

"Why not heroin?" Levi asked as he sat next to Willy and sniffed a line of cocaine through a rolled up fifty-dollar bill.

"If you do heroin, Levi, you can plan on going out of your goddamn mind, cause you'll never get off the stuff. Shooting that shit in your veins is like putting a gun to your head."

"Sounds good to me," Levi said after the line of coke was snorted. He reached for the bong filled with marijuana and inhaled as deep as he could. Then he coughed. Strobe lights flashed, candles flickered, Pearl Jam thundered. Levi floated among the psychedelic glow-posters he'd tacked to the walls of the nicely furnished apartment he'd rented on the afternoon Detroit Willy took him to Upper Haight.

Twelve days in San Francisco was all it took. Levi's transformation, helped by Willy and his girlfriend, was almost complete. His beard grew, his curls got cut and colored. The sides of his temples were shaved above the ears, and the fuzz on top of his head looked more like a skunk tail, black, with a white streak down the middle. Even Erica wouldn't recognize him now. He wore sterling silver bracelets, six fingers sported rings, and a necklace matched the dangling earrings that hung from three separate piercings of each ear lobe. Faded, dyed, used denims were only eighty dollars a pair. Baggy blue jeans, or tight denims with holes in the knees, weren't bad looking with the black, thick belt made of cable wire.

Levi thought the skinny sunglasses he wore day and night made him look cool. For one long moment, he wondered what his mother would think of his new look. And if Dad were alive? God, what would he make of this? But if Dad were alive…

It didn't matter. Dad was dead. *This* is who he was. Right now, Levi was in San Francisco, and he didn't give a flying fuck what anybody thought. The extended family of Detroit Willy, his girlfriend Virginia, and all their friends, welcomed Levi. Communal living in the new millennium, sixties style. They didn't live in the same house, but they seemed to live *together*. The artists and musicians had caravaned from Michigan, rented apartments in the same neighborhood, and hung out in the same places. Their children were Levi's age, and all seemed locked in a time warp. Carefree, loose, and loud. Levi fit right in, with a pint of tequila in his pocket and his wallet filled with cash. A constant party surrounded him, and Levi wanted to wallow with abandon in all of it.

"Who's coming over tonight?" Levi asked.

Willy's nose was running from the cocaine, and his eyes were bloodshot. "Virginia's bringing a few friends and a housewarming present. Jesus, I've never seen someone move so fast. In less than two weeks, you go from a Colorado cowboy to a frickin hippie, except for the money. I'm curious, Levi. How much money you got anyway?"

"Enough to buy all the dope we need."

Willy's fingers pulled at the beard around his chin. "Okay, your daddy's rich, and your mama's good-looking."

Levi winced but Willy didn't see it. "But you keep doin' dope and drinkin' like you been, and you gonna find your ass in a jail so dark, there ain't enough money in Fort Knox to bail you out. If last night's any indication, keep this up, and you're gonna get yourself killed."

Willy stared at the boy that was young enough to be his son. "You don't remember what happened last night, do you?"

"Not all of it," Levi answered, not sheepishly enough to satisfy Willy. Levi was making a Tequila slammer for an early morning hit.

"Then tell me what you remember," Willy scolded. "I'm on stage singing, you're in the audience, and all of a sudden, people are brawling and a bar stool flies through the air."

Levi's mind went back to the night before. Nothing had prepared him for combating the combination of pot, coke, and booze and all those people crammed into the place, pushing and shoving and trying to dance and talk.

"All I did was cop a feel from some chick's tit that was bouncing in front of my face. Bobbing up and down, and all I wanted was to see what it felt like."

She had been smiling, jiggling, gyrating like she was about to have an orgasm. Short skirt, skimpy and pulsating. She was a real live vibrator. Her hand had touched his crotch as she twirled to the music. Maybe it was an accident. Maybe not. But it was enough to get his blood hot. The only obstacle to whatever bliss Levi and the girl might have enjoyed was a short, yuppie type who took serious offense at Levi's hand on his girlfriend's nipple, challenging Levi to fight. What a prick. Levi vaguely remembered the anger welling up.

"So I bashed some guy. He was a punk."

"You hit him in the eye with a fucking shot glass." Detroit Willy had a small, rolled-up newspaper in his hand and he smacked Levi in the chest with it. "Says he was near blinded, right here in the fuckin' paper. You tore the top off some chick, and started pandemonium. And while I'm on stage."

"If I hurt some Napoleon's eye, I'm sorry. I don't remember why I got so pissed."

If Virginia hadn't pushed him under the stage and led him out the back door, Levi didn't know where he would have ended up. And he didn't remember much. Virginia filled in the blanks as they drank coffee together for three hours at an all-night Denny's. Levi admitted feeling cramped between the bodies and smoke and sweat. He remembered the pills and smoking a joint or two before Willy's ten o'clock set was beginning. Of course, he always had his tequila, so he must have drunk most of that. Then there were all those shoulders and long arms and legs and breasts that were calling to him, nudging him, urging and teasing and begging him to touch.

Detroit Willy looked at Levi with compassion as he put an arm around his shoulder. "I think you blacked out, boy. I been doin' dope forty years, and seen it all. Some of us handle it, some can't." He patted Levi on the back. "The question is, you prepared to handle the consequences if you can't handle the lifestyle?"

White Knuckle

"I can handle it, Willy." Levi was preparing another slammer.

"Ain't real certain 'bout that."

"With what I've been through, I can handle anything," Levi answered. Levi flaunted his arrogance and when the shot glass banged the table, he downed a drink.

* * * * *

New friends filled Levi's living room; a dozen adults looking to get loaded before they went dancing until the bars closed. For most, the priority was a party. Virginia's closest girlfriends, Ginger and Marsha, had other preferences. A party was fine, but the urgency for them was to find a friend to lie down with. *That* was their priority, and Ginger and Marsha didn't like not having their way.

"I wanna do a satanic thing," Marsha declared, her tongue licking the black lipstick on her mouth.

"What would you like to do?" Ginger asked. "Sacrifice a virgin, or carve a pentagram on some poor bastard's back?"

Marsha looked grim. "Can't find virgins anymore," she frowned. "and pentagrams are permanent. Let's get needles and stick'm on Bush's face. His picture's in the paper with him spouting off some shit about no gay rights, and drug dealers ought to go to prison for life." Marsha looked through her purse. "Find me a needle, so I can stick it up his hypocritical ass."

"He at least admitted to inhaling," Ginger said sarcastically, "and besides, needles are voodoo. I'm not into Satan, but if you find me a virgin over seventeen, I won't carve him with pentagrams, but I might fuck'm to death."

"Last virgin I had was in high school." Marsha sighed. A smile curled on her blackened lips. "He shook getting it up for the first time. After that, I didn't think his weenie would ever go to sleep."

"Boys are like that," Virginia said, as she gulped a glass of wine. "Once they figure out their prick is made for something other than pissing, they'll follow it around like a horse with a noose on its nose."

"Find me a virgin, and I'll take the fear of fucking out of him," Ginger bragged, pushing her hands under her breasts as if to make them larger than they already were.

A shiver went up Levi's spine as he watched and listened, anonymously.

"If you find a guy that's never been laid," Virginia popped in, "would you at least teach him how to do it right?" She pointed to Detroit Willy. "It took me thirty goddamn years to finally get laid properly. That's a lot of hand-holding."

Marsha's black eyebrows perked up. "That's why doing women makes for a good change now and then. Teaching guys how to touch you is work. They don't know what to do naturally, you got to show 'em. They don't have the same spots we women do."

"Doin' men's better." Ginger laughed. "If I got stoned bad enough, I'd probably do you, Marsha, but that's the virgin thing. Only I'd be the virgin in that one."

Marsha winked and quickly blew Ginger a kiss. "Don't matter if the virgin's a boy or a girl," she cooed. "One or the other, and I'll teach 'em exactly what to do and how to do it. It's a bloody cinch if you're in the right frame of mind. Here, have a line. Get with it, sister."

Marsha handed Ginger a hundred-dollar bill, rolled up like a straw. "Snort this," she said, handing her a face mirror with lines of cocaine already drawn. "If you get enough snuff up your nose, Ginger, you'll be tongue

White Knuckle

twisting til morning. The night will pass, virginity's history, and you'll think you're in the afterlife."

Levi moved closer, to listen without being too obvious.

Marsha looked like a thirty-year-old witch, Levi thought. Ginger looked ragged for someone leaning on twenty-seven. But the music and the cocaine and the booze were making Levi more confident. Marsha and Ginger seemed exciting, sexy, experts in their field, a field Levi wanted to plow.

The evening started to crackle, the witch in Marsha sparkled. For Levi. Marsha looked like she really did poke people with needles, and her black dress and black nails and lipstick made Levi think that she'd arrived on a broom. Riding a broomstick, like a rocking horse, riding with the stick stuck tight between her legs. Then again, Levi might have been hallucinating. On pot and hash and coke and on the new life he was fantasizing. Hallucinating on what did she call it? The afterlife.

What was under her black dress? If she had black hair, did she have black breasts? Levi burst out laughing, the marijuana was taking its full effect.

Levi found himself standing beside the two women. "White face, white legs, and white hips," he said as he giggled to Marsha. "But on top I see black hair, and on the bottom, there's toenails that look like soot."

He was laughing hysterically, but Levi's tripping out wasn't unusual. It was expected, and no one paid attention.

"Marsha," he said, "I bet you look like a goddamn checkerboard!"

Levi rolled on the floor, clutching his sides.

The witch and Ginger paid no attention to him. Marsha flicked her black nails under Ginger's chin, and Ginger swayed to the sensual sounds of the music.

"I need a man," Ginger said.

"Why not a woman?" Marsha asked softly as her fingers stroked Ginger's chin and neck and ears and went subtly across the top of her breasts.

"Why not?" Ginger answered, pulling Marsha's body to hers. They embraced and their lips touched, their eyes closed.

Levi thought it was the sexiest thing he'd ever seen. He stood right beside them, watching as they held onto each other with hands moving along their sides and hips and behind their backs and down.

Marsha and Ginger were so wrapped up in each other, neither of them heard Levi's hoarse whisper, "I want in."

Gently, he pulled the two women apart, putting one hand on each of their shoulders. Their faces flushed, and both of them were surprised to find him standing there.

Ginger and Marsha stared at Levi, wondering what he meant.

"Were you really serious about sacrifices and virgins?" The tone in his voice was cautious, but sincere. "I mean, really?"

Curious glances bounced from Marsha to Ginger to Levi. The two women still had their arms intertwined.

Marsha looked at Levi, but spoke to Ginger. "Well, well, well, what do we have here, girl?"

"I'm sayin' I'm fresh, and I want in." His shoulders lifted and fell.

Ginger grinned. "You lying? A handsome buck like you, saying you never done it before? I don't believe it."

"True," he said. An innocent twist curled on Levi's lips.

Ginger looked at Marsha, smiling. "If this boy's real, for me, the challenge would be extraordinary."

Levi knew the stares of both women were actually questions. Their look said it all. As they held each other, Ginger and Marsha stared at Levi, waiting for an answer.

Levi's voice was quiet, almost inaudible. "If you're serious, I…I'm ready for the sacrifice," Levi stammered. He took a deep breath. "Nobody knows it but…I am a virgin. I've never done it with anyone."

Both women took a better look. They studied Levi standing beside them, shivering.

"No way," Marsha blurted.

"Honest," Levi answered.

"Are you really telling the truth?" Marsha asked. It was more of a warning. But she could see it in his eyes. She could hear the truth in his voice.

Ginger's hand went to Levi's thigh. "Swear it," she demanded.

"I swear. I swear to God, I…I'm a virgin."

Ginger smiled at Marsha who nodded almost imperceptibly. The two women were hot and curious and ready to take on Levi and each other.

"I think," Marsha said softly, "that it's time we moseyed elsewhere." She took one of Levi's hands and Ginger took the other.

Levi looked like a toddler being led down the hallway as the three of them headed for the bedroom door.

*   *   *   *   *

Levi stood, watching the two women taking off their clothes.

Marsha *was* a black and white checkerboard. Black hair, white forehead. Black eyes, white neck. Small, firm, popping breasts. White, with nipples so dark, black looked beautiful. White waist, and then a black spot between her legs pointing to a tunnel of blackness that would lead him to the light. Long, white thighs and legs and toenails painted black. A checkerboard for sure.

Ginger's body was bigger, everywhere. Long red hair and brown eyes above mountainous breasts that wobbled as she wriggled out of her jeans. Her breasts promised wonders to Levi as she bent toward the floor, hastily pulling the legs of her pants over her ankles. Kiss me, caress me, see if your hands can cover all my terrain, they said.

Together, Ginger and Marsha unbuttoned Levi's shirt and unzipped his trousers.

"You're the most beautiful women I've ever seen," he said. And his eyes closed as he took in their touch. Ginger's fingers caressing his back and shoulders and chest while lips tongued his neck and ears and the small of his collarbone. They took off his shirt and his pants fell to the floor. A mouth and lips and tongue went down on the pyramid between his legs. His hands blindly reached for the mountains on Ginger's chest.

Marsha slowly rose up, licking Levi's belly and chest and shoulders as she stood. Her black lips moved. "If you two don't mind, I think I'm going to be in charge of this *ménage à trois*," she said as she went to the bed and laid down on her back.

White Knuckle

"Ginger, come lay beside me, on your stomach." Ginger grinned and obeyed.

"You swear you've never been with a woman, Levi?" Marsha challenged.

"I swear to God, never."

"Leave God out of this," Marsha ordered. She smiled. "That being the case, you can have control the first time. After that, me and Ginger take control. We're going to teach you everything you'll need to know, and we're going to have a damn good time doing it."

"What do you mean I can have control?" Levi asked innocently.

"It means that the first time, you can have it any way you want it." She spread her knees apart, as she rubbed the tip of her clitoris. "You can fuck me, Ginger's ass, and we'll both blow you first. Your choice, what do you want?"

Levi moved to the bed, and as he crawled between her legs, his lips and hands and chest touched the little, black nipples that poked their eyes toward the ceiling.

Her hand went to his penis, and she positioned the head of it just inside the tip of her vagina.

"Don't move," Marsha said, stabbing her black nails into Levi's buttocks. She paused, looked confidently into his eyes. The wetness grew as her pelvis pushed upward and her black nails clawed him down, down and deep and in and thrusting. Pelvis up, and Levi had his ticket to ringside, twirling in a three-ring circle of lust.

Levi felt the juice. He felt Ginger kissing his back, her fingers gently massaging his scrotum while Marsha's black nails dug at his arms and neck. The groans and moans turned into cries.

He climaxed inside Marsha's body underneath the black, curly, matted hair, deep inside and down. With just one bite of a sensuous pie, Levi was hooked on the gastronomic taste of his first piece of ass.

Marsha's legs were still hooked around Levi's hips; he felt her soft skin next to his. Ginger's mouth was grazing on his shoulder blades, whispering sighs on the back of his neck and into his ears.

As the fervency ebbed, so did Levi's fear. He wasn't an impotent coward or a snivelling little boy anymore. He gently moved off Marsha as his fingertips fondled Ginger's rolling breasts. Big and soft and dough-like as he squeezed and rubbed.

His erection never faded. Levi felt a sprinkling of titillating pleasure building again, and without asking or caring or thinking, he spread Ginger's legs and pushed into her softness with a desperate urgency.

His body buzzed as pins and needles pricked his entire being. Large and growing, gushing out juices that filled the hollows nestled between Ginger's thighs, his orgasm caused her to bubble and soon to burst as she cried out, "Levi, Levi!"

Marsha laughed when Levi finally rolled to the middle of the bed. "You might be a stud, Levi, but you've got lots to learn before this night's over."

He watched as Marsha guided Ginger's mouth in and around the curly black hair surrounded by the white skin below her belly button.

"Just the tip of your tongue, Levi. See how she does it? Quick, little flicks. You don't tongue it to death. Spread the lips, find the little knob, and flick the clitoris till..."

Marsha's breathing was heavy, her eyes closed. Marsha's hand went to the back of Ginger's head. "Now suck it," she commanded. "Now!" Her body arched as her legs curled around Ginger's ears. The clamor of Marsha's climax was deafening.

Watching the two women make love to each other aroused Levi. He was ready for more instruction.

Marsha smiled at her willing student. "Okay, Levi, let's talk about foreplay. Things to do before sex. It's called imagination; it's called erotic; it's called any number of other things. Just remember to do whatever your creative spirit leads you to do."

Levi nodded, and the three started to make love again. Twice during the night they took showers together.

"Remember," Marsha said, "the biggest turnoff is bad hygiene."

"It's worse than a small dick," Ginger added.

"What's the biggest turn on?" Levi asked as they dried each other off for the second time.

"Foreplay," Ginger answered.

"Intimacy," Marsha countered.

"I'll work on them both," Levi said.

"Work on them with us, Levi."

"Anytime, anyplace," were Marsha's parting words as she and Ginger left his apartment and walked out into the morning light.

"Thanks," Levi said. And he meant it.

"Thank *you*, Levi." Ginger winked. "You were my first virgin."

22

Judd's little Levi was gone. Kit's little Matty was lost. Erica's wonder boy was nowhere to be found.

Discovering that the little soldier inside his pants could pecker up on command was a profound revelation for a young man whose loved ones in Colorado Springs would never recognize. Now, Levi was constantly on the prowl.

"Willy, three nights ago, with Ginger and Marsha, that was the greatest night of my life."

"I told you, Levi, the family takes care of its own. You been accepted and they like you. Marsha and Ginger think you're pretty hot, but..."

"Spit it out, Willy." Levi didn't care if some pissy little thing was wrong. He'd heard enough criticism in Colorado.

"Don't overdo it, Levi. You're like a kid in a candy store."

"And I love candy, Willy. What's wrong with that?" Levi looked at his friend defiantly.

"You're overdoing this new lifestyle, and your attitude sometimes sucks. You don't seem to *really* care about anybody. Sure you're friendly and buy dope and pass it out, but you get loaded, and you change. Virginia says you get a scary look in your eyes. 'Evil-eye' she calls it."

"Virginia doesn't know shit!" Levi shot back. She's a woman, for christ-sakes! Sometimes she's got her head stuck…'"

Levi's evil-eye stare disappeared and was replaced with an astonished gaze as he watched Detroit Willy leap over the coffee table and reach for his throat.

This was no time for Levi to fight back. Too much adrenaline was venting in Willy's veins; his eyes were bulging, and his face flushed crimson. But Willy's voice was calm. Cool. Calculating and articulate. "Don't you never talk 'bout Virginia like that."

"I…I didn't mean to make…get you angry. I was expressing an opin…"

"No one disrespects Virginia." Willy said it like a drill sergeant. He strengthened his grip, pulling Levi's face closer to his own. "She's my best friend. You think women ain't to be respected?"

"I'm sorry, Willy. I'm truly sorry. I didn't mean any disrespect. Virginia's the best, Willy. I…I'm not thinking. Sometimes I'm stupid, and I wouldn't do anything to upset you or make Virginia think I don't respect her. You're really lucky." Levi's voice was meek, apologetic.

Willy's grasp loosened and then let go. Levi extended his hand.

After a moment's hesitation, Willy shook it.

"Don't do it again, Levi."

"No, I won't." Levi paused. "Do what?"

"Make Virginia mad. Don't make her nervous."

"I can't remember ever pissing Virginia off."

"It wasn't nothing direct. She just watches people and she says you runnin' too fast, chasin' too hard."

246

Levi's eyes rolled. "I'm running fast, but not fast enough."

"Maybe I'm not makin' myself clear, Levi." Willy lit his pipe and puffed. "You got to be nice to people. You can't drink and dope so much your personality changes and you lose control."

"I don't ever lose control," Levi boasted.

"Just remember that women are people, Levi. They ain't objects."

"I know, and I respect that," Levi lied.

"I'm warning you, slow down, cowboy." Willy said, as he pulled on his jacket.

"I can't. Marsha says she's got a movie and some toys for me to try." Levi walked Willy to the door. Willy shook his head.

"The girls ain't going nowhere. They'll always be here. Rest your jets."

His words fell on deaf ears.

*   *   *   *   *

"I've been here ten days," Sampson said, "and I'm not cruising for any more hookers with you."

Sampson was frying eggs and bacon in Levi's kitchen. He moved deftly from the refrigerator to the stove and to the toaster oven, where he flipped in two English muffins. "Detroit Willy's a gas." Sampson shot a disgusted look at Levi. "But if you don't stop the Jekyll-and-Hyde crap, he and his friends will diss you off and you'll be dust."

"They love me," Levi said defensively, and then grinned, "And they love me every chance they get."

"I can't believe you, Levi. You're a different person. The Tenderloin, Capp Street, the Saigon Palace Massage and Spa. If the low lifes you're chasing here don't kill you, AIDS will."

"You can't get AIDS from a blow job, Sampson, and most of the time, I'm careful."

"Goodyear doesn't make enough rubber to protect your penis."

Sampson was frustrated and angry. When he first arrived and saw his friend's "new look," he'd been concerned. The concern soon turned to disgust. He was still worried, but more out of loyalty for an old friend who was now nowhere to be found.

"I think you're an addict, Levi. If you're not one now, you will be soon."

"Addicted to what?" Levi asked, pouring a shot of tequila and taking a quick chug before sucking on a lemon. "So what if I smoke a little weed or take a line now and then?"

"Constantly!" Sampson snapped back. "It's eight in the bloody morning, and you're sucking lemons with tequila slammers for breakfast."

Levi grinned. "I'm gonna eat that bacon and egg stuff you're cookin'. Good thing you're here, pal."

"Are you still clueless, Levi? Look at this place, and you're having blackouts, my friend."

Empty bottles, dirty glasses, and smelly ashtrays filled with cigarettes and burned tobacco littered the apartment. The place hadn't been cleaned since Levi moved in.

"Last night you were a real prize, weren't you?"

White Knuckle

"I'm a prize wherever I go, Sampson."

"Yeah? Tell that to Ginger, if she ever speaks to you again." Sampson dished out the bacon and eggs and put butter on the muffins.

"Ginger?" Levi brushed the top of his head with dirty fingers holding onto a cigarette. An ash fell in his hair. He didn't notice. He sat down at the kitchen table and stared at the plate of food for a moment before putting a piece of bacon in his mouth.

"You know, Ginger?" Sampson continued. "The little Italian you've been banging in between every slut you find on the street." Sampson sat down across from Levi and attacked his breakfast.

Levi didn't answer. He stopped eating.

"You don't remember, do you?"

"Of course I remember." Levi took a swig of the coffee Sampson had poured into his mug.

"Then why did she leave here crying?"

Levi tried to think. "Because she found out I boinked Marsha again, I think."

"She left because you told her you wanted to watch me and her go at it, you idiot! She was trashed while you bobbed your head, laughing, and referred to her ass as a barn door just before you passed out cold."

"I was tired."

"You weren't tired, Levi. You were disgusting."

"I remember now. It was just a joke."

Sampson knew he didn't remember. And he knew his friend was lying. Lying like he always did in Colorado, except then he had reserved most of his lies for Erica. Now he'd lie to anybody, including Sampson.

It's no wonder Erica dumped him. Levi said it was her fault. Lie. Levi said he treated her like a candy cane at Christmas. Lie. He said he wore condoms and wasn't addicted to sex, drugs, and alcohol. All lies. And it seemed to have happened overnight. In less than a month, Levi acted more like a stalker than an excited kid hot on dating chicks and playing with the new toy he'd discovered between his legs.

"I think it's time you looked at yourself in the mirror, Levi." Disdain filled Sampson's voice. "You're sick, and you better figure out where it's coming from. Erica was a saint, compared to the sluts you're doing. And you'd rather do them than her. Don't make sense to me. Ever ask yourself why?"

"Erica's not any better than..." He stopped for a second to stare at his friend. "I don't care!"

Sampson hadn't moved. "Look at you, Levi," he said quietly. "You're outta control. Is this what Erica saw the day before you slithered out of town? You better figure out what's making you nuts."

"You're the one who's fucking crazy, Sampson."

"I'm not yelling and blacking out and beating up women, Levi. You are!" Sampson threw down his fork and jumped up from the table. "You're not just a liar, Levi. You're predatory. Predators don't make for good friends. Look in the mirror, Levi. See what a predator looks like."

Sampson hurried out of the kitchen and slammed the front door as he left the apartment.

23

After four months in San Francisco, Levi's extended family whittled itself down to just Marsha. Ginger, Willy and his wife, and the others had grown tired of Levi, the sugar daddy of Upper Haight. His money didn't matter. They unceremoniously dumped him. After Sampson returned to Colorado, he never called. Everyone deserted Levi, except Marsha.

"Did Willy ever tell about the doughnut hole in Detroit?" Marsha asked Levi as their taxi stopped on the corner of Sanchez and Market.

"Yeah, Willy told me about the doughnut hole," Levi said as they exited the cab.

He stared at a sign that read *Image Leather*. Beneath the sign was the window display. Manacles and shackles and whips and belts dressed mannequins smiling out to the customers on the sidewalk.

"Well," Marsha said with a broad smile, "welcome to the doughnut hole of San Francisco. If you're gay, and in the center of this hole, it's another universe. The world is outside, and you're in gay heaven. You're in the doughnut hole."

The Castro district was another world, a place where Levi had never been, a lifestyle he had never experienced.

Rainbow flags hung from every lamppost. The people in this doughnut hole had their own flag, their own marching band, and their own choir. A community of codes and colors. Total acceptance. Complete commitment to a living, breathing, lifestyle of proud independence. No one here was hiding in a closet. This closet was an open door – sometimes a circus, sometimes a zoo – all of it gay. Men and women and everyone in between.

"First," Marsha declared, "we're gonna buy some toys. Then, because it's Sunday, we're going to Moby Dick's."

Levi reached for her hand as they entered Image Leather.

"Don't!" she ordered. "We don't act like lovers here. Here, you act like a shtuper or a shtupee. Me? I act sassy, femme or butch."

"I'm supposed to act like what?" he asked.

"Jesus, Levi." Marsha put her cupped palm around her mouth. "You dolt! 'Shtuper,' the one who takes the top. 'Shtupee,' he's the bottom."

Levi paid little attention to Marsha. There was too much to see, and all of it leather. Leather restraints, fleece-lined for wrists and ankles and thighs. Harnesses and straps for necks and backs. Pigskin bikinis, and jocks, and side-zip shorts. Blindfolds and paddles. Thongwhips, and braided leather whips called Cat-O-Nine-Tails. Binders and spiked locking collars. What, he thought, in God's name is a cock and ball harness, a ring-a-dong, and who in his goddamn right mind needs a ball maul? Marsha picked up something called a Latigo ball stretcher, and that's when Levi recalled other ropes and locks. Levi thought about the exit as he turned toward the door.

"Wait, Levi," Marsha whispered, holding onto a T-Clamp 115A French Harness. "You've been using tweezers and fingernails on mine. I think this nipple clamp would work better, don't you?"

"I can't believe all this stuff," Levi said under his breath. "I'm not sure I'm ready for this."

252

White Knuckle

Marsha grabbed his arm. "You aren't going out, Levi. You're going down. We're headed for the dungeon," she said as she pulled him to the back of the store, taking the lead as she walked down narrow steps into a basement. Levi cautiously followed. Halfway through their descent, he saw a mannequin chained and bound and harnessed, absolutely powerless to do anything but his captor's command. The chains were silver, the harnesses black. Nothing was colored blue, and there were no ropes – just leather and metal.

Levi's alarm went off for the first time in months. He wanted to close his eyes. But if he closed his eyes, he knew that old images would crawl from their recessed corners. But you promised yourself you'd take risks, his mind scolded. You've got courage. Keep your eyes open. Stay awake and live and learn. Stay awake and stay alive like you've been alive for months. You aren't gonna die again. You're not going to wimp out any longer. Don't have another blackout. Keep remembering. Levi reached into his back pocket and took out the flask. In four large gulps, he emptied the tequila down his throat.

Marsha's eyes were wide as she surveyed the dungeon. Huge dildos were encased along the wall. There were chains and manacles, probes and plugs, some with batteries and some with ridges. All on sale, along with lubricating bottles of *Wet*.

The dungeon was dark, and Marsha reached for the zipper on the front of Levi's pants. "Doesn't this get you excited?" she asked. "See if there's a lock on the door. I'll do you for a bit, while you look at those toys, and think about which one you want."

Levi pushed her hand away. "I don't think I want any right now. But maybe someday."

Marsha backed away, a disappointed look on her face. She rebounded with a smile. "We could at least get those nipple things, and maybe the fleece leather cuffs, can't we?"

Levi clamped down on the camouflaged crawlers seeping out from the corners of his brain. Stomp them back in, push them into the darkness, and close the door.

Levi smiled back. "Sure," he answered. "Let's get the nipple-clamps and cuffs. In fact," the tone in his voice was suddenly enthusiastic, "let's get a whip or two, especially the Cat-O-Nine-Tails." He gave Marsha his most lascivious grin, and she laughed like a schoolgirl.

"I like having you all to myself, Levi. Without Ginger. You never knew who else she was doing."

"Yeah, just you and me, honey."

"It is just me, isn't it, Levi?"

"Of course," Levi lied. "After Ginger, it's always only been you."

"I'll let you in on a little secret. I've never been so monogamous before," Marsha giggled.

"Neither have I," Levi told her, returning her giggle with a small grin of his own.

* * * * *

When they left Image Leather, confusion ricocheted inside Levi's head as his consciousness tried to rearrange the realities of the lifestyle he *really* wanted with the one he was living. For the first time in four months, Levi thought he might be doing something wrong. But he was powerless, not knowing how to change it, how to stop. Beads of fear crept down his spine from his skull to his legs, even into his feet.

White Knuckle

As he and Marsha strolled to 18th and Castro, Levi tried to unscramble the conundrum in his brain, while the checkerboard witch at his side tried to conjure up the type of twisting they would do when the tweezers were replaced with the toys from Image Leather.

Marsha could sense that something was wrong. Levi seemed detached and withdrawn as they neared Moby Dick's. At the entrance, Marsha turned to Levi. "When we go in here, act macho. See if we can't get invited to their Sunday outing on the nudist beach where they go. They organize, and then go on Sundays.

"Too bad it's not on Saturdays," Levi said, sarcastically. "Think of all the priests who're missing out. They do it on weekends, don't they? Or does banging little altar boys interfere with confession?"

Marsha stopped. Her eyes were blacker than ever. "Why are you so cynical all of a sudden?"

"Because, all of a sudden, I'm thinking maybe I don't want this rope-and-bondage crap. All these guys, doing each other."

"I only want to do what makes you happy, Levi," Marsha said softly.

"You can't! You're not Erica." He spoke the name under his breath, but it shot into the air like a cannonball.

The sound of her name surprised even him. Just saying it made his mouth dry, his stomach tight, his heart sting. "I, I'm sorry, Marsha. I don't know where that came from."

"Who the hell is Erica?" Marsha asked.

Levi looked at his human checkerboard, standing in the center of San Francisco's doughnut hole with its rainbow flags and Velcro cuffs, leather shackles and shiny chains.

255

Levi's head twisted and turned; his gaze darted everywhere, searching for that familiar face, the nicotine-stained teeth, the bloated belly of fat, tubbing its way down the street. Approaching. Would there be a terrible scar on his forehead? Would he get close enough to string a harness around his swollen, stinking neck until he choked to fucking death?

"My God, Levi, I've never seen you look this way," Marsha said nervously. You're scaring the shit out of me."

Levi's search through the crowd ended as abruptly as it had begun. Master Bates wasn't out there, but he was in one of the many coffins, ready to push up the lid and crawl out when Levi wasn't prepared.

Levi came back to reality. He stared at Marsha.

"Who's Erica?" she asked again, annoyed.

"Nobody! She's nobody," Levi retorted.

"Levi," Marsha complained. "All I know is one minute we're going to kink around in erotica and the next minute you're acting like a shiatsu massage would be too weird."

"Detroit Willy said there's a line you can't cross, and there's a time to slow down," Levi answered. The look on his face was tired and worn.

"What about our toys, Levi?" Marsha whined.

"Save the toys for Friday. We'll do the toys and a few other things. There's a place to dance in Sausalito that should be safe for me to go back to."

"Anything more you want to see in The Castro?" she asked.

Levi shook his head. He didn't want to be with his checkerboard whore one more minute.

White Knuckle

Marsha stared up at him as Levi hailed a taxi. When he dropped her off, she asked, "Levi, is this the beginning of the end?"

"The beginning of the end of what?" He sounded irritated.

"Of us."

"Stop making a big deal out of this. Give me five days alone, and I'll see you Friday. And you can bring over all the goodies we bought. Don't forget the Cat-O-Nines."

"I don't care about that right now. Now, all I want is us."

"Me too," Levi said.

Marsha knew he was lying.

* * * * *

It took all of five days for Levi to whiteout what he needed. He did it with blackouts. Blackouts he used as whiteouts. Whiteouts Erica described to him the day they first met in the Alferd Packer cafeteria. He camouflaged the bloodbath of feelings with alcohol, a fifth a day; cocaine, one gram in the morning, two in the afternoon. Pot, all night long; tequila slammers for nightcaps, and finally sleep. Asleep in a blackout that held no memories. A blackout where nothing could be seen or felt or remembered. And then he'd wake up. Wake up, so he could start all over again. He did it for five days, five nights. He did it alone, and finally, he was happy with himself again. Finally, he was back to the man Marsha wanted.

On Friday, Marsha knocked on the door to Levi's apartment. When he didn't answer, she turned the doorknob and walked into the living room. He was asleep on the couch, looking like a transient who'd passed out in an alley next to a dumpster. He clutched an empty bottle of Jose Cuervo Especial like it was a teddy bear.

"A housekeeper you're not," Marsha said, as she surveyed the rubble of Levi's apartment. Dirty dishes, empty food containers, overflowing ashtrays. Not a surface had been dusted or cleaned, not a floor swept in weeks. Marsha noticed that cockroaches were taking up residence in Levi's kitchen. Can mice be far behind? she wondered.

The one surface that had some sense of order was the coffee table. There, Levi's drugs were carefully organized. A bong and two lids of pot were neatly tucked together on one side, while a family of cocaine paraphernalia huddled together on the other. A mirror, a razor blade, a little spoon, and a rolled hundred dollar bill circled around several ounces of white powder. Little acid drops were meticulously resting on a piece of clean, white paper. In the center of the table, a full bottle of Cuervo stood guard over it all. Marsha studied the sleeping Levi. She couldn't tell if he was merely sleeping or if a drunken coma stood in the way of getting him up and off to Sausalito. His beard was scraggly and dark hair lined each side of his head, with a white streak down the center. The skunk head on his streak stood straight up and looked like it was preparing to attack. Marsha bent over and shook Levi, then kissed him on his closed eyelids and his slightly open mouth.

Levi opened his eyes. "What time is it?" he asked, reaching for the Cuervo.

"Nine o'clock. Why don't you take a shower? It'll take us a half hour to get there."

"Plenty of time. Cut four lines, and let's go in the bedroom. Damn near been a week," he said, talking a swallow from the bottle.

Marsha could hear the slur in his words. "Obviously," she observed, "this isn't your first drink today."

The bored look on Levi's face told her he didn't care. Drunk again, she figured, but a little coke would clear the clouds, and if she could keep him away from the booze for a couple of hours, he'd sober up, they could dance, and then they'd rumble with the trinkets from Castro. But for that, Marsha wanted him sober. She didn't want a drunken Levi glaring at her bare bottom while holding a Cat-O-Nines firmly in his fist.

Marsha reached for Levi's arm, and he responded. This stage of intoxication made him compliant. A good sign. She led him to the shower, turned on the water and Levi stumbled in, apparently unaware that his underwear was getting wet.

Leaving him there to soak, Marsha went back and started chopping lines, double-barreled toots that would get them off, before they got off to Sausalito.

"I need another drink," she heard him say. Marsha turned and saw Levi leaning against the doorjam, fully dressed. His earrings were dangling, his hair was moussed, metal was around his neck, and he was drunk.

"Take a line," she said, approaching him with a mirror and the rolled up hundred-dollar bill. "Leave the bottle and dope here. We'll snort some now, and when we come back, the booze and pot will be here waiting."

Levi lowered his head and inhaled sharply, twice. The long, thick, white lines of cocaine disappeared up his nostrils. He looked into his lover's clear, black eyes. His own eyes were glossy and red, with lightning streaks bolting from the pupils to the outer edges of his eyelashes.

"We can leave the pot and acid," he said, "but I'm taking at least a gram of coke, and I don't go nowhere without my flask."

Levi pocketed the spoon and poured cocaine into a black leather pouch. He filled his flask with tequila and poured them both a drink. They drank and snorted, and when they left his apartment, they were both blissfully stoned.

Marsha drove past the Presidio and over the Golden Gate Bridge. Turning right into Sausalito, she slowed as they entered the small colony nestled on the other side of the bay. Levi took a swallow from his flask, lowered his nose, sniffed heavily, and smiled at his girlfriend.

The bar was hosting a benefit for the family of a singer who'd recently died, leaving a destitute wife and one daughter. The place was jammed with performers, patrons, musicians, and friends of the deceased. Dancing was at a fever pitch, beer chugged, music screamed and singers wailed. Levi and his checkerboard plunged into the middle of all the madness.

The sounds were so loud and the place so cramped, Levi couldn't distinguish any voices. He and Marsha were dancing to the rhythm and blues, not hearing or caring or thinking about anything or anyone but themselves.

"I'm gonna kill the son-of- a-bitch," was muffled.

"I, I know it's, it's him," a girl stammered.

"Break me a bottle; I'm gonna cut the bastard's face."

"No, wait! Not inside. Do it in the parking lot. Get him there!" was whispered in someone's ear.

"I want him, now!" was hissed into the night.

The thumping of drums continued to vibrate in the dancers' chests. And Levi, through his skinny, silly-looking sunglasses, saw only Marsha's black-eyed breasts, starting to harden. He could see them, as sweat dampened her T-shirt, showing the shape and firmness and the small, pointed nipples that he knew so well. Later, he thought for the first time, I'm going to clamp and pull and whip with blindfolds on and a scarf over her mouth to stop the shrieks of pain and joy.

"He's the guy, I know it!" The man's voice was raspy and accusing. It wasn't a guess. It was an indictment.

"Maybe not," another man said.

"Mack, you go behind him, hold him, and I'll bust his balls like a nut-cracker."

"Let the police bust him."

"Bullshit. He nearly blinded me!"

"Okay, okay, I'll sneak behind him."

"Don't need to sneak. He's bombed."

From out of nowhere, a huge, hairy arm grabbed Levi's throat. A chokehold. Some baboon was suddenly pretending to be a goddamn cop, and Levi was his prey. Another predator had caught him in a deadly grip.

The struggle began. Kicking and hollering and wrestling to get the arm off, to get the strangle out from under Levi's chin.

Had it not been for Marsha, Levi would have ended up unconscious on the dance floor. He should have. Just as he began to weaken, Marsha's teeth bit into the hairy forearm of the attacker and the arm let go. Levi struggled, flinging himself from his assailant's grasp and found himself standing in front of the stage. The throng of dancers scrambled to the sides. A fight was on; the music stopped, the bartender dialed 911, and screams ricocheted around the dance floor. Levi tried to catch his breath, clear his head, and find a place of safety. Where was his Pucker Patch when he needed it?

The aggressors weren't moving. They stood there, assessing their opponent. Levi's eyes focused, and through the smoke and disco lights, he saw himself in front of two men, ready to pounce. Two cocks were after him and he was already a ragged rooster.

The crowd rumbled, waiting for the cocks to kick, snare, and make the final attack on the rooster who was backing away, slowly.

"Hey, Napoleon," Levi slurred, "where've you been?" He wavered back and forth, watching, carefully assessing his two opponents. One looked like a sumo wrestler. The other was a runt, five-foot-two, but strutting as if bigger, because of his buddy. The hatred in Napoleon's eyes was palpable. Levi could see that he wasn't blind after all.

A man and woman held Marsha back as she twisted and turned, kicking and yelling, "Stop! Stop this! Somebody. Somebody do something!" She saw the smaller of the two men grab a long-necked beer bottle from an empty table. He flipped it menacingly from one hand to the other as he slowly closed in on Levi. A cat after a chicken, a wounded little chicken-shit.

Even without his buddy, Napoleon was a danger, crazed with anger and adrenaline, wanting to revenge the thin scar that encircled his nose and traveled up through his eyebrow and disappeared into his forehead.

Levi raised his hands in a Karate stance not knowing the first thing about martial arts. "Back off, asshole," he growled. "I've done nothing to you."

"You damn near blinded me, prick!" Napoleon shouted, crouching, moving closer, waving the bottleneck. "You're a low life coward, a grab-ass little snake. You hit me when I wasn't lookin'. At least you can see me coming."

Levi's back hit the wall when Napoleon smashed the beer bottle on a table, grasping a ragged piece of glass in his hand.

"Police!" someone screamed.

Napoleon vaulted, his arm straight, aiming the barbed bottle right between Levi's eyes. Levi turned sharply, but not sharp enough, not before the craggy glass struck just beneath his chin, lancing his beard and plunging up his cheek toward his temple.

Levi's face burst into a bloody mess, as red liquid gushed from the jagged fissure. Crimson rivulets cascaded down his face and onto his neck and clothes.

* * * * *

The police officers waited patiently for the doctor to come out of surgery. The cops hovered around like weary missionaries, waiting for yet another wayward soul to be captured.

Marsha too, sat outside the operating room while Levi was being stitched and clamped and sutured. A policeman stood in front of her, asking questions.

"Saranno's the kid who almost blinded the short guy four months ago, isn't he?" the officer demanded.

"I don't know," Marsha cried. "I didn't know him four months ago."

"You say he wasn't drinking much and the cocaine must've been planted. So how come his blood-alcohol level is about a .25, and there's so much dope in his veins pathology can't decipher it all?"

Her hair was disheveled, her makeup streaked from crying. She looked sad and pathetic. "Don't know. Honest. They just attacked Levi. He didn't do anything. We were dancing and minding our own business."

"Right, right." the cop said. "Where'd he get the cocaine?"

"It wasn't his, I swear."

"How come he started the fight, Ma'am?"

"He didn't!"

"Look, your friend's in big trouble. Just tell us why he nearly blinded the other guy months ago."

"I don't know." Marsha sank down into the chair looking frightened, tired, and much older than her thirty years.

"If you don't tell us the truth, Ma'am, we're gonna be reading you your rights in another minute."

"Levi didn't start any trouble. *He's* the victim!"

The officers exchanged snickering glances. "He don't look like a victim to me, lady. He looks like a strung-out felon who got what he deserves."

"He was attacked, for christsakes. There're witnesses!"

"Yeah, right. People who say *you* started biting the short guy for no good reason. They said you and your boyfriend started this, and *they* acted in self-defense."

"They're lying!"

"Stand up, Miss," he ordered, and Marsha obeyed. "You're under arrest for aiding and abetting a felony. For public drunkenness and disorderly conduct. Maybe possession, too. You've got the right to remain silent..."

Before the night had started, Marsha expected to be cuffed, but not this way. Definitely not like this.

* * * * *

When Levi woke up in recovery two hours later, he was groggy and nauseated. He had no idea where he was. Confusion reigned in whatever part of his brain was awakening. His beard had been shaved, and his face was swathed in white gauze bandages and compresses and tape. He felt swollen and numb. He couldn't see clearly. He could hardly hear.

Someone was asking questions, telling him to talk.

"Listen, kid, tell us why you nearly blinded that guy last time you saw him."

"Huh?"

"You're a dealer, aren't you? Drug dealing gets you in prison, not just jail."

"I...I don't...understand."

"Mr. Saranno, if you talk to us now, it'll be much easier for you. Talk, and then you can sleep."

Through the fog, Levi could distinguish some of the words, especially the word "sleep," and that's what he felt like doing. The cops shook him, but his eyes closed, and Levi blacked out.

"Shit!" one of the cops exclaimed. "Let's try to wake him up. He's only been cut; his health's not in danger. By tomorrow he'll have faked an alibi."

Once more the officers pushed on his shoulder, but Levi was engulfed in his anesthesia-induced sleep, where there were no dreams and no pain.

At seven in the morning, a nurse entered Levi's room followed by a member of the Sausalito Police Department.

"Mr. Saranno, how are you feeling this morning?" the nurse asked softly, the thumb of her hand, gently stroking his forearm.

Levi's eyes opened.

"Mr. Saranno, I'm Detective Thomas," said the man standing on the other side of Levi's bed. "I need to ask you some questions."

Levi peered warily from behind his bandages. Something told him he needed to be alert, but he felt numb and weak and tired. "Where am I?" he asked. "Did you get the guy who jumped me?"

"The guy you tried to blind?"

"You mean Napoleon?"

"So you have met him before, haven't you? You stabbed him with a glass, right?"

Levi struggled to speak. "I don't know what you're talking about."

"You just admitted you'd met him, Mr. Saranno."

"I don't know what you're…"

"You just admitted it!"

The nurse interrupted. "He didn't say that, officer. He's barely able to understand you."

Thomas ignored the nurse and turned back to Levi. "Now look, kid; we've got you for possession of cocaine with the intent to distribute, felony assault, public drunkenness, and a number of other possible charges. But understand, you've not been charged with anything, yet. You can still get out of a lot, but you've got to talk."

Levi reached out his hand and the nurse grabbed it. The detective looked apprehensive.

"I want a lawyer," Levi said.

"Fine, Saranno," Thomas said. "You'll need one. You're under arrest, and I'm getting a search warrant for your residence."

24

A few hours after Sausalito's finest had left the hospital room, the nurse came in to give Levi pain medication and to change his IV.

"How bad is my face?" Levi asked her as she worked.

"You had a good doctor. You'll have some scarring, but you'll be okay." She paused. "If I may be candid, Mr. Saranno, that's not your worst problem. Right now you need to get some support. I've plugged in the phone. Call your parents, or a friend – someone, and get help, because you're going to need it."

"Who?" he asked.

"You ought to know that; I don't. I've got a son your age, and I wouldn't want him to be facing what you might be. Good luck," she said as she closed the door.

Levi felt rotten and scared. What would be the consequences of the previous night's binge? Who should he call? He sat up in bed, his movements painstaking and slow. Under the bandages he could feel his face grimacing as he fought back the tears, fearing they would cause his face to burn and hurt even more.

Levi realized he was alone, terribly, frighteningly alone. His hands shook as he picked up the phone. He called Detroit Willy.

"Virginia bailed out Marsha last night, Levi," Willy said, with not a hint of friendship in his voice. "Cops told her your bail was going to be at least fifty grand. You crossed the line, ol' buddy, and there ain't nothin' I can do to help."

"But Willy."

"Levi, listen to me." There was a pause. "Even if I *could* do something, I *wouldn't*. You're over the edge. Ginger and all. You're abusive. Plain fucked up. I don't need it, and neither does the family. And don't call Marsha; she's got enough trouble, thanks to you. Call another friend somewhere else. Your friends here are gone." The phone went dead.

Dead, like Levi. Nothing on the line. No "Sure, I'll be there for you, buddy. Comin' right down." Quiet emptiness. Silence.

Levi's brain thumped and ached but he kept thinking. He dialed his mother in Colorado Springs. After four long rings, the answering machine clicked on. "Sorry I missed your call; my trip to Egypt is finally a reality. I'll be back in three weeks with pictures. Please leave a message at the sound of the…" Levi hung up before the beep could be heard.

He frantically dialed another number.

"Sampson! Hi, buddy."

"What's up, Levi?" Sampson sounded almost sympathetic. "Haven't heard from you in three months, man. Like you fell off the planet or something."

"I need help, Sampson." And the story was told. But what could Sampson do? He had no money, and he was in Colorado. Sampson didn't even know anyone in California. There were no connections within his circle of friends. Sampson didn't tell Levi how he really felt. Levi had become obnoxious and mean. A lying, self-absorbed, self-destructive, pathetic excuse for a person, much less a friend.

"Sorry, Levi," Sampson said, just before he hung up. "I hope everything works out. Let me know what happens. Write if they put you in the slammer." Click.

Levi paced in his hospital gown. His face ached and itched, pain stabbed his cheeks and forehead, and his hands shook. The pangs of drug withdrawal crawled all over him. His thoughts were in a dark eclipse, terror at every turn.

Rolling and drowning and gone. Choking, gasping, looking for a life-preserver. A line to pull him from the depths, up and back, into the living and the light. Of course!

Her voice was as soft and mellow as it had always been. Whenever she answered the phone, it sounded as if she were actually happy to hear from whomever was on the other end.

"Erica, it's Levi."

No response.

"I'm in the hospital, Erica. Don't hang up."

"Are you okay?" Levi thought there was genuine feeling and caring in her question. Worry too. Could she possibly want to be there, by his side? "I was attacked by two guys, got my face cut with a broken beer bottle."

"Oh, my God, Levi. How? Why?"

"It's not important, Erica. I need help. They say I'm going to jail for something I didn't do. It's Saturday, and I don't think I can get hold of Bill Barton, my father's old lawyer friend in Denver. Will you help me, Erica? Will you?"

"Of course! Levi, of course," she stammered. "I'll call Mr. Barton for you."

"As soon as the doctor releases me, the Sausalito police will probably take me to the county lockup. That's why I need a lawyer. I'll need bail, too, somebody to get me out."

"Why? What'd you do?"

"They're talking felonies. Assaults and drugs, all bullshit. I didn't do anything. Nothing, I swear. They're out to get me!"

"Sampson told me about the drugs, Levi."

Erica couldn't believe she said it. Sampson had sworn her to secrecy, but she'd pumped and pleaded, and finally he told her about the dope and booze and how Levi's appearance was a mirror image of the lifestyle he'd chosen. No word about the hookers, but it was enough. Enough to make her more confident in her decision to let go. Levi was going further into the darkness, and no matter how long it took or how hard and lonely and difficult it might be, Erica was determined to stay in the light and let him go.

"Sampson told you? What'd Sampson tell you?" Levi yelled, angry, a betrayed victim. "Erica, I'm in a goddamn hospital, and cops are outside the door!" He was almost shrieking. "I didn't hurt anybody. I've *never* hurt anybody!"

"Oh, really?" she said. Her composure and strength returned, and the defenses were up and strong. "You're saying you never hurt anyone? Is that what you're telling me, Levi?"

"Never!"

"Honest?" she asked.

"On my father's grave!"

"I'll do what I can to reach Mr. Barton, Levi. Good luck," she said, gently hanging up the phone.

White Knuckle

Levi couldn't believe she didn't even say goodbye. That bitch, he thought. His worst hour of need, and what does she do? Nothing! She hangs up the phone, while minute by minute he gets closer to being hauled off in a paddywagon.

Detective Thomas stuck his head into Levi's room and announced loudly, "Doctors say you're about to be released, Saranno. Take your nightgown off, save it for later. You've got ten minutes to get ready."

The door slammed shut.

Ten minutes? Damn, he needed a lawyer, a friend, someone to help him. Levi pulled open the drawer next to his bed. A Gideon Bible stared back at him. "I don't need you, God. I need a fucking lawyer who can work miracles!"

The telephone directory was next to the Bible, and Levi seized it. He sat on the edge of the bed and opened the phone book. As if out of nowhere, one name jumped – almost vaulted – out of the white pages, smacking him in the face. He felt the sting and looked into the phone book again. Closely. The name was still there, still hitting him. Levi shut the directory and flung it across the room, butterflying it against the wall.

"No!" he blurted out, instinctively, without thinking.

Levi had nine minutes left. He shuddered and tried to make a decision – a good one. He stared at the phone book lying open on the floor. He walked over, picked it up and carefully leafed through the pages. The name was still there with the number next to it, offering hope, offering… Slowly, he dialed.

The phone rang twice. "Good morning," a cheerful voice answered.

"Hello," Levi said with an awkward quiver. "Is this a good time to be calling? I mean…"

"Sure! Who's this?" The voice sounded warm and friendly.

"My name's, uh, I'm looking for…" Levi felt like he had to twist his tongue, turn it, rip it down his throat, and scoop the syllables out of his gut, turn them back around, and shovel them out of his mouth.

"I'm waiting. Who is this?"

"My, my name's Levi. Levi Saranno, and I'm looking for Asia Nichols."

The silence on the other end of the phone thundered through his ears like Niagara Falls. Levi thought he would have to scream above the roar, to be heard. For a moment, he wondered if he should say her name again. Or his own.

The soft, female voice finally spoke. "Levi?" Tentative and quiet. Ten years, and so many miles. Phone calls and letters and cards and presents. And time fading hope.

"Yes. That's me, Levi Saranno. Is this Asia?"

"Oh, Jesus!" She started crying as the phone fell out of her hand and dangled by the nightstand. She didn't hear him say, "I'm in trouble, Asia. I'm in a lot of trouble."

Asia quickly put the phone to her ear as her voice fought to remain steady. "What did you say, Levi?"

"I'm in trouble, Asia. A lot of trouble."

"I'm here, Levi. Just a phone call away. I remember the promise your father made, and it's my promise, too."

"I'm in a hospital in San Francisco or Sausalito, and now they're taking me to jail."

"Ohmigod! What happened?"

"An accident. I needed stitches. And now the cops want to take me in."

Detective Thomas opened the door to Levi's room. "Get off the phone, Saranno." He took Levi's hand and started to cuff it. "Time we left and got your dopey ass booked."

"Levi!" Asia shouted.

"Where are you taking me?" Levi asked. "I've got to tell my friend where I'm going."

"To the county jail, kid. Where do you think? We ain't goin' on a goddamn tour ride." Thomas took the phone from Levi and started to hang it up.

"She has the right to know where you're taking me!" Levi pleaded.

Thomas paused and nodded. Goddamnit, he thought, the dopehead already has himself a fucking lawyer. If he didn't give the lawyer ten seconds, it could screw up the arrest or at least give the slimeball attorney something to cackle about.

He lifted the phone to his ear. "Detective Thomas, Sausalito police."

"Where are you taking Mr. Saranno, and what's he charged with?" Asia asked.

"Who's this?" Thomas demanded.

"I'm Mr. Saranno's representative."

He wondered why she didn't say "attorney" or "lawyer." Still, she sounded professional.

"He's going to the Marin County jail. Charged with felony assault and battery. Add to that possession and distribution of a controlled substance."

"How long will it take to process him and have bail set?"

"Don't know. Couple hours, I guess." Questions. Lawyers and all them stupid questions. Interfering. Screwing things up.

"May I talk to him?" Asia asked politely but firmly.

"No." Thomas replied in a cocky, controlled voice.

"Why not?"

"Because it's time to go, lady. You can meet your client at the booking center." His words seemed to chuckle from his mouth. "Need directions?" he asked sarcastically.

Thomas waited for her to start yelling demands and hollering threats. When she didn't, he wondered how good a lawyer could she be. Christ, it was almost laughable.

"Then will you give Mr. Saranno a message, please?"

"Why not?" he said.

"Tell him that Vincent Morgan will meet him there personally within an hour. Mr. Morgan will be his lawyer, and you're not to ask him any questions in the meantime. Will you convey that message, please?"

"Ah, yes, yes, Ma'am. I'll do that. Yeah, sure. Did you say you want to talk to him? Here, tell him yourself." Thomas handed the phone to a bewildered Levi.

"Mr. Saranno," Thomas said, "you've got one minute to talk."

Thomas was dumbfounded, astonished as he mumbled to himself, "Vincent Morgan. Jesus Christ, the pissant doper's got the best fucking lawyer in San Francisco. How in God's name did that happen?"

25

Sitting handcuffed in the back seat of a police car wasn't Levi's idea of a good time. Good times like the ones he'd been having with Marsha, Ginger, and the North Beach bars. Willy and the family. The hookers and dope and tequila-slammers. Image Leather, and another line to cross. Who could he do it with now? They were all gone; even Sampson and Erica had abandoned him. So what else was new? People abandoned him, disappeared from his life. The players changed, the settings were different, but the conclusion was always the same. Everyone left – just like his dad. Ironic that the only one still around was Asia. Dad's whore.

At the booking center, Levi was fingerprinted, photographed, and processed. The mug shot was ten times worse than any driver's license photo. Red eyes, puffy face, bandaged and swollen, the skunk tail on his head, and they wouldn't let him pose with the skinny, silly sunglasses. Cops had no sense of humor, he thought.

An assistant brought a printed report to Detective Thomas. He read it and furiously crumpled it into a ball, then flung it at the wastebasket.

"No record?" Thomas asked, clearly annoyed. "I can't believe it. Check again," he ordered. "This is the guy who slashed Judge Cooperman's nephew. I need a search warrant. Saranno's got to get what he deserves."

"Good luck," the assistant muttered. "Maybe he's not getting what he deserves, but he is getting out. Vincent Morgan's here with some woman and a certified check for bail. There's another guy, too."

"Shit! Lawyers. We could clean up the whole goddamn country, if lawyers weren't mucking it up."

"What if he's not guilty?"

"It's Cooperman's nephew, for christsakes!"

"And now he cut up Saranno? They just switched places."

Thomas smashed his fist on the desk.

"Cooperman's clean." he insisted. "Only witness says he did it was cranked up on coke, and she's a friend of dopey here. Where's the fucking affidavit?" Thomas furiously shuffled papers on his desk.

"The affidavit's being typed. I'll go get it."

The locks were unlocked, and Levi was escorted into the waiting room wearing the skinny sunglasses firmly above his nose. He looked indifferent and insolent.

"Levi!" Asia cried, running to him. He put out his hand, waiting for her to shake it. But Asia grabbed him and hugged him like a lost child safely found.

Levi looked into her eyes. He couldn't escape the glamour of the glowing jade-green that looked him up and down, trying to make certain he wasn't a mirage, a fleeting image that would suddenly disappear. Her hair was long and shiny. Her creamy skin was touched by a hint of rouge, and her lips were a deep pink.

Levi couldn't help making the comparison. His mother was stately and dignified, someone with obvious class. But Asia had class, too. She also was a slender, wholesome, All-American girl who still caused men's necks to whiplash when she walked into a room. For reasons he didn't understand,

White Knuckle

Levi wanted to push her away, just like he did the last time he saw her, ten years before, at the funeral.

"Oh, Levi. I can't believe it's you. Who could've done this to you?" She delicately touched the bandages. She wished he would hug her back, so they could forget the past and begin all over again. But Levi stood stiffly, his arms dangling.

Two men approached, both dressed casually. One was tall, with silver-streaked hair, a dark tan, and an aura of supreme confidence. "I'm Vincent Morgan," he said, extending his hand, "and this is my investigator, Rick Bender."

Levi clasped Morgan's palm weakly. His client's handshake felt like a wet fish. Pathetic. Levi looked at Morgan. "Let's get out of this toilet. I need a drink."

"Where do you live, Levi?"

"Who cares? I told you, I need a drink."

"Don't fuck with me, Levi!" Morgan shot back.

Levi looked into his eyes and then to Asia's. "So sorry," he lied.

Better men get punched for less, Morgan thought. This was a punk with a bad hairdo and an attitude to match. He assessed his new client, wondering for a moment if this could really be the son of his former classmate at law school, the man he had always respected and admired. Too bad, Vincent thought, no matter how good the genes, some bad seeds just sperm their tails into the heat of living.

"What's your address, Levi?"

"Haight district. You like it there?" He nodded at Asia. "Ain't Lombard Street, but suits me fine."

"They're trying to hang your ass, pal, and I don't have time to play stupid games. They're calling you a drug dealer, and I'm asking where you live."

"I need a drink and a cigarette. I'm desperate for a slammer."

"Where, Levi!"

"Told you, Haight," he said defensively.

"How much dope you got there?"

"None," Levi answered. "I don't do drugs, and if I did, it wouldn't be any of your fu…"

Morgan wanted to slap Levi's bandaged face. "Lie to your girlfriend, Levi, but don't lie to your lawyer. Tell Bender here where you live, and tell him now."

Levi followed his instructions. As he spoke, Bender wrote down the address on a little note pad.

"Now give him the keys to your apartment, Levi," Morgan said, firmly but with less anger. Levi reluctantly pulled the keys out of the pocket of his jeans and handed them to Bender. Bender left the room in what Levi thought was a great hurry.

"I'm gonna smoke outside," Levi said. "That is, if you don't mind." Levi's voice dripped sarcasm as he walked out the door, leaving Vincent and Asia to follow.

Morgan knew he had his hands full. If it weren't for Asia and the memory of Judd, he would not have time for nonsense like this. Sometimes a lawyer needs to pick and choose. Good clients make for good results. Bad clients make for complaints to the Bar Association. The more you do for some folks, the less they appreciate it. Levi had immediately struck him as someone who didn't appreciate anything.

Morgan stared out the window and looked at the bandaged liar wearing jeans and a bloody shirt, with earrings dangling, and sunglasses plunked firmly above his nose, his black and white hairdo ludicrously atop his head.

"Asia, what the hell's he trying to prove?"

"I'm not really sure, Vince. But you've got to take his case. Judd always told me I could count on you. I'm counting this time. You know how long I've waited for Levi. I'm so sorry about his arrogance. You've got to help him."

"Asia, the charges are severe. More importantly, his attitude makes me want to punch him, not defend him."

"I know. But I think all this is really the symptom of other problems. He's troubled, disturbed. He needs our help, some guidance."

"I'll tell you where I'd like to guide him. Straight into a goddamn boot camp, where he belongs."

* * * * *

Rick Bender sat across from his boss in Morgan's opulent office in the Transamerica Building and shook his head.

"Truth is, I'm comin' down the steps with a box so full of dope and drug paraphernalia that if that Detective Thomas and the other cops hadn't been in such a hurry to get into the apartment, their dog could've busted me on the spot, and I'd be facing ten to twenty."

"You sure Thomas didn't recognize you?" Vincent asked, tapping his Montblanc pen on his desk with one hand, wiping his silver hair back with the other. Asia sat on the large leather chair listening attentively to Bender.

"Boss," Bender said confidently, "get the picture: I'm ploddin' down the steps; box's right in front of my face, and they push me aside like cops in riot gear, headin' for a gang war. Had I tripped, they'd of gotten it all. Bongs and pipes and bags of pot, coke, acid, and who knows what other shit was in the box. There was enough dope in that apartment to keep Levi and his friends high for months. I dumped it near the docks."

"How do you know the police didn't find more?"

"Kid kept it all in one big dresser drawer. Except for what he had on the coffee table, all the rest was in the dresser. Damn lucky, too. If I'd of been there for three more minutes, you'd be bailing me out. Levi's a real fucking loser."

"No," Asia defended quietly. "I don't believe that."

Morgan looked at Asia. She still had an innocence about her, an optimism, a believer in good. No wonder Judd had loved her so much.

"Judd's son is on a self-destruct mission, Asia."

"I don't agree, Vince. Some of Judd has got to be in Levi. Judd knew Levi would turn out great. I can't believe he could be so wrong. Levi's crying for help."

"Look at the facts, Asia. You bail him out; we take him into town, put him in a hotel to sober up, and give the cops time to do their thing. And he never even says, 'thanks.'" Vincent raised both arms over his head. "The little bastard hardly talks, and when he does, I get so mad I want to reach down his throat and yank out his tongue."

"You can't quit, Vince. Please." Asia had tears in her eyes.

The intercom buzzed and Vincent pressed a button.

"Mr. Saranno is here to see you, sir. Shall I let him in?"

White Knuckle

Levi walked into Vincent Morgan's office wearing blue jeans, a T-shirt emblazoned with "Shit Happens," his skinny sunglasses, and an old pair of sandals. A braided belt hung around his waist, and his earrings matched the necklaces above his chest. Although the bandages had been removed, the stitches remained, and Levi's face was still swollen and blotchy.

Vincent Morgan nodded to Levi, who avoided a handshake or any other pleasantries. Instead, he sank into the plush sofa and stared blankly at Asia and Morgan. He didn't even notice Bender.

"The D.A.'s had your case for four days now, Levi," Morgan said. "They're supposed to call me this afternoon and tell me exactly what you're charged with."

"That's nice," Levi muttered. "You'll get me off?" Then under his breath, but loud enough for everyone to hear, he said, "I haven't gotten off in ten days." He chuckled to himself.

Morgan gazed at Levi with disgust. "Why are you such a wiseguy?" he asked as he leaned forward in his overstuffed chair.

"Comes natural."

"Levi, cut the crap. Do you realize you could be facing ten to twenty years in prison? The least you'll get is a year in the county jail."

"You said I'd get off. What's their beef? I didn't do anything." Levi almost sounded innocent. Vincent Morgan could feel his stomach churn, a vein in his temple throbbed.

"You did plenty, Levi. The kid you hit in the eye with a shot glass is a judge's nephew. And you started a brawl. The cops found cocaine in your leather pouch. You were drunk and disorderly, had enough dope in your bloodstream to keep you high for a week, and when they went to your apartment, their dog went crazy."

Levi reached for his flask of tequila. Morgan saw what he was about to do, and Asia saw the look in Morgan's eyes. Levi saw both of them, really saw them for the first time. Vincent and Asia had offered to be his friend, and Levi was pushing them away. Just like he had pushed everybody else.

"I'm sorry," he said.

"Levi, get one thing straight," Morgan said, barely controlling his rage. "I'm only doing this for your dad and Asia."

Levi's chin bent to his chest. "I…I know." For the first time, a shred of repentance was in his eyes. A hint of remorse. The bravado was starting to melt away, not completely, but at least the shell had a small crack in it.

"I hate this," Levi said. "I hate what's happened. I hate everything and everybody. Guess that's why I live in the Haight." He giggled at his little pun. No one else in the room smiled.

Morgan stared at him. "Levi, you hate *yourself* more than you hate anything else."

The office intercom buzzed, and Bender picked up the phone. It was the D.A.'s office.

* * * * *

Vincent Morgan and the district attorney's representative talked for ten minutes. Sometimes friendly, sometimes not. A few times Morgan smiled; mostly, he frowned. Throughout it all, he took copious notes. Levi and Asia and Bender listened.

"You really think you can pin that rap on my client?" he said, in a mocking voice. "Try selling it to a judge, and by the way, it won't be Cooperman. I've got motions to quash the so-called evidence already typed. The motions will be on your desk this afternoon."

The expressions on Morgan's face changed with every other sentence. "I'm not pleading him guilty to a felony, Ms. Elkins. In fact, he won't be copping a plea at all. You've got the burden of proof, and you can't meet it." He sounded confident.

"Witnesses? Who?" Morgan looked distressed. Nonsense! My investigator's talked to everyone. The other kid got hit months ago, and the only positive ID you've got is a slasher himself."

Morgan continued to listen to the D.A.'s arguments. "There was no confession, and you know that. Detective Thomas will be lucky if I don't sue him for violating my client's civil rights." On the offense.

"Possession of cocaine? Prove it. And you know damn well they had no right to do a drug test, any defense lawyer knows that."

They talked back and forth. The expressions kept changing.

"I'll tell you what, Ms. Elkins, why don't we run all this past a settlement judge at a pretrial conference? If you're so certain about your case, see if you can convince him. I think you're out on a preliminary motion to dismiss. Certainly, you'll be gone with a motion for a directed verdict, should it get that far." Morgan listened to the voice on the other end of the line and then smiled.

"It's a deal." he said. "We'll meet in Judge LaMar's chambers sometime next week. If we can't wrap it up there, then I'll see you in trial." He hung up the phone.

Morgan looked at Levi. "You're probably going to jail, Levi. Only a miracle will keep you out."

"But, but I thought..." Levi stammered. "You said you could get me off." Levi's body shook. He needed a drink, but now wasn't the time to pull out the flask again. "I, I can't go to jail. All those guys in there, big guys."

Levi was crying, curled in his chair. Huddling. His knees were tucked against his chest, both arms pulled around his legs.

"No," he mumbled under his breath. "Not again. Never." His words were barely audible.

Asia's arms went around Levi's shoulders. Tears were in her eyes. "Don't worry, Levi. Vincent's the best, and he'll do something. No one will hurt you, I promise."

"No one will hurt you." The words felt like arrows in his ears. Did he hear that right? Another ambush. Shackles and ropes and greasy hands. Wet fat lips. Captured. Windows barred, and what would the guards do? Nothing!

"I promise, we're here to protect you," she said.

Levi jumped up, blistering with rage. "Promises?" he screamed. "The last time I heard a promise like that, you were involved, Asia! One promise, one Asia, and one dead Judd Saranno."

At the mention of Judd's death a searing bolt of pain shot through Asia. "I never thought you'd harbor so much hate toward me. Not after all these years."

Vincent stood there, shocked. He's so unpredictable, Morgan thought, so volatile.

Levi spun around, glaring at Vincent.

"I'm your client; she's not. Right?" he asked between clenched teeth.

"That's right," Morgan reluctantly confirmed.

"Then tell her to leave, please."

White Knuckle

But Asia was already at the door. "I'll phone you later, Vincent," she said to the lawyer. Ignoring Levi, Asia left the office.

As soon as she was gone, Levi turned back to Morgan. "Someday I might tell you the whole story, but in the meantime, you tell me what to do, and I'll do it. I've got enough money to pay your fee. I don't need Asia for…"

"I don't want your case, Levi." Morgan interrupted. "I don't believe you, and I definitely don't like you."

"Then do it for my father." The words were slow and deliberate. Calculated. This was a different Levi. A person Morgan hadn't seen. He stared solemnly at Judd's son – the pathetic legacy to a great guy.

Morgan took a deep breath, a sigh of resignation. "I'll call and tell you when the pretrial conference is set. You've got to promise to be there, Levi. That's when we find out if you're going to jail or not."

"I'll show," Levi said. "I promise."

"One more promise, Levi."

"What's that?" he asked cautiously.

"When you show up, look human. Clean yourself up. Dress properly."

"Why?"

"Do what I say, Levi!" Vincent Morgan was back in control. Do it, or I'm history. And bring your toothbrush; you might be going to the jug."

Levi nodded and looked at Morgan with a genuine smile. "Trust me, Vince," he said, "I'll dress so good, you'll think I'm my fucking father."

"I doubt that, Levi. I seriously doubt that."

Levi headed for the door, giving Bender a tiny salute as he went out. Bender stared coldly back at him. The investigator closed the door, scratching his head. "I don't get it, Vincent," he said. "You keep saying the kid's going to jail. Why're you going to let him sink? He's an asshole, but..."

"He's not going to jail, but he doesn't know that yet. Nor does the D.A. Levi is going to take a little trip, though. *That* much I'm doing for his father."

Bender looked at his boss quizzically as the attorney picked up the phone and dialed Asia's cell number.

26

Sometimes, when the doors are closed and lawyers enter a judge's chambers, deals are struck, and a client's fate is sealed. Forever. And it's irreversible. It's not that the client doesn't consent, they do consent, eventually, not knowing the cards have already been thrown on the table, the pot's been divided or there's a winner who takes it all. It happens behind closed doors every day, in every courtroom across America.

The client waits outside, wondering and hoping, eager for justice. If his lawyer is *really* on his side, justice is generally served. But if the lawyer is more concerned about his tee-off time or clearing his calendar, less justice is meted out, and once in awhile, the defendant simply gets screwed.

Inside Judge Christopher LaMar's chambers, Levi's lawyer and the county prosecutor put on the gloves and got ready to spar.

"I'm not going to let you hang this kid," Vincent Morgan said to Diane Elkins. "His father was a friend of mine, one of the best lawyers in Colorado. He died in a car accident, and Levi's obviously never gotten over it."

"Then send him to a shrink when he gets out of jail," Elkins said. "Your client damn near blinded Cooperman."

"With all due respect, Ms. Elkins, as a favor to an old friend, and for the woman he loved, I'll come at you with everything I've got. You'll spend tens of thousands of taxpayers' dollars, and when it's over, you'll still be a loser."

Judge LaMar leaned over his desk. "Now counsel," he said, "this is the time to see if we can *compromise* and work a deal that's good for the state and for the defendant. The docket of this court is already backed up. If we can reach an agreement, then justice is served, and a lot of time and money is saved."

Vincent and the assistant district attorney, Diane Elkins, sat in front of the judge's desk in chambers, trying to cut a deal.

Levi lingered in the courtroom, dressed in a suit and tie, wearing black loafers, sporting a new haircut, with the piercings nowhere to be seen. He looked like a graduate student waiting for an interview with a Fortune Five Hundred Company. Bender couldn't believe his eyes as he babysat Levi to make certain he didn't pull out his flask and get drunk before the three people in the judge's chambers had reached an agreement. Levi and Bender both wondered what was being argued in front of the judge.

Vincent smiled at LaMar. "How are your flying lessons going?" he asked. "Done your solo yet?" Trying to schmooze, without being too obvious. It was better than asking to see a picture of the grandchildren or commenting on the beauty of Mrs. LaMar, whose framed photograph stared at them from a long table behind the judge's chair.

"Going great." LaMar smiled back. "But I need to find a private landing strip that's got grass on it, instead of asphalt. Do some open-field landing."

Morgan leaned forward. "I know of a ranch with…"

Elkins interjected, refusing to let the judge or Morgan get too friendly or distracted. Elkins was a good lawyer, and one of the few female prosecutors who coped without making gender an issue every time there was an offensive or defensive attack.

"I'm trying to make sense of this, Mr. Morgan," she said. "What makes you think Levi Saranno can't get nailed for aggravated assault? That's a felony with a five-year sentence."

Morgan looked at the judge instead of Diane Elkins. "First of all, my client's a clean-cut, college student on a break. He's never been in trouble before, and he has an alibi. My investigator's interviewed everyone but Cooperman, who wouldn't talk to him, and no one can identify Mr. Saranno's picture. Nobody got a good look at the assailant at the bar. They said so in the original police report. It happened so quickly, the *real* culprit escaped. Besides, it was four months ago. I'll have psychologists and experts trashing any positive ID of Cooperman."

"We have a confession, albeit, somewhat weak." Elkins reminded him.

"The sweetest nurse on earth says there was no confession, Judge." He smiled at Elkins. "Besides," Morgan continued, "what jury's going to be sympathetic to some guy who slashes a good-looking college boy with a jagged beer bottle? On the assault charge, Counselor, you can't prove anything. Admit it."

Judge LaMar looked at Elkins. "Have you got a positive ID and confession, or not? Be candid, Diane; it'll save time."

"Not really," she said, squirming in her chair.

The judge leaned toward her, raising an eyebrow. "Mr. Morgan's making more sense, Diane. His arguments seem logical to me. You'd be better off going with your best case and forget a loser. If the jury doesn't like part of your case, it casts a shadow over the rest; you know that."

"Maybe you're right," she said, resignation in her voice. "But I've still got possession of a controlled substance and being drunk and disorderly."

"Oh, baloney," Morgan retorted. "My client may have been intoxicated, but he certainly wasn't disorderly. He got ambushed by two goons wielding weapons. They – especially Cooperman – were the disorderly ones, not my client. He's innocent."

"His blood-alcohol content was .25, and he had enough cocaine in his system to keep him high for a month," Elkins shot back. "He's probably still loaded. That evidence is clear as day."

"Unfortunately," Vincent countered, "*that* evidence is inadmissible. Here, Judge," he said, handing LaMar some papers. "This is our motion to quash with supporting affidavits. You'll see that Mr. Saranno never gave permission to have his blood drawn, the policeman got the permission slip signed by the girl he was with, when Mr. Saranno was fully awake and able to sign himself."

Vincent Morgan continued. "The defendant was obviously hurt, but Mr. Saranno's doctors have even affirmed that he was cognizant enough to make a decision and sign the documents to have his blood drawn, but my client was never asked. Cops *conveniently* forgot, but too bad for them. Some chippy girlfriend can't waive my client's constitutional rights; only he can, under these circumstances."

"Ms. Elkins?" The judge looked at the assistant district attorney.

"I, I really don't have an explanation, Your Honor. Mr. Morgan knows his client's guilty. He's arguing technicalities, minor details, instead of dealing with the overall picture here. His client shouldn't get off scot-free. The police went to the defendant's apartment, and the dog went crazy because of all the dope."

"Here's another motion to quash, your Honor." Morgan handed the judge more papers. "Under the circumstances, assuming the court rules that the blood tests were taken improperly, then the police had no probable cause to search Mr. Saranno's apartment. Even if they did have probable cause, which they didn't, there was no tangible evidence of drugs on the premises. The state doesn't have one sample of a drug that can be tested, except for traces on some carpet fibers. Any prior tenant could have been responsible for those, and besides, there's not enough residue to even rise to the level of possession within the definition of the criminal code."

Elkins was almost beside herself. "The goddamn dog went nuts, Vincent, You know that!"

"What're you going to do, Diane? Put the dog on the stand and have him bark once for a 'yes' and twice for a 'no?' Did you smell dope, Fido? 'Woof.' Did you get more than a lick of a drug on your tongue, I mean like, a joint of marijuana or a trace of cocaine that was measurable? 'Woof. Woof,' he barks. I rest my case, Your Honor."

The judge laughed. "'The state calls Fido to the stand. Will you raise your right paw, please?' 'Woof!'"

Even Elkins smiled, but quickly composed herself. "We're losing the big picture here," she argued. "Okay, so the cops made some mistakes, and there's not a whole lot to go on if the evidence is thrown out, but the fact remains, Levi Saranno is an alcohol and drug addict." She stood up, as if delivering her final argument. "He should be forced to pay for his crimes."

Vincent Morgan leaned down and opened the book on his lap. "This whole case stands or falls on the laws of evidence," he said. "It says right here in the book," he pounded on a page with a pointed finger for emphasis. "'If the search is illegal, the evidence is tainted, and the state may not utilize the fruits of a poisoned tree. Once poisoned, all tainted evidence is inadmissible.'" He handed the book to the judge.

LaMar glanced at the page and then turned to the prosecutor. "Let's face it, Ms. Elkins, the cops screwed this up. The trial judge will have to rule on Mr. Morgan's motions to quash. I'm just here to settle the case, but no judge in the county is going to deny the motion to quash. A girlfriend can't waive a defendant's constitutional rights, and if that evidence is gone, so is Fido's." He grinned.

"But," Elkins grasped for a final straw, "Saranno did have a coke spoon and a trace of cocaine in a leather pouch. We've got that, your Honor."

LaMar turned to Morgan. "What about that, Mr. Morgan? Any defenses there?" the judge asked.

"We can argue it was planted, Your Honor. Besides, the leather pouch wasn't actually in his possession. The pouch was in a coat that someone identified as Mr. Saranno's. If I don't call him to the stand to testify, the state can't authenticate that the coat was actually his. Even if they were able to meet their burden on that issue, the crime really constitutes possession of drug paraphernalia, a misdemeanor. With Saranno's clean record, no judge will give him more than a fine and probation. Besides, the jury's going to like this college boy with scars on his face. Are they going to find him guilty, or realistically, aren't they going to say he's paid enough and in all probability, give him another chance?"

"Ms. Elkins," the judge said, "Isn't it really true that when all's said and done and the evidence is washed clean, you don't have anything significant to build this case on?"

"He's guilty, Your Honor."

"So what? You can't prove it." Judge LaMar tossed the file to the side of his desk. "Vince has promised a Dream-Team defense because of old friendships. You'll never get a felony conviction, and if you do get a misdemeanor, the defendant's not going to get anything more than a small fine and probation. He's not going to spend a *single* day in jail; that's a foregone conclusion. Why waste the court's time? I suggest you dismiss all the charges."

Elkins breathed a heavy sigh. She sat in her chair, quietly resigned. "All these goddamn rules," she said. "Appellate decisions that make my job so fuc...so darn difficult. How do I explain it to Cooperman?"

"Don't worry about it, Diane," Judge LaMar consoled her. "Cooperman already knows his nephew's an ass with a chip on his shoulder."

White Knuckle

"That's exactly what my client says." Morgan chimed in.

"I'll tell Judge Cooperman the state couldn't prove its case and had to let the defendant go." Judge LaMar opened the file. "That is going to be your motion, to dismiss all charges, isn't it, Diane?"

"I suppose I have..."

"Wait!" Morgan interrupted. "The state hasn't moved for total dismissal, yet. Have you, Diane?"

"Huh? I don't understand. You win. I'm making a motion."

"Bullshit! Just a second. I don't want to hear any motion. I'm not about to get disbarred."

Elkins and the judge looked confused. "You haven't made a motion, Diane, and your Honor hasn't issued any orders. Am I right?"

The judge and the prosecutor nodded, still confused.

"Diane, you want at least six months and a misdemeanor, don't you? And Judge, you'd consider a diversion, correct?"

Again, the judge and the prosecutor nodded.

Morgan walked quickly to the door, smiling. "Then please give me five minutes with my client. I'll be right back." He hurried out.

Levi saw the lawyer coming toward Bender himself. Levi's face turned pale. "Shit!" he said to Bender. "He doesn't look good, Rick."

Levi was right. Morgan's shoulders slumped, and his head was down. He walked slowly, scratching his hair, his face and cheeks, and the back of his neck.

When Morgan reached Levi, he put his hand on the boy's shoulder. "I'm not going to lie to you, Levi." His eyes stared out a courtroom window. "Look at that," he said. "Birds are flying, and freedom's really something special, isn't it? Makes you wish you were an eagle or something."

"What...what's happening?" Levi demanded. He was wringing his hands.

"Like I said, Levi, I'm not going to lie to you. What the prosecutor's willing to do, and what I'm offering, are two different things, but I think if you agree, the judge can be convinced to go my way."

"What? Vincent, tell me!"

"The state wants to dismiss some charges. But at the same time, Ms. Elkins wants justice served and wants you to pay for your crimes. I told her we wouldn't cop a plea to a felony, and they'd have a hard time even convicting you of a misdemeanor."

"What about jail, Vincent? I told you, I'll skip the goddamn country, before I let them lock me up."

"That really scares you, doesn't it? Why, Levi? Why are you so scared?"

"I'm not going to take any chances, Vince. Never! Never," his words faded. Under his breath, he uttered, "Never again."

"Well, you're smart," he said. "Sometimes it's good to be afraid. Even paranoid people have some real enemies."

Levi stood, ready to bolt for the exit, but Bender stepped in his way. "What's the bottom line, Vincent?"

"If you'll give your consent, Levi – and that's what we need at these pretrial conferences, we need our client's consent – if you'll consent to my recommendation, I'll go in and talk to the judge and prosecutor. If they buy it, then I've done my best. I've done what's best for you."

* * * * *

"All rise," the bailiff said, as the black-cloaked judge entered the courtroom. Everyone stood. The judge pounded the gavel and said, "Be seated."

Elkins remained standing. Levi sat down in his chair, trembling from head to foot.

Judge LaMar cleared his throat. "Am I to understand that in the matter of *The State of California vs. Levi Matthew Saranno*, there's been a settlement or plea agreement?"

"Yes, Your Honor, that's correct," Elkins said.

"Please put it on the record, Ms. Elkins."

"Your Honor, the State of California moves to dismiss all charges against the defendant except for the charge of misdemeanor assault and battery. It is the state's recommendation that Mr. Saranno be sentenced to the county jail for not more than six months and pay a fine of not less than one thousand dollars.

"However, the state also recommends that this conviction and plea shall be abated and ultimately dismissed in its entirety on the condition that Mr. Saranno voluntarily, and at his own cost, enter into an in-resident drug and alcohol rehabilitation program until such program is successfully completed. If Mr. Saranno accepts this condition, and if he successfully completes the drug and alcohol treatment program, all charges will be dismissed, and the record expunged."

"Mr. Morgan?"

Morgan grabbed Levi's arm, and they stood together.

"May it please the court. I'm Vincent Morgan, the attorney for the defendant. Ms. Elkins has correctly stated the agreement between the parties, and the defendant is prepared to change his plea at this time."

Judge LaMar looked at Levi. "Do you fully understand the charges that have been brought against you, and have you been advised to your satisfaction with reference to the agreement which has just been placed on the record?"

"Yes, Sir," Levi said, his voice trembling.

"And is it your desire to plead guilty to the charge, as stated, because you are guilty, and that you are not acting under any duress, nor are you hampered by any medication or drugs?"

"That's correct, Your Honor."

"Very well, then. The plea of guilty is accepted and entered into the court's record. The other charges against the defendant are dismissed with prejudice." LaMar banged his gavel. "How do you wish to proceed, Mr. Morgan?"

"Thank you, Your Honor. I have talked with the defendant's friend, Ms. Asia Nichols, who's informed me that she's made arrangements."

Levi shot Morgan a look of surprise and anger.

Morgan ignored it. "She's made arrangements to place Mr. Saranno in the Betty Ford Center in Palm Springs, California. Ms. Nichols will pay the entire bill, about twenty thousand dollars. They are expecting him this evening. My investigator, Mr. Bender, will accompany Mr. Saranno to the Betty Ford Center on the first available flight."

Judge LaMar stared down at Levi. His grave expression and deep voice reduced Levi to quivering Jell-o, the cowardly lion standing before the great, all-powerful Wizard of Oz.

"Are you willing to go to the Betty Ford Center, Mr. Saranno, and complete the program?"

"Yes, Sir."

"You understand that if you don't complete the program successfully or if you walk out, I can reconsider and put you in the county jail for up to six months?"

"Yes, Sir." Levi couldn't control the shaking in his hands.

LaMar nodded, his voice deeper and more somber than ever. "All right then, it's the judgment of this court that the defendant be allowed to enter a diversion program, and that upon successful completion, all charges will forever be dismissed."

As the judge rose, everyone in the courtroom stood. He leaned over toward Levi. "Mr. Saranno, without Vincent Morgan, this opportunity never would've been at your disposal."

"I know that, Sir."

"Mr. Morgan's input in chambers changed everything for you, Mr. Saranno. And you know that your sentence could've been a whole lot different, were it not for Mr. Morgan."

"I know that." Levi's right eye twitched.

"Do you, now?" the judge's eyes twinkled as he nodded his approval to Vincent Morgan and Diane Elkins. "I'm glad you know your lawyer made this result happen and that you won't forget it."

Levi could hardly get the words out. He was feeling faint. "I won't forget it," he stammered.

"Well, in that case, good luck, Mr. Saranno. You'll need it." He stepped down and opened the door that led to his chambers. Levi was no longer aware of the judge or Vincent Morgan. He was too busy wiping away tears.

* * * * *

Levi and Morgan stood in front of the courthouse, waiting for Bender to bring the car. Without Levi's knowledge, the investigator had been to Levi's apartment. Bender hadn't known Morgan's plans in advance, but he did what was asked and packed enough clothes for at least thirty days of what Morgan said would be, "confinement in someplace not so pleasant considering Levi's state of mind."

"Vince," Levi said, "Bender's not gonna know all the stuff I need."

"You mean drugs?"

"Maybe," Levi answered. "Thirty days at Betty Ford is a long time to go without."

"Why don't you just accept the help you've been offered?"

Levi pulled his flask from his jacket pocket and took a long, deep drink. "I don't need any help, now. Now I need tequila."

Bender stopped the car in front of the courthouse, its engine running. Morgan grabbed Levi's arm, opened the door to the front seat, and almost pushed him inside. "Bender will sweep out your apartment again, before you get back." Vincent leaned in, "You want me to convey anything to Asia?"

"Yeah," Levi said. "Tell her thanks, but nothing's changed. She's paying for this with my father's money, therefore, my money, and I'll chalk it up as a debt partially paid."

Bender shook his head as he sat behind the wheel. "You're a real piece of work," he said quietly.

Vincent Morgan slammed the door shut, then put his head through the open window. "I should've let you hang, Levi. Asia took nothing from your father, and you didn't take anything from him either. You're nothing like him, and never will be."

Morgan gave Levi one last angry look and pulled back.

Levi hit the button that closed the window, and the car sped off toward the airport. He looked at the investigator. "Don't suppose you packed any weed, did you?"

"Not a chance."

Levi saw a store as the car neared the entrance to the freeway. "Stop here, please. I've got to get a carton of cigarettes. At least I can smoke those."

Bender reluctantly pulled to the curb. Levi opened the door and walked across the street, away from the store. Bender instinctively reached for the door handle, but stopped when he saw the liquor store where Levi was headed. Bender waited, almost hoping Levi would flee out the back door and be gone, only to have a warrant issued for his arrest. Levi walked into the store empty handed, and walked out with a carton of cigarettes and two pints of tequila.

"Care for a drink?" Levi said as he got back into the car. Bender silently shook his head. Levi twisted open the cap and lifted the bottle into the air as if making a toast. "Here's to good lawyers."

As soon as the plane was aloft, Levi chugged down more tequila, and by the time the jets' wheels slapped themselves on the Palm Springs' tarmac, he was drunk enough for another blackout. Bender considered getting a wheelchair, but opted instead to coax and drag what was left of Levi Saranno to a taxi.

Even if he couldn't walk or talk straight, Levi managed to stuff the remaining pint of liquor into his suitcase as they sat in the back of the cab for the short ride to the Betty Ford Center. Levi continued to pat his trusty flask, making certain it was safely secure in his coat pocket. Bender looked at him with disgust. "Thank God you're not my son," he muttered under his breath.

Finally, the taxi turned from the main street and cut past the grounds of Eisenhower Hospital. A narrow, paved road led them off the highway, past fences of tall arborvitae and into the parking lot.

Two men lifted Levi from the cab, and carried him through the double doors of the rehabilitation center. Bender pulled the tequila from Levi's suitcase and put it in his own back pocket. Levi was still asleep, not knowing he had arrived.

BOOK THREE

You must die in order
for your soul to be saved.
A Promise is given: His name
is Jesus. Hear His voice.
PEACE.
When you hear the voice, death
and sin are no longer present.
He is constant in His love.
It is His promise that
you will have peace.

Nothing Missing.
Nothing Broken.

Daniel J. Gatti

27

Levi's mouth felt like it was stuffed with clay. Desert dry dirt. He needed a drink, he thought. He rolled out of bed, fully clothed, and opened his suitcase. He remembered hiding a pint of tequila in a side panel, and it was gone. Gone! How could it be missing? It had to be there!

A nurse walked into his room without knocking. "Good morning, Mr. Saranno," she said. "My name's Lois Jean. I've got to take some information down, and we're going to do a few simple tests. Here." She handed him a green and black pill. "This is Librium. You'll be taking it four times a day for two days. After that, no more pills."

Levi looked at his suitcase and then patted his jacket.

"We did a search last night," she said. "Alcohol and drugs aren't allowed here, as you must realize. Not even cold pills or mouthwash. Nothing." She reached for a piece of paper and handed it to Levi. "Please sign this consent form. We're going to test your blood for everything imaginable, and the doctor will be here shortly for a physical."

Levi looked down at the paper. "Can I get my girlfriend to sign this?" He smiled, not expecting an answer. Lois Jean handed him a pen. He signed. She took his blood pressure, asked a few questions, and left.

The doctor followed, put him through a routine physical, and dialed a number. "Mr. Saranno's ready for placement," he said. The doctor turned to Levi. "You can wait in the sitting area outside. We're overloaded with new arrivals, but someone will get you shortly."

With suitcase in hand, Levi walked down the hallway. He found a chair in the sitting area and waited. Waited as he stared at the most beautiful woman he'd ever seen. She was black and tall and she had green-grey eyes, pouty red lips, and glistening white teeth. She had a small backside, and her miniskirt revealed a pair of legs that Levi would follow anywhere.

Lois Jean came out and said to the woman, "Willow, the doctor is ready to see you, now."

Willow stood up, her thighs parted, and Levi's heart pounded. When he pulled his eyes off of her legs, Levi noticed there was no life or expression on Willow's face.

"Looks like we're checking in together," he said, trying to be friendly. She barely noticed him. No smile, no nod, no nothing. But he would remember her name. He watched as she picked up her suitcase and followed Lois Jean down the hall.

A loud voice came crashing into Levi's fantasy. "Mr. Saranno, I'm Gregory Martinez, your resident manager."

He had watched Willow walk away, along with Levi. "She's got a nice ass, buddy, but forget it. No fraternization's allowed at Betty Ford. They've placed you in Fisher Hall, so you might find that difficult, but count on it, if anybody starts screwing anybody, we'll know about it, and you're out of here."

Levi stood and shook the man's hand, weakly. "I'm Levi Saranno."

"Nice to meet you. Grab your suitcase. I'll take you to your quad." They walked out of the main building. "You're lucky to be here, Levi," he said. "I hope you make it. We only take eighty patients, twenty to a quad. McCallum and Pocklington are men only. North, over there, is for women. You're in Fisher – it's co-ed, where Elizabeth met her last husband. Over there's the Cork Building, donated by the Kroc family – you know,

McDonald's. 'Cork" is 'Kroc' spelled backwards."

"Where do the actors stay?"

Gregory laughed. "You're all actors. No superstars here this week, but you never can tell who's going to tumble through the door. Don't matter, though. Everyone's the same here. Addicted. Fucked up, strung out, with your lives out of control. Wouldn't be here, otherwise."

"I'm here because of a hanging judge. Last thing I need is this place."

Gregory smiled as they entered Fisher Hall. "Still in denial, huh? When you admit you're powerless and your life's unmanageable, you'll have taken the first step. Till then, you'll stay fucked up, and it'll get progressively worse."

"All I've got to do is stay sane for thirty days," Levi said.

"That's the second step, Levi." Gregory laughed. "Sanity. There's a power out there that can restore your sanity. Find it, and maybe you'll find your way out of here a different person."

"I'd rather find my way into Willow's panties."

Gregory just looked at him. The smile had vanished, and his voice turned deadly serious. "This is not the outside, Levi. In here, you don't get away with anything. Trust me. Don't test it."

Levi saw her again that afternoon. Like him, she was just another patient, waiting for the psychological interview and testing. But to Levi's delight, Willow was a patient assigned to Fisher Hall, his quad of twenty.

"My name's Levi Saranno. You feel like talking?" he asked as he sat on a couch across from her chair.

Willow looked up from her magazine. She saw the scar on his face. "No."

It was a word of dismissal, but those legs were long and lean, and he knew they would feel better around his neck than any tequila slammer down his throat. Now there's progress, Levi thought. Getting rid of the obsession for booze and replacing it with an obsession to get laid by Willow. Maybe under a tree. Under a willow's where he wanted to be.

He sat down. "Your name's Willow. I heard Lois Jean say it. It's beautiful."

"I said, 'no,' and when I says 'no' to a man, I mean 'no.' How come you men don't get it? If I wanted to talk, I'd of said, 'yes,' but I didn't, did I?"

"No," Levi stammered.

"That's it! That's what I said, 'No!'" She stood, towering over the seated Levi like a naughty schoolboy with the teacher hovering over his desk. Except this teacher looked like a beauty queen. Miss America. Miss Black America.

"They said we're supposed to make friends here," Levi said. "Remember, mingle with the people in our quad, but not the others. I'm just doing what they told us to do."

"I don't talk to no man, if I don't want to," Willow said. "They was supposed to put me in North, with women only, but it's full up. I'm in this joint 'cause of creeps like you. I'm here 'cause the modelin' agency says I got to be. But I don't need no help, and I don't need someone lookin' like *King-baby*, holdin' a little weenie in his hand. I don't need you or no one to be my friend."

Willow looked at Levi's fresh scars. Then her red-nailed finger gently touched the bottom of his chin.

"I'm sorry," she said. She sounded sincere, but the look in her eyes was still distant, weary. "I just don't want to talk to no one. And I don't want no one

306

near me. No man, ever. Ain't nothin' personal. Actually, I noticed you, too, and I've a hunch you're not so bad. Maybe not much different than me."

The palm of Willow's dark hand, barely grazed over the side of Levi's wound. "At least I can see you're scared. Aren't we all?" She turned to leave. "See ya around," she said and was gone.

*　*　*　*　*

After the interviews and psychological tests, the time for rehabilitation began. Of all the people at the Center, Levi was probably the least ready and willing – let alone able – for the process to start. Wake-up was at 6:15. Breakfast, without patients from the other quads, was at 6:50. There was time for a meditation walk around the pond before the morning lecture at Firestone Hall. Lectures at Firestone were three times a day, the only time all eighty of the patients were gathered together in the same room at the same time. Group therapy, without the counselor, was in the afternoon for the twenty patients in each quad. Supervised exercise followed, and after the evening lecture, patients were instructed to write in journals. About feelings.

It was enough to make Levi sick. It was such bullshit. No television. No phone privileges for the first week. Pizza on Saturday night. Visitors on Sunday. No time for golf lessons. All they had time for was to hunt down and extract feelings, as if they were magical insights into recovery.

If Levi thought he would have time for a round of golf, he soon realized that the very idea was just another hallucination in his head. Another one. Like the ones he had suffered for the first four nights of trying to sleep without alcohol or drugs sifting their venom through his system. Without the Librium, he would have gone into deliriums. But the Librium worked. The doctor said he'd sleep, and eventually, Levi's body got used to nights without downers and mornings without a slammer to get him started. With the Librium, his withdrawal pains consisted of shakes and sweat as the poison oozed from his pores.

But illusions nevertheless continued. Fantasies and images and apparitions of what it would be like to be on the outside again, out on the streets of San Francisco, free to do what had made him feel alive and in control, even when he wasn't. At least there he had the illusion of power.

An illusion that was blended and filed and folded among all the others scrambling in his brain. For the last ten years of his life, Levi had been the scrambler. Mixing and churning and dishing out servings that he deemed appropriate. At Betty Ford, they took care of what recipes were to be used for the daily menu. Clinicians at Betty Ford decided what was on the patient's tray for the day. Three times a day, they served up food. About five times a week, they served up a person. A person with *feelings* – feelings ready to be exposed.

The exposure happened in the small group therapy sessions after the morning lecture at Firestone. That's when the twenty patients to each quad were put into a room, and then they were seated in a circle, supervised by a counselor. No one could hide, and no one could be excused. That's where the stabbings and scramblings took place, that's where people were served up, carved up and then exposed. Exposed for who they really were. Confidential confrontation. "How does it make you feel?" *That* was the big question. The biggest and most important. Looking in and speaking out about feelings. Lunch was served after the feelings were gnawed raw. Like onions, the therapy sessions pulled off one layer of skin at a time until they got to the inner heart of a person's soul. Tears were a natural part of the onion-peel process.

Martin Thoms was Levi's group therapy counselor, the leader, the guy who decided which person would be exposed and served to the others as the *entree du jour*. Levi seldom participated in group discussions. Willow never said a word.

Levi watched and listened as he sat in his circled-chair. He listened to the patients in their quad. They all had a story to tell.

White Knuckle

"My mother and two sisters were killed in the fire, and I escaped. I was the sole survivor," someone cried.

Martin smiled. "How did that make you *feel*?" Martin asked. Next?

"I saw him beating her, every day, every night. But he didn't beat me. He just visited my bed afterwards," someone wept.

Martin smiled. "How did that make you *feel*?" Next?

"He was drunk every day; he never took me to the Park Plaza. His quality time was spent with his *other women*," someone sobbed.

Martin smiled. "How did that make you *feel*?" Next?

"I caught her in bed with my brother, and..." A cry.

A smile. "How did that make you *feel*?" Next?

"I felt like a goddamn duck, and I wanted to be a hawk. But hawks don't have webbed feet, and I didn't have any claws. How the hell do you think it made me feel?"

"Anger? Do you *feel* anger?"

"No! I feel like breaking your fucking neck! That's how I *feel*." A tear.

Smile. "See, we're making progress!" Next?

They sat around in a circle, five mornings a week with Martin Thoms. Twenty chairs with patients, and one chair for Martin. Eventually, each would have a chance to sit in the middle. Pull the chair into the center, and let each patient-vulture take a turn at peeling away another layer of skin until *real feelings* could be felt. The outside personality was just a facade. The insides had to be exposed, like turkey bones after Thanksgiving dinner.

309

But how does a woman talk about her feelings with men in the group? How does a man express his innermost thoughts, with women sitting there, laughing and mocking? Catty under their breath. Happy to see men feel anguish, the same type of pain they'd been dishing out all their lives. Men and women, sitting in a circle, looking at each other, and the rules were this: one person talks at a time, and no one's allowed to attack physically. Mentally, take whatever punches you'd like. Blind side 'em! Hit below the belt! Bruise, kick, and bite. Harder. Deeper. Crawl inside and rip out their innards with words and insights.

"I hate you, you little prick! Not true!"

"Is so. It's your fault. You started the fire; no wonder you escaped. Coward! How does *that* make you feel?"

Smile. Next?

"He didn't beat *you* because...because you really did like fucking him, isn't that the *real truth*?"

"No! No! No!"

"Liar!" Smile. Next!

"Who did *you* bang at the Park Plaza? You were doing the same thing, weren't you!? You're a victim? Bullshit. I think you've been a slut all your life, and your husband was just another John. Admit it! You were fucking in the Plaza long before he ever did!"

"How...how did you know?"

"But why? Why have you acted like a slut all your life?"

"Because I'm addicted, you idiot! What are you, a goddamn moron?"

White Knuckle

"I think you like acting like a slut."

"I like drugs and booze and sex. Cross addictions. Because I'm an alcoholic! But it's a disease, isn't it, Martin? An illness. It's not my fault, is it?"

"But how does that *really* make you feel?" Smile. Next?

"If it's a disease, then how come there's no cure?"

"You're sick! Your brother probably made her feel like a woman, something you never did. Selfish and spoiled. One little rich boy who never gave a thing in his life, just took!"

"I'm gonna take you outside and beat the..."

"Nothing physical, remember? Just words. Remember, we're after feelings. Peel off the skin and get to the feelings."

"I quack like a duck. I look like a duck. I act like a duck. Then how come I feel like a hawk?"

"'Cause you're a duck, you fucking idiot. Quack! Quack! Quack! Start swimming in the right pond, and you won't hate yourself anymore."

"Promise? Do you really, really promise?"

"Read the Big Book, pal. That's where you'll find the promises. I'm not promising anything but another peel on another layer of skin. I like ripping it off, one layer at a time."

They all did. Taking turns. Enlightening. Insightful. Fun, when *you* weren't in the center of the circle.

After seven or eight more sessions, Levi peeled off a few of his onion skins. He expressed some shallow feelings, cast a few judgments, and put an exposed toe in the water of the process just to see if it came out scathed or deformed. Nothing serious, nothing too deep or too revealing. He tiptoed around the edge of the circle, but never dove in head first.

Willow never said a word. She just watched, listened, and slowly simmered. Getting angry and boiling alone in her own little world. A world black and dark. Isolated and quiet. Levi kept his eyes on her constantly. Just looking at her made him feel sorry for the scars she carried alone.

At first, Levi wanted Willow physically. He wanted to touch and caress the glistening softness of her black, silky skin. But then, as he watched Willow from a distance, his feelings began to change.

As the days went by, he stopped wanting her body. The fantasy stopped, replaced with feelings he'd never experienced. Time passed, and he wanted to protect and defend and even respect and trust her. Respect? Trust? She didn't do anything. She hardly said a word. Willow was obviously alone and wanting to hide. Why did Levi want to trust her? Why did he want her to trust him? Where were these feelings coming from? How did the feelings get inside Levi? Could they have been there all along?

Levi wondered and waited. He didn't know the answers to a lot of questions. But he did figure out one thing in the first ten days at Betty Ford. Levi figured out for certain he felt one real thing, and he couldn't escape it. Levi was certain he felt afraid.

Afraid of the circle. He wasn't putting his chair in the center of the group. Not in this lifetime. At least not while he still had some control.

Levi waited for the fear to pass, but it didn't. It continued to grow as the circle bit into one patient at a time. His time was coming, and he waited his turn, afraid.

He also waited for Willow's turn.

28

"Today is Women's Day," Martin Thoms announced to the therapy group. "We're going to start out talking about safety, what makes a woman feel safe and secure, from their perspective. Men don't speak; just listen."

Damn, Levi thought, men don't get to talk, and he had to listen to the women babble. Willow probably wouldn't utter a word, never had, and he didn't care about the others.

But attendance was mandatory, and everyone had to abide by the rules. Levi sat back, trying to think about something other than a woman's feelings about insecurity.

One lady talked about baking bread in an old brick oven from Italy. "Freshbaked bread makes me warm. It smells good, and I feel fine."

"Long-Island Iced Teas made me feel safe. After I'd get bombed at the neighborhood bar, I felt like I could take my pick. Booze was my friend; it made me loose; it made me feel sure of myself. Then I nearly lost my mind."

"My mind was lost," piped in another, "when my husband hanged himself on a telephone cord while he was talking to his mother." She sighed and slumped, like she was falling into a cushion of bad memories.

"His chair was right under the wall phone. He was so drunk. He must've been leaning back, when the chair legs slipped, and he went down. Somehow, the cord was around his neck, and I found him dangling like an old goose on a clothesline. I blamed myself, so when I thought I had control over the quiet, I took Valium in the morning, drank wine for lunch, and had a vodka-bottle nightcap."

That's when Willow spoke her first words. Out of the silence.

"I remember the first time I was raped. It was on Fat Tuesday during Mardi Gras. I grew up in Louisiana." Willow murmured the words so softly, almost no one noticed. Then, one by one, the people in the circle began to listen. Levi sat on the edge of his chair.

"The mask is really what saved me," she said. "But it didn't save me 'til that night when I saw he didn't recognize me, even though we was ten feet apart from each other. That skinny, pompous bastard just sat there. He didn't even know who I was. The mask covered me and made me feel safe.

"I can't remember *exactly* how old I was, maybe ten or eleven, in New Orleans. I always knew I'd be a party girl. I know I was pretty young, 'cause I was so scrawny, I looked like a boy. But I got through it. Men kept trying to fuck me after that. It's like I had a badge on, or a neon sign that said, 'Go ahead and fuck her; she's easy lickin'.

"In high school, my stepfather kept sayin', 'She ain't no good. She'll get her ass knocked up before she can drive.' He tried. He was the next old bastard that kept grabbing me, talkin' trash, and jumpin' in my bed when my mother was drunk or sleeping. She was always drunk or sleeping or whining and crying.

"But I got through my teens with only two boys gettin' inside my panties." Willow paused and looked bewildered. Her eyes squeezed shut, and she slapped her chin as if swatting at a mosquito. A memory was zipping into her head, and memories were covered with layers of onion skins. Onion skin memories started to peel.

"But as a kid that skinny, white fuck got to me," Willow said. "I had long, scrawny legs and nappy hair, and a chest as smooth as an ebony stone.

"I remember telling my mother I wanted to see the Mardi Gras parade on my way to school that night. I was going to be Cinderella in our school play, and my mom and brothers and sisters was all going to be there to see me. I was so excited, I was skipping everywhere. It'd be the first time all the attention was on *me*. And I was Cinderella.

"I can still hear Mama saying, 'Don't you go downtown, girl.' I heard her. But I didn't listen good. Instead of goin' straight to school like I was supposed to, I went skipping downtown, smiling and acting like hot shit, because I was going to be like white people. Cinderella. Big time.

"I was skipping and laughing, and then this skinny white man steps out from a door onto the sidewalk, right in front of me. He held two small ropes, about a foot long, with a loop at each end. Like handcuffs. Only they wasn't made of steel.

"'See this rope, sweetie?' he said. I remember standing there on one leg like I was a one-legged chicken. Sort of stupid. I jumped back, wondering what the honky meant. I was supposed to be doing Cinderella, not Debbie Does Dallas. And I stared at him. All I could see were those big, gnarly teeth. Then he laughed and says, 'Let's play, Baby. You and me are going to play a little game.' Then with a whisk of his arm, I found myself inside the doorway.

"It was kind of dark inside, but I could see a candle burning, and I remember a whip near the bed. A small one, but big enough to cause welts like the ones I got from the switches my stepfather used. The man locked the door and grabbed my wrist. My bag with the Cinderella dress and mask fell on the floor, and he slipped one noose of the rope around my fingers and pulled it so tight on my wrist, I could feel my hand swelling. I remember thinking, 'Hand, don't get bigger. You can't get out, if you get bigger. Shrivel up, girl. Get small and hide!'

315

"But there was no gettin.' I was already a goner, and I knew it. In the dark room, that white bastard, he looked like a sweaty cowboy. I remember he was sweatin' hard. Wet forehead, wet hands, and wet dick. Dripping. A little calf roper. White trash, and my first 'lover.'

"I was like a rag doll when he threw me on the bed and sat on top of me. He threw my arm up to the headboard, and in the middle of the headboard was a wooden post. He put the cord around the post and stuck my other hand in the other noose and tightened the collar. I was strung, with my arms over my head, tied to a bedpost.

"I was sweating," Willow shuddered like a dog shaking water off its back. "and the last thing I remember seeing, before he fucked me, was his clenched teeth over my face. This time his teeth weren't smiling. He was hateful and hungry. And I thought, 'I didn't do nothin' to make you mad. All I want is to see a parade.'

"But he looked so angry, I thought he was going to swallow my neck when he sucked on it. His teeth – what he had of 'em – were brown and pointed and ugly. Mean. His breath smelled like beer and nuts. And after slobbering on my collar bone, he just lifted up my skirt and covered my face like I was in the morgue, and he was ready for another part of the autopsy.

"He didn't say nothin' at first. But I knew. I was so scared. But when he put my dress over my eyes it made me feel better, safer in the darkness.

"He was anxious, he ripped his zipper when he pulled his pants down." Willow laughed. No one else did.

"It's funny, that rip sounded like the scream of a fighter jet. I still remember that. At night, I remember. Sometimes I wish I was deaf, so I wouldn't hear that zipper zip in my ear making such a terrible, loud noise.

"And then he touched me. I could feel his fists and his fingernails pushing into the skin above my nipples. Then he put his palms underneath them and squeezed and squeezed. He pulled and squeezed and lifted my whole body up with both hands on my chest and skin.

"'You ain't got toots.' he yelled and jerked at my chest. Seemed like he wanted to pull tits right outta me, but I didn't have no tits, and he couldn't pull tits out, no matter how hard he tried. And he tried, but it didn't hurt. It didn't hurt 'cause I was hiding too far away in the darkness, with my head underneath that dress. Then he punched me, hard in the stomach, and called me a crazy bitch. He hollered. 'You dirty, little whore, you ain't got no toots!' I think he meant tits, but he said, "toots." If you ain't got toots, I ought to turn you over and fuck you proper. Boys don't have toots. You're supposed to have something to suck on! Something to slap around, to roll my nose in like bread dough.' He sounded real pissed off."

Willow glanced blankly at the other patients surrounding her. She looked mystified. "I didn't know white people liked toots and sticking their noses in bread dough," she said. Her head turned back and forth, trying to understand.

"He hit me a few more times, and then ripped my panties off and tried to poke me. I could feel his dick bouncing up and down, but he couldn't get it in. That's when he stuck his head down there and spit on me.

"I didn't like that part. I didn't like him spitting on me. That dirty, skinny, slimeball – spit!

"I heard him gurgle it up, just like my brothers did when they was having luger contests. Big wads of snot and saliva. Gross. And now, this bastard's dirty fingers pulled my twat apart so he'd get a good shot! And he did.

"Then I felt his dick. Spit was all his dick needed. After a few jams, the tip of his dick was wet like the rest of him. He plugged me like a javelin. Then, he spit again. Or so I thought. His prick spurt inside me. I didn't know nothin' about sex. He was coming, and I thought he was spitting again. That's why I don't let men come inside me. They got to get it off on the outside.

"Then his dick wilted and shrunk. He got off me, and I heard him putting on his pants and shoes and humming Dixie. I laid there in all his mess and my blood and his spit. I was laying there, hurting, waiting to see if it was safe to move. The pig had just spit on me, and he was humming like a canary.

"When I realized the fucking was over, I finally peeked out from the dark hole I'd crawled into inside my head. I could feel his eyes looking down on me and on my tootless body, but I was so far away from him, inside myself, that I wasn't really afraid anymore. Where I was, he couldn't hurt me. Hell, he couldn't even find me.

"I don't remember how I got out of the ropes and that room. I don't remember getting to school and putting on my costume or even my Cinderella mask. I forget how I felt, or why I didn't call Mama or the police. But I remember wearing my mask. That's what I remember most."

"I found safety that night," Willow said. "When I first woke up to reality, I was on stage in my Cinderella dress and my mask was on. Lights was shining. People were clapping and laughing. I saw my mama and brothers and Grandma sitting there real proud." Willow Dawn paused.

"Then I seen that bastard again. Him and his prick were sitting right in the front row. I remember wanting to run. I wanted to scream and yell for help. But suddenly I realized that the calf-roper and his dick didn't know me. They didn't know who I was or nothin'. He was so close he could've grabbed me and fucked me again, right there, if he wanted to. But he didn't want to, 'cause he couldn't see who I was."

Willow smiled, as if she knew something nobody else did. "You see," she said, "he didn't recognize me because I was wearing my Cinderella mask."

Willow Dawn's tone turned confident and stronger. "It's what keeps me safe today. The mask. All you've got to do is find one that fits, and then wear it. Wear it wherever you go."

White Knuckle

Martin Thoms shook his head. "You can't *always* hide behind a mask, Willow. It's just not possible. You can't hide the past and go through life without coming to grips with your demons. Sometimes, you've just got to come out."

"It's always worked for me," she said.

"Has it?" he asked. "Has hiding behind your mask really worked? Or are you just barely holding on to your sanity? Eventually, you'll lose your grip. Maybe it's time to deal with your anger and guilt."

Willow looked at Martin, then over at Levi. Tears were streaming down his cheeks. Their gaze locked into each other from across the circle.

"Levi, without our mask, they'll just hurt us, won't they?"

He shook his head back and forth.

"I don't know," he said. "I don't know."

* * * * *

Levi's love for Willow Dawn was like nothing he'd ever felt. He didn't love her body and legs and breasts. Her grey-green eyes, soft mouth, and smooth ebony skin. Levi loved Willow's heart, and she loved his spirit. They walked around the pond each day and spent every free moment together. Together, they rambled through each other's thoughts and feelings and hearts. Levi and Willow Dawn were friends.

"How come I always thought I was the only victim, or that no one else's problems mattered?" he asked.

"How come we go it alone, never telling, never being honest?" she wondered.

"If you're honest, Willow, they'll hate you. It's safer to lie – then no one will laugh at you."

"Have you ever tried being honest?"

"No."

Willow turned and held his hands in hers. They stood by the pond, facing each other. "Until I spilled my guts in the circle, Levi, I never told no one, and I was never honest, either. I was afraid, before I spoke up, but it just poured out. And now it don't scare me anymore. No one laughed, and no one blamed me."

"I saw Martin smile, Willow. I saw it."

"He wasn't laughin', Levi. He was smilin' because he knew I was lettin' go of the mask. I was gettin' sane."

"How did it feel?"

"Like nothin' I ever felt before. Like a weight was lifted, and I was free."

"It's a mighty hard decision, Willow. It's real fucking scary."

"Be honest, Levi. Just tell the truth. I'll be there listening – I'll even be sittin' in your corner."

He pulled her body next to his. As they embraced, she could feel him tremble.

29

For nearly three weeks, Levi kept most of his feelings to himself or he shared them only with Willow. In the group sessions, he was an outsider, watching and listening, auditing a class, not a real student. Not participating.

But on this day, and in this group session, Levi finally felt like talking – he wanted to be honest – for the first time.

"The truth is, I died the same day my father did." Levi's voice was low and shaky. "The tomahawk is what saved me, but now I know it only postponed the real fucking I got. I remember running so hard my heart felt like a bomb, ready to explode. And carrying all those quarters, putting 'em into the phone while my mother stood beside me crying. What good's a quarter when there isn't nobody to call?

"Quarter after quarter. I pounded on that fucking phone till my hand bled. And no answer, no response. And he had promised! My father promised he'd be there, and I needed him. I couldn't go back into Small Pox, not without Dad. I only cracked Bates's skull open – Dad would've ripped off his goddamn head."

Levi put his face into the palms of his hands, his eyes closed. The group listened. No one said a word.

"When I was fifteen, I decided to go back to Small Pox. It was a vision. I wanted it more than I wanted anything." Levi raised his head and looked at Martin. "But my brother Joshua was a coward. Even if he'd known the truth, he wouldn't know how to fight. You understand that, Martin? Do you? My whole world was filled with cowards and liars.

"Joshua wouldn't take the time to even drive me there, and he didn't know the plan, or ask why I wanted to go. I had a club and a hatchet. I wanted to see Bates with his dick hacked off and shoved down his throat. I wanted to watch him choke to death. That vision stayed with me for years. It's still there, sometimes."

Levi looked out the window. He stared at some distant place beyond the room, past the people in it, who sat quietly listening to him.

Levi's mouth curled with disgust. "Joshua was too busy to drive me to the camp. And you know what?" He shook his head, looking down again at the floor. "He was my mother's favorite. She liked Joshua best. Sure, she tried to hide it, but I wasn't that dumb. She saw too much of my father in me, so she distanced herself. And I tried – really tried – not to be like my father. My father got buried, and so I tried to bury everything he ever said and the memories of everything we did. See, he was the biggest liar of the bunch. He promised he'd be there. Instead, he croaked. That was really stupid."

Levi looked at Willow. "Yesterday, you said the creep spit on you. It made me sick. Sick because everybody's been spitting. They been spitting on us all our lives."

"Why blame yourself?" Martin asked. "That's the real problem, isn't it Levi? You blame yourself."

"Fuck you, Sherlock!"

Levi stood abruptly and started toward the door.

Willow's stare caught his, and she nodded. Her eyes motioned for him to sit down again. They reassured him that he would be okay, and that he had much more to say.

White Knuckle

Levi returned to his chair and sat like a stone statue, not moving, not talking. Thinking. Memories raced through his mind behind his eyes, like a picture show on panavision. Images, dreams, and thoughts. Dry tears. Darkness. A glimmer of tears, and then they closed. Levi took a deep, cleansing breath. His shoulders straightened, and he opened his eyes.

"It was my mother who forced me to go to camp. Dad left the house, and I blamed her for everything. I didn't blame my father for Asia or for leaving my mother. I blamed both my mother and Asia for Dad's death. I figured the two of them caused it. They were women. Women were traitors and couldn't be trusted. But then, Dad couldn't be trusted either. I was nine years old. Raped by a fat man with peanut brittle, and my father was nowhere to be found.

"Dad made promises. They all did. All of the promises were broken. Everybody turned out to be liars. So there was only one thing I could do. Dad said I could be the best. I believed him at the time. He said he had faith in me. And so I worked to be the best liar in town – in the world. The best at fucking people over before they fucked me. I was fucked by my father, my camp counselor, my mother, Asia, and everyone after that. Pretty soon, it was just safer to stay in my box." Levi fought to hold back his tears.

"Kit called it a Puckerbush Patch. Kit was another woman I loved, and she left me, too. I loved Kit, Mom tossed her out, and she disappeared, and never kept in touch.

"That one really floored me. I could understand my father not staying in touch, after all, he was a goddamn dead man. But Kit? Why didn't Kit call me or write, or try to come and visit, if she loved me so fucking much? I finally decided she was a liar, too.

"All of them. Men and women. Women were the worst, though. They lied about everything. And they weren't even subtle about it. Makeup, false eyelashes, padded bras, and prick-teasing charades that called for a dick, but when you got right to it, they just wanted to see if you'd fall into their trap. Getting you aroused was more fun than actually getting you off. They made me sick, so I stayed away. And you're right, Martin," he said, staring at Thoms. "I did blame myself. It *was* my fault. Bates did what he did because of me. I knew it all along. It was my fault for being stupid, for letting myself be vulnerable. For letting anyone love me when love was just a four-letter word. Another dirty, dangerous word."

"How did that make you feel?" Martin asked. "How did it *really* make you feel?"

"Alone, goddamnit!" Levi's face turned crimson with rage. "I'm alone now, and I've been alone my whole fucking life!" He started crying. Choking sobs came up from his deepest recesses.

Willow started to move from her chair. Martin smiled gently and gestured for her to remain seated. Levi's dam was overflowing. The floodgates of pain and memories and nightmares had been opened.

"Getting raped by Bates was not your fault, Levi," one patient said.

"Neither was your dad's dying," said another.

"Your mother had her own pain. She had the right to deal with it her way," someone else observed. "Especially 'cause you never told her what happened. How was she to blame?"

"Hey, Levi. Look at me!" The man speaking to him was a patient who had already confessed to the group that he'd abused his wife and practically every girlfriend he had ever met. "Look at me!" His voice was rising.

Levi stopped crying. His composure returned. He stared at the other patient. The man smiled, a smirky, sort of all-knowing smile. "Ain't it true, Levi," he said. "Ain't it true you're really no better than Bates? You're a liar, you're a cheat, and you've been fucking with everyone who's ever come close to you. You're a predator just like he was, only you ain't been fucking little boys, yet. You've just been fucking yourself."

The room fell quiet, filled with tension. Levi's expression changed. The squinting lines in his face smoothed. The red hot anger softened to a pale pink, and the bulging muscles in his neck calmed. Levi smiled at the confessed abuser, in rehab for his own transgressions, his own addictions. Levi looked around the group, then at Martin, finally at Willow. "The truth is, I feel so angry that if I had a gun, I'd blow my fucking brains out."

"That's because you've been holding on to life and your knuckles are turning white," Martin said. "White knuckles, and it looks like they're about to lose their grip."

Willow rubbed her chin, and her words were hushed, but clearly audible. "Why hurt yourself, Levi, when everyone's been doing it for you? But mostly, you been doin' it to yourself, haven't you? For all these years, haven't you been hurting yourself, 'cause you won't let anyone else close enough to hurt you anymore?"

Levi stared blankly out the window, thinking. He turned and looked back at Willow. "I don't want to be hurt anymore," he said, staring at her.

"It comes with life," she answered.

"But who do you know, Willow? Who's worth trusting?"

"I trust you and God, Levi," she said. "And if I can trust you, maybe you should start trusting yourself."

*   *   *   *   *

"Hello?" A lifting voice answered the phone.

"Is this Erica?"

"Yes. Who's this?"

"You don't know me, Erica, but I've got to tell you something. I'm breaking a promise, but it's the right thing to do. I know it."

"I don't understand," Erica said.

"My name's Willow, Willow Dawn. I'm calling because I have a friend, someone I care about. Someone who's changed like nothing you ever saw. Seems like overnight, but really, I think he's always been there. Kind of hidden like. He loves you, Erica. Levi Saranno loves you."

"I don't care, I…it doesn't matter."

"Don't hang up, Erica. I've got to tell you a story. It's breaking every rule, but if I don't tell you what I know, you might never find out. You might never be told."

"I said it doesn't matter. Levi's not a part of my life anymore. I, I just don't care. Except…"

"Except what?"

"Except if he's okay. I mean the thing in the hospital. Levi's okay, isn't he?"

"That's just it, Erica. Levi's not just okay. Levi ain't Levi anymore. He's – you got to believe this, Erica – Levi's the most gentle, loving, and honest man I've ever known."

"Oh, really? Are we talking about the same person?"

"Not the one you know, Erica. There were two Levi's. Now there's one. Look, he's not the guy you knew, Erica. He doesn't know I'm calling. I'm doing it for him, but I'm also doing it for you. I'm telling you, Levi isn't Levi, and you've got to listen, Erica. Listen for your own good."

"Why should I?"

"Just let me explain, Erica. Then you can decide what you want to do. And how you really feel."

30

"You called Erica? No!" Levi looked shocked. "I can't believe it. Why would you do that to me, Willow? You're not supposed to do that."

"This ain't no betrayal, Levi. I'm your friend, and I did what friends do. They help each other when they can."

Levi's hands were clammy as he walked with Willow on the path around the serenity pond. "What'd she say, Willow? What'd you tell her?"

"She ain't easy, Levi. Her walls are like King Tut's Tomb. You'll need to dig mighty hard to get inside."

"Did she listen to you?"

"For the first five minutes, Erica didn't respond to nothin'. Then I said something about you being honest, that you weren't a liar."

"What'd she say!?"

"She hung up the phone so hard, I figured she broke it. Slammed it right down without another word."

"Oh, Jesus." Levi looked pale. "This is hopeless."

"So I waited a bit and called her back in ten minutes. I let her stew. She's hurt, but she's still curious."

"What'd she say when you called back?"

"Hung up again. Twice in fact." Willow stooped and picked a flower. "But it kind've reminded me of when I got my first runway assignment at the fashion show in Milan. I always wanted to go to Italy. I kept bugging the agency, and they kept saying no. After awhile, they finally got curious and listened."

"I don't get it," Levi said.

"Curiosity, Levi. If you make people curious about yourself, then maybe they'll stop long enough for you to work your charm. I made the top man at the agency curious, told him I was a virgin and I'd do *anything* for a show in Italy. He got curious, and I got what I wanted." Willow laughed, something Levi noticed she did often these days.

"What happened with him?"

"Nothing. He was gay. He just wanted to know what a virgin model looked like. Never seen one before."

"What does this have to do with Erica?"

"When I called next, her curiosity kept her on the line, but christ, Levi, damage control wasn't easy. She didn't believe we were talkin' about the same guy."

"She's gone, isn't she? I know it. Feel it. I was such a loser when it came to her."

"Erica says you never *once* told the truth. That lying covered you like white on rice."

Levi shook his head sadly. "Next to you," he said, "she's the most honest person I've known. I never could figure out how to deal with it. She was always trying to get inside my head. Always scheming to figure me out." He stared at Willow's bright eyes. "Lies were easy my whole life. Facing the truth was like getting naked in front of your mother. It's just not something you do."

"You did it okay when you put the truth out to the circle," Willow observed. "And you don't have any trouble talking to me."

"I'm not afraid of you, Willow. Erica scares the shit out of me. Always has."

"Why?"

Levi looked at the water, then back to Willow. He paused, and carefully chose his words. "Willow, I've never told a soul, and I...oh, forget it."

"Don't, boy, or I'll push your ass in the water. You're talkin' to Willow here, so spit it out. I'm no one to be afraid of, remember?"

Levi hesitated. "She scares me, Willow. She scares me..., because she's like my Dad. Erica reminded me of him and Kit. They were the only two people I really, really loved."

Willow raised an eyebrow, as if trying to squint inside Levi's thoughts. "Are you still afraid of Erica, Levi, or are you afraid of yourself?"

"I'm afraid of losing again." Levi bent down and picked up a smooth stone. He threw it hard, skipping it over the water. "See that rock?" he asked. "You throw it out there, and it skips for a while and then just sinks. Drops to the bottom and drowns. Alone and by itself."

Willow leaned down and picked up the biggest rock she could find. She threw it as far as she could. It sank, waves circled around where it went under. "I'll bet if that was a diamond, you'd go after it and bring it back," she said.

"Probably," he answered. "So what?"

"So no one's divin' in after you. But I suspect," a curl cornered her lips, "Erica saw a diamond somewhere in your relationship. If you polish it up and let it shine, my guess is she'll do some dredging."

"And if she doesn't?" he asked.

"Well, at least you went down shining this time." Willow grabbed his hand. "We've got to stop our lying, Levi. Especially to ourselves. Stop being afraid. Maybe then people'll quit spitting on us. Maybe then we won't sink to the bottom."

* * * * *

Willow called Erica again, but convincing her to visit Levi at the Betty Ford Center was tough, even though Erica had already made plans to vacation in California with Reni.

Erica's curiosity grew when Willow asked, "Did Levi ever *really* talk to you about his father? What they did together and how it made him feel?"

"No. Not really. Maybe once, I can remember."

"Did you ever hear about a place he calls the Choke Hole? A spot where he and his father went fishing? And the skid trail that leads to the river?"

"Yes. Actually, it's one of the few good memories I have." Erica's tone changed. A softness echoed through the phone line. "That...that was the day I..." She stopped talking.

"The day you what?" Willow urged.

"I don't even know you, Willow. Why should I tell you anything personal?"

"'Cause I know Levi, and I know you're hiding something. So what happened by the river, Erica?"

"That's the day I fell in love with him." The words were soft. Clean and pure and honest. "He was such a different person there."

"He's back, Erica. He's practically wading in the water, and he's the person you saw way back then. The change is real. And Erica, it's honest."

"I...I just don't know. I need to think about it. How can someone change?"

"Maybe he didn't change. Maybe he was always the Levi he's been hiding. Levi's unlocked memories. He remembers things now, and that's where he's found the change. It's where he's found himself."

"I, I don't know what to do, Willow. I don't..."

"Come meet the new Levi," Willow said. "Your instincts were right. Your timing might've been wrong. But if you had courage before, muster it up again, girl."

"I, I don't know. This isn't easy."

"Erica, there's more. There's a reason Levi was hiding from you. But he'll have to tell you about that himself. Then I think you'll understand everything."

"You tell me. Please, Willow. Tell what you know."

"I can't, Erica. It's Levi's place to tell you the truth. There was good reason for his actions. If you're curious about that reason, you'll have to ask him yourself. He's here, and he's different, I promise."

*   *   *   *   *

Addicts are never cured. Their disease is sometimes held in remission, like diabetics who need daily shots.

For Levi, his daily shots were of support and knowledge. He was being insulated – not with insulin, but with insight. He was getting a life. But Sundays were a waste of time at Betty Ford. On Sundays, Levi could watch TV, take all the walks he wanted, and piddle the day away until visitor's hours were over. An A.A. meeting took place at Firestone Hall on Sunday nights, where outside alumni could stroll in from the desert around Palm Springs and pick up their medallions to celebrate the number of months or years of continuous sobriety.

Levi didn't have visitors on Sundays. His mother and Joshua didn't know about his vacation in the sun, and Vincent Morgan called only once to see if he hadn't gone A.W.O.L. Leaving was the last thing Levi wanted. Levi wanted more group sessions, more walks with Willow, more affirmations about fault and guilt and anger and repression. The demons started to disappear. Predators hate exposure. Publicity turns them yellow. They hide. When fully exposed, the predators die, and Levi's demons were not immune to the light.

Nightmares were fading as the locks on Levi's memories constantly opened. When Levi wasn't talking to Willow about his past, he talked to himself. Solitary walks around the serenity pond – tossing stones, skipping into the laps of memories – rocking chairs and fairytales. Conversations bounced back and forth between hope and times forgotten.

From age nine to twenty, Levi had carried chains on his heart. At Betty Ford, the chains became ropes; the ropes became strings. Strings faded into tiny, silk webs, and the webs floated softly away on the wind.

Levi walked. Thinking silently, or whispering out loud. At first, he thought he was alone, but the fragile feeling of loneliness slowly diminished. Isolation and loneliness began to disappear.

White Knuckle

As the days passed, Levi sensed someone was beside him. Someone was there. He reached back. Timidly he touched a thought; carefully, he opened the door. With delicate caution, he let in the light.

Finally, Levi started talking to his dad.

For years Levi had repressed the childhood memories and feelings, the sense of friendship and protection that vanished before he could say good bye. Gone. The ultimate promise had been broken.

You promised you'd be there, Dad. A phone call away. Instead, you died. That's no way to keep a promise, Dad. I loved you. You were my life.

Levi sat on the bank of the pond, throwing pieces of bread to the mallards swimming up to him.

Okay. So it was an accident. But there was no one else I could trust, Dad. You didn't leave me anyone in your place. I was left with Mom and Josh, and they wouldn't have helped. No one had your strength, Dad. And you were gone. Why Asia? Why leave us for her?

Levi looked deep into the water. He remembered the big house in Denver and seeing his father on television. Some guy went on trial, and his mother and father were always fighting. Then camp. Anakeegee and Bates and running, running for the telephone. Levi clearly saw himself dashing through the woods, knowing that when he found the phone, he'd find safety.

I knew you'd get him, Dad. I knew for certain you'd make him pay. But you were already dead. There was only one thing I could do. So I did it. I died, too.

"Can I change, Dad?" Levi said out loud. "Can I be as strong as you? Would that make you proud?" He threw another stone and watched it sink. "I'll try," he promised. "I'll try to change. I can do it, if you stay with me. Please don't leave me."

335

Levi ran out of bread, and the ducks paddled away. Sun shimmered on the water's surface as small ripplets waved against the shoreline. Some visitors and patients walked quietly around the pond while others spread blankets on the grass, watched children play, or ate from picnic baskets brought in from the outside.

Willow's gentle touch startled him. "I've been looking all over for you, Levi," she said, grinning. Willow was happy, almost giddy. She reached out her hand. "Stand up, boy. You and me are takin' a walk over to reception. I want you to meet a friend of mine."

Levi's face clouded over. "I don't feel like meeting people right now, Willow." He stood up and faced her. "It's not going to be easy. We get out of here in three more days."

Pulling gently on his arm, Willow walked toward Firestone Hall. He followed beside her. "I know. And you're afraid people won't accept you."

Levi hesitated and looked at her. "No," he said. "I'm afraid people won't think I'm being honest. I never have been, so why should anyone think anything's changed?" He kicked at pebbles on the path. "I won't know what to say, or how to start."

"Even if you don't know what to say or how to start, Levi, you still got to try." Willow pointed in the direction of a woman, sitting inconspicuously on the deck of Firestone Hall. "Start there," she said.

Levi's stare finally focused. "It's not possible. This isn't real," he said looking back at Willow, then up again at the blond woman in the distance. She saw him too, and gave him a slight, nervous smile.

"Start being honest with someone who just might love you," Willow said. She gave Levi a gentle push. "Go on, guy. Introduce the Levi I know to Erica."

31

Erica reached out her hand as Levi sank his shaking body into the chair next to hers. "Willow suggested I see you, Levi."

He burst into tears.

"Last time I saw you, you were crying," she said, as she adjusted her body, trying somehow to make it comfortable. "I told myself I'd never see you again, Levi."

He didn't answer.

A part of Erica wanted to soothe his hair, and touch the long scar on his face. She didn't. She stayed silent, not knowing what to say or do.

Was she merely curious about Levi, or did she really care? Did she feel pity for him? Love? Was she just a gullible adolescent, or courageous and wise to come and face this man?

"I'm out here on a little vacation with Reni," Erica said, trying to make small talk. "You know, Disneyland, Hollywood, Beverly Hills."

Levi stopped crying. "Does Reni know you're visiting me in this place?"

"No. I don't even know why I came, but your friend Willow's pretty convincing."

"I...I'm glad you're here. I understand why you wouldn't want Reni to know."

"Reni met a surfer in Balboa. She's spending the day with him. I'm supposed to be shopping at some mall by the Crystal Cathedral. Obviously, Palm Springs is a slight detour in a different direction."

Erica looked into Levi's red-streaked eyes. "How've you been?" she asked. "You look different from what I expected. Sampson painted one picture, Willow another. I didn't know who to believe, so since I was in the neighborhood, I thought I'd see for myself."

Levi fidgeted. "Erica, I never expected to see you here. I didn't even know if you'd ever see me again in Colorado." His voice trailed off. He groped for the words. "How can I explain what's happened, how things have changed?"

"Well," she said with a hint of reprisal in her voice, "I guess we all change. Some better, some worse. You got worse, I hear, and I didn't think *that* was possible."

"I don't know what Sampson told you, but I'm sure it was true."

"Sampson said you're not worth having as a friend anymore. He said I should stay away from you, that you're probably infected."

"Sampson's right about a lot of things, but that one's not true. Definitely not true. They test you here like crazy."

"The pictures Sampson painted were so...so ugly."

"I've made a lot of changes, Erica. I know I have."

His hand reached to hers. Erica resisted the urge to open her palms and let him in. Her fingers held firmly to the glass of iced tea in her hands.

This was a time to be tough, she thought. Patient. Time to listen and observe. To look for the cracks and hints and evidence of guilt. The lies and deception. Look beyond the neat appearance and superficial words that flowed like a new lover's lies. Search beneath the exterior.

White Knuckle

"So you've changed, have you?" Her tone was matter-of-fact. "Tell me how."

Levi looked toward the pond and saw Willow lying on the grass, eyes closed, her face directed into the sun and sky. He turned to Erica. "I'm not afraid to be a friend," he said thoughtfully. "I'm not afraid to have one, either."

"That's not what Sampson told me," Erica said, sounding like a mother with a recalcitrant child. "Sampson said you've gone sideways. Off the deep end, and into a world of darkness. Even he couldn't trust you. Is it true or not?"

Levi didn't hide the resignation and regret. "The truth is that since I was nine, I couldn't trust anyone, not even myself. That being the case, there's no way anyone should trust me, whether I wanted them to or not." His eyes closed as he turned away from her. He looked ashamed.

"I don't get it, Levi. You have talent. I've always sensed it, and so many hidden gifts you were born with. But I never saw them, I just suspected they were there. But you blew them away. You'd never talk to me, never let me in."

Erica stood up and reached for her purse. Levi got up from his chair immediately. "And I...I tried," she said.

"If I said I'm sorry, would you believe me?"

"I still don't trust you, Levi. I came out of curiosity, that's all."

"You're lying," he said with a smile. It wasn't an accusation. His tone was warm and kind. "Now you're the liar, I'm not."

Levi's hand went firmly to Erica's wrist. His pull was strong yet gentle as he stood beside her. Levi moved closer and softly touched the tips of his fingers to her chin. He stared deep at her face, not saying another word. He waited for the cool air to blow away the tension.

"Lying doesn't suit you, Erica. Don't start. Trust me on that one."

Could this be the boy who had left Colorado Springs, the snooker-playing hustler with dirty nails and chalk marks on his jeans? The drunken doper with dangling earrings that Sampson had described? The last Levi she'd seen was a whimpering weasel. How many lives did this guy have?

"You're acting different, Levi," she said. "I don't know what it is – your voice, or how you're dressed."

"Asia bought me these clothes. She bought them just before my lawyer sent me here."

"Did you say, Asia? I thought you hated Asia. You said she was the reason your father died."

"Don't act so surprised, Erica. I know now the accident wasn't Asia's fault. I've just blamed her, because she was an easy target. It's how I've treated everyone. Anyone who's tried to get close. Blamed them for my problems and kept 'em at a distance."

"I can't help but ask, Levi. What did I do wrong?"

"Nothing. You were just a victim of my problems. You had nothing to do with why I acted the way I did."

"Why were you so hard to love, Levi?"

"I'll tell you in Colorado, Erica. It's a long story, but I promise to tell you everything. Can I see you there? Call you sometime?"

"I…I don't know if that's what I want. I've got to think about a lot of things."

Levi nodded. "I understand."

And for the first time, Erica thought that maybe, just maybe, he did.

32

"'Bred and born in a briar patch! There's no place I love better!' I heard that when I was a kid, Willow, and I always thought it was true."

"It's a fairytale, Levi," Willow said. "Leave it back at Betty Ford."

The taxi drove toward the Palm Springs airport after leaving the Betty Ford Center. Levi laughed. "Brutal honesty isn't going to be easy for me."

"Just try being yourself." Willow took Levi's hand in hers.

"Who's that?" he asked.

"The guy I know."

"Willow, we've been cloistered in a goddamn shell for thirty days. Now we're facing reality again. I can't let *all* my defenses down."

"Why not?"

Levi thought about the question. "Because it's still not safe."

"Neither is lying. Isolation in some stupid patch isn't the answer, either."

"Is there a compromise, you think?"

Willow squeezed Levi's hand. "No," she said. "There ain't no compromise. Go make your amends, Levi. It's one of the steps we've been taught. But if you can't be honest doing it, then there's no point in doing it at all."

Daniel J. Gatti

"Since when did you become a shrink?" Levi smiled.

"This psychological stuff don't mean nothin', Levi. Nothin' if you don't accept that you're human, you got flaws."

"I've got plenty of those."

"I hope you left most of 'em back at the Center."

"What if I didn't?"

"Listen, Levi, the moment you stop hiding, the moment you stop being afraid of getting close, that's when you're gonna be reborn. Yeah, born again. Get God. He's got promises, and He don't break them. "You're gonna start coming from a place of light instead of a place of fear. Everything you do and say will come from love, not fear. And then, it will be honest. No more lies or bullshit. You'll see."

"Get God?" Levi asked. "How do I get God when all I've ever done is sinned?"

Willow smiled. "Just ask Him, Levi. God loves sinners, wants them in His House. Jesus said, 'Love God first, and do unto others as you'd do unto them.' Start there."

"I dont know how to talk to God, or if He'd talk to me."

Willow smiled again. "Levi, she said. "Don't you get it? God's always been with you. He's Who got you through the darkness. You've had an angel on your shoulder all your life, protecting you. Now, all you got to do is open the lines of communication. He'll listen, and eventually, you'll hear back."

Levi grabbed Willow and hugged her tightly. When the cab pulled up to the airport curb, he didn't want to let her go.

Willow gently extricated herself and kissed Levi on the cheek. "We're both gonna be fine," she said. "And we'll stay in touch. We only got a couple of friends we can trust. At least we got that, and that will always be ours. We'll keep it special."

Once inside the airport, they waved good bye and the two of them walked in opposite directions. Levi searched for his gate and turned back for a final wave at Willow. She was gone. His friend had disappeared into the crowd. He smiled, knowing she wasn't disappearing forever. He looked upward and said "Thank you, God. Thank you for Willow, and thanks for saying 'hi."

*   *   *   *   *

The pilot's announcement that the plane was making its descent to the airport in San Francisco woke Levi from a deep sleep. He had been dreaming, but not dreaming nightmares.

In the baggage claim area, Rick Bender was looking for silly sunglasses and a sullen look. The investigator barely recognized the young man that came up to him, hand extended. "Thanks for coming," Levi said, shaking his hand firmly.

"Boss's orders," Bender answered, reaching for Levi's suitcase.

"I'll carry it," Levi said, gesturing him away. "Sorry I was such an ass last month. I don't even remember you dumping me out of the cab at Betty Ford, but if I was rude or obnoxious, I apologize."

Bender laughed. "You were just your normal self." He stared at Levi. "Before you get back to your apartment, you might as well know, it's been cleaned. No booze anywhere."

"Thank you," Levi said. "I really appreciate the help, and I mean it."

Bender scratched his head, wondering. "Betty was good to you," he said. "But maybe you didn't understand. I said the booze is gone, Levi. You've paid the piper. Charges will now be dismissed; you're free to go back where we found you."

Levi nodded. "You found one guy, Rick. You're now with another one."

Bender drove Levi to his apartment, unlocked the door, and watched as Levi entered.

Levi put down his suitcase and surveyed the surroundings. "Doesn't look the same," he said. "Doesn't even feel right."

"Asia had it cleaned. Thought you might like it."

Levi turned to Bender. "I hate it," he said.

"Figures," Bender replied. "I'm glad she didn't order flowers."

"I hate it," Levi said, "because it's the place where I almost died. This isn't me, anymore. I don't plan on staying here. I'm not going back to where I was."

"We'll see." Bender said. "People don't change overnight."

Levi smiled. "Maybe it's not a change," he said. "Maybe it's a rebirth."

Bender smiled cynically. "Good luck," he said as he went out the door.

"Well, there's one you didn't win over, old boy," Levi said to himself as he walked into the bedroom. Instead of unpacking, he opened another suitcase. As Levi packed his clothes, he noticed the red light blinking on the answering machine. He hit the button.

"Call me, you creep. There's a few things I've got to say." Marsha's voice was filled with anger. But there was no way to tell whether the message was left last month or in the last few hours. Maybe she's calmed down, he thought, as he dialed her number. She answered on the first ring.

White Knuckle

"Marsha, this is Levi."

"About time!" she screamed. Instantly, Levi knew it didn't matter when the message was left. His checkerboard sweetheart needed to vent.

"I've been gone, Marsha."

"They threw me in the fucking slammer, Levi! Said I was a goddamn accomplice to a crime – yours!"

"What happened?"

"Detroit Willy bailed me out, and they dropped the charges after you went off on some stupid vacation! You didn't even call me to see."

"I'm sorry, Marsha. I just called today to tell you the apartment's open and the rent's paid to the end of the month."

"So fucking what?"

"So I'm moving back to Colorado, and I'm telling the manager to expect you and the others to be taking out what's left of my possessions. You can have it all, divide it any way you want. Ginger should get some things. Just get it out before the end of the month."

"Fuck you! I'm not a moving van!"

There was a long pause, and Levi waited for the hangup. The click didn't come, and Levi waited.

"What do you mean, Colorado?" Marsha's anger turned to desperation. "You can't just up and go to Colorado. We bought toys, remember? We never got to use them."

"I'm sorry if I hurt you, Marsha. Really I am. But I have to leave."

"But, Levi."

"You'll meet another guy."

"You fucking loser!" was the last thing he heard her say. He hung up the phone, picked it up again, and dialed Ginger. Ginger seemed to accept his apologies. She was certainly less angry.

"Will you help Marsha and the family sort out the furniture?" he asked. "You can have whatever you want."

"Are you leaving the dope behind?" Ginger asked.

"I'm leaving *everything* behind," was the last thing he said, laughing.

Levi left the apartment an hour later. He didn't look back.

After checking into the Clarion Bedford Hotel, Levi settled into his room for the night. He knew what was happening on the streets of the Tenderloin and he didn't care. Instead, he made plane reservations and thought about his future. Dinner was brought to his room. Before he went to sleep, Levi picked up the telephone and dialed Asia's number.

* * * * *

Levi felt nervous as he stood at the top of the crookedest street in the world, looking down at the house with its vines of purple bougainvillea draping the rails on the deck of Asia's terrace. Lombard's red-brick road still twisted its corners around flower beds and tourists.

The Friday afternoon sun was high as Levi waited on the sidewalk, and the trolley car behind him screeched to a stop at the top of the hill on Lombard. When Levi called Asia and told her he'd be there at three, the next day, she said it was perfect timing. "We'll have company," she said brightly. Levi wasn't too happy about that. He wanted to talk to her alone.

He looked at his watch. He'd gotten there an hour early, but Levi wanted extra time. He needed to get his feelings and fears and anticipated words under control. His words were rehearsed, and he wanted to make certain that his gut wouldn't turn them into a nervous whirlpool of mixed emotions and superficial cliches.

"Levi?" Asia said. A hand touched his arm.

"Asia! I…I was just waiting. It's not three, and I…"

Asia stood with a bag of groceries. She smiled as she pulled out her keys. "I went down to the wharf and picked up some fresh crab. We need an appetizer. I'm glad you're early, actually. Here," she said, handing him the bag and unlocking the front door.

When Levi entered, he was instantly greeted by *Lovers*, the sculpture Judd had bought for Asia in Carmel. Levi passed through the foyer and looked around. Plush carpets; Italian marble and granite; original art work; comfortable, elegant furniture. Everything was light and colorful. Inviting. Like Asia.

Flowers and plants adorned the corners, and photographs in magnificent frames were perched on top of end tables, the mantle, in nooks and crannies, and in every room. Levi avoided looking at the photographs. He knew his father would be there. He could feel his father's presence all through the house.

Asia took the groceries into the kitchen. Levi surveyed his surroundings, the view, the water and the wharf and San Francisco Bay. He was thinking about his father and Asia, what they had planned together. For the first time, Levi got a true sense of what his father really wanted before he died.

Asia returned from the kitchen, and handed Levi a soda. She was drinking a glass of iced tea.

"I've waited for so long, Levi."

"Before you say anything, Asia, I have to tell you. I have to be honest. Oh damn, I don't know how to begin."

"Begin at the beginning," she said gently.

Levi nodded. "The truth is, Asia, I always hated you. Not when we first met, but after Dad died. I hated you for taking him away, I blamed you for letting him be in the car and getting killed. I wanted you to die, instead."

Asia sat down on the beige velvet sofa. "I'm listening, Levi, even if it hurts. You have the right to feel the way you do."

"But I don't hate you, Asia, not anymore. And I don't blame you, either."

She smiled slightly.

"I don't have anything but respect for you. I understand now that Dad loved you. I understand *why* he loved you." Asia's eyes misted, but she fought back the tears.

"My father never would've left me for someone who wasn't wonderful. And Dad was right. Otherwise you wouldn't have kept sending cards and letters and kept trying to stay in touch. I…" Levi's voice choked up and wavered. "I was jealous. And I wanted to hurt you. Make you pay."

"What can I say? I can't defend myself. I had hopes and dreams. I wanted a family, and for you to be in it."

"I can't make it up to you. Asia, I'm sorry. I'm sorry from the bottom of my heart. I can only thank you for what you've done and ask for your forgiveness. There's nothing else I can do."

White Knuckle

"There's one thing you could do," Asia said softly.

"What?"

Asia put her glass of iced tea on the coffee table and extended her arms. "Let me hold you, Levi. You could let me hold you. And you could hold me back."

And he did. Levi held her close and tight and cried. It was one of the easiest things he'd ever done in his life.

* * * * *

They stayed in Asia's living room overlooking the Bay, and talked for an hour. At three o'clock, Asia began to glance at her watch. Levi went over to the mantle and stared at a picture of his father. A smiling, happy Judd beamed back at him.

"You know, Levi, I was always sorry that your dad and I started our relationship while he was still married to your mother. It wasn't my style, believe me, but I couldn't control the timing. I felt terrible, but I loved your father like I've never loved anyone, before or since."

"Not even Vincent?"

Asia laughed. "Don't be silly. Vincent was your dad's friend, and my lawyer and financial advisor after your father died."

Levi heard the front door open and then close with a loud bang. Shoes dropped to the marble floor. He wished he and Asia weren't going to be interrupted. Not just yet.

A pretty nine-year-old girl rushed into the living room. Asia greeted her with a warm embrace, then turned to face Levi.

"Levi." Asia smiled. "Meet your sister, Shelby."

33

Shelby flew into Levi's arms. "I can't believe it! Oh, Levi, you're so handsome!" Joy hallowed her face. The nine-year-old daughter of Judd Saranno couldn't have weighed more than seventy pounds, but when she jumped into her brother's arms, the momentum carried them both to the couch and then to the floor. Levi hugged her back, his face registering a mixture of shock, happiness, and gratitude.

Asia watched, smiling as the brother and sister laughed and talked and touched in a seeming hurry to make up for the lost years in fifteen minutes. Finally, Asia told her daughter to wash for dinner, and as Shelby dashed from the living room, she called back to Levi, "This is ten times better than Disneyland."

When Shelby disappeared, Asia said, "Come in the kitchen, Levi. You can help me with the crab and crackers."

Levi followed her quickly. "Asia, why didn't you tell me?"

"What could I say to you?" Asia said as she took out the cocktail sauce from the refrigerator, along with fresh lemons and celery sticks. "I had no idea I was pregnant until after your father's funeral. I'd caused enough pain in your family, and I couldn't put your mother through more. You were only nine years old, Levi. You'd never have been able to understand, and you were already so angry. You hated me. I just had to wait, hoping that the day – this day – would come."

"But I got older, you could've said something."

Asia arranged the crab meat and crackers on a tray and began slicing the lemon into wedges. "I couldn't do anything until you came to me. In California, it's safe to acknowledge Judd Saranno as Shelby's father. In Colorado, it would've been impossible, and I wouldn't have done that to your mother."

"But what about you? How did that make *you* feel?"

"Knowing I was pregnant and your father dead. It was awful. Then I knew Shelby was a blessing. She was my link to Judd; I had a part of him. But you know, Levi, it's ironic. You said you were jealous of me, remember?"

"Yes."

"The truth is, I was always jealous of you, too."

"Jesus, Asia, how could you be jealous of me?"

Asia's voice cracked. "Because your father always loved you best, Levi. It was something I always knew was true."

Levi was jolted.

"Loving a man or woman is one type of love," Asia said. "Loving a son or daughter is another. The love your father had for you was like nothing I ever saw. His last words were about you, not me. His last thought was of you and how much he cared and wanted to be there as you grew up. That's why I stayed in touch; tried to, anyway. It was a promise I made to your father, when he was dying. If *he* couldn't keep his promise, I would, even from a distance."

"Asia, I, I treated you so badly." Levi was awash in remorse; Asia's words felt like a blanket, a comforter that surrounded him and soothed an old wound that was still aching.

White Knuckle

Asia went on. "I raised your sister to believe you were like a storybook hero, off doing battle with dragons and devils, and that one day you'd come back."

Levi finally got up the nerve to ask Asia the question that he'd wanted to ask ever since they'd been talking. "You never married. Why?"

Asia smiled. "I've had my chances. But until I feel for someone like I did for your father, there's no point in getting seriously involved. And men don't knock every day, not when they have to compete with your father."

Levi bit into a cracker as Asia squeezed lemon juice on the crabmeat, put a small bowl of seafood sauce on the tray, and picked it up. As they headed back into the living room she asked, "Have you got a girl you like?"

Levi's smile vanished.

"I...I'm sorry, Levi. It was..."

"Her name is Erica," he answered. Levi looked down, and the expression on his face was sad. "Erica reminded me of lots of people, Asia. She reminded me of my father and Kit. And now," he paused, looking into Asia's jade-green eyes. "Now Erica reminds me of you. God, Dad was lucky."

Asia put the tray on the coffee table and touched his cheek with her palm. "If Erica's anything like me, Levi, and if she feels at all like I did about your father, then trust me," she kissed him on the side of his mouth, "you're very lucky, too."

* * * * *

Shelby had long, dark, brown hair tied in a ponytail that flowed below her shoulders. She was lithe and light, with skinny, tanned legs and black eyes that looked into Levi's as if he were the most important person in the world.

"You look like me." She laughed. "You look like Daddy, too."

"You're prettier than both of us." Levi said. "You look like your mom, and she's as pretty as they come."

"Tell me about Daddy, Levi. You had him for nine whole years. That's old as me." Levi smiled and nodded. "Tell me everything. Was he as great as Mom says? Did he really teach you how to shoot and fish? I've seen pictures of you and Daddy fishing. Will you take me fishing, Levi? Can we go places, and you show me where you and Daddy went? Can we?"

"Of course we can. Anything you want, and I mean it. I'm not going to lie to anyone, especially not to my little sister."

Asia had pizza delivered, and the three sat in the living room, eating pizza and going through photograph albums. Levi delighted Shelby with stories of fishing trips and what it was like to be with their father.

"I was your age when Dad died, Shelby. I'm sure he went to heaven. He liked kids our age. As far back as I can remember, Dad and I played all sorts of sports, except for soccer. Dad hated soccer. He didn't like boxing, either. But Dad loved the mountains, and he loved me. I know he loved your mom, and I'll bet he's watching us and is happy. I know he's loving you."

Shelby smiled at Levi and hugged him, her smile turning into a yawn.

Asia frowned. "It's eleven o'clock, Shelby. Way past bedtime. But tomorrow, you can stay home from school, and you and Levi can spend the day together. That is," she turned to Levi, "if your brother's got the time."

"I've got to get back to Colorado." Levi bent across the couch and kissed Shelby on her forehead, "But tomorrow, I'm spending the day with my sister."

White Knuckle

Asia looked at her daughter. "Get your pajamas on, and I'll read a story, but just a short one tonight."

"Can Levi do it?" Shelby asked.

Asia glanced at Levi.

"I'd love to," he said.

* * * * *

Levi saw the photographs and books that lined the shelves in Shelby's bedroom. Encyclopedia and classics. *Grimm's Fairy Tales, The Frog Prince, The Velveteen Rabbit, Charlotte's Web,* and dozens more.

In the center of her desk, Shelby displayed several framed photographs. Levi saw his father in one of them, standing in front of a courthouse, looking like a lawyer. Asia was in several other photos, sitting on the veranda with Shelby at her side. In one picture, Judd and Asia were standing on a beach, staring into each other's eyes. In the middle of the arrangement of photos was a picture of Levi, wading in the shallow water of a river, smiling with the flyrod and an empty fishing net beside him.

"Someday, Shelby, I'll take you to the Choke Hole that's in this picture. It was the last place Dad took me, before he came to California."

"Promise?" Shelby asked.

"I promise," he replied. "I'm gonna go back soon, and see if it's still there. If it is, I'll find the trail, and I'll send more pictures. Someday, we'll catch a fish there, and if it's not too big, we'll fry it, and then catch some more."

Shelby was cushioned in bed. As Levi stared at the picture of his father, Shelby asked, "Levi, would you read me my favorite story? It's not very long. Please?"

"You're too old for fairytales, aren't you?" he said. "Some fairytales are better left unread, I think. I think sometimes they just aren't good 'cause they leave you with wrong impressions." Levi sat, tucking in the blankets around his sister's shoulders.

"Read me something," she pleaded.

"Have you ever heard a story about the Puckerbush Patch, or Brier Fox and the Tar Baby?"

"Sure. Brier Fox got outfoxed, didn't he?"

"For a while, at least." Levi said, lying down beside her. "Let me tell you what I think, and then you go to sleep, okay?"

She put her hand into his. "Okay."

"Once upon a time, a long time ago, kids were told about places where they could hide. The patches were supposed to be safe places, places only kids could find. Bad people couldn't get into these places, and kids could be there all alone. Some people called them briar patches, and some said they were Puckerbush Patches. Patches with thorns and nails and spears, but kids could get into them without getting hurt, and bad people couldn't get in, so the children would be safe.

"But these weren't safe places. Not really. They weren't safe if you hid there and stayed there and never came out again. In fact, they aren't good places to stay, because the way to keep bad people away from you is not to hide and stay hidden. If you do that, Shelby, then you'll be alone. And you'll be afraid. You can hide for a little while if you have to, but only hide until the coast is clear. Then run out. Run as fast as you can."

"Where do you go?" his sister asked. "What should you do?"

White Knuckle

"Holler, Shelby. Holler and scream and yell and shriek. Go find your mom. Find the police or Vincent. Or me. Anyone. Find someone you can trust. And keep on screaming your whole way out, screaming so loud that the bad people will run, and then they'll be the ones hiding. Maybe they'll try to jump behind the patches, and maybe hurt themselves on the way through the thorns and prickles."

"What if the bad people don't let you scream? What if they don't want you to tell?"

"Bite them! Bite them hard and keep on screaming. Get a crowd around you. Make such a commotion and racket that people will start coming, just to see what all the fuss is about. Remember this, little Shelby: Bad people don't like crowds. Bad people don't like the truth to be told, for everyone to know. If everyone knows they're bad then you don't have to hide anymore. They don't want their neighbors and friends and relatives and people to know the truth. Once bad people are exposed, then they're the ones who have to hide. They're the ones who have to suffer and slither away into some swamp where they can't be bad anymore. If you expose the bad people, Shelby, and if you tell everyone about their lies and threats and the mean things they do, then you'll be safe; you'll be free."

"That's a scary story, Levi," she said, holding his hand tightly.

"I know, Shelby. But it's the truth."

Levi kissed his sister goodnight, and turned out the lights.

34

Shelby slept as Levi and Asia talked far into the night. Levi told Asia about Small Pox, the ropes around his wrists, the broken hinge, and the tomahawk that should've scalped the son-of-a-bitch. Running to the phone, knowing his father would be there, only to find no answer. Finding out later that his father had died, and then coming to the realization that Bates would live and Levi would be alone.

"Everything Dad ever told me became a lie. Any love I had for him, I tried to bury. I distanced myself from my mother, too. She was weak, but it wasn't her fault." he said. "Weak and lonely, and she blamed Dad for her unhappiness, probably because he'd always taken care of her. It made sense to me. But I found comfort in myself. I felt as if I was the only one I could trust."

Asia asked questions, gently, like a nurturing friend.

"Why did you lie to everyone, Levi?"

"Because it was easier than the truth."

"Why did you keep hiding?

"Because I didn't want to be hurt again."

"Why didn't you ever tell Erica?"

"Because I was ashamed."

"Why did you push her away?"

"Because I was afraid."

"Why did you stay with those awful people, like Marsha?"

"Because I had control."

"Why did you let Willow in?

"Because she was just like me."

"Are you any different now?"

"Yes."

"How?"

"Because now I can remember. I remember all the things I forgot, the things I pushed into darkness and kept hidden, because they made me unhappy and angry and frightened."

And he did remember. He remembered how he felt on the river and how he felt about his father. His father made him feel secure and strong, invincible and good. Tough. Able to take on the world and slay all the dragons. His father gave him hope and wisdom and joy and a feeling of closeness. A feeling of love.

Those were the things he'd forgotten. Now they were what he remembered. "The way I figure it, Asia, I grew up on my own, not having a clue how to go about it. At Betty Ford, they said I aged – chronologically, but I stopped growing emotionally at nine. My mind never grew with my body. I didn't trust anyone, and I tried to whiteout the memories. I tried very, very hard."

White Knuckle

"Levi, I'm terribly sorry."

"It's okay, Asia. Now I understand. My reaction was no different than most kids who go through this. It's how most of us deal with abuse or tragedy, if it's not dealt with at the time. Abuse occurs thousands of times every day. Thousands of people hide it in closets. There's nothing unusual about me or what happened."

"Yes there is," she insisted. "It's horrible, and maybe how you dealt with it in the past isn't unusual. But what *is* unusual, is how you're dealing with it now, and how you'll deal with it for the rest of your life. The rest of your life is what's going to be unusual."

"I can only hope so." Levi looked weary. "I want to believe in people and promises. I want to believe in God."

"You'll do it, Levi," Asia said. "I think you'll have the kind of life your father always envisioned for you." Asia hugged him. "You'll have the life you want, Levi, and I hope you'll let Shelby and me play some part in it."

"A big part, Asia. I promise."

Those were the last words he said to her before going off to bed.

*   *   *   *   *

Saying good bye to his little sister wasn't easy. It wasn't easy to for him to leave Asia, either. All three cried at the airport, tears of sadness and joy and relief.

"I won't be gone long. I'll see you both soon," Levi promised.

"Don't forget," Shelby said.

"I won't."

361

Asia hugged Levi one last time, then whispered in his ear, "Now I'm begin-ning to see what I always dreamed of."

"What's that?" Levi asked.

Asia looked straight into Levi's eyes. "I'm beginning to see your father in you."

The boarding call came over the speaker system, and Levi gave Shelby a final hug and headed onto the plane, eager to get back to Colorado, to get home.

* * * * *

Sheryl and Joshua stood stiffly, waiting to greet Levi when he got off the plane. As soon as they spotted him among the arriving passengers, Sheryl waved, and Joshua reached out for a handshake as a smiling Levi came up to them. Surprise and embarrassment crossed Joshua's face when Levi grabbed his brother and embraced him, instead of shaking his hand.

Levi kissed his mother and said, "Mom, I love you."

Sheryl, too, looked shocked. Levi grinned at Joshua. "I love you too, Josh. Did I ever tell you that?"

"My, God," his brother said, "I thought you quit drinking."

"I did. I quit a lot of things. Let's go home, and I'll tell you about it."

It wasn't difficult for Levi to talk to his family about San Francisco and his stay at the Betty Ford Center. He left out his encounter with LaToya and some of the gory details about his San Francisco escapades. Sheryl and Joshua didn't need to know everything.

"The truth is," Levi said, as the three of them sat at the kitchen table, "my drinking got me in trouble, and I landed in jail. Sure, Vincent Morgan got me out, but I didn't know Vincent, Mom; you did. And you were in Egypt when I was arrested."

"So how'd you get his name?" Joshua asked.

Levi looked at his mother. "Mom, you always said God has a plan, and we've got to accept it."

"You're home, Levi," she said. "I've never seen you look better. I've never seen you so relaxed and confident."

"Mom, I had no one else to call, so I called Asia."

Sheryl nodded. Her tone was compassionate, wise. "Who else could you call? Actually," she shrugged, "I kind've thought you might visit her."

"You're not angry?" Levi asked.

"Not anymore," Sheryl said. "What happened, happened. Levi, I know more than you think I do. Vincent and Sally Morgan were friends of your father. Remember, they were at his funeral." Levi nodded. "I've kept in touch with Sally over the years. Christmas and holidays and such. And she's told me some things about Asia."

"You called her Dad's whore," Joshua reminded her.

"I was hurt – very hurt, Josh," she said. "I got over it, thank God. I even felt sorry for her. She'd send you boys letters or cards, and neither one of you responded. I know that must have devastated her. Especially since…"

"Since what, Mom?" Levi watched his mother's hesitation and waited for her to continue.

Sheryl's eyes welled up. She fought back tears. "Especially since she wanted you both to know your sister, Shelby."

Joshua stared at his mother. Levi was speechless.

"A sister?" Joshua stammered. "I got a sister?"

"Yeah," Levi answered. "A nice one, too." He turned to his mother. "How do you feel about that?"

"At first, I was angry. Now, it's in the open. Now I can deal with it and you boys can as well. I'm no longer jealous."

"How did you find out?" Levi asked.

"It's not something Sally Morgan could hide from me. But I've got to tell you boys something," she said, reaching out her hands, touching each son. "I'm sorry I kept the secret from the two of you. You had the right to know, and I was wrong to not tell you."

Levi walked to his mother's side and put his hands on her shoulders. Massaging her, he said, "We all got things to be sorry about, and we all got a lot of forgiveness to give."

"Mom," Levi said, "I'm sorry I went into a shell for so long."

"You went into a hole, Levi," Joshua interjected. "I went into my computer, feeling guilty myself."

Levi was startled. "Why, Josh?" he asked.

"Because I hated you," he answered matter-of-factly.

"I don't understand." Levi looked confused.

Joshua's lips trembled.

"I was jealous," he said. "And angry because," Joshua's voice faded as he struggled to get out the words "because Dad loved you best, Levi. You and him did everything together. Me and him did nothing, nothing important. I wanted to please him and never could. You were the only one that mattered to Dad. That's why I hated you."

Levi watched Joshua wipe away a tear. Levi moved from his mother and touched his brother's shoulder. "I'm sorry, Josh," he said. "I'm really, really sorry."

"So am I, Levi. I'm sorry too."

* * * * *

The three talked into the night. Levi told his mother and brother what happened at Camp with Barry Bates.

"Dad's death took precedence over everything and everyone. I couldn't say anything about Bates, because it didn't seem important, compared to Dad's dying. By the time the funeral was over, I figured it was all my fault, anyway. I was guilty, and Bates didn't matter. I was the sinner. Besides everyone had their own pain to deal with. I didn't think anyone would understand, and no one could do anything about it without Dad there."

"That filthy, fucking bastard!" Sheryl cried. Tears of shock and dismay rolled down her cheeks. "My son. My Levi. Oh, my God. "

Neither son had ever heard their mother swear like that. Both had seen her cry, but never like this. "I'm so ashamed, Levi," she said. "I should have figured it out, asked the right questions. How could I have been so blind? And all those years, thinking you were acting like you did because of your father's death, and only that."

"Mom, you had no way of knowing. There were too many other reasons to explain how I behaved. I'm sorry for all the trouble I caused along the way."

"I'm so sorry too, Levi." Sheryl took her son in her arms and hugged him tightly. "Forgive me, Levi."

"Mom, there's nothing to forgive. There never was."

* * * * *

"Vincent," Levi spoke into the phone, "I just wanted to apologize and to thank you for what you did."

Sheryl stopped to listen outside of Levi's bedroom.

"There's one other thing, Vince." Levi's voice was hesitant. "I know I don't deserve it," he said, almost stammering, "but I don't know many lawyers. Not like you, anyway, and I need to ask one last favor. You can say no if you want, Vince."

Levi saw his mother and smiled. He waved her into the room. Sheryl sat down beside her son on the bed. She watched him as he took a deep breath.

"I've decided to go to law school," he said, his hand tightly clenching the receiver. "I've got a few years to make the grades and get in, but I'm serious now. Now I know I can be the student I should've been, and when the time comes, I hope I can use you as a reference. May I?"

Levi paused, waited, listened and then slowly he broke out into a grin, from ear to ear. He thanked Morgan and hung up the phone.

"Yes!" he cried out, pulling his fist back in triumph. Sheryl looked at her son with unabashed pride.

"Since when did you decide to become a lawyer?"

"Just following the footsteps of my old man," he replied.

Sheryl hugged her son. "And you'll be as good a lawyer as he was. I know it.

Your father was one of the finest trial lawyers in the state. I can't remember a case he lost."

"Mom," Levi challenged. "Even I remember Dad losing the one that involved his friend who pulled the plug on his son."

Sheryl smiled. "He didn't lose the Bernie Panzer case, Levi," she said softly as her eyes closed and her voice lowered.

Levi looked at her quizzically.

"Your father was right all along, Levi. It's too bad he didn't live to see the final result. The court of appeals remanded the case, saying Panzer couldn't have killed someone who was already dead. His biggest crime was interfering with the hospital's decision to stop the machines that kept the poor boy's body breathing."

"Panzer served eighteen months, waiting for the appeal process to work its way up the court's ladder. Eventually, Bernie was resentenced for the time served, and when he got out of prison, he and his wife went to New Mexico and started over. Last I heard, the Panzers have a nice family, and he's a big developer outside of Santa Fe."

"I can't believe it," Levi said. "I thought Dad lost you and us and his last case as well."

Sheryl shook her head. "Levi, regardless of whatever problems your father had as a husband, parent, or lawyer, he always tried to do his best. Your father was never a loser, Levi. Judd Saranno was the best at whatever he wanted to do. And you can be, too. You've got his genes, Levi. Just do your best, and it'll be better than most people ever do."

35

"God, give this girl Your blessings, 'cause she's going to need them," Reni frowned, sitting across the table from Erica. "You can't really be serious about giving Levi a second chance, not after what he did?" She took a deep swallow from her glass of lemonade.

Erica glanced at the ducks and flowers and the beauty outside the window at the Lakeside Terrace restaurant. She shook her head back and forth, clearly thinking. Wondering.

Erica turned to Reni. "You ever been in love? You've dated nice guys, bad guys, and guys in between. Slept with who knows how many. But have you ever been in love?"

"Every time." Reni smiled. "But I pretend. Pretend like I'm in love so it feels better."

"So the answer is no?"

"Answer is, it feels better. But what's love anyway? I've not found it, and I've got experience; enough experience to know you're not going to find love from Levi, and why would you want it from him when there's fifty million better and you could pick and choose from the lot?"

"Like I told you, Levi and I have been talking. Levi's not who you think, and certainly not like he was before leaving for California."

Reni's eyes rolled. "It's no wonder there're so many blond jokes, Erica. You're blond – and acting like a joke." Reni's tone was serious. She couldn't hide the perplexed expression on her face. "So you and Levi have been talkin'. About what? About his escapades in San Francisco? Even I'd be gettin' him tested for AIDS after what Sampson said. He's such a fucking loser and a drunk besides."

Erica looked at her friend knowing she couldn't tell Reni the truth. The truth about Camp Anakeegee and the wounds and feelings and honesty Levi expressed over the phone. Levi had finally confessed his secrets to Erica, trying to make her understand.

"We've been talking on the phone, Reni. I'm amazed at his ability to communicate when he's seldom been able to in the past."

"Look, Erica," Reni said, tapping her nails on the table top, "listening on the phone is one thing. Letting Levi into your life again is another. You can hang up the phone and his lines of bullshit go silent. What does the thought of letting your guard down feel like?"

"It brings on the chills. I feel afraid."

"So why even think about it, Erica? Love hurts; makes people crazy. When I'm acting nuts, you tell me to listen to your advice, so listen to mine."

Erica's expression turned inquisitive. "What I don't understand, Reni, is why you hate him? Dislike is one thing, hate's another."

"What's to get, girl?" Reni lifted her hand and reached across the table with her palm in front of Erica's face. "Look in the mirror, Erica. You remember seeing that pretty face looking like desolation from a tornado striking you damn near dead? See my hand? Look in the mirror of my hand and remember how dejected and angry you were after Levi's ditching. You looked ragged, beaten, betrayed, and now let's pick at your heart."

She pointed a finger toward Erica's chest. "How did your heart feel?" she asked. "Do you forget telling me your insides were plowed and planted like an onion field." Reni smirked, and the nostrils on her nose squinted upward. "Levi ripped up your heart and bulldozed it into squash."

Forgetting those feelings wasn't easy, and Erica knew that. She remembered. When Levi left her parent's bedroom, shock set in and ravaged her for weeks. She was horrified. Anger helped relieve the pain. Resentment and emptiness and stupidity – she felt them all. The feelings of indignity flowed inside her veins like spewing lava. With indignity came remorse and guilt. Erica was helpless and frozen – a naked child in a snowstorm of shame.

"Do you know what abuse does to children?" she asked Reni.

"Fucks 'em up I suppose, so what? You never had abuse except from Levi."

"Shame," Erica answered, lowering her head, speaking softly. "Abused kids live their lives in shame and anger and with a loneliness only they can feel, not understanding why."

"More shit from your psychology class? What's that got to do with you and Levi? If you weren't abused, was he?"

"No," she lied, "but when his father died, Levi felt abandoned. He's told me so many things, Reni. Levi's open and kind and gentle. It's like I was right all along. My instincts told me Levi was worth loving, and I did."

Reni's eyes opened wide. Her forehead furrowed. Three fingers touched her lower lip. "You're not telling me you're still in love with him, are you? Please don't be telling me that, Erica."

"No," she was quick to respond. "I'm saying that maybe I should give Levi a second chance because of what he's been through. I know who I am; I'm just not certain who he is."

"He's a lout, Erica. Told you that before." Reni's fingers brushed through her hair. "I'm bewildered. You're smart, but this Levi's got your head and brains twisting like that old tornado."

"Reni, you could be more forgiving or at least more understanding."

"I understand his dad died. Too bad. All parents die. Get over it."

Erica glanced out the window. The sky was blue while fluffy white clouds floated on the horizon.

"I had a vision," she said.

"Don't tell me the vision had Levi in shining armor on some sort of galloping stallion, okay?"

"No," Erica answered. "I was told prayers were being answered. Jesus made a promise. He promised peace. Nothing missing. Nothing broken. It's Jewish, but it's real."

"Was Levi the vision?"

Erica tilted her head, and put the palm of her hand at the side of her face. "I don't know," she answered. "I honestly don't know. But someone was in my presence, and I don't know who he was. There was a shadow next to me, holding me close and I was safe. I felt secure and tender. It was surreal, but I touched the feeling of closeness. There wasn't passion, but there was love. It felt like an angel of God."

"Get over it, Erica. You're daddy's a preacher but that don't make Levi holy. That doesn't change anything. Levi's an ass, and he's not worth your time."

"I once made myself believe that, Reni. But after the visit at Betty Ford, and talking with his friend, Willow, I'm not sure. Now Levi's calling, we're talking, and I'm talking with someone I hardly know."

Reni leaned closer to Erica. "What motivates you into ever thinking about caring for Levi? Honestly, I don't get it. Can you explain?"

"I wish I knew the answer myself. Forgiveness? Closure? Revenge? All those things come to mind. Maybe it's just wanting to know the truth."

"About Levi?"

"No, the truth about myself, and why I feel the way I do."

"You said Jesus made a promise, right?"

"Yes, He did."

"Well promise me this then. *If*, and I hope you don't, but if you see Levi, promise me you'll not fall in love with the guy. He's just not worth it. Promise?"

"I'm not Jesus." Erica paused, then smiled. "Reni, I'm just Erica, but I do promise you this: if I see Levi, I'll make certain I don't fall in love with him, not with the Levi I *once* knew. That's a promise I know I can keep.

* * * * *

There is peace to be found out of chaos. Levi, there are lessons to be learned out of hatred and betrayal and abandonment. Deceit. Lies. Deception. All of those things are real. But as real as they are, your soul and spirit and wisdom and insight and strength can, and will, overcome.

"I can't fucking believe it, Levi." Sampson was shaking his head, marveling at Levi and the letter Levi held in his hand. "I saw you in San Francisco! You hated Asia and loved the lifestyle of Detroit Willy's family. Now you're reading a letter from Asia, telling me she's right and that you love her, your sister, and Erica, too."

"Do you want to hear more?" Levi asked sitting in Sampson's living room, drinking coffee.

"You're back, Levi. And different." Sampson hunched in a chair, staring at Levi, remembering how he looked with the skinny sunglasses and metal piercings surrounding his face like cheap silver around a clock. "How does Betty Ford change a gnat into a warrior of righteousness? I don't get it."

"God does it, Sampson, not Betty Ford. The Betty Ford Center is just the conduit through which energy flows if you'll let the gates open." Levi grinned. He looked fresh and clean. Tan. Confident. Sober. Mostly, Levi had an aura of strength Sampson had never seen.

"So do you want to hear what else Asia has to say in her letter or not?" Levi asked.

"Go for it."

Levi read from the letter,

> You are everything any lover could ever want or hope for, Levi. God's real blessing. Now, and in the future. A cherished one. That's what you deserve – and someday, you'll have someone who is like you, can love like you, can feel like you, and who can give like you. One and together. A spirit that radiates kindness and goodness and strength. Power. Over those who would hurt you or take from you. I want to protect you from all this misery others will want or feel the need to inflict. But, I can't – and so – you can and will. Hopefully. And not just by yourself, but with the help of others who love you, deserve you, and who recognize the power that's within your heart and soul. Your mind. Insight. Instincts. Yourself. And God.

For many years, Levi, you've been feeling alone. But, Levi, you're not alone. Always, He's been with you. There's no need to be in the desert, hiding. You have the right to live and be happy. Giving and sharing. To be loved unconditionally. And why?

Why, because you are a chosen child. Not the ordinary. Not the apathetic. Not the taker or mediocre follower. Instead, the complete opposite. You are the caregiver. The generous one. A leader among leaders. And nothing you do will be without passion. A great and powerful passion that glorifies a need in others to follow you, to believe in you, to trust you. And in time, to love you – like only you can love. You deserve all of that. You deserve more than anything to be loved. And I love you. With God's help, good choices, and an open mind and heart, you will find and keep what you deserve: unconditional love and passionate serenity.

Love,
Asia

Sampson stood up, scratching his head. He watched Levi read Asia's letter silently to himself.

"I wonder," he said, "if what she says is possible. How can all those nice things be true? I know you, Levi, known you forever. I see changes, but don't know how long they'll last or even if they're real."

Levi glanced up. "Suppose all I can do is try. Someone said friends can be friendly if not used. I'll start with honesty and not using people."

"Like you used Erica?" Sampson reminded him. "How are you going to get her to buy into Asia's so-called insight? If you show Erica the letter, she'll just think they are words from someone who's really talking about your father, not you. The person that's in that letter hasn't been seen by any of us."

Levi stood up, extending his hand to Sampson. "Thanks, pal," he said as their hands clutched firmly. "All I can do is try. Actions are louder than words. Patience might help. But getting Erica to give me another chance hasn't come easy."

"That don't surprise you does it, Levi?"

"Of course not," Levi said. "But at least she's talking to me without hanging up the phone. Erica's one of a kind, Sampson. Her heart's innocent, and her body shines."

Sampson patted Levi on the shoulder. "I'd stay away from her body, Levi," he cautioned. "She's not about to expose that again."

"I don't expect her to. In fact, that's the last thing I want from her right now."

"Then what do you want from her, Levi? What do you *really* want from Erica?"

Levi slowly paced the room with his arms and hands clasped behind his back. He looked at the floor and then raised his head as if looking to heaven. The words were like a prayer.

"I want her to know that a Puckerbush Patch has been burned. I'm willing to be vulnerable; to be honest and open. I want Erica to see the someone that's been hiding because he was too afraid of getting hurt."

"So when's that going to happen, Levi?"

"Tomorrow, Sampson." Levi smiled, took a deep breath, and blew out the air as if he was about to shoot the biggest free-throw of this life, and the game was on the line.

"Erica's taking a chance, and in the morning, I'm driving her up Pike's Peak and we're going into the mountains, fishing. There's a place I haven't been to since I was a kid, and I know I can find it. It's always been there, and Erica's going with me."

A cautious look crossed Sampson's face. "Levi, if Erica goes with you, I hope you'll be different than you've always been. I'm your friend, but even I'm not convinced. You look new, seem new, talk about things I've never heard you mention, but if I'm not convinced, how's she going to be?"

Levi stared at Sampson and sheepishly shrugged his shoulders. A look of hope and wonder enveloped his face.

"You haven't answered me, Levi" Sampson said. "If I'm not convinced, how do you convince Erica?"

"I don't..." Levi paused. "It's in God's hands, not mine."

36

Curiosity. That's what Willow said might do it for Erica.

"Erica," Levi had said, "you were always the curious one. The one with courage. Way more than me. Now I've got the nerve. Just let me show you. One step at a time."

She hesitated, and Levi continued to press forward. "What've you got to lose, Erica? Weigh it against what you might find. At least you'll find out what's real, one way or the other."

Still she wasn't certain.

"Are you afraid, Erica?" he asked.

"Of course," she answered.

"Of me?" He paused. "Or afraid of yourself?"

"I don't know," she said.

"Then you should at least find out. It's certainly not going to hurt you to find out what's real, and what isn't."

Erica finally agreed. Reluctantly.

He was someone else, he told himself, when their conversation had ended.

The one thing he wouldn't do now was lie. He would be honest. She can't be afraid of honesty, he thought. But as he knocked on Erica's door, Levi was petrified.

Erica smiled. "You're on time. How refreshing."

"Hello." He reached out his hand and she instinctively took it. The handshake was firm. "I don't think we've really met before. My name's Levi Matthew Saranno. Some people call me Matty, and I'm here to take you fishing."

"I'm Erica Lynne Jacobson. Some people call me Sunny."

"What should I call you?" he asked.

"Stupid, probably. But let's go fishing. Actually, I've never caught a fish before. You'll put the worm on the hook, won't you?"

"We're not fishing with worms. Fly fishing's more aesthetic. I think you'll like it better."

"And where, Mr. Saranno, are you taking me?"

Levi looked at her. "To a river I haven't seen in years. To the Choke Hole."

"Is that because you choked?"

"Not the last time, I didn't. I hope I don't, today."

Erica was radiant. Her blond hair was tied back in a ponytail, underneath a baseball cap. She wore a cotton, long-sleeved shirt, tight blue jeans, and comfortable hiking boots. In a duffle bag, she had shorts, a halter top, tennis shoes, and her wallet. The cell phone, too, in case she needed a taxi.

White Knuckle

Levi grabbed the duffle, opened the door for her, and quickly got into the jeep, smiling at her the whole time.

In Manitou Springs, Levi parked in front of a small store. "This place opens early. They used to serve lousy coffee, but then they got some fancy equipment, and now they call it lattes and cappucinos. It's not lousy anymore. Would you like one?" he asked.

Erica nodded. "With nutmeg and chocolate, skim milk, and vanilla," she said as she pushed open the car door. She laughed. "I think I'd better make it myself."

Inside the store, they were greeted by a ponderous fat man, leaning heavily on the counter. "What can I get you?" he asked with a chuckle. The man was huge. Jovial and big.

"I'd like a vanilla steamer with skim milk," Erica said.

"And I'll take a tall, double latte," Levi added.

"Comin' right up." He pushed his belly back from the counter and slowly turned to fill their order. His movements were slow. He weighed a ton. Sunny watched as Levi surveyed the candy jars.

As the man placed the coffees on the counter, he said, "You kids look like you're dressed for mountain climbing. Goin' up the Peak, are you?"

Levi smiled. "No. We're going fishing. Know any good spots or tips on what flies are catching fish?"

"I know a spot that's got German browns, son. But I can't tell you where it's at. Favorite fishin' holes are secret, you know. I'll take my grandson, but I can't take you."

Levi laughed. "I understand," he said, handing the big man five dollars. "May I have the change in quarters?" he asked.

Erica watched and listened. She wasn't crazy, she had a plan. Watch his every move, listen to his every word, look at his eyes and face and listen for inflections and tones and clues. Consistencies. Differences. Thoughts. She watched carefully, thinking Levi was genuinely friendly. Outgoing and open.

The fat man counted out six quarters and handed them to Levi. Levi handed four quarters back and put the other fifty cents on the counter. "I'd like a dollar's worth of peanut brittle," he said confidently. "The other quarters are for your grandson. He's lucky to have a grandfather who knows where fish are hiding."

The gentleman bagged the brittle and put it on the counter. "Have a great day, pal."

Levi was still smiling. "You too," he said. "Have a really great day."

"Care for a bite?" Levi asked Erica as they left.

"Levi, you don't like fat people. I remember you saying that. And you don't like peanut brittle either. I'm surprised."

"That was a long time ago," he answered.

As the two got back into the jeep and Levi revved the engine, Erica said, "You're not acting like you used to, Levi."

"I hope that's good." Levi smiled.

"I'll let you know."

White Knuckle

Levi glanced over at Erica. "What made you say yes?" he asked. "I mean, what made you decide you'd even give me ten minutes of your time? I don't deserve any of it. I'm aware of that, you know."

Erica looked out the side window. The forest was green and healthy. Huge trees, rocky mountain cliffs, and tall peaks were rising toward the morning sun. "I don't know what draws me, Levi. I don't know what drew me in the first place. But it was a feeling I had. I can't explain it. Then Willow called, and, well, that made a difference. What she said."

"So you think I might deserve a second chance?"

"Almost everyone does."

"Maybe, this could be a first chance," Levi suggested. "Let's pretend that today's our first date. You don't know me, and I don't know you. But I do know how to fish, or at least I once did. And today I'll take you fishing. I don't want anything from you, and I don't expect a miracle. I just want us to try our luck at the river."

"Fine." Erica's voice rose. "But I'm not Kit, whoever the hell that was, and I'm not Willow or Asia or your mother, either."

"I know. I do know." Levi's eyes misted. Erica gave his hand a quick, reassuring pat.

They drove a long way, and then Levi stopped the car and pointed. "Look up there."

Erica had looked, knowing she'd seen it before. And then she remembered how Levi acted that day. How they had walked down the skid trail and then stopped, only going part of the way. Maybe that was it. Levi could go only so far. Stop. Turn. Halfway or part way, but never down to the bottom, never to the very end. Never to tell the whole story, never to tell the whole truth.

Erica stared at the rocky ridge that jutted from a nearby cliff, and pointed to the hidden trail leading down to the water. Levi said the ridge reminded him of a rainbow trout, with rock sides of pink, purple, speckled grey, and brown. He was right. There were spots of black, and the rock rainbow's snout glistened red with Colorado clay, pointing to the skid trail. And at the bottom, Levi's Choke Hole.

"Tighten your seat belt, Erica. We're going for a ride," Levi said, looking over at her and smiling.

*   *   *   *   *

Levi was glad he'd carefully gone over the wench to remind himself how it worked before he picked up Erica. Now, he took off the wench cover, opened the back door of the jeep, and made certain his ropes were there and the chain saw was cinched. His tool box was tied securely, and after he put his jeep into low, four-wheel drive, the vehicle veered from the rocky mountain road, and Levi slowly headed down the hillside. Nothing looked familiar. Levi stopped driving. As the jeep sat perched on the edge of the mountain ridge, Levi knew that if he'd taken the wrong path, there would be no place to turn around, and the only way out would be a tow truck, with a cable hundreds of yards long.

"Levi," Erica sounded alarmed, calm, but cautious. "Are you sure we can do this? Ten more feet, and the only stop's going to be on the bottom."

"Do you want me to turn around?" Levi asked.

"No."

"I love your pizzazz. Dad said if I was ever gonna do this, you'd better have pizzazz."

White Knuckle

The jeep dropped over the edge. All four tires were on the ground, most of the time. Brakes on and rolling anyway. Over rocks and trunks and vines and holes. Ditches. Tree limbs smacked the windows; bushes scratched the sides; another bump, and Erica's hat went flying.

Wow! she thought. "Oh, my gosh!" she screamed. The dufflebag popped to the front seat; the paper cups flew to the floor. Levi's hands were on the steering wheel, and Erica's heart was in her throat. Bushes. Trees. Branches. A scream. Wide eyes, searching for the trail, knowing it would lead them to safety, and just before Erica was convinced the roller coaster was about to fling them into an empty abyss, the bushes opened, the ground flattened, and she found herself in God's park. The jeep stopped in a cloud of steam from its hot, gasping engine.

Levi grinned nervously. "Welcome to the Choke Hole, Erica."

"My God, Levi! What's the wench for?"

"It pulls us out when we go up – fifty yards at a time. Doesn't do diddly coming down."

"And the chain saw? What's that for?"

"Don't know. But Dad always had one; he just never used it." Levi looked at their tire tracks leading up the hillside. "Doesn't look like the skid trail's been used in a while."

"Levi," Erica said, breathing heavily, partly out of fear, "I never knew you to take a chance."

"Erica, you never knew me. Let's go fishing."

She had seen pretty rivers and streams before. Places for picnics and wild flowers in beautiful canyons. But Erica had never seen anything like Levi's Choke Hole. This was the most breathtaking, magical place in all of Colorado.

"This is how I remember it," Levi said. "This is where I caught the biggest German brown trout in Colorado state history. This is where..." He started to stammer. "This is where, where..."

Suddenly, Levi was crying. Tears flowed down his cheeks.

Erica reached for him. Her arms went around his shoulders, and she pulled his face to her chest. It had never happened. She had never seen it. Willow had said that Levi had finally unleashed his feelings, his pain and passion, and now Erica finally saw it.

"Tell me. Tell me, Levi. This is where, this is where...what is this?" He looked sad and lonely and troubled.

Levi looked at Erica's sunny face. Here is where it all came back, and in such a torrent and fast and faster and so unexpected and now back, remembered and sad. Like an open book. Suddenly clear. Clearly sad.

Levi pointed to a tree, next to the white water outlet, its current shifting swiftly. "See? Over there," he said.

"Yes."

Levi looked into her blue, brilliant eyes. "This is the place, Erica. All of a sudden, now I know it's where..."

"Where what?"

"This is where I left my father, Erica. This is where I left him. Right at this spot. Holding on to him. Listening to his promises and words and feelings. Love. I didn't leave him at the funeral or at camp. I left him here. And he's been here all the time. He's just been waiting, waiting for me to come back."

* * * * *

Erica remembered as well. She remembered them standing at the top of the skid trail many months before, and the glimpse she had gotten into Levi's feelings that day. He wasn't rotten and hard and cruel like Reni said. Those were symptoms. Levi's real problem was that he was wounded, a wound that had never healed. For all the months she'd known him, Levi had always been bleeding.

And now, Erica knew the bleeding had stopped. Some pain remained, but the wound was starting to heal.

"Take off your hiking boots," Levi said. "and put on the tennis shoes. You won't have to go into the middle of the river for the biggest fish in this puddle, so let's first get the hang of hanging a fly out to dry." His old rod was in her hand. "Let out line, and let it drift. Then pull your arm back fast to just above and in back of your head. Pause on your back stroke, and fling the rod to ten o'clock. Ten o'clock to two o'clock. Pause, then two to ten."

She practiced. He helped. And soon they were fishing. Erica took to the sport naturally. Within an hour, she acted like an expert.

"You've caught four fish," Levi said. "How many do you think I can clean and fry?"

"There isn't one bigger than eight inches," she complained. "And you helped me too much. I'm catching one without your help. Where's the big one? I want a big fish, one really worth frying."

"You don't have hip waders, Erica. You'll get wet and freeze your ass off."

"Big deal. I've got a change of clothes."

"Erica?"

"Where's the big fish?" she insisted.

"Okay," he said. "Try above the white water run, or close to the shoreline, under extended branches and dead trees. Or try the calm water behind those boulders. We'll go there or below the white water rapids. Come on, I'll help."

"Stay put, Levi. In fact, why don't you start collecting firewood and getting your pan greased. Make yourself useful. I'm catching lunch."

Levi watched Erica head upstream. She didn't cast perfectly every time, but she had grit and determination. And pizzazz. She headed for the calm water, just behind huge boulders. After several unsuccessful attempts, one cast landed perfectly. Erica waited, the fly disappeared, she pulled back, and the fish was on. She let out a wild whoop of joy.

It was the most beautiful sight Levi had ever seen. His father's words echoed in his ears, as clear as the day he said them years ago. "Look for someone just like yourself or like Kit," his father had said. "If you ever find a woman who loves you as much as I do, then you'll be safe, and you'll be happy."

I screwed it up, Dad. Erica was like Kit, but better. I told Kit I loved her. I never told Erica. And she's like you, Dad. If Erica isn't like you, then she's like Asia, and Asia made you happy. Erica loved me once, Dad. Really did. And I pushed her away. What can I do? What can I say?

"Say you're sorry," Erica yelled. "I've got lunch, and you haven't picked a stick for the fire yet. What a sorry-sap you are, or do I have to make the fire, too?" Erica stood in front of him, proudly displaying an eighteen-inch rainbow tucked within her net.

"Sorry, how could I have been so dumb?" Levi said. "I thought you'd at least give me more than ten minutes. You were great out there. That was beautiful. Give me the fish, I'll clean it and then show you how to cook by a river."

* * * * *

White Knuckle

After starting the fire, Levi pulled the cooler from his jeep, along with the box that held utensils and an old, heavy steel skillet he'd cleaned and oiled the night before. Carefully, he had picked stones and placed them around the fire. He took out the grill, placed it securely on the rocks, and put the skillet on top of the grill. Levi pulled butter and salt and pepper from the cooler. He placed a lemon nearby as the butter melted. It took but moments to clean the fish.

After cleaning the trout, Levi put Erica's prize inside a large, freezer bag filled with flour. He shook the bag until the fish was covered with white powder. He added salt and pepper. The fish was then put in the pan. It sizzled. Hot. And crisp. The air filled with the scent of a frying rainbow.

Erica changed her clothes on the other side of the car while Levi fried the fish. When she returned to the fire and the cotton quilt blanket that Levi had spread on the ground, he already had carefully scooped out applesauce and potato salad from the bowls he took from the cooler. The fish turned a crispy brown, and when Levi pulled it from the skillet, he deftly removed the bones and placed half of the fish on one plate, the other half on another.

"Lunch is served," he said proudly, as he handed Erica the trophy that minutes before had been swimming in the water.

It tasted like no fish she'd ever had. Fresh. White. Light and delicious. It was better than any restaurant in Colorado. "I could really get used to this," she said to Levi, as she looked all around, then back at the tastiest lunch she'd ever had.

Levi grinned. He had given her something special, at least he knew that much.

After they finished eating, Erica stood up and reached down for Levi's hand. He got up, still holding on to her. They walked to the river's edge.

The two were standing at the same place where Levi and his father had stood when Levi freed the huge German brown he had caught, years before.

"Levi, why did you say that this is the very spot where you left your father?"

"Dad said that it wouldn't be the last time he and I would be together. That he'd never get so far away that I couldn't reach him. He was the one person I could count on. He promised. And when he died, he broke that promise."

Levi looked into the water and back to Erica. "It was the promise I remember. I remember the very words. He called me Matty. He said, 'I love you more than anything in this world, and I'll always be with you.' I believed him as we stood here, and then after camp, he was gone forever. So I left him here. This is where I put him, and I've never been back. Until today."

"Why did you bring me here, Levi?"

They faced each other. Levi stared at Erica for a moment, then his gaze drifted over the water and up the skid trail, into the rocks and bushes and trees.

For a second, Erica thought she was losing him, but he turned back to her and said, "When I looked around just now, I was looking to see if my father was here somewhere, in the same way. My father was my world, you know. He was the only person I really loved. I thought he was the only person I would ever love. I was wrong."

"Why did you bring me here, Levi?" she asked again.

A softness came into Levi's eyes. They almost sparkled with light and kindness. "Because I wanted my father to meet you, Erica. I wanted you to meet him. I wanted the feeling of closeness. I didn't know if it would be possible, but if, if it was, then it'd happen here. Here is where I felt my deepest love for someone. Here's where I last felt like I was loved."

She pulled him close. Her face looked up to his. "Thank you for letting me meet your father, Matty."

"Only people who love me call me Matty."

"I know," she said. "But I can't say, 'I love you.' Calling you Matty was frightening enough. I just wanted to test it. See how it felt, and how you reacted."

"How did it feel?"

Erica hesitated, thinking about her answer. "Strange," she said. "Right now, I think I like Levi better, but Matty seemed okay. Different, but okay."

"Will you try again?"

"Maybe." She stopped and thought. Carefully.

"Most likely" she said, "is a better answer."

"Erica." Levi's voice was steady; his eyes never veered from hers. "I love you more than anything or anyone in this world."

"Then let's be friends, Levi. Let's really be friends."

"Do you think you could ever love me?" Levi asked simply.

"I don't know. Anything's possible, but I don't know. Not yet," Erica replied.

"Then I'll wait," Levi said. "I'll wait. I'll wait for as long as it takes."

Erica smiled, and Levi did not reveal what he knew in his heart would someday become a reality. Levi was Matty, and that reality was not going to change. He pulled Erica close, and held her as he watched the river flow, knowing his father was watching as well.

The two of them stood there, near the river and in the sun. They stood there. Close. Holding on.

This novel is dedicated to the millions who have been tormented by child abuse and who, nevertheless, grew up to be warriors of righteousness and justice. This is for the redeemed – God bless you in your journeys.

About the Author

Daniel J. Gatti is an attorney practicing in Oregon and Arizona. His case against a major insurance company was the subject of a documentary, "The Paper Chase," featured on *Dateline*, which won many television awards including the Polk, Peabody, Edward R. Murrow and Dupont-Columbia awards. Dan was a guest on *20/20* with Diane Sawyer and was invited to appear on *Good Morning America*.

Gatti is the co-author of four legal books, with his brother, Richard, and is listed in *Who's Who In America* and *Who's Who in American Law*. He is a member of The President's Circle of the Oregon Trial Lawyer's Association, The American Trial Lawyers Association, and he is admitted to the US District Court, the Ninth Circuit Court of Appeals and the United States Supreme Court. *White Knuckle* is his first novel.